Deadly Flames:

Dragons in Combat

Bayonet Books Anthology

Book 11

Michael Vance   Eddie Spohn   Jordan Campbell   M.D. Boncher
Axel Quintana   J. R. Handley & Jena Rey   Baden M Chant   Dan Kemp
Jesse James Fain   Parker McIntosh   Stephen W. Chappell
Kenneth E. Givens II   Nathan Pedde   Matthew C. Lucas   Sevanna
Wells
Jack Gallegos   Fulvio Gatti

Bayonet Books
Virginia Beach, VA USA

Bayonet Books Anthology: Deadly Flames: Dragons in Combat
Is a collective work of contributing authors and Published by Bayonet Books
anthologies@jrhandleyinc.com
869 Lynnhaven Parkway, Suite 113-129, Virginia Beach, VA 23452
https://jrhandley.com
Copyright © 2024 by J.R. Handley

Credits:

Cover art by: [Artist]
Edited by: Bayonet Books

Bayonet Books: Deadly Flames: Dragons in Combat
by Bayonet Books – 1st edition, 2024

Ebook ISBN: 978-1-960016-19-5
Trade Paperback ISBN: 978-1-960016-20-1

Other Books by Bayonet Books

Anthologies

Contact This!
Storming Area 51
From the Ashes
On Deadly Ground
Deadly Enhancements
Slay Bells Ring: Operation Klaus
Fire for Effect!
The Monster Within
Zombie! Patient Zero
Clash of Steel

Singles

Wolfoid
King's Commission
Vacuums Suck Hard!: Adventures of the USS Big Stick
Savage Skies

Table of Contents

The Wizard's Gambit 1

The Dragon of Wychsbreath 15

Back in the Saddle 41

The Piper of Strath Dubh 67

Dragon Drops 101

A Death of a Dragons 117

Feeding the Dragon 131

Altitude 149

The Dragon and the Horse 167

The Fellowship of the Unlikely 189

The Jotunni: The Zombie Dragon 211

Curse of the Scaled God 235

The Wrath of the Bride 257

On a Wing and a Prayer 281

Ashes to Ashes 307

The Scourges of Ojunland 331

Fire in the Land of Wolves 359

The Wizard's Gambit

By Jack Gallegos

In the city of Elderrock, defined by sleek skyscrapers and modern convenience, there is one last plot of undeveloped land in the heart of downtown. The reason? An immortal dragon has squatter's rights. For centuries, the creature has claimed the space as its own, the city growing up around it, and any attempts to reclaim or buy the land have ended in fiery disaster. The city and even the biggest corporations have long given up on developing it, and no sane person would dare approach the beast. Yet Cormac, a desperate real estate agent, sees opportunity where others see certain doom. Facing a bleak future, he decides to do the unthinkable. He must confront the dragon. Whether he gets the fire-breathing monster to listen to his proposal or simply becomes its next victim, Cormac has to try. This deal, if successful, could save something far more important than his career.

The Wizard's Gambit

By Jack Gallegos

"You're out of your mind!" Bryndhilda said, handing Cormac the proposal he had worked on all morning. It was freshly printed on good stock and bound neatly inside a forest green plastic covering.

"Maybe," Cormac said, examining the proposal, nodding at the quality and professionalism. "*Probably*. But if I can convince the owner to give up the lot... Whoever owns that lot is, by default, one of the richest people in the city. Could you even *imagine* if I snagged it?"

"No, actually, I can't," Bryndhilda replied. "Because it's a stupid idea."

Bryndhilda wasn't a real estate agent like Cormac, but she was head of the agency's graphics and design department. The dwarf managed and maintained those big printers and sign presses with the same mastery as her ancestors who had stoked the Brightforges.

"Don't get me wrong –" She spoke over the sound of the large color printing press as she worked to get the charts Cormac asked for done. Usually, people had to wait at least twenty-four hours to get color charts printed, but she was a friend, and he was calling in a favor. "– it's a nice fantasy, but that doesn't make it any less stupid."

"Tell me how you really feel," Cormac said.

"Do you even know how many people have tried to get their hands on that plot over the years? Me neither. Hundreds? Thousands? Not just the *Real Estate Agents of the Quarter*, either." This was a reference to an award Cormac received back in June. She didn't actually roll her eyes when she said it, but the expression was definitely implied. "Misery! There's not a single powerful person in Elderrock that wouldn't *kill* to get their hands on the last undeveloped plot of land in the city! But nobody even tries anymore! They haven't tried in years. You know why?"

"Because people who tried stopped coming back." Cormac waved the danger away. "I know the rumors. They also say that the people who *did* come back came back extra crispy."

"Exactly my point!"

"But –"

"But *nothing*," Bryndhilda snapped and then composed herself. "Look. It's dangerous at worst and a waste of time at best. The owner of that lot has squatted there... *forever!* He might be the *original* squatter. Some people say he was there before Elderrock was even a city! What makes you think you can do what others have failed to do for *centuries*?"

One of his charts came off the press and she held it up for him to admire. It was a bar graph of projected profits versus costs over the course of ten years, then fifty, then a hundred.

"I know you're just trying to look out for me," he said, "and I appreciate your concern, but I'm on a hot streak and it's now or never."

"I never pegged you for being suicidal."

Nobody in their right mind would encourage the type of stunt Cormac had in mind. Even if he told her the truth, the real reason he had to do this and do it without delay, she'd still say he was out of his mind. He turned his gaze back to the top page on his clipboard, the Daily Leads, and read, and re-read, the undeveloped plot's address:

1107 Karthanc Ave

His bosses always put it at the top of the list. Not because they expected an agent to secure the lot, but because it was what the old epic poems called a wizard's gambit. It was a goal to shoot for even though it was far beyond any mere mortal's ability to obtain. Cormac had seen that address at the top of the Daily Leads page every single day since he started working here, but before today he had never once actually considered going after the lot.

Before today?

Everything that had happened before today belonged to a different life. Cormac wasn't the same man he was yesterday.

There were corporations that would pay… Hell, they'd pay all the gold in the city and more for such prime real estate – for the last undeveloped plot in Old Town! If Cormac was able to flip the lot his cut of the sale would be just a tiny percent of the total and yet it would also be enough to live forever in the lap of luxury, maybe even disappear…

You can't disappear from them, he reminded himself. *The Mage Corps can always find you, no matter how far you go.*

There was only one person the Mage Corps feared.

Not to mention everyone else.

If the owner of the lot had been literally *anyone* else, the corporations themselves would've found some way to squeeze him out long ago, just like they had the owners of every other property in the area. Cormac wouldn't put assassination past the corpos. But the owner wasn't just *anyone*. It was

Calixto, and no one had the balls to fuck with a dragon. Not the richest, most ruthless corpos, not the head of the black magic mafia families, not the mayor or the Mage Corps itself.

That's where Cormac's idea came from.

It was a wizard's gambit type of idea, a suicide mission type of idea, but for his son he'd do anything.

Once his third and final chart was printed, he said, "I'm going to go talk to him. Right now. Before lunch."

Bryndhilda packed up his charts in a black bag along with a light wooden A-stand — what an artist would've called an easel — to help him with his presentation. The dwarf might not approve of his plan, but that wouldn't stop her from doing her job. She even slipped him a laser pointer for good measure.

Lastly, she held out a manilla envelope. When he went to take it from her, she clamped down, not letting go at first. "Clearly, nothing I say is going to stop you. Just… Make sure you say your goodbyes."

"I will."

"Also, tell the bosses I get your parking spot when you die."

———————

Cormac unlocked the apartment door and found his son and daughter, seven and five respectively, playing in the living room. They both greeted him excitedly with big hugs and kisses and then promptly forgot about him as they returned to their game. Cormac watched them play with a smile on his lips a bit longer, and then retreated to the bedroom.

Lacie was sitting in bed with the covers pulled around her, draping her like a cloak, only her tiny white face poking out. The door was open so she could still see into the living room and hear the children at play, but the room was dark, and her bloodshot eyes shied away when he flipped the light switch.

He sat on the bed next to his wife and pulled her into him. She leaned over and he wrapped his arms all the way around her, like he could shield her from all the badness of the world with just one embrace. He could hear her breath catch as she fought back yet another bout of sobs.

"Has there been anything else?"

"Not since last night," she said. "Not since…"

And she was crying again.

Lacie was a former Marine and now she worked on construction sites, no job for the weak hearted. That was how they met, in fact – she was the on-site building manager of a property Cormac had flipped about eight years ago, back before he was a full-time realtor. To this day, she still handled his permits and took on most of his construction projects. In this marriage, she was the tough one. But since last night – when they had been woken up by alarming sounds coming from their son's bedroom – she had been a mess.

"I found a way to fix it," he said. "Maybe."

She pulled away and looked at him, tears streaking her pale cheeks. Her expression was a mixture of hope and disbelief.

"How?"

"I –" He wanted to tell her the truth, but he couldn't look into those big beautiful blue eyes brimming with tears and tell her she might not just lose her son but her husband as well. He *couldn't*. "– know some people. We have enough of a nest egg that I think I can get us – all of us – out of Elderrock, out of the country. We have about a week before *they* find out. Maybe longer, but we can't delay. We need to stay one step ahead."

The lies tasted like bile.

"Do you really think…?"

"I promise," he said. "I will fix this."

"Don't make a promise you don't intend to keep," she said. "That was the deal, remember? All those years ago? Never make a promise if –"

"Lacie," he cut her off. "I promise."

She looked at him for a long time. Finally, she nodded. It was time to go. If he stayed any longer, he might lose his nerve, and then what?

Their goodbye kisses were salty from her tears, but he took comfort in the fact that she seemed stronger now than when he first walked in. At the very least, she had shrugged the blanket off her shoulders and now sipped from a cup of ice water she got off the nightstand.

Before leaving, Cormac hugged his children one last time, holding them close, holding on for so long that they both squirmed to get away. Finally, he let them go, with one extra kiss for his eldest, his beautiful son who didn't – couldn't – understand what was happening.

Cormac left the manilla envelope – the one with his life insurance policy in it – on the table by the front door. Then, he was back in his car and on his way to Old Town to make a deal with a dragon.

Not a deal, he reminds himself. *A presentation.*

The dragon stood when Cormac entered the small gap in the tall privacy walls at 1107 Karthanc Ave. Calixto put his snout right up into the real estate agent's face. Cormac clutched his presentation materials to his chest and thanked the gods he took a piss before coming here.

Calixto's shiny ruby eyes stared at Cormac over nostrils that were bigger than a human head. The dragon **BREATHED**.

A barrage of scents, warm and cold, more than Cormac could quantify or qualify, ranging from brimstone to the smell of the knockoff wax pastels his mother used to buy him when he was a child. His mind reshaped the dragon's language, scent, into language and emotions, and the words cascaded into Cormac's mind one letter at a time and yet so quickly it may as well have been instantaneous.

You're brave to come here alone.

The dragon pulled away and circled around itself, massive talons digging into the dirt. Cormac, fighting down a bout of frantic humor, was reminded of a cat except, of course, a cat didn't make the Earth shake. The dragon settled, relaxed but ready to level a city block at a moment's notice.

Cormac forced steadiness into his voice. "Trust me when I say being brave is new."

He gestured around the empty lot. The skyscrapers to either side were different from the rest of the ones in Old Town because they were spaced out more and the sides of the buildings that faced Calixto's lot didn't have windows. As for the black privacy walls along the border of the lot itself, Cormac suspected these were more for the benefit of the people *outside* than the dragon. The skyscrapers dwarfed even the magnificent Calixto who, tail to nose, was at least eight stories long.

"Yesterday," Cormac said. "I *never* would have done this."

Bravery from desperation, then.

"Yes." He held up the bag with his charts and graphs. "Desperation and preparation. Never discount either."

I won't sell.

"I know. This isn't about selling. And I'm not here to convince you to leave, either. In fact, for my proposal to work, you *can't* leave. But I'm getting ahead of myself. Before we get to my proposal, I need more information. So, start by telling me your story, and then –"

The dragon moved faster than Cormac would've thought possible. One moment, the dragon lounged, the next Cormac was raised into the air by a giant talon, brought close to the gaping maw of the dragon. This time the dragon's **BREATH** smells like a burning forest and dirty copper, and it sets his fillings to vibrating.

Don't mistake bravery with brashness, little mortal.

"I'm sorry, I'm sorry," Cormac said. He couldn't tell how much of the fear was his and how much was his emotions being manipulated by the dragon. Either way, his whole body shook with it.

"I didn't mean… I didn't…"

The dragon dropped him, and he landed and let out a huge sigh of relief. He picked up his bag off the ground, patted it with shaking hands, hoping his charts and graphs inside hadn't been ruined.

Why do you want my story?

"Well, uh, well…"

Taking a deep breath, he composed himself. He forced himself not to think of the real stakes, about his son. He reminded himself that this was just a client. A rather large and deadly client, true, but still *just a client*. Cormac was here to give a presentation, just like the hundreds of presentations he'd given before. This was business.

He began again, "Nobody knows why you care about this place. We don't know why you always come back here even if you leave for years at a time or why you guard it at all. I have my suspicions, and if the details of your story line up with my hopes…"

And if I don't meet your prerequisites?

"I'll go away and you'll never see me again."

The dragon moved so that just his left eye stared into Cormac. The vertical iris blinked and dilated as it focused on the real estate agent's face, like a camera lens spinning to get a clearer picture.

You say that like it means something. If I saw you every day for the rest of your life, I would forget you the day you died.

"I don't know about that," Cormac said. "I can be really annoying."

This, I believe.

Scorching steam erupted from the dragon's nostrils.

You're really not going to offer me riches?

"I don't have any riches to offer. I work for an agency, and they have a lot of money, but I imagine the richest people in the world have already made you offers. More than my agency can offer."

Then, what *do* you offer?

"Nothing. At least not until I've heard your story." It was time to gamble. "I need to make sure I can trust you first."

More steam, and the dragon made a rumbling sound deep in its massive, green scale covered breast. Cormac thought for sure it was going to start blowing dragonfire and turn him extra crispy, but then he realized that the sound was laughter.

You want ME to prove myself to YOU?

When the dragon said ME Cormac saw, and smelled, and *felt* an erupting volcano. The heat almost broke him, but then the sensation was gone like it had never been. Conversely, when the dragon said YOU Cormac saw – or, rather, sensed – a single insignificant ant in a desert, indistinguishable from the grains of sand around it.

"I guess you could put it that way."

Others have asked for my story, and still, nobody knows why I stay here... Does this not tell you something?

Cormac swallowed, feeling less confident by the moment. But wouldn't the dragon have killed him already if he were going to? He swallowed and said something his grandma used to say all the time:

"Three can keep a secret if two are dead."

Another of those rumbling laughs.

Shall we see if I am worthy, then?

Cormac knew better than to answer.

The dragon brought his nostrils close again, flaring less than five feet from Cormac's face. If he wanted to do it, Calixto could snap and eat Cormac whole. Instead, the dragon **BREATHES**.

Hear. See. Live.

———————

Fire. Vengeance. Death. Glorious death.

The screams are music.

But they are so tiny, those screams, so small the voices of human and elf and dwarf and all the other insignificant creatures that were not the glorious Obscure. Voices so tiny, music so small.

Music is an addiction. But he doesn't want small, insignificant music. He wants a symphony *that will feed the addiction.*

The more he kills, the louder the music, the more delicious the melody. More death. More vengeance.

More…

More…

It's like storm clouds suddenly clearing when the Curse breaks. Dazed for a moment, it's Calixto's own internal cries of triumph that tip him off, but he knows it's over. The Curse is broken, and…

…he's…

…free…

Finally, finally *free!*

There's no time for elation, though, because his surroundings come into focus. Where is he? What is this place? Angry and scared faces stare up at him. He's surrounded by little trolls and even smaller elves in armor and brandishing weapons and warcries.

What –

They're trying to kill him! Arrows bounce off his face! Spears jab into his sides! He roars as one of the spears gets lucky and slips beneath one of his scales. Ropes fly overhead, and –

– and he remembers….

He remembers a peaceful life. Then the Obscure. Then the Curse. Then years of war during which time he killed everyone who dared step in his path, anyone the Obscure sent him to kill. He created beautiful music out of death and destruction, and he did so with a laugh in his belly. How many had died by his claw and flame? Impossible to count. Thousands. Tens of… Too many. Far, far too many…

Even now he is surrounded by smoldering corpses.

No…

It wasn't me; *he wants to tell them.* I didn't want to do it!

But it doesn't matter. They've seen his hesitation, and they pressure him. Elves and trolls try to kill him, their hatred for the Obscure – and for him – drawing them together, forcing them into an alliance that never would have existed otherwise. He is their enemy and if he doesn't move now, doesn't fly right now, *they are going to overwhelm him, pin him and they will kill him.*

They won't believe for a moment that the psychotic dragon they've fought all these years was a puppet of the Obscure. Even if they do *believe him, would they care? No, they'd still want to kill him, and they would be right. He wouldn't blame them; their hate is justified.*

I deserve to be hated; *he thinks.*

Wings explode outward, accidentally killing more because they are crowding him so close.

I'm sorry. I'm sorry!

But it doesn't matter as he launches himself into the sky. Spears and arrows fly after him. The ropes almost *snag him, but he's able to slice through them with his teeth and talons and get away. In the air, he picks a direction at random, and he flies. He is himself again, but who is that now?*

I'm sorry, I'm sorry, I'm –

––––––––––––––––––––

"I'm sorry," Cormac said, picking himself up off the ground. "It was… I wasn't ready for… for *that*. It was so real. I could *smell…*"

He put the back of his hand to his nose and shook his head rapidly even though it was still swimming from his tumble.

You're only human. We will stop.

"No!" Cormac swallowed, realizing he probably shouldn't shout at a dragon. He held up a hand and tried not to vomit. He had experienced every moment along with Calixto.. "I mean… I'm sorry, I just mean… Please keep going. I can handle it. And if I can't? Well… That doesn't matter because I need to know more."

Though, truth be told, didn't he know enough already?

This isn't about me anymore, he thinks.

"Please," he said, picking his presentation materials up off the ground a second time.. "Please, tell me the rest of your story."

No. Not the rest but some.

––––––––––––––––––––

The war ends. Time, as it always does, passes. The world says the Obscure is gone, defeated. So why is it that Calixto can still smell the vile creature out there in the world? The monster that turned him into a killer?

I know you're out there.

And so, he scours the lands, looking in the most likely and unlikely of places. He searches the Obscure's tower and the metal city where his followers lived while they ravaged the world during the war. But the scent is wrong. Faded. Some of his followers remain, but the Obscure hasn't been here since the war ended.

Calixto's anger at being used all these years burns inside of him hotter than any fire, and he wants to enact vengeance on the Obscure's followers, but would that mean he's no better now than when he was Cursed? And how many of them had been used like he was? He'll let the other races sort through that mess.

I've seen enough death; *he tells himself when he can't sleep. The compulsion to rage, to destroy, to create music, burns inside.*

Those few who will speak with him, mostly trolls and goblins, say the Obscure is gone, that he's wasting his time, but Calixto can smell him still. So, he keeps searching, keeps flying, weeks, months, until…

There!

A tiny village. No, not even a village. A patchwork farming community nowhere near the front line. The place is completely abandoned, though the fields are still green or lush and close to harvest.

This is the first time since his hunt began that the Obscure's scent is actually stronger, like he's finally getting closer.

He circles and lands.

He's here!

Where are you!

Anger spills over. Dragonfire streams into the sky, declaring his challenge.

Nothing. But the scent is unmistakable. If he takes a step in any direction, the scent grows weaker. The same if he flies. There's only one thing left to try, and so he digs into the soft earth.

He will *find the Obscure and make him pay. Talons tear into the dirt, and — yes! The Obscure's scent* does *get stronger the deeper he digs! He digs, and digs, and —*

"Hello? Can you hear me down there!"

The shouting finally breaks through the haze of determination. He looks up at the sound only to realize he can't see out of the hole anymore. He cranes his neck at the opening above. A tiny head pokes over the edge, smiling down, waving at the dragon.

"Hi there! Can we talk?"

I'm busy.

"Yes, I can see that. From the looks of it, you've been busy for quite some time. Found any buried treasure?"

I don't care about treasure.

"Well, that's good because there's none down there. For that matter, you won't find the Obscure that way, either."

Finally curious — and annoyed — enough, Calixto climbs out of the hole that he must've spent days digging without noticing the passage of time. Disconnecting from time is nothing new for him — it's the only way to stay sane as an immortal being — but it usually doesn't happen when he's actively doing something.

Back up on the surface, the farming community is mostly crater. He recognizes the man, an elven hero from the war.

Theodysus.

"Call me Ted," the elf says. "I'm honored to finally meet you, Calixto."

We've met. On the battlefield.

The memories of those battles make Calixto sick to his stomach. While he and Theodysus had both survived, so many others had not.

"Doesn't count," Ted says. "Based on the color of your aura, I'm talking to a different consciousness altogether. Unless, of course, the bloodthirsty version of you I did meet is the real you, and this —?"

No!

"Didn't think so. How did you find this place, anyway?"

I can smell the Obscure here.

"Interesting." The elf sniffs but then shakes his head like he's being an idiot. "I've had the world's greatest mages searching for this place night and day, and none of them have sensed it yet. I even had some other dragons trying to sniff the Obscure out, but they found only cold trails. Nobody I tasked with finding him has come within a five-hundred miles of this place, and they all say the same thing: The Obscure is gone. And yet here we are. You, me and the truth."

The truth…? So, he is here!

That rage, again, at his very core of being.

"In a manner of speaking. I don't think the monster we knew as the Obscure exists anymore, at least not as a conscious being. But I think his essence lingers. A portion of his power is trapped here. I don't know why. Maybe this is where he originated. Maybe he had a plan."

We must destroy him.

"Why?"

The dragon is taken aback by this question.

For what he did! So he will not rise again!

"I suppose so," Ted says. "Unfortunately — or, perhaps, fortunately — there's nothing left for us to do but wait and watch and guard this place. You and I don't have the power to destroy him any further than he's already been destroyed. Even with the power of the Elven War Hymn still pumping through me… Perhaps if we revealed he was here, we could find enough people to help us, to lend us their power, but I think even that is a wizard's gambit at best. And if we do tell other people the truth, then everyone would know his power lingers here. Everyone. Not just those who want to destroy it. Then what?"

More war.

There's always more war."

The dragon snarls. Fire burns in his belly.

Then what?

"The war might be over for the rest of the world, but for me… My newest war is now against time itself. So long as his power remains, I can't let anyone have it. Not ever."

I know about it.

"Indeed. And I'm choosing to be thankful for that. I thought I was going to have to fight this particular war by myself. That is… What I mean to say is…" The elf hesitates but not from indecision. Calixto senses an unspoken threat in those pauses. "I'm hoping that since both of us now know the truth, I don't have to bear this burden alone?"

———————

"And you've been here ever since? Guarding this spot?"

I used to leave. For decades at a time, but I came back once and found a whole town, the hole filled in. I had to scare everyone off. I didn't leave for extended periods after that. Eventually the city that is now called Elderrock began to form, but it was miles away at the time. I should've stopped it, but I didn't. And now this is my life. Preventing evil people from putting a skyscraper on the dark lord's grave.

"What about Ted? The elf?"

He's an elf. He found other causes, other dark lords to fight. He still checks in, but I haven't seen him for a century.

"So you've been guarding this place, alone, for all this time? Why? It can't just be because of revenge, surely."

I haven't been alone.

"What do you mean?"

Insofar as dragons can shrug, Calixto did so.

It's time, Cormac told himself. *Now or never.*

He reached into the black bag Bryndhilda prepared for him and he pulled out the wooden A-frame, which he set up with practiced ease. Then, he brought out the three charts, wishing he had had time to make more, and placed them on the frame. He rolled up the proposal long ways, implying increased preparation based on his disregard for the paper itself, and held it in his left hand like it was a navy green bludgeon. He left the laser pointer in the bag. Not his style.

The plan was to begin by showing the dragon his own fiscal worth. He did not come with a typical offer, but this was different. Showing the client their own worth was a good way to put them at ease. After that, Cormac would move onto the proposal, making sure to frame it like the best possible alternative as times were changing. There'd also be projected earning reports over the course of five, ten and fifty years.

Cormac felt confident.

This was where he *shined.*

"First and foremost," he said, standing with the A-frame to his left, gesturing toward it with the rolled-up proposal. "I just want to say thank you for letting me speak with you today. I wish to begin –"

The world exploded with heat.

Dragonfire burned white and hotter than the sun.

You try my patience. I thought you were brave.

Cormac blinked. Again. The lot came back into focus, the dragon, too, slowly, as his eyes readjusted. There was a shadowed streak directly across his vision that wouldn't go away no matter how many times he blinked, the after image of the thread thin stream of fire.

What was left of the wooden A-frame and his charts were smoldering on the ground. He held his left hand up to his face, the one with the rolled-up proposal. About a quarter inch from the skin of his hand, the proposal just… stopped, blackened, like the fire sliced through the plastic and the paper instead of burning it away. He opened his hand and the remains of the rolled-up proposal fell to the ground, not even warm. How had the dragon been able to destroy with such pinpoint precision? He touched his eyebrows, surprised to find them still intact.

Voice far steadier than it should've been considering he had thought he was dead, he said, "I didn't mean to offend you."

Why are you really here?

"I have an idea for a building," he said. He didn't need his materials. He could still do this. He could! Was he not the *Best Real Estate Agent of the Quarter?* Gods, he'd do anything for a glass of water right about now, though. "But not a corpo building like all these. I'm talking about a halfway house, a place for those shunned from society, a place for those who want to be *redeemed* or saved. Based on what you told –"

Before he knew what was happening, the dragon had reached out, grabbed Cormac by his feet and lifted him so that he hung upside down. The world blurred as the dragon lifted him, higher, higher, until he dangled above Calixto's upturned maw.

"Wait! Please! No! Please!"

Much like how the Curse on Calixto broke all those years ago when the Obscure died, Cormac also broke. He had come here because it was the only option. He had prepared all morning the best way he knew how. He came with logic and numbers to prove that he could make it happen, that he'd be a good business partner. That he was *professional*. He practiced his proposal, leaning on preparedness to carry him through, using professionalism to override his fear.

Now, all that remained was fear.

Why are you here?

"You've stayed here all this time because you want to be redeemed! That's why I think a halfway house would —"

LAST CHANCE!

He felt the dragon's grip loosen!

"My son!" The words were ripped from Cormac. He knew his mistake. He should have come as a father, not a real estate agent. Everything else, the grandstanding, the proposal, the charts. It was all meaningless. He was not here with a proposal. He was here to *beg*, beg and hope. "This morning! He used magic. Do you know what that *means* for a human?"

The Mage Corps.

"Yes! They'll take him from me. From us! The children they take aren't allowed to go back to their families, not ever. That's why I need you! I need you to protect him because I can't. Because there is nobody else in this city the Mage Corps fears. But you? They fear you. Even —"

Yes.

"— if I convinced you to sell so I could flip the lot, it wouldn't matter. All the money in the world won't make a difference. Nothing *mortal* will stop the Mage Corps. Only a partnership — Wait. Did you say yes?"

Yes.

The world around him blurred and then Cormac was once again on the ground, laying on his back, with the dragon towering over him. He stared at the darkening sky beyond. When did that happen?

Where had the hours gone?

I kept my promise, Lacie, he thought, tears of relief pouring down his face. *Just like I said I would. Our son is safe.*

About Jack Gallegos

Jack Gallegos lives in Roswell, NM with his wife and three beautiful children.

The Dragon of Wychsbreath

By Stephen W. Chappell

———————————————

Three siblings journey through a desolate valley on a quest from their king: to slay a mighty dragon that is terrorizing the land. A surprise attack separates the trio, leaving them reeling and vulnerable. Their journey takes them to the village of Wychsbreath, where an unexpected welcome pits them against the very village they have come to save. It is a trial by fire as the siblings are forced to battle both man and beast in a desperate attempt to carry out their mission and escape with their lives.

The Dragon of Wychsbreath
By Stephen W. Chappell

The road led them through a valley of embers and the charred remains of dead things. Blackened, broken trees reached for dark storm clouds as they swayed in the wind. The clip-clop of the horses echoed eerily, the only sound of life in this desolate place. Helen pulled her cloak tighter, but it offered no comfort against the palpable dread that shrouded her soul.

"The dragon's work, no doubt." The deep timbre of Daegel's voice broke the traveling trio's grim reverie. His callused hand drifted to the hilt of his sword as if the dragon's return was nigh. A drab woolen cape billowed behind him to reveal heavy, battle-worn armor. A scuffed shield painted with the red and gold of the kingdom hung at his side.

The silvery voice of Orvyn floated back to him. "Your grasp of the obvious is excellent." Though his words were lighthearted, he spoke them in gloomy, subdued tones. The youngest of the three siblings adjusted the ornate staff slung over his back. He shook his head to release a bit of his long, brown mane from beneath it.

Chestnut hair framed the annoyed look on her face as Helen turned to glare at her younger siblings. "Hush, you two, before you draw someone's attention." A wooden bow hung at an angle on her back. Quivers beat against her black stallion, keeping time with the gait of her steed.

A lone vulture circled, a dark, feathery movement against the tempestuous sky. It settled high in the remains of an old, dead oak and cast its brooding gaze upon them.

Orvyn looked around theatrically, a hand outstretched towards a skeletal corpse at the side of the road. "Perhaps we attract the attention of that poor elk? Do you think it prefers the monotony of the wind whistling through its ribs?" The animal's white skull grinned at them from its resting place on the barren sand. A scrawny rat emerged from an eye socket, drawing the vulture's scrutiny.

"Enough." Daegel's tone brooked no argument, Orvyn's sarcastic mimicry notwithstanding.

Helen sighed. "Will you never grow up?" At nearly eighteen summers, Orvyn was the youngest and often acted the part.

Daegel scratched at his beard as he searched the foreboding sky. "We'll need to pick up the pace. Those clouds promise a miserable night if we don't make the village."

"It looks like we're approaching something. A farm, perhaps," Helen said. Indeed, a short, rickety fence graced the side of the road ahead. "Perchance they'll agree to shelter us."

Beyond the fence, a patchy, poorly tended field of barley stretched across the valley floor. Some of it had been harvested, but most of the field was stricken with blight. A ragged scarecrow stood watch over the withered, dying grain. Gangly chickens clucked on the ground, pecking at the occasional bug that happened across their path.

At the edge of the field stood a dilapidated farmhouse. The ramshackle structure wore a sagging roof and a porch full of broken floorboards. Behind it stood an open barn with a large hole smashed in its roof.

"Is it possible that someone lives here?" Daegel asked as they dismounted.

Orvyn shook his head. "Someone may exist here, but I wouldn't call it living."

Helen strode towards the building, the hulking Daegel trailing behind. A skinny cat ran away as they stepped onto the creaky porch.

Helen rapped on the door. "Is anyone there?" she called as she lowered her cowl.

There was a scuffling sound from within, but no answer to her call. Daegel swept back the fabric of his cape, revealing the cold, polished pommel of his blade.

The door creaked open, but only a crack. "Yes?" a gruff voice drifted out to them.

Helen cleared her throat. "We're travelers heading for Wychsbreath. We're in need of shelter. The weather, you see, it's no night for camping." Distant thunder rumbled as if to underscore their plight.

The door swung open just enough to reveal the farmer's whiskered, gaunt face. He spared a glance skyward. "The weather is the least of your worries, methinks."

She raised her eyebrows in an unspoken question, but he did not elaborate. "May we come in?"

He thought about it for a moment before shaking his head. "No, I'd not..."

Thunder rumbled across the valley floor, joined by a nervous neigh from one of their mounts.

"Are those horses you've brought?" His eyes lit up as he spotted them by the road.

Helen raised her eyebrows at Daegel questioningly. "Yes," she said at last. "We, ah, we rode them here."

The farmer licked his lips. "We don't see many horses hereabouts." He pulled the door the rest of the way open. "You can stable them in the barn. Yes, the barn will do. You can stay here in the house. I've an extra room in the back."

A curt smile crossed Helen's lips. "Thank you for your kindness. I'm Helen."

"Ivan."

A cold sleet began as they led the horses to their home for the evening. Though there was a gaping hole in the rickety barn's roof, enough remained to provide some shelter for the animals.

The gray light of the stormy day faded as they prepared their steeds. Orvyn said a brief incantation and a bright orb appeared to light the barn as brightly as the daytime sun. "Does that man strike you a bit odd?" he asked.

Daegel grunted in reply as he untacked his black stallion. "I don't trust him."

"You don't trust anybody," Helen groused as she hung her saddle. "We can accept Ivan's hospitality, or we can spend the night in the tents."

"We should press on to the village," Daegel growled.

"Not in this rain," Helen said. "We've no choice, really."

Orvyn shuddered. "It's good that it is only for one night." He put down a bag of feed for his mare. "There you go, Matilda," he said softly to the horse. "Eat up."

Daegel glowered at them. "It would do us well to sleep with one eye open." He nodded at their steeds. "Ivan is a bit too interested in them."

Helen turned to Orvyn. "Can you do anything about the door?"

He shrugged. "The master has taught me some wards. I know one that'll keep Ivan out." He glanced at the hole in the roof. "I have no magic to seal up that hole, though."

They finished in silence. Orvyn waved his hand, extinguishing the floating orb. A flash of lightning heralded the start of the downpour. "Go," he said. "I'll catch up."

While Helen and Daegel dashed for the farmhouse, Orvyn latched the barn door. He traced a shape with his finger and said a few words. The ward flashed brightly, then faded to a dim, blue glow. Though it took only a moment, he was thoroughly soaked by the time he rejoined his siblings.

Ivan was waiting for them. He showed them to a room in the back. "I haven't beds for the lot of you."

"This will do," Daegel said.

With a smile, Ivan pulled the door closed. "A pleasant night to you, then."

"Strange man," Orvyn reiterated as he prepared his bedroll.

"Shut up and go to sleep," Daegel grumbled.

They slept fitfully, the storm frequently rousing them. When sleep took hold, they dreamed of gilded treasure just beyond their grasp and a dragon moving sugar-dusted pawns in a grand match of chess.

In the morning, the horses were gone.

———————

Candles kept the cold, dim window light at bay. The steady pelting of rain showed no sign of slowing, though the thunder had finally ebbed. Ivan stoked the fire in the hearth, filling the room in warmth and light.

"The chickens haven't given me any eggs lately, but there's a loaf and a bit of jam."

"Thank you." Helen broke off a piece of bread and handed the loaf to Daegel. He tore off a piece of his own and placed the rest on the table in front of Orvyn's empty chair.

"You live here alone?" Daegel asked.

Ivan nodded. "Wife died a few years back, and my sons, well..." He trailed off, the faraway look of a painful memory in his eyes.

Orvyn burst into the room, dripping wet with rainwater. "Ivan! What happened to our horses?"

"What!" Helen and Daegel both exclaimed.

The farmer shifted his gaze towards Orvyn. "Not in the barn, eh?"

"Where are the horses?" Helen snapped.

"Thieves, maybe," Ivan mused. "Predators."

Orvyn shook his head. "The doors were warded, and they were unbroken this morning."

The table shook as Daegel stood and drew steel. "Where are they? And what was your part in it?"

A pale-faced Ivan pushed back, Daegel's blade at his throat.

"Save it for the dragon!" Helen said through gritted teeth. Daegel lowered his weapon but didn't sheath it. "If they're gone, we'll have to make do."

Orvyn scowled at her. "Make do? How do you propose we carry all of our gear?"

"You're after the dragon, are ya?" the farmer asked. "Why, may I ask?"

The siblings looked at each other, then at their host. "Are you daft?" Orvyn said. "It's a dragon!" He gestured towards the window. "Look at the damage it's done here."

"And it's been ranging further," Helen added, "encroaching on more populated lands."

"That's not the dragon's doing," Ivan said. "It's our own. For doubting its strength and wisdom."

"You're addled," said Orvyn.

"How far is the village?" Helen asked.

Ivan raised his eyes to the ceiling, considering. "Laden with grain and leaving at dawn, I'd make it on foot by midday."

They all groaned.

"I'll not go on foot," Orvyn announced.

"Do you propose we turn back?" Daegel growled. "It took a week to get thus far with the horses. How long do you think it'll take without?" He sheathed his sword. "With the dragon's wealth, we'll have no trouble replacing them."

"If we can kill it, you mean," Orvyn said. "And don't you mean the King's reward? Its hoard belongs to the people from whom it was plundered."

"And the remainder is for the King," Helen added. "We're moving on, and I'll not hear any more about it. Horses or no, we've a job to do."

With no further dissent, they gathered their things and started on their way.

"I'd think twice about going," Ivan called as they walked out the door. "Ain't nothing there for outsiders except death."

Misery clung to them as they trekked to Wychsbreath. A headwind fought against them while its ally, the cold rain, battered their spirits. Even the rutted, muddy road opposed them, sucking at their feet with every step. Chilled beneath their sodden clothes and burdened with all the gear they could manage, the trip was slow going. Though the rain had tapered off by midday, the village remained out of sight.

Helen led them down the soggy road, her mood as foul as the weather. The withered landscape weighed on her; she made her home in lush, vibrant forests, teaming with life and infusing her with energy. Here, the desolation drained her, a stifling fog that severed her connection with life and surrounded her with its impenetrable misery.

Her brothers' bickering didn't help one bit.

"We never should have stopped there," Daegel said as he side-stepped a deep puddle.

Orvyn rolled his eyes. "We couldn't have gone on in that storm," he said. "And the dragon would have gotten the horses anyway."

"You don't know that," his brother snapped. "How did the dragon even know the horses were there? The farmer, I bet."

Orvyn sneered at him. "Dragons have a very keen sense of smell."

Daegel snarled disdainfully. "Did you learn that from your wizard-master in Fair Haven?" He grunted as he pulled his foot out of the mud with a slurp. "The least you could do is cast a spell to dry the road."

"I've had about enough of you two," Helen said. "You're bickering is making me insane."

"You may be the eldest," Daegel rasped, "but that doesn't mean you're in charge."

Her eyes narrowed at him. "The bounty was granted to me, Daegel." She had earned respect in the kingdom as a hunter, both for food and for bounty. Her track record had caught the attention of the Royal Court and earned her the right to this warrant. "That puts me in charge."

"Really? Then why do you think Father sent me along?"

Their father, the King's Master-at-Arms, had had his own plans for dealing with the dragon. When the warrant was instead granted to Helen, he was livid. The thought of a woman, even his own daughter, collecting this bounty was anathema to him. He forced her to disband her hand-picked team and instead include Daegel; he would collect a portion of the reward and all of the credit.

"You know why," she snarled, her face red with anger. "I'll not discuss it further."

Her father, she had learned over the years, had little use for her except as a political tool and fodder for an arranged marriage. It appalled him that she shunned such a path and shamed him that she was as skilled a hunter as any of the men under his command.

"Speaking of Ivan," Orvyn interjected, interrupting her ruminations. "Why does he support the dragon?"

Helen harrumphed. "People are drawn to power and wealth." She gave Daegel a pointed look at Daegel. "Dazzled beyond sense by it."

"But what does he get out of it?" Orvyn protested.

She glanced at Orvyn. Her father's reasons for including Orvyn on this team rather than a seasoned warrior were a mystery to her. He was a wizard's apprentice, an occupation their father found distasteful. She would have to ask him about it sometime.

"Who knows?" She shook her head sadly. "Protection, maybe? The illusion that some of it will eventually trickle down to him?"

"Dragons aren't givers," Daegel noted. "They're takers. As much as Ivan has lost, if he believes the dragon takes more from someone else, then maybe that's enough."

They walked quietly for a few minutes before Orvyn interrupted the peace. "Strange," he mused. "We've passed many farms but have seen no oxen to work them. Nor cows, nor pigs. Not even any goats."

Daegel harrumphed. "The beast has been here a long time. When it runs out of game, what do you think it is going to eat?"

"Haven't seen a lot of people, either," Orvyn said. "You think it's eating them?"

"It can't have eaten the whole valley clear, can it?" Helen asked.

Daegel sidestepped a deep puddle, landing instead in a slippery bit of mud. His foot squelched as he fought its grip. "Never underestimate a dragon," he replied. "And it is ranging further."

Helen turned to address Daegel. Instead, her eyes grew wide at a figure that appeared in the sky behind him. "What's that?"

Orvyn followed her finger. The figure was closer now, close enough to see the beat of its enormous wings. "It's the dragon!"

With a low, terrifying screech that echoed through the valley, the dragon dropped out of the sky, flying fast and low and trailing a stream of black smoke.

"Orvyn, stand behind us!" Daegel demanded as he lifted his shield and drew his sword.

Orvyn ignored him. He pulled a pinch of ash from his cloak, waved his hands, and chanted an incantation. A shimmering curtain formed in front of them.

The dragon shrieked, and a ball of fire screamed through the air. They cringed, but for naught; the fireball splashed harmlessly against the shimmering barrier that Orvyn's magic had erected.

Helen unslung her bow and loosed an arrow at the oncoming beast, then three more in rapid succession. Though they flew true to their target, the arrows could not penetrate the dragon's scaly hide.

Smoke flared from its nostrils as the colossal serpent soared towards them, a terrible maelstrom of power and fury. Yellow eyes peered out from a face of blood-red scales and framed by a crown of deadly horns. It folded back its powerful wings and extended razor-sharp claws like a raptor approaching its prey. Daegel raised his blade and prepared to strike.

The creature let out an ear-splitting screech as it passed over the trio, so close they could smell its fetid breath. Orvyn was knocked over by the draft of its passage. Helen drew and released, then knocked an arrow for a second shot but stayed her hand; with its speed and a sudden climb, she had no chance to strike her target.

They turned to follow the dragon's flight but were startled by a heavy thump and a splash.

"What is it?" Orvyn cried as he pulled himself out of the mud and watched the dragon head to the mountains.

Helen approached the bundle. A battered horse's head stared lifelessly at her beside its chewed, mangled remains.

"It's Matilda," she said with a note of disgust. "The dragon's eaten her."

He stared at the remains of his horse in shock. "Is it some kind of message?"

"A warning." Her brow furrowed as she scanned the area. "Where's Daegel?" She looked around frantically. "Daegel!"

They searched the area, more frantic with each passing minute. They found only his longsword mired in the mud. Daegel was gone.

————————

A sullen Orvyn turned towards Ivan's farm and started the long journey home.

Helen sniffled and wiped her tear-streaked face. She felt forlorn, defeated. Lost. She spun slowly in the center of the road, searching for some sign of Daegel. The sight of Orvyn walking away stopped her. "Where are you going?" she asked. "We can't stop now."

He didn't turn around. "'Tis a fool's errand we pursue, Helen. He was the strongest of us." He wiped at a damp eye. "With him dead, what chance have we?"

She stepped in front of him and held out a hand. "He's not dead!" she insisted. She wiped her nose and glared at him with puffy, fiery eyes. "If the dragon wanted to kill him, it would have killed him here. And us, too." She sniffled and blinked away a tear. "No, he's not dead. The beast has carried him off somewhere. Alive."

Orvyn shrugged, his youthful face as hard as stone. "You're delusional. He's gone now. In pieces, perhaps, or at the bottom of the dragon's belly."

Helen shoved him. "Don't talk like that! He's not, I tell you." She searched the ground around them. "Do that thing you do. That thing with the puddles."

"Scrying?" he scoffed. "I haven't the skill; 'tis not an easy thing."

She poked a finger into his chest. "I've seen you do it."

He shrugged. "That doesn't mean I can do it now."

She stepped towards him and got in his face. "That doesn't mean you can't try."

He sighed and dropped his gaze to his feet. "Alright." He searched the area, eyes darting from puddle to puddle. "Over there. I'll need something of his."

Helen spied Daegel's sword where it had fallen. She stalked over to it and pulled it out of the muck, then marched back and held it out to Orvyn.

Orvyn took it from her and nearly dropped it. "Oof! How does he manage this thing?" With a groan, he cradled it in his arms and knelt before the puddle. His reflection regarded him from the muddy water, gray clouds floating by overhead, and Helen's impatient reflection beside him. He closed his eyes and breathed deeply, then muttered a few words. A moment later, he opened his eyes.

A hazy view of gray clouds appeared in the water, indistinguishable from those overhead.

"Nothing happened," Helen said.

"Something happened," Orvyn corrected. "Our reflections have abandoned us."

She uncrossed her arms and put her hands on her hips. "What of Daegel?"

"I don't know."

"Well, shouldn't you mumble some more words?"

"It's not just about the words!" he snapped. He closed his eyes and inhaled deeply, then continued in a steadier tone. "It's intention. And focus. Energy. And other things too, sometimes." Irritation wrinkled his face. "This isn't easy, you know."

"Well, do something!"

"Something? Right." He stood, grabbed the sword by its hilt, and pointed the tip at the ground. He lifted it, red-faced, then thrust it into the puddle while shouting something that, to Helen, sounded incoherent. Muddy water splashed in all directions as the sword sank into the earth. He took his hands away, leaving the sword standing straight up from the puddle.

"There's something," he said wryly.

A mist rose around the sword, swirling and expanding, covering the road and rising until the landscape around them was completely obscured. The temperature dropped precipitously as the wind picked up. A rhythmic flapping sounded above them.

"What's happening?" Helen asked, worry creeping into her voice.

Orvyn shrugged. "Something?" At Helen's dirty look, he added, "This has never happened before."

A dark shape appeared in the mist, not five feet away. Orvyn swooshed his hands, and the mist cleared to reveal a red-scaled leg and a fist full of claws. Clasped within, Daegel beat against it.

"Daegel!" Helen yelled.

"He can't hear you," Orvyn chided. He withdrew the sword from the puddle. The mist cleared and the vision faded, leaving them alone on the muddy road. "But you were right, he's alive."

Determination hardened her features. "Then our only choice is to go after the dragon. We've got to help him."

"How do you expect that we two can achieve such a lofty goal? Daegel was our strongest."

Helen sneered. "We were never going to defeat it with steel alone, Orvyn. We'll think of something."

"Of course we will," he said, resignation creeping into his tone. "We shall *think* it to death."

"Don't be an ass." She stalked off in the direction of Ivan's farm. "I've got to retrieve my arrows. Then we're off to Wychsbreath."

The road sought refuge in the shadow of the northern range as the valley narrowed. Abandoned farms stood watch over blighted fields. Mutilated carcasses stood like macabre statues, whispering of their unseen, violent ends. The air was heavy with the pungent stench of decay; with each breath, it dampened their souls and shrouded their hearts with foreboding darkness.

Their arrival at Wychsbreath, a peaceful farming community far from the Kingdom's enemies, should have lightened the blanket of oppression that had followed them. It did not.

The first sign of trouble was that the village had erected a wall. The makeshift barrier was a simple construction of logs and rope stretched across the road in each direction. Sharpened poles jutted from the ground every few paces. Bowmen watched them from platforms at the top of the wall. A wooden arch marked the village's entrance. Two gaunt, weary guards stood beneath it, their pikes crossed to bar entrance.

"State your business," one said brusquely. Their weathered, drawn faces were suffused with a pale gray pallor.

"We have a warrant from the King," Helen said. "We're to slay the dragon that plagues his subjects in this valley and the village of Wychsbreath. The burgher is ordered to provide whatever aid and comfort are necessary for us to complete this mission."

"Our village has no burgher," one of the guards said.

Orvyn looked to his sister as he reached inside his cloak. "His Majesty has told us..." he started.

The men tightened their grip on their weapons. "Your Majesty is mistaken."

"He is your King as well," Orvyn chided.

The guards shook their heads. "We recognize no king."

Helen placed a calming hand on her brother's shoulder and met the guard's stony gaze with soft, firm tones. "Perhaps we might speak with whoever is in charge."

"The High Priest." This from the other guard, who had not yet spoken.

Helen adopted a disarming smile. "Perhaps His Eminence would grant us an audience?"

The first guard nodded at the other. "He is a busy man, but you may seek an audience." The guards raised their pikes to allow them to pass. "Know that his authority here is absolute."

Helen and Orvyn exchanged a look. "We thank you," she said to the men. "On behalf of His Majesty the King."

The village was small, and they had no trouble finding their way to the guildhall. But the uncanny stillness of the empty streets made them uneasy. From every darkened shadow, Helen could feel the villagers' eyes upon them, sending chills down her spine.

The guildhall looked as though it had been the site of a devastating battle. The pitted stone walls were stained with black soot, and broken shutters clacked against the building as they swung in the wind. Spires rose from each corner of the building, but one had been shorn off as if cleaved off by a giant axe. The unguarded, open door beckoned them to enter.

"Dare we enter?" Orvyn asked, leaning heavily on his staff.

Helen nodded slowly. "Stay on your guard."

Inside, torchlight provided dim illumination. The walls were covered with dark tapestries, giving the hall a dark, oppressive atmosphere. A smoky haze swirled and infused the air with an acrid, sulfuric stench. Rows of pews faced a blood-stained altar, behind which a human skull grinned at them from atop the high back of a black, wooden throne.

"Good afternoon."

Helen jumped at the eerie voice that greeted them from the shadows. She cleared her throat as she sought out its source. "We seek an audience with the High Priest?"

A figure emerged from the darkness; a stooped, ancient man draped in blood-red robes laced with golden filigree. Long, wispy hair dangled beneath a black cap while he studied them with yellowed, rheumy eyes. "You have the advantage of me." A crooked smile was pasted on his lips like a costume.

"We have a warrant," she said. "From the King."

The man raised a skeletal hand to the skull. "Have you met the town burgher?" The painful creak of his voice tumbled across the room. "He was loyal to your king."

Helen swallowed. "We are here to dispatch the dragon."

"He blasphemed," the man continued, stroking the skull as one would a pet. "He suffered the fate of all blasphemers, as was his due."

"The dragon," Helen said. "Where is it?" With a shift of her hips, the folds of her cloak fell open to reveal a worn hilt and a sliver of cold steel.

"Scalithrax protects us," the man said. Doors opened at the back of the hall. "He has delivered us from the hordes of ogres that would ravage our town."

Orvyn raised a nervous eyebrow. "You've, ah, seen these ogres, have you?"

The man spread his hands before him. "Scalithrax enriches us with its wealth." Behind him, four guards strode forward, each holding a sword.

"Ah, perhaps you've not noticed the desolation that surrounds your, ah, your fine village." Orvyn tightened his grip on his staff. "I'm not sure I'd call that enrichment."

The High Priest's grin became a sneer. "Enrichment takes many forms. We want for nothing here in our peaceful utopia." He clapped his hands together. Behind them, the doors to the hall slammed shut. "We want nothing from you or your king," he snarled.

The soldiers passed by the priest and stepped around the altar.

"You have come at an opportune time," the man continued, rubbing his hands together. "Our tribute to the mighty dragon Scalithrax is overdue. The two of you will do nicely."

Daegel struggled against the dragon's grasp. He pushed and pulled. He beat his fists against it. But his efforts were for naught; he could not overcome its iron grip. He reached for a weapon, but the dragon's thick, leathery toes denied him access.

The air grew misty as they gained altitude, and dizziness clawed at his consciousness. His fists pounded even as his head swam and his vision went dark. He gasped and slumped, succumbing at last to the rarefied air.

He was lying on his back when his senses returned to him. He breathed deeply of the thick, smoky air around him. Nausea gripped his stomach as his head spun with vertigo; he shut his eyes tighter until the feeling ran its course.

When he felt well enough, he cracked his eyes open a sliver. Firelight provided dim illumination but gave no clue as to his whereabouts. Beside him, something yellow glinted in the faint light. He moved and was greeted by the tinkling sound of shifting metal. His hands rested in a sea of small metal objects. He grasped one of them and examined it. The face of the King stared at him, stamped onto the side of a gold coin.

His eyes flew open as he pushed himself up. Not twenty feet away, the dragon's narrowed, yellow eyes stared at him as he floundered atop its hoard.

He scrambled back, coins flying as he struggled across the mound. He slipped and stumbled his way to his feet, fumbling to reach a blade as he did.

The dragon laughed.

"You mock me?" he yelled with as much bravado as he could muster.

"I pity you," the dragon replied in a resonant, slithering voice that shook the cavern. "To stand amidst such wealth and grandeur while under the sway of fear and misplaced loyalty."

Daegel's eyebrows curled into question marks. "What?"

The dragon lifted its head to a set of braziers placed high in the cavern walls and exhaled a breath of fire. The braziers roared to life, filling the lair with a warm, flickering light. The dragon's blood-red scales shimmered as the firelight danced across them, but even its deadly beauty shrank next to the dazzling display the flames revealed.

Mounds of gem-studded treasure towered above them while half-buried chests spilled their riches into the hoard. Rubies and sapphires, diamonds and exotic gems he couldn't name. The air glowed with dazzling brilliance as the firelight danced across them. It was more treasure than the awestruck Daegel had ever seen. He ached to touch it, to hold such brilliance in his own two hands.

"Magnificent, isn't it?" Its voice slithered to him across the cavern and enticed him with its warm embrace.

He forced his gaze back to his captor. The serpent was draped atop a mound of gold. It sprawled and spread, rolls of scaly flesh cascading over its hoard. Its head was longer than Daegel was tall and yet appeared too small for its immense body. Gluttony on an unmatched scale, Daegel thought.

"Why do you show me this?" he breathed.

Scalithrax lifted its great bulk from the mound. It dipped its head and buried its nose in the golden treasures, then tilted its head back to shower itself with its riches.

"Answer me!"

The dragon laughed. "I wonder at the wealth your king has promised to dispatch poor Scalithrax." It lowered its head yet again, this time nudging a small pile of the treasure towards Daegel. "I wonder at the price for you to dispatch someone for Scalithrax."

He eyed the stack sliding towards him. Small when compared to the riches around him, but much larger than what the king had offered. "Why would a mighty dragon like you need others to do their dirty work?"

Scalithrax chuckled. "To snack on a troublesome human can satisfy a craving but sabotage a goal."

Daegel lowered his sword. "But were I to take care of your troublesome human..."

"A new leader for the human vermin that dwell below would serve me well."

He averted his eyes from his captor. No matter where he looked, though, he saw only incredible wealth. And it could be his to share. Or, his alone, perhaps. He adjusted his grip on his sword. "My warrant is clear. Why shouldn't I just slay you now and be done with it? The villagers below would be better off without your tyranny."

The beast threw back its head and let out a great guffaw. "The villagers welcome Scalithrax. It is your King who is a tyrant. He taxes them into poverty. For protection, your King claims. But he gives them no protection. He gives them nothing."

Scalithrax narrowed its gaze and put its nose right up to Daegel. "Your King's 'protection' is to hunt my kind. To add the heads of my kin to his wall. To grind our horns and smash our eggs for his sorceror's so-called 'magic.' To breed more vermin and sully our hunting grounds."

The dragon slid another pile towards Daegel. "Scalithrax tires of fighting the human vermin. A partnership with the humans, I have offered. A partnership with Scalithrax, they have accepted." The dragon sat back, looking at him expectantly. "The King will oppose it at his peril."

Daegel eyed the offering. So much treasure! With such wealth, even his father would bow down before him.

Scalithrax clucked in amusement. "You wear the stench of avarice like a fine perfume." It closed its eyes and inhaled deeply. "Its bouquet is intoxicating."

Daegel shook his head but could not turn his eyes from the gold. "The humans below already follow you, dragon. Of what use am I to you, then? Why should I help you?"

Scalithrax snorted derisively. "Their priest follows his own agenda. But you. Ah! Unstoppable, we would be. Even your King would tremble with you at my side."

Daegel reached a hand towards the dragon's offering. His fingers touched the gold and caressed a ruby the size of his fist. He pondered the dragon's words, the warrant drifting from his mind and fading into a distant memory.

The guards threw themselves at the siblings. Helen dodged their attacks, a blade in each hand. She blocked and parried, thrust, and jabbed, driving the men deeper into the hall. She stabbed one man, slipping her blade beneath his armor. He gasped and fell, his life gone before he hit the floor.

Orvyn was a whirlwind of motion, his body flowing with the lethal dance of the warrior-mage. He leapt and kicked, a fountain of blood spurting as the man fell. The crack of a rib left another man wheezing as Orvyn twirled his staff. With the sweep of a leg, the man's head smashed into the floor. A look at his face and Orvyn knew the man would not again bother them.

"Orvyn!" His head snapped up at Helen's strangled plea. She clutched at her throat and struggled for breath, her face beet-red. The remaining guard advanced, hand outstretched in a bid to capture and subdue her.

Orvyn's staff crashed against the man's forearm with a satisfying crack. The man cried out but slumped in silence when the staff struck the base of his skull.

Helen's knees crumpled as Orvyn reached out to her, but she shook her head. She pointed weakly at the High Priest. A gleeful glint in his eye, the priest chanted, wringing his hands, and staring at her.

With a snarl, Orvyn reached into his cloak. "Quiet!" he yelled as he threw a simple, black cloth towards the priest.

The cloth vanished in a cloud of smoke. The priest's mirth transformed into shocked surprise as silence befell him. He worked his jaw, but his mouth would not open. He clawed at his face, frantically working to peel apart his lips.

Helen gasped, sucking in huge lungfuls of air. She stood unsteadily and retrieved her swords, then took one swaying step toward the struggling priest.

"Helen, no!" Orvyn warned. "We've got to get out of here."

The sounds of rushing footsteps echoed around them. Soldiers streamed into the back of the hall, joined by villagers wielding axes, pitchforks, and clubs.

They bolted for the doors. Helen slammed into them, twisted the handles, pulled, and pushed, but they were held fast.

Behind them, the priest smiled gleefully, his lips parted to reveal his yellowed teeth. He grunted and groaned as he worked his jaw; his silence would not long continue.

"Stand aside," Orvyn said. His eyes lost focus as he chanted an incantation and punched at the empty air. The doors rattled but held firm.

The first of the soldiers ran past the altar, slashing with his sword as he reached them. Helen parried and buried her knee in his groin. "Orvyn, hurry!" she said as she clubbed the ailing man in the side of his head.

His chants dripping with anger, Orvyn punched again at the empty air. The doors shook. With a shout, he shoved with both of his palms. The doors exploded off their hinges and landed several yards away.

Helen grabbed Orvyn by the wrist, and together they fled.

The trail to the dragon's den was obvious and well-worn. But while it provided them with a clear direction toward their goal, it left little mystery about their flight.

Helen turned and loosed several arrows towards the villagers. She checked her quiver but was dismayed by its dwindling supply.

"Orvyn, it would do wonders for our chances if you could send a few lightning bolts their way."

Orvyn ducked a branch as he continued upward. "It would, wouldn't it? But as Master Izinoth has said, why summon a lion when a house cat will do?"

Helen risked a glance over her shoulder. "If you're going to summon cats, it better be a lot of them."

He chuckled. "Lightning needs a rod to guide it. We'll have to try something else."

The storm had downed several trees. With a muttered chant and a wave of his hands, the trunks quivered and slid a few inches, then rolled and tumbled down the mountain. His eyes rolled up in his head as he continued. More trunks rumbled down the slope in a great, billowing cloud of dust, joined by loose rubble from higher up the slope. When the dust settled, the clamor from below had become cries of anguish.

Helen glanced back. Most of the villagers were on the ground nursing injuries; those who weren't were fleeing towards the village. For the moment, at least, the siblings had evaded them.

———————

The trail wound a meandering path up the mountain, stealing time but taking no great effort to follow. Dusk had fallen, and a light mist enveloped them. Around a bend, the dirt and stone of the trail met a flagstone path leading into a darkened cave.

An unlit brazier rested in the center of the chamber. With a pinch of ash and a brief incantation, Orvyn lit the firepot, filling the space with warmth and light. A dais stood to one side, and a nook in the back wall held a bloody altar. Beside it, an opening led deeper into the mountain. The air wafting from the corridor shimmered and stank of sulfur. Orvyn conjured an orb of light to guide them as they crept into the passage.

"Something feels...off. Don't you think so, Helen?" She shook her head, her attention consumed with their mission.

At the end of the passage was the dragon's lair.

They stepped from the rocky corridor into the gold-filled cavern. The malevolent gaze of the dragon Scalithrax greeted them. Beside him stood their brother, a cold smile on his face and a sword held loosely by his side.

Helen held her bow at the ready. "Scalithrax, we come by order of our King to rid the land of your pestilence."

"No." Daegel stepped forward. "The dragon and I have reached an agreement."

She scowled at him. "What agreement?"

Orvyn surveyed the cavern and its treasures. "Something's not right here."

"He offers a partnership and considerably more gold than the King."

"No," Orvyn objected. "It's a lie."

"You should know better than to trust a dragon," Helen said.

A tendril of smoke escaped the dragon's nose as it watched, its scales glistening in the flickering light.

"I assure you, there's no deceit here." Daegel held out a hand. "You can join us. Rule the valley and share in the dragon's wealth."

"You're blind," Orvyn said through gritted teeth. "There is only deceit here." He closed his eyes and started an incantation. His chants grew louder and more urgent as he raised his arms. The treasure rattled as his voice echoed about the chamber, reverberating and building until they had to cover their ears. As his incantation reached its crescendo, he brought his hands together in a mighty clap.

A bright flash of light filled the chamber and momentarily blinded the siblings.

"What have you done?" Daegel breathed. Behind him, the dragon growled menacingly.

Where once there had been a cavern-filling hoard of gold, now there was garbage. Bones and rotting corpses were piled high along the walls, the true scope of the dragon's gluttony now apparent. Beneath the dragon, a small mound of gold and silver coins formed a bed on which the gluttonous beast lay.

"It was all a lie, Daegel." Orvyn wheezed, exhausted from the effort of dispelling the illusion. "There is but a paltry treasure. Dragons are deceitful creatures, and you fell for its lies."

"What have you done?" Daegel shouted. Fire blazing in his eyes and sword held high, he charged. Helen ran to intercept him, a blade in each hand and fury etched on her face.

"You have been so easily swayed by this foul beast that you would attack your own brother, Daegel?" she shouted.

The dragon lifted its massive bulk from its bed of coins. Its yellow eyes burned with fury as it drew in its breath.

Orvyn threw a pinch of ash in the air and began a chant of protection. The air shimmered with Orvyn's protective barrier.

As the dragon's flames splashed against Orvyn's barrier, Helen crossed Daegel's sword with her own. Sparks flew as their blades met. A thrust and a parry, a swing and a block, each deftly countering the other's attack. Their skills were well-matched, but as Helen was forced back, she was reminded that their strength was not.

Daegel swung at Helen's head. She ducked and jabbed but couldn't connect. He thrust with his shield, striking Helen's hand and forcing her to drop a blade. She deflected his follow-up swing but stumbled as he pressed her.

The dragon swiped at Orvyn. He ducked the worst of the blow, but still, a claw raked painfully across his arm. He rolled behind Daegel, blood from his wound staining the ground where he rolled.

Daegel pressed his advantage, advancing and swinging. She retreated, parrying each blow. But her foot caught a rock, and she stumbled and fell, the breath knocked from her as she landed on her back. Daegel stood over her, wild fury in his eyes. He lifted his sword overhead, the tip aimed at her heart.

Helen gasped as she waited for him to plunge his blade into her waiting chest. His mouth dropped open as he jerked with a sudden spasm. He staggered and coughed, blood trickling from his mouth. The tip of a sword emerged from his chest. His own blade fell from his hands as he dropped to his knees. He slumped and fell over on his side, dead.

Helen stared at her fallen brother. She recognized the blade that skewered him; it was her own dropped sword. She turned her gaze away and found Orvyn, eyes glazed and face pale. He reached out an unsteady hand to her.

Then she saw the descending maw of the dragon behind him.

"Get down!" She grabbed his arm and pulled. Scalithrax bit, catching only the folds of his billowing cloak. The dragon lifted its head, drawing Orvyn into the air. He shrugged off his cloak and dropped to the ground next to Helen.

The beast shook its head and threw aside the empty cloak. The cavern shook as the dragon bellowed a fear-inducing roar and pushed itself up to its full, terrifying height.

Its jaws snapped as they rolled and regained their feet. It swiped as Orvyn swung his staff, landing a harmless blow against the creature's thick hide. Helen charged at it with a sword raised high but was knocked aside with a flap of its wing.

Orvyn raised his hands and began a chant. The dragon swung its head like a club, sending him flying and puncturing his leg with one of its deadly horns. He screamed as he struck a wall.

Helen unslung her bow and loosed three shots as she advanced on the beast. She reached for a fourth, but her quiver was empty. The dragon stomped, barely missing her as she rolled under it to avoid the blow. She drew a dagger from her boot and thrust it deep into its soft underside. She let go and scrambled away; the dagger remained.

The dragon swatted her, sending her across the room. "Ah!" She rolled as she landed but was slow to rise. It swept its tail, again launching her across the cavern. She landed face first and was slow to get up. "Orvyn," she moaned. "The dagger!"

Orvyn shook his head and staggered as the dragon turned its attention to him. He could see the dagger protruding from its underside.

The dragon inhaled, its lungs inflating and tendrils of smoke drifting from its nose.

He concentrated on the dagger as he chanted an incantation, pounding one fist on top of the other.

The sound of thunder reverberated in the cavern as storm clouds formed above. Darkness clouded his features as he chanted. The air roiled around them. With the thrust of his hand, he pointed at their attacker.

The dragon leaned forward, belching fire.

The air sizzled as a cerulean bolt of lightning cleaved the air and struck the dagger. The impact hurled the dragon across the chamber. Flames splashed against the walls as its head was jerked every which way. It screamed as tendrils of energy crackled around its colossal form, searing blackened trails across its hide. Tremors shook the cavern as it crashed to the ground. It landed on its side, its legs spasming in a desperate but futile attempt to right itself.

Orvyn screamed and collapsed to the cavern floor. He rolled over and over, extinguishing the flaming remnants of his clothes, then lay still on his back, gasping.

Helen staggered to her feet. Somewhere along the way, she'd lost her remaining sword. She limped to Daegel's still form and retrieved the blade that had dealt him the fatal blow. Holding it high, she ran at the dragon, screaming an incoherent battle cry.

Scalithrax wailed as she plunged the blade into its chest and pierced its foul, deceitful heart. It kicked feebly at her, tried weakly to lift its head. She pulled out the blade and thrust again, twisting as it penetrated the beast's chest. Its eyes, once filled with malevolent fire, dimmed as it recognized its fate. A tremor shook its massive frame, and then, finally, it lay still, a final whimper coming with its dying breath.

Helen knelt beside her brother and tended his wounds; she knew a bit of the healing arts. She staunched the flow of blood and bound his wounds and said a few mumbled words that helped to ease his pain.

"My cloak," Orvyn croaked.

Helen scanned the cavern, finding the cloak among the bones and debris along one side of the cavern.

From a pocket, Orvyn took a poultice to salve his red, blistered body. He winced at every touch of it. Terrible burns covered his face, chest, and legs; parts of one arm were blackened with them. When he finished, he started to lie back down, but Helen stopped him.

"We can't stay. The villagers will come soon. Can you travel?"

He nodded weakly as he gingerly pulled on his cloak, assuring Helen that the poultice was already working its magic despite his groans.

They were pleased to find that the entrance they had used was not the cavern's only exit. The gaping egress used by the dragon was high and inaccessible, but another exit led to a point out of view of the village, with a game trail that ran in a different direction.

She dragged the body of their fallen brother as far from the dragon's lair as she could manage, an arduous journey that lasted until near dawn. The funeral pyre burned brightly as the stars faded and the sky began to light. The exhausted siblings grieved and wept as they watched the flames embrace their brother and carry his spirit into the heavens.

"I can't believe I killed him." A tear ran down his blistered cheek as he stared into the flames.

Helen put an arm around him. He winced but did not shrug her off. "There was no choice; he was already gone. The dragon took him from us."

Orvyn sniffled. "What of the villagers?"

Helen shook her head. "The dragon is dead. The truth is there for them to see. They will do with it what they will."

The sun crested the horizon, spreading its rays across the fog-enshrouded landscape. They hugged as they watched the brilliant pinks and oranges of dawn, lying down to rest under the bright blue sky of the new day. Later, they would set off to face their father and report to the King. But for now, the warmth of the dying embers guided them to the land of dreams, where dragons were always vanquished and brothers never fell.

The High Priest picked his way past the tumbled debris and up the mountain, his entourage not far behind. He entered the temple they had built for the dragon and held up a hand.

"Wait here. None may enter the sacred chambers whom the mighty Scalithrax hath not anointed."

He slipped into the passage next to the bloody altar and emerged into the chamber that now served as the dragon's tomb. Startled by the sight of the slain dragon, he let out a gasp.

"But the gold, your reverence! You told of us such riches!"

The High Priest scowled. "You were to wait outside," he grumbled.

"I'm sorry, your reverence. I thought I might assist you," he said in a trembling voice.

The priest grunted in annoyance. "It is obvious. They took the gold with them when they murdered the mighty Scalithrax." He stalked past the half-eaten carcass of a horse.

"But there was so much!"

"And so you see the depths of their depravity," the High Priest replied. He turned to face his follower. He recognized the man from the village but did not know his name.

"None may know what has happened here," he said, reaching inside his robes and stepping closer to the man.

"As you wish, your reverence, but why?"

The priest withdrew a dagger from his cloak and thrust it into the man's chest. "It would weaken me," he explained.

The man gawked at the bloody dagger in his belly. "Sir?" he said as he looked at the priest beseechingly.

"The dragon gives me power," the High Priest continued. "They follow me because they fear him." He looked over his shoulder at the dragon's carcass. "Though I fear that Scalithrax and I did not quite see eye to eye."

The man gurgled, and his eyes glazed over as he fell to the ground.

"Perhaps they have done me a favor," he said, wiping his blade on the dead man's clothes. "It was becoming increasingly difficult to satisfy. And I have my own ambitions."

He left the tomb and rejoined his entourage in the cavern. "Scalithrax has demanded a sacrifice," he announced. "And your brother has graciously accepted the honor."

The members of his entourage bowed their heads in respect. "What of the interlopers, your eminence?"

The High Priest smiled. "Scalithrax has vanquished them," he said with a glint in his eye. "As I knew he would. Now, Scalithrax sleeps. He must not be disturbed." He led them outside. "Tomorrow, we seal the cavern."

"Seal it, your reverence?"

"Yes. The dragon must not be disturbed." A smile ruptured his face as he started down the mountain trail. "Until then, you shall follow me without question. So Scalithrax commands."

About Stephen W. Chappell

Steve Chappell is the chosen servant of four feline overlords who grudgingly tolerate his service. They live in the outskirts of the NJ pine barrens with his wife, whom they also tolerate. He currently works as a systems engineer. His writing credits include stories published in Dark Horses Magazine and in the anthology "Ruth and Ann's Guide to Time Travel." Besides writing, he enjoys reading, photography, and hiking. He can be found online at https://www.facebook.com/stephen.chappell.author/.

Back in the Saddle

A "Tales From the Dream Nebula" adventure

By M.D. Boncher

———————————

Dawson VanderZee was fed up with media fame and wanted to return to his former life as a professional hunter. When the Big Double M Ranch hired him to remove some dangerous megafauna that threatened their tourist operation, it seemed a perfect way to restart his old career. Now, he was a million miles from home, in the strange skylands of the Chimera Belt. Where uplifted animals and exotic creatures were every day occurrences. Dawson was ready to hunt down a nest of Ursipines. Creatures so chemically dangerous they could spawn cultists. Addicted to their toxins, the poor souls were willing to kill to protect the animals he'd been hired to cull. A detail his employer conveniently forgot to mention. This job was going to be far harder to keep himself, and his young stowaway fanboy, Bucky, alive!

Back in the Saddle

A "Tales From the Dream Nebula" adventure

By M. D. Boncher

.

1

As Dawson Vander Zee stepped down onto the depot's platform from the sky train, an excited teenager popped out of the crowd in front of him. The kid's brightly embroidered shirt dripped with fringe and glittering rhinestones. Fancy boots and leather chaps added to his over the top outfit, capped off with a broad brimmed white stetson hat. Dawson was so focused on the kid's clothes at first, he missed the cat ears jutting through holes in the hat's brim.

A felimorph, Dawson thought wearily. *I am so far, far from home.*

The boy tipped back his hat, his orange tabby face beamed with a starry-eyed grin. A long tail stuck out through his britches and swished with excitement.

"Mr. Vander Zee, I watched all four seasons of "Greatest Hunts"! It's my favorite! My dad watches too from time to time, but thinks you need to be out here where the real challenging hunts are."

Oh, my Xiao… he's a fanboy, Dawson realized with growing horror. *I didn't charge them enough.*

He'd gone back to contract hunting to avoid this sort of thing. No publicists and their tours. No directors or executives giving notes on how to hunt cinematically or be more authentic. No more questions about specific hunts he didn't remember. Just pure craft. He didn't care what anyone said, he was not going to utter the show's catch phrase. Not even with a gun to his head.

"Thanks for being a fan. We appreciate it," Dawson's face tightened into a practiced smile, as he hoped to stem the avalanche.

After ten days over two point nine million miles through human-occupied space, regardless of how comfortable the sky train was, he was a bit edgy. Baking in the heat rising off the hot railroad tie platform was a pleasure. No more sterile 68 degree air. The breeze was saturated with dust and creosote.

Looking around, he was impressed with their commitment to the rustic American Southwest ambiance here. The depot's post-conquest design interpreted in adobe and raw timber gave a pleasant faux old west aesthetic. He smiled at what he saw. Half the people standing around wore replica dress of the period or modern clothes heavily influenced by it. A giant silverback primamorph walked by wearing only a hat, gunbelt and MOLL-E gear packed with pouches, and nothing else. Dawson couldn't help but stare

At least the kid was wearing pants. Not all felimorphs do out here, Dawson remembered, pursing his lips, his mind still distracted by his bustling surroundings. *They prefer to go "au naturale". Dunno if I'll get used to that.*

The sky train's locomotive reactor began venting steam and the chaos of passengers loading and unloading became deafening and he no longer could hear the boy talking.

"Yeah?" Dawson said, squinting at the noise. "Sorry, kid. It's been a long trip. What'd you say?"

"I said, I'm your ride to the Big Double M Ranch," the teen shouted, paws-hands cupped around his muzzle.

His attention went back to the boy. "Oh good," The venting ceased.

A canned announcement from the depot's speakers cut off the kid's babble. "Hail Xiao, and welcome to So Lo Gulch Skyland, in the Carotella Drift. All disembarking passengers, remember to present your ticket when you collect your belongings at the baggage car. Don't forget to check out with the Imperial Travel Office in the waiting room. They're expecting you. Next stop for boarding passengers is Rio Marto! Exclusive spa resort skyland. Thank you for riding Dream Union Skylines. Your premier choice for budget travel."

Another clump of tourists pushed by and climbed into the carriage. They were standing in the way.

"Now that you're here, those Ursipines're dead for sure! You ever hunt those before?"

"No kid. I haven't," Dawson muttered. "First time out here."

The pair stepped aside and let embarking passengers through.

"Uh huh. What's yer name, son," Dawson asked carefully, half expected the kid to introduce himself as "Hop-A-Long".

"Buckminster, but everyone calls me Bucky. Some call me Buckaroo," he gave Dawson a sheepish look. "You can call me that if you want? I think it sounds more like a real cowboy."

Dawson said as he looked toward the front of the sky train. "Look, I need to get my gear from the baggage car before they leave, a'right?"

"You bet Mr. Vander Zee! I'll help haul it to the yute for you," Bucky said as he started leading the way.

"Yute?"

"The air truck," Bucky said as if it was the dumbest question in the world.

"Right." Dawson sighed, and followed along, opening up his datapad and pulling up his claim ticket as he walked.

The scuffed and dented baggage handlers were pulling the last of his gear off the car when he arrived. A small crowd blocked his way, but Bucky had somehow managed to slip in-between the crush getting right up front.

"Rollo!" the kid called out, "Gimme Mr. Vander Zee's gear, will ya?"

The big mechoid displayed a rude emoji on his digitized face screen when he recognized Bucky. "C'mon, Buckster. You don't got a ticket you don't get bags. Them's the rules and you know it."

"Come on! Help me out here." Bucky whined petulantly.

"No way. Not getting yelled at again," Rollo said, giving a 'poop' and 'eyeroll' emoji flash instead of facial features. His servos groaned as he lifted a pallet of machinery off the baggage car.

"Here ya go, mench," Dawson addressed the mechoid and shoved his arm between two chatting people, oblivious to their surroundings. They scowled as he pushed his way between them, not bothering to apologize to the rude pair. Rollo did a quick scan of Dawson's datapad.

"Hail Xiao, and thank you," the baggage handler burped in a deep voice.

"Hail Xiao. Give my bags to Bucky, I gotta check in with the depot agent."

"As the gentlemench wishes," Rollo said adding a thumbs up on his face.

Dawson nodded, then laid a hand on Bucky's shoulder. "Take my kit and load up your yute. When you're done, find me in the depot. Okay, son?"

"You bet, Mr. Vander Zee!" Bucky said as he unfolded his carry-all wagon. Dawson had to give the boy credit. He came prepared for the job.

Striding toward the depot waiting room, he rolled his shoulders to get some of the kinks from the trip out of his muscles. As the door opened, a good recreation of a nineteenth century American train station greeted him.

Modern conveniences like the security scanning line, a small VR amusement room to one side and the diner on the other ruined the immersion. Holo-screens projected schedules or rule loops and advertising above sentients' heads.

"Travel to exotic Conongabo!"

"Choose Dream Union for your next pilgrimage to Aegibria this X-mas."

"Visit exciting Metroballis!"

Passing through a few holo spokesmodels that tried to engage Dawson with sales pitches, he walked to the imperial travel window.

A gila monster reptimorph in an imperial officer's uniform waited with friendly expression. "Hail Xiao and welcome Mr. Vander Zee," She addressed him.

Dawson blanched for a moment. Her cultured soprano voice catching him off guard. He never could tell reptimorphs genders. They all looked alike to him, sadly. At least she seemed used to first timers' reactions to being near the Chimera Belt.

Crap, he thought. *She recognized me. Here we go, round two.*

"Hail Xiao," he said stepping up to the counter and bracing for more fan reactions.

"I'm checking in for special hunting permit #14792-HM. Any new advisories?" He waved his pad over the countertop scanner.

"Sso you're the man Mr. Morsskane hired to rid us of those toxic Urssapiness roaming around?"

"Yes'm." Relief grew that she wasn't going to gush on him.

"Good newss. There'ss no new alertss or updatess. Your original liccensse downloadss are sstill accurate."

"That's just dandy," Dawson said with a smile.

"For your ssafety, I must assk the following questionss."

"Fire away, darlin.'"

She licked one eye and smiled. *A nervous tick?* Dawson guessed, grateful at her professionalism and indifference to his celebrity.

"Do you have your field dresssing drone with the 'Toximax 14' Hazzmat protocolss?"

"Yes, ma'am."

"Do you have any additional weaponss you intend to use during your hunt other than those lissted on your application?" she asked reading the next question from her script.

"No, ma'am."

"Do you intend to use your contractor sstatuss to include any off liccensse bounty hunting?"

"I don't intend to, but if some behnger interferes with my duties, I will defend myself according to Xiao's law," Dawson said without any prejudice or excitement.

The factor smiled with her eyes, or was that a disapproving squint? Reptimorphs were not common back home, so he wasn't sure. "As any good ccitizen sshould do."

"Anything else, ma'am?" Dawson gave her his off kilter heart-melting grin. It seemed to have the desired effect on her as a genuine smile bloomed.

"Nothing at all Mr. Vander Zee, but I'll give you a sspeck of perssonal caution for when you're out there," she leaned forward. A deep protective instinct kicked in despite himself and he hesitated a moment.

She's not going to bite me you idiot, he thought. *Although, her mouth is still poisonous.*

"Watch out for Jumbo Magumbo. The bounty on him iss up, and local law enforccement would happily pay out if ssssomething "untoward" happened." She lick-winked at him.

"Ma'am, if we tangle horns, I'll bring him back. Don't expect him to be breathing." Dawson's eyes were dark and sparkling. His lop sided grin oozed confidence and danger.

"Then y'all have yoursself a ssucccesssful hunt in Sso Lo Gulch. When you see Mr. Morsskane tell him Officer Ssaunderss ssendss her besst."

"You have my word," Dawson agreed and turned around almost tripping over Bucky.

"Ready to go?" He asked?

"Yeah, all tied down!" the boy said.

"Then let's git while the getting's good."

"Yeah! I have a million questions!" Bucky said, leading the way.

Xiao kill me, Dawson thought, as they walked out the door.

2
———

Dawson flew over the rolling land back to ranch headquarters in one of the work yutes. There, an imposing Texas hill country farmhouse rose into view, surrounded by a decorative picket fence, glowing in concert with the colorful clouds of the evening. He banked slowly over the outskirts of the homestead and parked the yute back at the machine shed with the other vehicles.

The "MM" tourbus lumbered back to the machine shed by him while a batch of exhausted tourists made their way into a guest bunkhouse, pulling their luggage on anti-grav coasters over the scrubby sand. Various tourists awaited the dinner bell, relaxed together over cocktails and beers on the sprawling wrap-around front porch. He caught sight of Bucky walking with his father Darius up to the main house for dinner. Bucky took off like a shot toward Dawson once he stepped out of the vehicle.

"Can I help you with anything? Carry your bags? What'cha need?" Bucky asked almost frantically.

"I'm good, son," Dawson said. He didn't want to take advantage of the boy's hero worship. It was bad enough that the kid made a spectacle of himself. He didn't need accusations of abusing such a state of devotion.

Dawson shouldered his tac bag and the rest of his gear, shaking his head. "You heading up for supper?"

"Buckminster! Leave him alone!" came the bellow from Darius, a giant black patheramorph. Bucky's ears swept back, his eyes got wide, and his tail popped into a bottle brush.

"We'll talk later. I'm good for now, but you best mind yer pa," Dawson nodded toward the head foreman whose ears were flattened to his skull.

"Oh... ok, Mr. Vander Zee," Bucky said and walked back, his back hunched. Poor Bucky clutched his tail as he trudged in front of his father to the house.

He must be getting an earful, Dawson thought and shook his head. *Can't fault Darius though. Bucky's abuse of the spillover perks of his Dad's position isn't a good habit to let alone.* Dawson did think Bucky's assumptions of his dad's authority was relatively benign, but if not squashed fast, it could grow.

That kid makes me feel so old. Dawson sighed with the thought. His muscles aching as he walked.

Dawson finished changing clothes and made his way back to the house as the triangle dinner bell rattled.

Mr. Marvin Morskane, owner of the Big Double M Ranch had a hefty dining table capable of seating fifty guests. Common practice had the senior men eat with the tourists and help field the questions of the greenhorns there to experience "living history". Dawson's presence as an actual celebrity made it an extra special occasion.

Family style western cooking at its best was on the table. No snobbery or fancy frills, only classic dishes done exceptionally well. Dawson's seat was a few down from Mr. Morskane. The big human looked like a piece of tooled leather. His skin was tanned and wrinkled from decades of hard work outdoors. His wife was as glamorous and stylish, clearly a paragon splice with perfect genes, but age was giving her a dried apple woman's appearance. Together, they were like cute salt and pepper shakers, perfectly matched.

Across from Dawson sat Darius with Bucky at his side. The boy sat stiffly in his chair, elbows conspicuously off the table. The rest of the nearby places were filled with premium guests followed by the band of cowboys going out with them in the morning for their cattle drive experience.

"How went the scouting, Mr. Vander Zee?" his host asked.

"Went fine, Mr. Morskane. We're all set to go."

"Call me Marvin." He gave Dawson a sparkling smile.

"Sure thing, Marvin," Dawson said.

"Did I hear correctly that you've been called in special to deal with some Ursipines?" a mechoid guest asked. The gold plated mechoid felt out of place at a dude ranch. Apparently self aware robots liked to get away and have vacations, too.

"Yes, Mechster Gildabrent," he answered, then started right into his stock spiel he gave for his entire stay. "Ursapines are very dangerous to biologics. Cattle in particular. They're a weird mashup creature probably created by Xiao the Eternal to pester humanity. Others say they are a side effect of evolution going off the rails in the Dream. Scholars fight over what's true, but how else would you explain it? A Grizzly bear the size of a buffalo, covered with long porcupine-like quills and little hedgehog spines underneath that are so toxic, they poison their environment? Breathing its musk can maim a person at a range of a hundred yards?"

"My! That is something!" the mechoid said. Dawson suspected he was some sort of imperial court staffer. Not an actual courtier noble.

"It will make for an interesting hunt, but you won't have much to worry about. Ursapines prefer meat over servos." A chuckle went around that end of the table.

More random small talk sprang up. Dawson and Darius shared a glance of relief as the guests put their questions to Marvin.

"Mr. Morskane, what about this eco-terrorist we've been hearing about? A Jumbo Magumbo?" asked a harried looking businessman who Dawson never bothered to remember his name.

He'd expected it sooner or later. Darius' eyes narrowed.

"What sort of name is that?" added his wife with an irritating titter.

"Calling him an eco-terrorist misses the mark. He's a kook shaman of some self-created, drug-based fake religion. Like the old drug cults of pre-conquest Earth. How someone could think intoxication brought on by exposure to Ursapine poisons baffles me," Marvin said, his lip curling into a sneer.

"Hail Xiao that they were declared criminals. At least they can be dealt with swiftly," the businessman's wife sniffed haughtily.

Dawson held his tongue and took a big bite of pot roast. He felt the same way about her worship of Emperor Xiao.

"Are we in any danger from him?" Mechster Gildabrent asked.

"No," Dawson said. "That dangerous honor belongs to me. Every Ursapine I can kill will motivate him to come after me personally. This assumes Jumbo is in the area at all. I suspect he's pestering someone else because my scouting hasn't turned up hide nor hare of him. Which reminds me, Darius. I have two new poisoned waterholes marked on the map so you can keep clear of them."

"You are coming with us?" the businessman leaned toward Dawson.

"I'll be all over the place with the air truck, keeping you safe by taking down these critters."

"Don't expect to see much of him, y'all," Darius added. His contra-bass voice commanding attention. "The drive passes near networks of slot canyons. They're hell to track in, so he'll be airborne ranging far out and around checking things out. We're on horses with the herd. Of course, if you see an Ursapine, get clear and holler out. These beasts are dangerous."

"I'll be around the chuckwagon with you for meals most times. Don't nobody call me late for supper." The joke caused a few big laughs around that end of the table.

———————

With dinner concluded, guests and ranch hands filtered outside. Some went to enjoy the night around the giant bonfire ring for drinks and cigars. Dawson was tempted to join them, but it would be best to prep for tomorrow.

He pondered what a real desert night on Earth was like with stars and the moon shining down. Like everyone he'd seen pictures and videos. "Night" in the Dream Nebula was really more like deep civil twilight. This shade was as close as they ever got to it, except during a particulate storm. Everything turned nearly into silhouettes with dim illumination from the dark orange, red and purple washes of clouds as the skyland rotated to face the dark cold deeps of the Dream Nebula.

They would be heading out at what used to be called "first light" which now meant 0500 hours. His sensors marked the waterholes reporting if any Ursipines were drinking there. Gamecams now covered several caves that might serve as ambushes. There may be some he'd missed, but enough of them were covered along the drive's course with plenty of warning.

Dawson let out a huge sigh and scratched his head. *Perhaps it'd be best to make final checks and hit the hay. Best be as rested as he can be,* he thought.

"Dawson?" came a voice behind him.

He turned and saw Marvin and Darius approaching through the lit path from the house.

"Yes, Mr. Morskane, uh… I mean Marvin?"

Marvin took a look around to make sure no one was within earshot. "I didn't want to say this in front of any other guests, but you best be careful out there," Marvin said, his face grim.

"I will, sir." Dawson said.

"No. It's more than that. Jumbo Magumbo called you out personally on the network," Darius said and projected a holoscreen from his personal assistant on his wrist.

The video that materialized was a juvenile psychedelic meme. Lots of drugged out threats, trolling and halfwit philosophizing mixed with doctored images of Jumbo Magumbo killing Dawson, like a self-styled holy avenger.

It ended with a direct personal challenge, like a little boy demanding they meet and have some sort of fight after school on the playground.

A chuckle and lopsided grin bubbled up from deep in Dawson's throat. "That's an amusing attempt to terrorize me. He shouldn't post things while fried on his own supply."

Darius clearly agreed with the sentiment. "We're not worried about it so much. We just wanted you to know," the big panther-man said.

"Yeah. It's hard to intimidate someone who is apathetic to your threats. Looking incompetent doesn't help either," Dawson said, feeling more confident in his chances of earning a nice bounty if this loser showed up.

"Forewarned is forearmed," Marvin said.

"Absolutely." Dawson agreed.

"Personally, I'd rather have done the job myself, but as you can see, my time is spoken for. I think Marvin chose well this time."

"This time?" he asked pointedly.

"Well... you're not the first person I hired for this job. There were four others," Marvin admitted.

"So, four other hunters have already taken a shot at your Ursapine problem?"

"Yeah," Marvin said, scratching his jaw and looking up at the clouds intently. "I admit I made mistakes. Tried to do it on the cheap... use local talent, you know? None of us realized Jumbo's persistence in protecting his holy critters."

"Uh huh. He's a religious fanatic. You should have taken that into account. How many died by Jumbo's hands?" Dawson's words were sharp as a razor.

Darius answered first. "He shot two. Local boys who ignored the warnings. One was former animal control and the last was a hunting guide who happened to be in the area. They both vanished. It's possible the Ursapines got them."

"And you let the local authorities know about this?"

Darius gave his boss a sidelong glance that screamed "I told you so".

"No. We didn't. The local boys were chalked up to accidental death by the sheriff, and the others might have just run off. Technically they may still be alive, but we can't find hide nor hair of them and they never came back for their belongings."

Dawson fixed the pair with a mildly disappointed look. The shame expressed by Darius' whiskers and tail swishes gave Dawson a good idea that he was ordered to keep quiet about the others.

"Well, gentlemench, I think it's time I called up imperial security and see what they can tell me about Jumbo so he's less able to surprise me. At least I have time to get some good sleep, but really wish you'd told me this three days ago."

"I'm sorry," Marvin said. "I really didn't think it would matter considering your reputation and skill."

"I insisted you be told about the personal callout at least," Darius threw his boss under the bus.

"Tomorrow, you take care of your tourists, and I'll see if I can't get lucky and bag Jumbo before he does something. Marvin, I'm going to ask that you have your veterinarian come along. He at least could patch me up or administer anti-venin should I need it, okay?"

"I'll see to it," Darius said.

"Depending on what I get back from Imperial Security, I'll need to use the house nano-fabricator to make some extra gear I didn't expect to need."

"Absolutely," Morskane agreed.

"See you at breakfast, then," Dawson said and walked to the bunkhouse for a long night of study.

3

"Long Rifle to Trail Boss, over?" Dawson commed. while zooming in on the beast with his rangefinders.

Ursapines weren't terribly hard to track by air thanks to their size. Having covered the most likely routes from their lair with gamecams reduced his search pattern considerably. The brute lumbered out of a cave and made its way toward a watering hole, its nose scenting the approaching cattle drive.

"A lot smarter than the average bear," Dawson thought with a chuckle as he watched the animal prepare a trap and ambush.

Hovering a thousand feet up and a quarter mile back from the watering hole, the big animal never knew there was an air truck near by. Something that far away didn't register as a threat. It began to bathe.

"Man, these things are cunning!" Dawson thought. The water rinsed through the beast's spines, poisoning the water. Small fish began floating to the surface. Their bright white bellies flashed in the light.

"Trail Boss to Long Rifle, go ahead," Darius' voice crackled over the connection. Must be a mineral deposit interfering with the connection.

"Avoid hole #7. Eyes on an Ursapine poisoning the water. Use alternate stop #7b."

"Copy, Long Rifle," Darius said. "Are you getting interference on your end?"

"Roger that, Trail Boss. I suspect a mineral deposit or maybe an incoming electrical storm." Dawson looked at the sky. Lemon yellow and brown dust plumes colored the Dream Nebula. No unnatural disturbance seemed to be happening. He couldn't spot any flares, glowclouds or lightning. Just the typical distant chunks of planets floating along.

"Maybe. Keep an eye out for bad weather. It might be coming up from underneath the skyland. Surprise storms have been known to come that way, but meteorology says we're clear for now."

"Will do. Long Rifle out," Dawson said. "Now let's drop this big lummox and earn our pay."

"Trail Boss out." Dairus closed the link.

Dawson set the autopilot to hover and rolled down his driver's window. He grabbed his massive blaster rifle. A single bolt could fry all the neurons in that animal's body leaving nothing more than small burns at the impact point and where it grounded out.

He flipped up the scope covers and drew a bead on his target. The range was around 3500 feet. An easy shot for his rifle setup.

Once the Ursapine was done frolicking in the water and eating a few fish, the beast sloshed back to shore going toward a little copse of willows to hide and wait. A growing ring of dead fish speckled the surface of the waterhole.

"Good, you're nice and sopping wet," Dawson murmured as he took aim at the critter's back. He wanted to land the shot where he had the highest chance of grounding out through the heart.

Finger contact with the trigger turned his red dot into an ionizing beam. He hoped the creature didn't notice it and flicked the safety off. Everywhere the ions touched on the beast's body made its fur stand up in a little patch revealing the little barbs and pale flesh underneath. He engaged the rifle's stabilizer gyro, and the crosshairs stopped jiggling from his pulse.

He held his breath.

A purple-white discharge streaked toward the Ursapine at the speed of light, a clap of thunder chased after it. The shot hit the critter's back, above the heart, followed by a secondary flurry of pops and sizzles from the grounding points. The grass beneath the monster's feet burst into flame as the creature shook, in a series of violent spasms. It crashed to the ground, thrashing with desperate attempts for retribution, flinging sprays of foot-long incense stick like quills, hitting nothing.

"Wow!" came a muffled voice in the truck's tarpaulins on the flatbed.

"What the?" Dawson burst out and spun to look over his shoulder, out the rearview window.

From an open end of some tarps protruded a set of small furry paw-hands clutching rangefinders, looking toward the dead animal. They vanished back under the folds.

"Bucky!" He exploded.

With a few quick moves, Dawson rapidly descended to the ground. He heard a high pitch shriek from the boy as he dropped to the ground almost at terminal velocity, leaving the two feeling nearly weightless. He landed and threw the truck door open. It groaned, hyper-extending the spring and jamming open. With snapping fury, he whipped off the folded tarpaulin and saw a hunched up Bucky there with a few rations, his own small caliber quadrail musket and a little flying drone camera.

"I'm sorry! Don't be mad! Don't be mad! I wanted to help," Bucky pleaded. He jerked his riding goggles down around his neck revealing an inverse raccoon mask of dust on his face.

"This isn't a game, Bucky!" Dawson roared. "I can't be looking after you and do my job!"

The desire to scruff the boy was so powerful his hands clenched into fists repeatedly.

Bucky's fur stood up on his back puffing up, his shirt as his ears smashed down to his skull and he cowered.

"I know it's not a game, Mr. Vander Zee, but I knew I could help you."

"We're nine hours out, and with a dead creature on the ground causing a hazmat situation, You can't *believe* how upset I am with you, Bucky! You put your life in danger." Dawson threw his hat to the ground with a dusty puff and scrubbed his face with his bare hands and walked around the truck.

"I'm sorry," Bucky whispered, clutching his tail, tears welling in his eyes. "It's just I thought you might need-"

Dawson's hand shot up, one finger commanding silence. He walked over and looked at what the boy had with him, desperately seeing if he could make an omelet out of these broken eggs.

"You don't have hazmat gear, so you can't help me with that. Plus, I can't risk you being on back of the flatbed anymore." Dawson opened the passenger door and moved bags and gear around from his kit. The gap between the seats was packed shoulder high now. His stowaway had a small cluttered spot to sit next to him. "I've got work to do. Get in and stay there, the air purifiers should keep you safe till I'm done field processing the corpse. I'm not going risk telling your father you died from Ursipine poison."

Bucky nodded a lot. He grabbed his tail tight and nestled into the cab. Dawson got out his hazmat suit and mask. Just in case, he slapped an anti-poison nano patch on his shoulder and handed one to the miserable boy. "Put this on, just in case. It's all I got."

Bucky obeyed, putting it where his fur was thinnest on his belly.

"I know you wanted to help," Dawson explained through the closed window and his chemsuit. "You don't know what this is all about. This job is not only hunting big game."

Bucky slumped as deep into the passenger seat as he could, looking over the lip of the window with big ashamed eyes.

Once sealed, Dawson looked around, pulled out the field drone from the toolbox and fired it up. The device floated on its tiny grav fans whispering like little breezes through grass. It bleeped and blooped as Dawson gave orders from his data pad, took up his rifle in a ready carry and started toward the dead creature. Any twitch and that thing was getting another blast.

"Check vitals," he commanded the drone. It zipped over and pressed a probe between the bear-like body's shaggy coat of quills, to its undercoat and those poisonous spines. The outer quills gave off a toxic musk considered to be aromatic by connoisseurs who burned them like incense sticks. Research last night reminded him this purified the musk reducing the danger, but it became heavier became more hallucinogenic. Apparently that's how the drug's devotees used it in their drug cult. On the other hand, the quill organic compounds were medically beneficial. The inner spines were where the lethal toxins you really didn't want poking you resided.

"The animal is deceased. Zero brain function," the drone blurped.

"Excellent. Skin it. Seal it up and break down the rest."

There was no bounty for it being alive or any use for the carcass. Just the quills and the little spines underneath. The hide would be packaged up and hermetically sealed. Once it was skinned, the drone would nano-disassemble the rest into polymer blocks and rare earth distillates.

Dawson turned around, scanning the horizon, looking for the drive's scouts. Hopefully they would keep the herd far enough away, ensuring no animals got poisoned. If there was a mate or cubs nearby, he would spot them.

"Know what? Save the head. Preserve it for a trophy," he ordered the drone. It 'beep-booped' back an affirmative. May as well have something personal for this hunt. Could be worth selling to someone if not for his own collection.

"Mr. Vander Zee?" Bucky asked through the window. Dawson did a check of the wind direction and motioned for him to roll down the window and took his hood off.

"Yeah?"

"What're you going to do with me?" Bucky leaned a little out the window, his fingers tightly curled around the door.

"I've been thinking about that Bucky. Guess you'll just have to come along. I gotta stay out here till the drive is done for the day. We'll meet up with the rest and settle in for the night."

It didn't take much to figure out what that would mean for Bucky. In his excitement, he'd been nothing but trouble since Dawson showed up. Darius would probably hide his son at the very least. A pang of pity went through

Dawson, but it wasn't his place to shield the boy. Bucky needed to learn to accept what he earned.

There was a snap like a dry twig. Dawson's left hip jerked, and an explosion of polymer shrapnel peppered the airtruck's door. Shocked, he looked down to see his ruined datapad. Then three points of pain exploded from his kidneys. The wind was knocked out of him and with barely a gurgle, pain crumpled him to the ground.

"Dawson!" screamed Bucky.

In that moment, Dawson knew Jumbo Magumbo had gotten the drop on him.

4
———

"Ho-kah-YEEE!" came the terrifying scream followed by a set of triumphant yips and shrieks.

Dawson could barely breathe. His mind was scrambled, angry. Why didn't anyone tell him were playing 'Cowboys and Indians' at recess today? No, that couldn't be right. He'd been shot! This wasn't school. Pain throbbed throughout his torso and down into his groin with every move. A cold trickle ran down his lower back.

Please, let that be sweat, he thought.

Hoof steps thumped softly up to him. A shadow fell across Dawson's face. Twisting his neck, he saw a man sitting on a horse. An expressionless face twisted by chemicals and failed genetic splices stared back. Jumbo Magumbo, the lunatic shaman, self proclaimed protector of the Divine Ursapine. The drugged out holyman got down on a knee over Dawson examining his prone victim.

"Penance... penancepenancepenance I must do- penance. I was too late. Too late-too too late," the genetic abomination muttered to himself.

Either the Ursoid genetic graft had not taken proper hold to turn him into a bear-man, or it went sour due to his use of the hallucinogenic quills. This left the shaman with semi-melted appearance somewhere between man and a bear. As a spliced humanoid, he had none of the natural bulk and elegance of an uplifted Ursamorph. Spliced Ursoids looked something more out of ugly mythology in comparison.

Instead of a feather headdress, this nutcase had stuck quills shed from an Ursapine into his scalp giving him the appearance of the animal's small mane, leaching the toxins into his scalp. How was this guy not dead yet?

Bucky tried to go for his own rifle, but Jumbo Magumbo was faster. His little military coilgun carbine shoved through the open window.

"No-no, no little cub! No, you don't! Hands up. Up, up Uuuuuupp!" Jumbo babbled.

Bucky did as the shaman ordered.

"Get out or I'll splatter you all over that cab," Jumbo threatened.

Dawson only squirmed weakly on the ground.

"Big game hunter," Jumbo said looking down as Bucky got out and backed away from the truck. Jumbo's carbine never left him. "You infidels sicken me. No respect for the holyholyholy divinity of life beneath your consciousness. None. None. No!"

Dawson gave out a burbling groan as a heavy shove of his boot to the ribs, Jumbo kicked him off his side and onto his stomach. The burning lead pain of his wounds made him scream out. This startled the horse, and it ran off. Jumbo hardly paid attention.

"Good, good," Jumbo said with a malicious titter, then reached down and poked the holes in Dawson's jacket.

"These will bleed out nicely. Or you will feed the mate. No worries. There are more. Many more. Soooo many more."

Dawson was furious at his helplessness. His sidearm was in the truck. His blaster rifle, by dumb luck fell a few yards away.

A new searing pain shot through Dawson's lower back as it felt like a needle was being inserted into one of his wounds. He twisted his neck and saw Jumbo plucking another quill out of his scalp, then sticking it into the second wound. Dawson hissed with a delicate pain that burned and went numb. He could not escape Jumbo inserting the third quill.

"There now," Jumbo cooed to Dawson. "Soon you'll have a new understanding of life."

Dawson's rational mind felt like it was about to crack. Would the anti-poison nanopatch stop it? What would these toxins do to him? Cranberry fire radiated out from the quills in the wounds, and his thoughts were getting very slippery.

"What're you gonna do with the kid?" Dawson spat into the dusty soil.

"I think I need a hostage. Yes. Oh, yesyesyes. Vvvvvtt!" he let out a bizarre spasm and shook his head. "Maybe that will securekeep my holy masters safe from the likes of you heretics! Take him back into the caves and raise him up. Grow the faith… lovely.

"I'm not coming with you!" Bucky shouted at Jumbo. Dawson looked up at the boy.

The shaman turned, a sad, clown-like frown on his face. "Who said you had a choice, little kitty? I'll give you all the best milk you can drink, yarn to playplayplay with… And something better than catnip!" Jumbo promised.

"And assuming you find yourself able later, let's keep you from following us," Jumbo said to Dawson.

He fired several bursts into the engine block of the air truck. The reactor went into emergency shutdown and scrammed. They heard a few pops and a strange sensation like they were falling in three different directions as the gravity generator went dead. The air truck was now an immobile chunk of metal, polymers and ceramic.

"If you survive the next few hours, greatest hunter man, you aren't wandering far. Is that okay with you? Yes yes yes? I thought you'd like it."

Rolling himself onto his good side, Dawson growled but felt his strength breaking free from pain's shackles.

"So fierce, but so impotent," Jumbo taunted.

The mad shaman made his way over to Bucky, gun leveled at him. The shaman approached the boy like he was a dangerous animal. His free hand out in front, looking to grab hold.

Bucky sidestepped away from the air truck, readying to run.

"Don't!" Dawson said. "You just keep yourself alive, Buckaroo." He prayed that the boy had enough good sense to listen.

"Listen to the smart deadman, little Buckaroo," Jumbo said. He slide-stepped forward a little more, almost touching the cowering Bucky.

A hardness fluttered in the boy's eyes. Bucky shot Dawson a look.

Am I hallucinating now? Dawson wondered as the boy's fur was starting to pulse and flow with new colors along his stripes. But his back felt much better.

Much better? Dawson realized he didn't care that it felt like a trio of fiery nymphs were cooking sausages over the hot and toasty barbecue pits in his kidney. At least the pain no longer radiated down his legs.

Bucky looked at the cab and back to Dawson, then to Jumbo reaching to take hold of him. Bucky slid a little more away from the maneuvering Jumbo into giving his back to Dawson.

Smart kid. Slicker than I thought, Dawson felt a smile creep over his lips.

Slowly, Dawson rolled onto his stomach, ready to launch himself. As Jumbo grabbed hold of Bucky's wrist, Dawson leaped up and launched himself toward the cab, and his sidearm.

Jumbo spun around, aiming his carbine toward Dawson as he dove through the open passenger door. It was enough to stop the few musket balls that hit the door instead of blowing through him.

With a snarling yowl, Bucky launched himself at Jumbo, blindsiding him. Dawson looked up as he heard the impact of two bodies on the ground. He saw Bucky was barefoot, and had missed the lethal throat bite, getting

Jumbo's cheek instead. Jumbo couldn't get his rifle around for Bucky's body blocked it. His claws hooked Jumbo's armored jacket and pulled it wide open. The pair hit the ground and Bucky began rapid jackhammer kicks into the shaman's exposed belly, raking him with his back claws from his navel to his knees. The screams and yowls made the hair on Dawson's scalp stand up.

He pulled his pistol out of his belt holster on the cab's floor, then slid to the ground as agony and drug induced vertigo overwhelmed him. He slumped against the door frame. Jumbo managed to push Bucky away and the boy took his chance to run, cresting a short rise and vanishing behind a thicket of mesquite, leaving only him and the badly mauled Jumbo Magumbo rolling in the dirt.

Dawson smiled and thought *Good for you, Buckaroonieoooni, You'll make it. Oh, mench! These quills are melting my brain.*

Dawson forgot which of five swirling multicolored shamans in the kaleidoscope was real as they smeared across the landscape and kept changing his mind. The synesthesia from his wounds felt-smelled-tasted like sweet burned marshmallows with bacon jelly.

Maybe I should do something about those quills immyback, he thought. *This can't be a good way to taste pain. I don't wanna hear that no more.* he ruminated.

Jumbo was spouting a jumble of unaligned vowels and consonants. Bucky's painful rakes were probably not deadly but left Jumbo in an awful mess.

"Just shut up, you mashup!" Dawson shouted drunkenly. "M' tryin' ta git these quills out." His mouth wouldn't form words cleanly.

Sloppily, he switched hands with his U-beamer sidearm, and rolled a bit to his side. Feeling for the long flexible quills in his wounds, he tugged. It felt like a knitting needle coming out, and so he held it up to make sure that's what happened.

Jumbo looked horrified as Dawson held the foot long quill up in the air, about a third of it steeped in his blood.

"You ruined everything!" the wounded shaman shrieked. "Ruined ruined! All ruined! Why can't you stand the beauty?" Jumbo's blubbering trailed off.

Dawson drew out the next quill, and Jumbo moaned like it came out of his own flesh.

"Quiet, you can't feel this," Dawson mumbled, unable to keep his pistol on target.

"Stop it! Keep the beauty inside you!" Jumbo hissed.

Dawson drew out the last of the quills.

Jumbo stared, openly perplexed at the act.

Smiling, Dawson held the bendy blood-covered quill silhouetted against the sky. *Oh, that's what's going on!* Dawson realized. *I must be in anaphylactic shock.*

"Heretic!" Jumbo shouted and aimed his carbine at Dawson.

Dawson's own pistol went "snap-buzz", and he stared at it in shock, realizing he had pulled the trigger. The carbine flew out of Jumbo's reach as the U-beam from Dawson's pistol obliterated the shaman's hand and trigger assembly. With a wail, he fell unconscious from shock.

There was a low sound from the thicket of willows. The dead Ursapine's mate was coming.

"Bucky?" Dawson called out. "Where'd you get to, son?" He groaned as he got to his feet and started rummaging around the cab for his first aid kit. Time for a wound patch, a big dose of broad spectrum antibiotics and painkillers. The anti-toxin patch he put on earlier was now black. Dawson pulled it off and put a fresh one on.

That curious grunting was approaching fast.

"My arm," Jumbo groaned as he regained consciousness. "Cannnn't feel... finners."

Proper painkillers helped instantly, allowing Dawson to slowly rise and brush off some bloody mud. His focus returning, he looked around for Bucky again, and sang out.

"Get back here son! Another Ursipine's here!"

Jumbo started laughing. "You're not going anywhere. Your blood will draw the holy beast right to you."

Then the dark shaggy shape of an Ursapine pushed through the willow thicket. It's baleful eyes locking on to the blood-soaked men. The quills hissed like a thousand twigs as it walked.

"You know what, Jumbo?" Dawson asked. He picked up his huge blaster rifle off the ground and started walking away from Jumbo. His feet dragging through the dust. "I'm going to give you your fondest wish and let you commune with that beast... internally."

"You mean eternally," Jumbo corrected "Eternal internal eternal internal," the wounded shaman sang to himself.

"No. I'm gonna let that monster eat you, first."

Jumbo didn't seem the least bit displeased with that.

"And when you've achieved whatever transcendental form or paradise you thought you were gonna get, I'm going to kill that critter dead and collect the bounty on both of you."

That cut through Jumbo's addled brain, and he gasped, "No!"

"Oh, yeah. The way I figger it, we all get what we want,"

"You can't kill the holy Ursapine!"

"I can, am and will. I'd say watch me, but it's gonna eat you ass first. If you want me to make sure you don't suffer, I'll shoot you while it's doin' the job. I doubt you were so merciful to the other people you murdered," Dawson said.

His hunting drone flew between them, ignorant of everything that transpired. Slowly, it towed the dead Ursapine hide pack onto the air truck's flatbed using it's anti-grav tractors. Dawson chuckled as it started back for the head still ignoring everything going on.

The Ursapine mate started trotting toward Jumbo, licking it's drooling maw.

"Get back! Nononono no!" Jumbo screamed at the beast "It's a trap! Don't come closer! Run away! Killkillkill him first!"

Man, what a blasted fool, Dawson thought as he took position behind a low scrubby bush. His back fought with the pain meds, nearly overwhelming them for a bit before it simmered down.

Unable to escape, Jumbo continued to try and warn the creature. His sainted beast fell upon him. The shaman did not scream, as the animal went for his belly first.

Dawson tasted bile as he watched the horror. *Eat the damned fool's head,* he screamed inside at the beast. The Ursipine tore Jumbo's diaphragm, and the shaman's voice became incoherent gurgles, and started to suffocate. Despite his hatred for everything Jumbo stood for, common decency forbade him to let even this madman suffer.

Another thunderclap and purple-white flash. The electricity coursed through the beast's mouth and into Jumbo, mercifully electrocuting both in one shot.

Dawson stood up and observed the pair of corpses. He felt sick to his heart, but relieved. *Not the most glamorous way to get back into this line of work.*

Hoof-steps approached from behind.

"You killed 'em both?" Came Bucky's unsure voice.

"Mmm-hm,"

"Poor guy," Bucky came alongside as Dawson continued to stare at the mess of man and beast.

"I can't say that yet, Buckaroo. He got what he earned."

"I found his horse. It ran off farther than I thought. We need to get you back to the drive, and we don't got comms to call for help."

"Good job. That truck's not going anywhere. The veterinarian's with the drive. Man! I knew I'd need him."

"You want to ride on front?"

"Pro'ly best. Let's go get some of our gear. We'll leave the drone to process out this other Ursapine and prevent it from poisoning the area." Some of the more sensitive plants were dying already.

Dawson looked at the horse next to him. It was a fine quarter horse. Jumbo had good taste in mounts it seemed. He let out some hisses and groans while getting into the saddle. Bucky handed up Dawson's gear, and then hopped on back, getting his own rifle at the ready, just in case.

"You think my dad's going to be mad at me?" Bucky asked as they rode off toward the drive's camp. They should reach them about the same time.

"Without a doubt, Buckaroo,"

Bucky gave a satisfied giggle at Dawson's using of that name. As they rode slowly away, the drone began field dressing the Ursapine.

"But I bet he's gonna be proud of you something awful, too. I know I am."

About M.D. Boncher

M. D. Boncher is an author, artist and composer who has lead a "Writer's Life". With several careers in many industries to provide a wealth of experience to draw from. He is passionate about, philosophy, civics and his faith. His hobbies include RPGs, videogames, camping, reading or watching movies. A former Wisconsinite, he now lives deep in the mountains of West Virginia with his wife, four very fluffy cats and small flock of feisty but naïve chickens.

His series include "Akiniwazisaga" a dark epic fantasy and "Tales From the Dream Nebula" A sci-fi pulp-punk adventure serial. You can find all M.D. Boncher's social media connections, books for sale, music, art and more at www.resonantmedia.art.

The Piper of Strath Dubh

By Matthew C. Lucas

Poor Bean Baird. The bagpiper for Lord Hugh Lamont has been sent to act as a "squire" for Lord Hugh's son in his quest to find a dragon. Dragons are scarce in the fourteenth century, though. After three days of poking around the Highlands, Bean is cold, and soaked to his bones, and, worst of all, out of whiskey. But when young Hugh stumbles upon a dragon pup's nest, the adventure takes a dark and uncanny turn—one that will forever change the piper's life.

Matthew C. Lucas

The Piper of Strath Dubh
By Matthew C. Lucas

Bean Baird rubbed his tired thighs through his kilt. Three days on a nag's saddle were three more than he'd ever spent astride a horse. Three dank, dreary winter days clopping about one of the dankest, dreariest corners of the Highlands. Three days of rain, and saddle sores, and having his manhood mashed unmercifully against a wet saddle he had no earthly business riding upon.

"Whoap, whoap. Easy, beast," he chided the old horse no one had ever bothered to name.

The horse flicked some droplets from her ear and kept right along on her business, plodding up a steep and winding goat-path. He gave the reins a tug, but the nag was as indifferent to Bean's clucking and rein-pulling and fretting as the mountainside they climbed.

Bean hacked a cough and stretched his calves as best he could and squinted through the low-floating clouds and waves of mist.

God save him, but traipsing through the heath and over the hills was no business for a man four and fifty years old. No hearth fire, no thatched roof, and, worst of all, no cellar from which to fetch another bottle of whiskey to replace the one he'd finished had left Bean in an unusually foul mood.

"Keep up, Bean," a man's voice called from a little farther up the mountain.

Bean made a face and mouthed, "keep up, Bean," before replying:

"Coming, m'lord."

The horse hooves clacked across the stones at the same unhurried pace as ever. A short clamber over a mound of tumbled down rocks and then the path took Bean and his nag along a slow sweep by a cliff's edge that was more than a bit too perilous for Bean's comfort. By and by, the ground leveled and then they came to a stony plateau on the mountainside where the one who called for Bean awaited.

A young man tilted himself as high as he could on a steed and waved a mailed arm at Bean.

"Just look at this place, Bean!"

Bean wiped the wetness from his eyes as his horse drew closer and did as his lordship requested. A more gray and desolate blot of bleakness Bean had never seen. Cold, lifeless rocks jutted from the ground at every angle. Murky puddles filled the dips and cracks in between the stones. A lone hedge had sprouted once upon a time, spread its brambles a couple of feet, and died, leaving behind a bramble of thorns. Gloom seeped from the ground.

Bean wasn't at all sure what he ought to say. So he fell to his most trusted answer. He gave a single, meaningful nod and declared:

"Aye. And there it is."

Hugh Lamont's smile widened.

"There it is," he repeated with a note of satisfaction.

Hugh the Younger, as he was often called, stood tall for his age, a proper height befitting a would-be nobleman, though young Hugh still bore the gangly awkwardness of an adolescence he hadn't quite outgrown. He had a long, narrow nose and thoughtful eyes. A mop of red hair dangled soaking wet over the ermine trim of his cloak. A coat of chainmail, too big for his frame, hung limply underneath it. He was as drenched as a carp and by rights should have been just as road sore and weary as Bean, but of course the lad didn't seem to mind the discomforts in the least.

Hugh was, after all, young. And he was in love.

Which was all well and fine, Bean reflected, except when youth and love drag old men out to chase dragons into the Black Cuillin mountains of the Highlands.

———————

It had been a much finer evening a fortnight past when Hugh the Elder hosted Sir Ian MacFarlane at the Manor of Strath Dubh.

"Manor" was a trifle generous of an appellation for the Lamont home. As was bestowing the preposterous name "Strath Dubh"—or Black Valley— on the place that, truth be told, would scarcely pass for a large farmhouse. But Hugh Lamont the Elder had pastures in the valley and hands to work them and a dozen tenants who paid him more or less regularly. In their poor part of Christendom that was sufficient to count Hugh a noble and to call his home a manor. In Hugh's estimation, at least.

Bean had happily gone along with old Hugh's pretending, addressing him and his son "m'lord," and bowing whenever they called for him, as it had earned him some of the easiest money he'd ever made. For Bean Baird was the only bagpiper in the valley. And it went without question that a self-styled nobleman in the Highlands had to have a piper in his employment.

So, when the day came that a *knight*—a proper knight, mind you, dubbed by an earl and blessed by a priest—called upon the Lamont's with his pretty blonde daughter, Mary, old Hugh had flashed a shilling at Bean. That kind of payment put a spring in a man's step. For a shilling, Bean went to the trouble of cutting new reeds for his pipes and taking a bath for his patron.

Bean remembered that night as if it were yesterday. Old Hugh was arrayed in his finest tartan and broke out the good whisky for the occasion, as he was trying to get his guest good and plied. The younger Hugh had perhaps enjoyed a dram too much as he seemed to be swaying in his chair. While Bean was taking a brief reprieve from his performance and enjoying his patron's spirits (just to keep his mouth sufficiently moistened for the next round of tunes), he overheard the younger Hugh wooing Sir Ian's lovely daughter.

"How many times have you been to York, then?" asked the lad.

"Eight, nine," Mary replied as if such a journey were no more trouble than a jaunt to a well. "Father takes me with him whenever he has occasion to visit court. Which is quite often."

"Oh."

"I'm a lady in waiting."

"What are you waiting for?"

Bean had nearly spat out his drink at that gaffe. The young lady twirled a strand of her hair in her finger and laughed in the way only a young maiden can—a siren sound, enticing and mocking all at once.

"You are such an earthy fellow, Hugh." Mary leaned close enough for her shirt to brush against his hand and dropped her voice low. "I think I'm going to like you."

"I ... oh! That—that would be ... lovely."

Hugh was beaming. If there hadn't been a thatched roof overhead, that grin would have floated the poor boy off into the clouds.

"You know," said she, "my father means to see me married."

Sir Ian cocked an eyebrow in her direction, while Hugh the Elder rubbed his hands together greedily.

"D-does he now?" Young Hugh stammered. He'd squirmed in his chair like a half-drunken eel, and that had gotten a chuckle out of the lass.

"He does." She paused meaningfully, a mischievous grin playing at those pink lips of hers. "In England."

Both Hughs looked ashen; the younger one might have crawled under the table if he could. Sir Ian attempted to assuage his hosts:

"Now, Mary. My only concern is that you will be maintained in a manner that suits our station. York has wealthy lads aplenty. Indeed, it does. But if a similarly situated suitor could be found in Scotland …" He let the thought trail.

"Scotland is a rather poor place," Mary observed.

The color rose in Hugh the younger, and Bean could see the red hairs prickling on the back of the boy's neck, but to young Hugh's credit, he held his tongue.

"Well," said he, and he paused to give his next words a proper thinking over, "what we may lack in gold, we make up in valor."

"Well, said, son!" Hugh the Elder thumped the table. "He's a clever lad, you see, Sir Ian? Sure to make a mark in the world with that kind of pluck."

"Indeed." Sir Ian stroked his moustache, turned to his daughter, and declared in the tone of a father who was inclined to spin proverbs and witticisms in all instances. "There is an ancient more in these lands, Mary, not without its merits, that must always be borne in mind. The Scots hold their heroes more precious than their treasure."

"Aye, and that's well said, too," old Hugh drained his cup, filled it again, and proposed a toast. "To the heroes of Scotland."

The four nobles and Bean the piper hoisted their cups to toast Scotland's bravery. Then Old Hugh called for a medley of patriotic tunes and, as Bean played his bagpipes, the talk of the table turned to those feats of heroism the Gaels of Hibernia were so fond of retelling. The conversation was pleasant, the pipe tunes were stirring, and the whiskey flowed like a stream. Young Hugh seemed to be making progress with the knight's daughter. She'd tittered no less than twice while Bean played. But when Bean paused for another minute to rewet his parched lips, Mary gave the pot another stir.

"You know," she said musingly, "for all their songs and ballads, the Scots' bravery is lacking in one respect."

"Whatever do you mean?" young Hugh asked.

"Well." She tilted her chin and smiled coyly at him. "All these desperate charges and bold duels and getting slaughtered to the last man, that's all well and good. But there's not a single story of a Scotsman ever slaying a dragon, is there?"

The table went silent as the men sat and puzzled on that for a bit before the older Hugh tried to brush aside the lass's question.

"Mistress Mary," he chuckled. "It's the Year of our Lord 1331. There's not been a dragon sighted in the Highlands since the time of the Picts. How's a man supposed to kill a creature that's not around anymore, much less have a story told about it?"

But the girl wouldn't be so easily deterred.

"The English managed it. They have their St. George. So did the Germans with Sigurd. Those men slew a dragon and cut off its head and brought home its golden horde as a gift for a beautiful princess. I read it in a book."

"Well," old Hugh allowed, "that's a fair accomplishment to brag about, I suppose."

"Indeed," the girl replied and steepled her fingers beneath her chin as she gazed hard into young Hugh Lamont's face. He couldn't break away from her stare, just as couldn't help but smile at her whim. For she had him wrapped as tight as a bug in a spider's web. Bean clicked his tongue in pity for the boy. The devilish glint in that young woman's eyes would have made a faerie blush for shame. "A Scot who did such a thing as *that*," said she, now resting a hand on Hugh's elbow, "is a Scot I could love."

Hugh was done for. His bonnie lass wanted a hero. And sitting next to her was a young man more than willing to try to become one, or willing to die in the trying.

Oh, indeed he was.

"You see it, don't you?"

Hugh was hunched before a slab of rock, examining its dimensions from every angle, as enthusiastic as a terrier who had just caught a scent.

"See?" He pointed excitedly.

With an ache in his ass and a grimace on his face, Bean slid off his saddle and joined his companion. He knuckled at his lower back, bent over, and pretended to study whatever it was Hugh was staring at.

"M'lord?"

"It's the surest sign yet we've had of a dragon."

It looked to Bean an utterly unremarkable piece of gray-flecked boulder about the size of a tombstone, no different than any of the million stones strewn across the mountainside. But he dutifully replied:

"M'lord."

The young man faced Bean, his cheeks aglow, his words a babbling brook of enthusiasm:

"Mary told me to look for things out of the ordinary." He gestured at the hunk of stone. "Now at first glance, this rock wouldn't seem extraordinary. But it's *too* flat, if you take my meaning. You'll not find its kindred anywhere around here. All these other stones, what we've been climbing over, they're all shaped like, like—"

"Like haggises?"

"Just so. But not this one. This one is different. Because this one was carefully placed here. Vouchsafed by a mother dragon to protect her young. This." He slapped the face of the stone with his palm, sending a spray of droplets flying. "*This* is a dragon's nest, or I'm a fool."

"As you say, lord."

"Right." Hugh nodded. "Let's move it over."

An unwitting groan escaped from Bean's throat. He tried to cover it up as a fit of coughing, but Hugh wagged a scolding finger.

"Now, Bean. Father sent you to be my squire. A good squire mustn't shirk his duty."

More particularly, old Hugh had sent Bean to keep an eye on his moonstruck son and to see that, after the boy had tired himself out traipsing around the Highlands to look for Mary's dragon treasure, he got home safely and with his pride relatively intact. Bean was more of a chaperone than a squire; but he was not at liberty to share that with his charge.

"As you say, sir, but this here's my first piece of squiring. And I'm a bit old to be learning a new trade. That and my knees, you see …"

Hugh's face clouded. "Father told me I'd have a squire. He paid you like a squire. You will act the part. Now grab that stone and move it aside so I can see if there's not a dragon's nest underneath."

The lad had a fair point about the payment. The half farthing old Hugh had slipped into his hand had been generous, and Bean had already spent it.

"Aye, sir," Bean grumbled. His fingers frozen, his joints creaking, Bean crouched low, gripped an edge of the slippery stone, and gave it a heave.

The damned thing could have been a millstone.

"C'mon, Bean. Give it your all."

Bean tugged and strained until his whole body shook.

"I … am … m'lord …"

Slowly, the stone lifted. No more than the span of a little finger, but he'd gotten the edge of it up.

"Smartly now, Bean! Just move it aside a few feet."

It was on the tip of Bean's tongue to roar in the boy's face to lend him a bleeding hand if he wanted this behemoth moved an inch, much less a foot. Bean let out a groan that turned into a curse, which did the trick. He lurched all his weight to one side and let go. The stone landed with a thud, about a forearm's length over from where it had been. Bean collapsed alongside it. Hugh brushed past him and pressed his face against the side of the stone.

"There's a hole under here," he announced.

Bean was sprawled on the ground with his hands behind his head, gulping air. Every muscle in his body was on fire, as if he'd been wracked.

"A hole … m'lord?" Bean managed.

"Aye. I can just make it out. It's the edge of a deep hole." He sniffed and made a face. "There's a strange whiff in there. Like rotted eggs."

"Eggs." Bean nodded. Still on his back and panting, he gazed up into the sky, wondering how it was he could see so many stars in the daytime.

"Don't remember reading anything about eggs," Hugh said to himself. He rubbed his chin and ran his fingers through his sodden hair and, for the first time, seemed unsure of himself. "No magical door. No runes. No azure flames or ancient temples. At least, not from what I can tell." Hugh stood upright and looked down at Bean. "You'll just have to have another go. And this time finish the job."

"Now, see here—"

Bean's words were cut short by an explosion. A plume of dust and ash billowed out of the ground. A gusting breath of whooshing air was followed by a piercing, bestial cry and then a shadow burst out of the partly uncovered hole. It soared into the sky, stretched a pair of leathery wings wide, and swooped back down.

"Holy Christ!"

Bean rolled to his side, the stones scraping his face. He scrambled to find cover. The horses reared with fright. Before Bean could blink, a creature— a nightmare—that Bean's tired, addled mind could scarcely conceive, was lunging at his nag. The old horse tried to kick back, but whatever fighting days the nag ever had in her were long gone.

A single word formed in Bean's brain and pierced through the confusion. *Dragon.*

Only slightly larger than a he-goat, but a dragon all the same. With a scaly, crimson hide, and jaws full of sharp teeth, and eyes like pools of midnight. He'd unearthed an honest-to-God, legend-come-to-life—in miniature.

The piper couldn't take his eyes from the horrible apparition. Neither could young Hugh. The lad stood rooted to his spot, gawking like a boy at a fair. His horse, a younger and swifter mount than Bean's, had more sense than its master and went galloping off as fast as it could down the mountain. Alas, Bean's horse couldn't join it.

The dragon clamped its claws onto the nag's flank, curled a forked tail around her chest, and sank its teeth into her neck. A feeble bray was cut short in a strangled gasp as the old horse's legs buckled. Down it fell into a tangled, bloody heap. The saddle bags it carried along with Bean's bagpipes went tumbling to the ground in a clatter.

"My pipes …"

The creature slithered atop the fallen mount, flicked its tongue, and started to gorge, paying no mind at all to young Hugh, who still hadn't moved an inch.

"Hugh!" Bean peaked around the line of rocks and hissed at his lordship.

The lad turned and looked at Bean. Bean made a motion, as if he were pulling something free from his belt.

"Your sword!" he whispered as loud as he dared.

Hugh blinked at him.

"Sword!" With his hand, Bean sliced through the air.

"Huh?"

The boy was impenetrable.

"You," Bean pointed at him, "have a sword," he thumped his side, "that you," an emphatic point with his finger, "can kill it with." He made a vast, sweeping swipe with his hand.

Hugh shook his head sluggishly, like a man trying to wake from a deep slumber.

"Oh?" he said. Then, after a pause, more firmly: "Oh."

Hugh's fingers slowly clenched the handle of the weapon he had at his side, the sword his father had lent him along with his coat of mail. The young Lamont set his jaw and unsheathed the blade.

Much as naming Strath Dubh a "manor" was a wee bit of a stretch, calling Hugh Lamont's blade a "sword" could also count as something of an exaggeration. A good, heavy dirk was what it was, but the old man had had the blade fixed with a grip, guard, and pommel, so that, from a distance, one who didn't know better might have mistaken it for a truncated broadsword. The steel was sharp, though, and more or less free of rust. Drawing the weapon must have helped Hugh find a measure of his manhood. He lifted the blade in salute and announced with a reedy, shaking voice:

"H-hold there, foul worm. And, um, and harken thy doom."

If Bean had been shocked by the dragon's appearance, its reaction to that bit of claptrap almost made him faint. The dragon paused in its carnage. A strip of furry flesh dangled from its mandible. It cocked its wicked head, as if to say, "You have my attention, now what do you want?"

"What the hell are you doing?" Bean squeaked. "Why didn't you just kill it when it wasn't looking?"

Hugh's face was white as milk, his eyes as round as gourds. He replied to Bean from the side of his mouth:

"Had to—had to issue a challenge. Only proper. Knight's code of honor."

"Oh sweet, weeping Jesus ..."

The dragon craned its neck and studied the man who had addressed it. It flicked its tail thoughtfully against the nag's carcass. Its jaws cracked open, a trickle of blood dripping from the dragon's teeth. It replied in a stilted English,

"*Who ... are ... you?*"

The boy gulped and nearly dropped his blade. Bean gripped the edge of his rock.

"Who am I?" Hugh repeated. It took a rather long moment for him to recall that bit of information, but at last he responded: "I—I am Hugh Lamont of Strath Dubh. A-a noble knight, strong of heart and pure of arm— I mean, strong of arm and heart of ... Well, you understand me."

"*That I do.*"

Bean's spine turned to ice at the wee dragon's smile.

"*What would you have of me, Hugh Lamont of Strath Dubh?*"

Hearing his name from the dragon's lips almost did the boy in. He looked like he might faint. Bean came around the rock, just a step, to aid his lordship.

"I ... what do I want from you? Well. Your horde, I suppose. And, um." An embarrassed blush came to the boy's face. His eyes dropped. "And also ... also your head. If you please."

A low, rumbling laughter, and then the dragon brought a clawed talon to its chest in what, Bean supposed, was meant to be a mock salute.

"*If you please, I'd rather hold onto both. Have at you.*"

The dragon beat its wings like a hawk taking flight, and then up it went, launching from the perch it had made of Bean's dead horse. Though it was no bird, the dragon moved deftly through the air, slithering to Hugh's left, then his right, searching for an open flank to strike. Hugh drew back and spread his feet into a swordsman's stance. The dragon made another feint, veered high, and then plunged straight down; its front talons opened wide to catch Hugh's head.

The young Lamont let out a yelp and swung his weapon. The flat of the blade glanced off the dragon's foot. Not enough to draw blood, but the blow sent the dragon twisting away mid-air to beat a retreat.

"Well struck, lad!" Bean cried.

Hugh made another wild lunge. He yelled at the dragon, "Strath Dubh!" and swung again.

The dragon fluttered just beyond Hugh's reach. The lad gave chase, whirling his blade about like a madman. After a minute or so, Hugh had to stop and catch his breath. The moment the boy let down his guard, the dragon swooped down like a gull on a fish. This time, though, instead of trying to claw him, it peeled up at the last moment and avoided Hugh's parry. As it flew by, it whipped its tail like a scourge across Hugh's eyes.

"Aach!" the boy cried.

Hugh stumbled backwards and waved his dirk blindly about. The dragon flapped its wings, circled overhead, and landed a few feet behind Hugh, stealthily as a cat. Before Bean could shout a warning, the red devil leaped onto the young man's back, clawing and biting and pulling his lordship to the ground, just as it had to Bean's nag. The fight turned into a scrum. Dragon and man rolled over one another, their limbs all intertwined, each wrangling to dominate the other. Thank God for that chainmail, Bean thought, or else the boy would have been clawed to ribbons.

Bean clenched his fists. He felt helpless just standing there watching. A swirl of thoughts raced through his mind.

On the one hand, he was no warrior, nor had he ever claimed to be. Besides which, battles were a young man's game; all the more so when they involved dragons. On the other hand, Bean was a kind soul by nature, and he'd always been fond of his love-struck lordling, despite his folly. Bean knew he'd never have a proper sleep again if the boy ended up in a dragon's stomach. And on the third hand (if he'd been blessed with such an appendage), there were also his bagpipes to consider. Lying over there on the bloody ground, sure to be stomped into twigs in all this fracas. A fine set of pipes he'd had since his boyhood, worth more than a pair of milking cows.

That last hand settled the matter.

And it gave Bean an idea.

Hugh and the dragon were still wrestling. Hissing and cursing and grunting, they seemed stuck in a stalemate. Young Hugh had managed to wriggle a leg free and lever himself over the dragon, but he couldn't quite free his sword arm, for the creature had clamped its wings and back legs tight around the right sleeve of his mail. Hanging upside down, the dragon curled its neck backwards and tried to bite at Hugh's exposed face, but he was just out of reach. Sooner or later, one or the other would strike a fatal blow.

Bean hurried over to where his pipes had fallen. Saints be praised, none of the drones had split (though there were some nasty new scrapes in the woodwork). He picked up the instrument.

The dragon inched its head closer to Hugh's face and snapped. His sword arm still pinned; the boy had to buffet it with his elbow to keep from being bitten. There was no time.

Bean tucked the leather bag underneath his armpit, draped the long drones over his shoulder, jammed the blowstick in his mouth, and blew. There was a warbling wail as the three drones struck in. He squeezed the bag hard with his elbow to bring in the high-pitched chanter, the music-making pipe he held in his hands and launched into a quick march.

Not two bars into the tune and Bean got his wish.

The dragon paused its clawing and biting and looked over at Bean. In the span of a moment, its black eyes twinkled at him, almost as if ... as if it liked what he was playing. Bean thought he detected a smile playing at the corners of the beast's scaly lips.

Then it was gone.

A dirk's blade thrust into the underside of the dragon's chin, up its jaw, and pierced through the crown of its skull. The dragon made a gargling noise and then it went still.

Hugh gave the blade another push.

The dragon's tongue rolled out of its mouth. A bilious, gray ooze trickled between its teeth, down the gilded pommel of Hugh's sword and onto his forearm. Hugh held his sword fast, panting madly and flushed as red as a cherry.

Bean let his pipes sag. The drones gave up a moan and went still. Silence swallowed the mountainside.

"I did it ..." Hugh finally breathed.

Bean slumped to the ground. All he could do was sit on the cold, hard mountain and stare impassively at the corpses of a magical creature and the old nag it had killed. The wetness of the rocks began to seep through Bean's kilt, but he didn't get up. Bean felt detached and somber and very tired.

"I did it," Hugh said again.

"Aye," Bean replied irritably.

The boy stepped back to admire his handiwork and gripped his blade's handle with both hands. It took him a few pulls before he could free the sword from the dragon's skull.

"I slew a dragon," Hugh announced. As if Bean hadn't been there and played a part saving him. Hugh wiped the gore from his blade and blathered. "I killed it. A real live dragon. It had teeth and claws. And-and it flew. And smelled like eggs. And it *spoke*. Christ's blood," he made the sign of the cross, "the thing spoke! You heard it, didn't you, Bean?"

"Aye."

The boy's chest was more puffed than an overblown bagpipe. His gaze went from the dragon to his sword then back to Bean.

"I saw a dragon," he said, still in disbelief. "And I killed it."

Bean looked up at the boy, at the glow in his cheeks that hadn't dimmed in the slightest, and that made Bean frown.

"Aye," he said in a voice flat and old. He leaned his head back against a rock and closed his eyes. "That you did …"

———————

While Bean rested, his thoughts took leave of dragons, and mountains, and eerie mists, and roamed for a while through that border realm between dreaming and thinking. A memory came to him, like a vision.

It was the night before he and Hugh were to set out on this journey, some four days ago. He had been in his cottage, packing what effects he had for the fool's errand he was being sent on, when Bean heard a knock at the door.

He opened it, and standing in his entrance was none other than Mary MacFarlane. She was draped in a woolen shawl to ward off the cold. Bean was struck dumb by her sudden appearance. She tilted her head.

"Why, yes, Bean." Mary smiled coyly. "I would love to come inside."

"Oh." Bean stepped aside and showed her to the best seat by his fireplace. "Please, um, make yourself at home."

Bean's was a humble cottage about a hundred yards from the Lamont manor. A round room covered with a thatched roof, it had a window, a table, a bed, and a couple of mismatched chairs. Which had always been ample for

Bean who had always lived alone; but at that moment, he felt the crudeness of his abode most keenly. Mary, however, glided across the rushes on his dirt floor as if she were in an earl's castle and settled in the chair she had been offered.

"Busy packing, then?" she inquired.

"Aye, ma'am. We leave at the dawn."

"As do we. Now that my father and Lamont have finished their business, we'll be returning home."

"I hope you enjoyed your stay, my lady."

She said nothing for a long while but stared at the fire.

"My lady?"

"Why did you look at me the way you did when I was talking to Hugh?"

"Look at you?" He had no idea what she could have meant. "I—I never—"

"Don't deny it, Bean." One of her eyebrows cocked. "You gave me a hard look at supper. Like I had done wrong. Why?"

Sitting there by the fire, her golden hair gleaming, her eyes sparkling, Bean could well imagine why a younger man would go off on a wild adventure for her sake. Though why she should wish for such an undertaking remained a puzzle.

"Well, ma'am," he said carefully, "with all due respect, your talk about slaying a dragon and bringing you treasure as a means to gain your affection—well, it wasn't right. No, ma'am, it wasn't. And there it is. I can't think of any plainer way to say it."

He feared he had far overstepped his bounds, but Mary simply crossed her leg.

"How so?"

"Because a young fellow in love will take that as the gospel. He'll go and try and do it because you said you'd like him to. Only you've put him to a task that can't be done. He'll search high and low in the Cuillians for a dragon, but he'll not find one. No, never." Bean leaned closer to make his point. "Because there are no such creatures anymore… Which I think you know."

"Of course, I know."

That had been a surprise to Bean. His face must have showed as much, for Mary let out a long, fruity laugh. "Oh, Bean. Bean. You should see your face!"

"I don't—I don't understand."

"Bean Baird, you're a simple man. But you're also a dear one, so I'll not have you think ill of me. I don't expect Hugh is going to find anything more fearsome than a deer, and that's if he's lucky."

"Then … then why'd you tell him all that?"

Mary grew pensive for a moment and stared into the fire. The log crackled. The orange embers floated up into the chimney like spirits on their way to heaven. She turned to Bean.

"I've been betrothed. Father will have me wedded to Hugh."

Bean was about to wish her congratulations, but she talked over him.

"I shall wed Hugh Lamont the Younger because my father has no dowry to pay. And a well-off Highland farmer won't ask for one, not from a knight. That is the plain truth of the matter."

Mary went quiet again, and Bean didn't know what to say. He studied her for a bit but could make out nothing. Was the lady sad? Happy? Something in between? The way she had spoken and the expression that held her lovely face were as inscrutable as the flames in the hearth. So he could only answer, "Aye … There it is."

"Yes, aye. There it is." She shifted in her seat and smiled. "Hugh is a decent sort. He's even a bit handsome. But in his heart, he's just a Highland farmer."

"And what's wrong with that?"

"Nothing at all, Bean. But I want a little more from a husband. Your so-called lord has never strayed beyond this farm, never seen any new places, never met any different people. The farthest he's ever ventured is St. John's Kirk for Easter mass." She heaved a sigh. "If I am to be stuck in a farmhouse for the rest of my days, I want it to be with a husband who has had an adventure. Even if it's a farce."

Now it was she who drew herself closer to Bean. She took one of his hands in hers, and his old heart flipped a somersault. "I want something to talk about with Hugh besides the weather, or the sheep, or how the wheat's coming in. I want him to have an adventure. So *we* can have something to say to each other. Even if it's, 'remember that time you went chasing through the mountains to find me a dragon's treasure?' and we can both share a laugh. I would be content with that."

Bean rubbed at his chin and thought. "I suppose," said he, "a little adventure might do the lad well. There's no harm in it, at least."

"No, Bean. There's not. And he'll be the better man for it."

———

Whether or not he became a better man for it, the thrill of Hugh's victory proved short-lived.

Together, Bean and Hugh moved the flat stone that had covered the dragon's nest all the way over, a far more manageable task with the eager help of a pair of young arms. Hugh had crept down into the hole, which turned out to be no deeper than a shallow grave and searched every cranny within. Twice for good measure. All he had found were eleven silver pennies (old ones from good King Malcolm's reign), a bowl, a brooch, and a thimble. The two men stood over the trove and said nothing while a light rain misted down. Hugh's shoulders sagged, the color in his cheeks faded.

The piper cleared his throat.

"Well, it's, um—" Bean sought for the right word.

"Pathetic." Hugh snapped.

He would have called it "a bit lean," but no point debating the lad when he looked to be on the verge of crying.

"Aye," Bean nodded. Droplets of water trickled down Bean's scalp. He waited for what he thought a suitable length of time before he blew out an exaggerated sigh. "Still," he said. "Eleven coins is eleven more than you had. And what a story you've got to tell. Your Mary will be marrying an honest-to-God dragon-slayer. And the lads at the farm will—"

"No," Hugh cut over him.

"M'lord?"

Hugh turned to Bean "We came to find a proper dragon. With a proper horde. This was just a warmup."

Bean had to bite his tongue to keep from cursing. The boy would be the death of him.

"But sir," he pleaded, "we've been at this for three days. And that beastie you killed over there's the best we found. Which, mind you, is a pretty bloody big miracle, no matter the size …"

Bean went on and on, trying to make Hugh see some common sense, but the young lord was only half-listening, he could tell. While Bean talked, Hugh stared up the mountainside, up the steep rocks and the low-lying storm clouds and the curtain of fog and rain. The look on his face was much too determined for Bean's liking.

"… So with all due respect," Bean raised his voice to gain Hugh's attention, "but you've done what you set out to do. You killed a dragon. No different than those Saxons Mary told you of. She's sure to be impressed, I promise you."

But Hugh was already adjusting his belt and tightening his bootstraps as if he meant to do some more climbing in the waning daylight.

"Sorry, Bean," he said in a way that didn't sound the least bit apologetic. "But there is another dragon up at the top of this mountain, a bigger one. A real one. And I mean to slay it."

Mist-veiled mountaintops spread before Bean Baird. The night sky, so close he could touch it, sent a howling wind cutting through his clothes like a knife. This high up, the climb had become steep and treacherous with ice. Bean had felt like an ant, slowly clawing his way up over frozen rifts, inching towards a summit he still couldn't see, clutching his bagpipes for dear life while trying his damnedest not to miss his footing.

But, at last, at long last, they had reached the top.

It had taken a great deal of wheedling on Hugh's part, and five of the eleven pennies along with the brooch from the dragon's horde, to keep Bean engaged. But here he was. At the summit. With his fingertips frozen and his head spinning from the thin air.

"M'lord," Bean huffed and wiped the cold sweat from his brow. "I said I'd see you to the top. Here we are. And there's no sign of any dragons. Can we be heading back down, for the love of God?"

Hugh squinted.

"There's one up here," he said, though with not the same conviction as when they'd started. "The dragon said so. It wasn't lying."

Bean had heard this story a half dozen times during their climb. While Hugh and his dragon had been locked in combat, knocking each other about, they had conversed, after a fashion. Hugh told the thing he would take its head to give to his lady. While the dragon, according to young Hugh, had replied: "It's your head I'll be taking to the top of the mountain. To mother."

Stuff and nonsense. The kind of bluster men will say when they're fighting in hopes of denting their opponent's courage. Hugh, however, had convinced himself that a "ma dragon" awaited him at the top of the mountain. One that would have a horde worthy of presenting to his future bride.

So here they were. At midnight atop a cold, barren mountain. Bean had had about enough of this adventure.

"You cannot take the word of a dragon, sir. That's a fact. It's in every tale that's ever told of the beasts. Besides which, I'm cold, sir. And tired. And need a drink and a proper sleep. My lord? Where are you going now?"

Hugh had started to shimmy around a boulder.

"Dragons may speak in riddles, Bean. But they never lie. That's what's in all the tales. I want to look about the other side over here."

"Jesus, Joseph, and Mary save me. No. I'm not turning over every rock in the Cuillins. I'm done. I tell you, I'm—"

"I promise, Bean." He shot a glance over his shoulder at the piper and smiled. "Just a quick look about in the shadows over here. If I don't find anything, we'll find a place to camp and head home at first light."

"Thank God."

Bean grumbled and settled himself into a crack that more or less shielded from the breeze. He didn't have to wait long before Hugh came scrambling back. His eyes were as big and wide as the moon above him. Like he'd seen a ghost. Or a ...

"Dragon's lair," he hissed through his teeth. "A *ma* dragon's lair."

―――――――――――

Heathenry. That's what Bean would have called it.

On the far side of that jutting boulder, Hugh had found a fissure in the top of the mountain. A crack twice as tall as young Hugh and longer than an ox train. It was dark as coal save for wisps of white steam trailing out that rose like tendrils into the night sky. The air about the fissure felt as warm as a campfire.

Which all made for a strange enough sight, but it was the columns in front of the mountain hole that had Bean make the sign of the cross.

Two marble columns. Alabaster. Each ten feet in height, with fluted sides and flowering tops, and festooned with sculpted dragons, all writhing and worming like a troop of demons in flagrante. Two great pillars as fine as any that might have graced St. John's kirk.

Except they were here. On top of a mountain. What the devil were two marble columns with all the markings of witchery upon them doing up here on top of a mountain? Heathenry was the only explanation that came to mind.

Bean traced another cross over himself. Hugh strolled around one of the columns, seemingly quite pleased with himself.

"Still think that dragon was lying, Bean?"

Bean shuddered under his cloak. "I think," he said flatly, "we've come to a place where angels might fear to tread."

"That may be. But Hugh Lamont the dragon-slayer of Strath Dubh has a horde to fetch." He took a couple of steps closer to the crack in the mountain and crinkled his nose. "Ach, that smell again." He yelled into the hole: "Hello! Hello in there! I say, *hello!*"

Hugh's "hello" echoed back from the cavernous void. The lad called out a few more times, then paced in a circle. He drew his sword.

"My lord," said Bean, "you're—you're not meaning to head down there, are you?"

"No, no, of course not."

"Oh, good."

"Pipes up."

"Pipes ... Beg pardon?"

Hugh's blade tapped impatiently against his thigh.

"Your bagpipes. I want you to play them, loud as you can. If there's anything alive in there, the pipes will flush it out."

Bean started to argue, but once again, the lad had a point. The piper was in no mood to play, nor were his fingers feeling nimble. But if a quick tune was what was needed to assure his lordship that this eerie hollow in the mountain was, God willing, bereft of life, then Bean could belt one out.

So, he licked his chapped lips, blew his bag full, and played. Just a run up and down the scale and the opening of "The Battle of Caerbannog." As Bean was about to wrap up, a jet of white flames belched from the fissure. It was followed by a deep rumbling in the ground.

"Ah-ha!" Hugh cried.

A single clawed talon appeared from within the crack. Like the hand of the Devil himself, it came forth, stretched wide as if awakening, and rested on the base of the left marble column. It was a horrible appendage to behold, enormous, fearsome, and yet somehow lithe. Deep within the darkness of the crack, a pair of eyes, blacker than their surroundings fixed upon the two men.

"Shyte!" whimpered Bean, staggering backwards.

The eyes in the hollow flicked from the young man and his dirk, to Bean cringing with his bagpipes. A voice reverberated deep within the mountain.

"*That was ... lovely.*" The voice purred like a siren's call and stormed like breakers on a shipwreck. An ancient womanly voice that was both fell and fair at the same time. "*Could you play some more?*"

"I ... I ..." All the thoughts went tumbling out of Bean's head. For though he could not see its shape, he was conversing with a dragon now, of that there could be no doubt. A dragon as high above the one they had unearthed before as Bean was above an ant. The blowpipe nearly slipped from his lips.

"*Do you know 'Azrael's Tail?' Or 'The Wyverns Reel?'*" One of the claws on the talon lifted. "*Oh, perhaps 'The Fall of Parzifal.' I always loved that one.*"

Now Bean had learned a fair number of tunes over the years, but none of those sounded familiar, or at all pleasant. He stammered, fearing he might give offense:

"I, um, I'm afraid I'm a bit rusty on those. Begging your pardon, my lady."

He gave a nervous bow and nearly fell over, which made the dragon chuckle.

"*Then play any tune you like.*" The dragon's eyes narrowed for a moment before one of them winked at him. "*Fear not, little piper. So long as you play well, I won't eat you.*"

She laughed, and it dawned on Bean that this great, fearsome beast might be having fun with him. It puzzled him and scared him all at once. There was a smile he could hear in her voice that overcame the terror of her veiled presence, so that Bean was able to soldier through a reel he'd picked up not long ago from a York piper. While he played, the dragon hummed within the fissure and tapped a claw in perfect time. When Bean had finished playing, the dragon let out a contented sigh.

"*Oh, but that was grand. Grand. May I trouble you for an encore? Perhaps something funereal?*"

Hugh, who had been standing by all the while, twirling his dirk, interrupted.

"Dragon," he proclaimed haughtily, "I've not climbed this mountain for my piper to entertain you. You'll harken to *me* now."

The dragon's eyes regarded the young Lamont much in the way a she-bear might regard a jackrabbit standing high up on its hindlegs, scratching for a fight.

"*And who are you?*"

"I am Hugh Lamont of Strath Dubh. I'm a knight. Pure of arm and strong of heart. Damn me, why can't I get that right? Strong of arm and pure of heart. Yes. That's what I am, and I've come to claim your horde and your head."

A more insipid—and absurd—spectacle, Bean couldn't imagine. He wrung his hands over his head, for he was certain the dragon would simply come out of the dark, squash Hugh for his impertinence, and maybe do the same to Bean for good measure. Instead, her eyes rolled and the lone talon that had emerged thumped the ground and shook the whole mountain.

"Ugh! You bestirred me—and halted this gentleman's fine piping—for the sake of a challenge?" Tendrils of flame burst from the hollow.

Now it was Hugh who found himself stammering. For it must surely have dawned on him that the pup he had killed was not even a tenth the size of the mother in that fissure.

"Um." He shuffled his feet. Feet he suddenly seemed keenly interested in studying.

"Boy," the dragon snarled, *"you have no magic blade. I sense no omen or prophecy on you."* She paused meaningfully. *"Your armor is too big for your body, and your body's no bigger than a twig. You must be a fool. Run away, little fool. Run back to your court and count yourself blessed to have awoken a dragon and lived."*

In the waxy light, Hugh's cheeks beamed pink. He straightened his shoulders and drew a deep, incensed breath. "I-I'll not run. And I'm not a fool." He sniffed indignantly. "I have made my challenge in the customary form. Will you accept it?"

"Oh, very well. If you're so eager to leave this world, I'll oblige you—in the customary fashion. Shrieve your soul and meet me here on the morrow's dawn." The claw withdrew back into the dark of the mountain. The eyes turned away. Before she had disappeared, her voice echoed from within the bowels of the mountain, *"Keep your pipes warmed up, piper. You'll have a funeral to play soon."*

———————

No amount of persuasion would turn young Hugh from his lunacy. Facing that she-dragon would be suicide. Plain and simple. Surely, Hugh recognized as much. Why, just her claw was as big as Hugh's horse, the one that had had the good sense to save itself and run from this cursed mountain. There would be no loss in honor for Hugh to follow his steed's example.

All through a meager supper, Bean spoke to Hugh thus, at times cajolingly, other times lovingly, and once or twice, quite forcefully. All to no avail. Hugh's mind—addled with love and legends—was made up. And no appeal to God, or God's Blessed Mother, or Hugh's blessed mother, or the lass Hugh would wed and make a mother would turn him from his deadly course. He was a Scot, through and through, and stubborn as a stone.

So, Bean left Hugh to "hold his vigil," as he called it, which entailed passing the rest of the night on his knees praying for his soul's salvation. Given what tomorrow likely held, that was probably a good use of the lad's time.

Not for Bean, though.

While his lordship prayed, Hugh crept into the mountain's fissure. He kept his pipes clenched tight against his chest. As he stepped inside, he discovered there was light within. Though there was no source. A faint glow that seemed to hover, untethered to any candle, or lantern, or window. It was unnerving, and yet Bean was grateful for the light, for the inside of the cave was jagged and strewn with loose stones, and Bean would have surely bumped his noggin if he had had to stumble blindly in the dark.

As he made his way further into the mountain, the hollow sloped downward. Step by cautious step, he descended. The light never wavered. He lost track of time at some point. But finally, when he had thought he must surely have reached the roots of the mountain itself, the passage he had been following widened into a great chamber. The ceiling soared and the walls opened wide into a room almost as vast as a castle.

In the center, resting upon a hill of glittering gold, lay the she-dragon. Long as a fallen tower and covered in scales that shimmered ochre, a warm glow emanated from her body and sent waves of heat eddying into the air. Her head was knobby and riddled with scars of battles long past, but it had not lost the elegance of its curves. A tuft of shimmering silver hair sprouted from her crown. A wisp dangled between a pair of eyes that were as deep and terrible and wise as the sea.

"God save me," Bean breathed. He had never known fear like this, a dread so thick and heavy it choked his very soul like peat smoke. His body stood frozen, even as sweat rolled down the back of his neck.

The dragon had seemed asleep on her horde, but then without looking up, she spoke to Bean.

"*Well met, piper.*"

Bean fell to his knees.

"*Have you come to give me my encore?*"

It was no less terrifying speaking to her for the second time. Bean gulped, and hawed, and trembled so hard his teeth chattered. The whole walk down, he had been rehearsing what he would say if he should happen upon the dragon (and she should happen not to kill him). It took every ounce of Bean's courage to finally summon the lines:

"Um. Begging your pardon, my lady. And by your leave. I respectfully seek your, um, dragonship's audience. For a tune—and a talk."

"*Oh?*" She seemed amused. "*What kind of talk?*"

"A friendly one, ma'am."

"*Mortal man,*" her voice shook the walls around him, sending down a rivulet of dust. "*Do you how many friendly talks I've had with your race in all the eons of my life?*"

"Um. Um." How the devil was Bean supposed to know such a thing? He'd have to confess his ignorance. "No, I don't."

She lifted a single claw, as long as a halberd.

"*One.*"

"Oh, dear."

"*And you're the one.*"

It took Bean a moment to work out her meaning, but when he saw the way, she rested her chin on her shoulder and considered the fact that she'd done him no harm yet, he felt a small sense of relief. "Oh," he said.

The dragon craned her head to face Bean fully. The heat radiating from her body played tricks with the air. Her whole form seemed to waver, as if Bean were looking at the dragon through a shaky looking glass.

"*You have better manners than the man you serve,*" she said. "*He's rude and stupid. There's not enough meat on him worth the trouble of picking. If he's a knight, I'm an adder. I'll kill him quickly tomorrow, but it puzzles me why your man wants to die so young. And so needlessly.*"

"That's actually what I'd like to talk to you about."

She cocked her head thoughtfully, but then twirled a claw in a circle.

"*First, the tune.*"

"Your dragonship?"

"*Music before business.*"

"You want me to play? Now?"

"*Yes. I assume you brought your pipes for that very purpose.*" Her gaze went far away, and her voice sounded wistful. "*I should like to hear your finest medley. Something quick, but pensive. Contemplative, but not complicated. Familiar, but novel.*"

"All right." Bean brought his bag beneath his arm. His mind raced, for of course he had no idea what music she had in mind. His fingers, though, knew just what to do, returning to the familiar march medley he always started his practices with. Which was neither pensive, nor complicated, nor at all novel. It was steady and stirring, like all good bagpipe music should be.

When he had finished, the dragon's eyes fluttered. A gray tongue flickered, as if she could taste the fading echoes of the final strains. When at last the chamber had grown silent, she let out a contented sigh.

"*That,*" said the she-dragon, "*was a fine piece of piping.*"

Bean stuck a leg out and tried to bow in the courtly fashion he had seen once or twice before. "You're too kind. I'm glad you enjoyed it."

"*That I did.*" She stretched her great limbs and lifted herself upright, sending coins and jewels tinkling down like a waterfall. "*Ah, me,*" she said musingly, "*'Tis a quiet, lonely life dragons lead.*"

"Ma'am?"

"*We eat. We horde. We sleep. We wake up and lay an egg somewhere and forget all about it. Eat again. Sleep again … More and more sleep. Until by and by, even our dreams become tedious. Once in a century, a happenstance hero might come round. But they're always fools, like the man you serve. Tedious. Stupid. Poor company who makes poor entertainment. They always die in the end.*"

Bean did not know how he ought to respond, so, once more, he resorted to his standard observation, "Aye. And there it is."

"*There it is.*" She nodded once. "*You at least have acquired some wisdom—what was your name again?*"

"Bean, ma'am."

She giggled. "*Bean. That suits you well. Bean the piper, you have given me entertainment. So, I'll give you the boon of a chat. What words would a mortal man have with a dragon?*"

For the first time, Bean smiled. He grasped his pipes firmly.

"Words of business, your dragonship."

"*Really?*" The dragon cocked an eyebrow. "*I am intrigued.*"

Bean knew well she was, for Bean was a shrewd fellow when it came to bargaining.

"You like the bagpipes?"

"*Aye. Since the first time I heard their skirl calling from a hillside. They've touched me like no other instrument.*"

"Then I've a proposition for you …"

An oily, purple light crept over the eastern mountains. Steel-colored clouds covered most of the sky, but the coming dawn held the possibility of a morning without rain. A small blessing, as the air still stung with bitter cold.

Hugh Lamont stood between the two ornate columns before the mountain's fissure. The statuary dragons that decorated the pillars gazed down with churlish indifference upon the would-be knight in the ill-fitted chainmail.

Much like the real dragon who had just emerged.

She sat upright, her front legs extended, wings furled, teeth gleaming, as silent and still as the mountain underneath her. Her chest and shoulders were like a castle keep. Her eyes were bottomless wells. Orange heat pulsated from her body. She was a force of nature. An ancient power.

She looked slightly annoyed.

Hugh looked like a man standing before his gallows. As he beheld the dragon in the fullness of her awful might, his eyes refused to blink. His face turned green. Thank heaven they hadn't had breakfast or else the boy would have surely spewed it out.

The dragon's tail slithered behind her, a long, silver-maned appendage as wide and winding as a river. It flicked as her dark eyes glowed warningly.

"Would you see this affair through, then? In accordance with the customs?"

If Hugh had gone tearing off down the mountainside for dear life, not a man in the world would have blamed him. Nor counted it as a mark against his courage. No more than if a fisherman put his boat in from a storm, or a forester fled from a woodland fire. But Hugh didn't move.

Between the lady he hoped to win, and the silly stories he had filled his head with, and the guidance of a good-hearted (if somewhat vain) father, Hugh Lamont the Younger had acquired that peerless, and often utterly pointless, bravery that was both the curse and the crowning glory of the Scots. He stood his ground. His voice squeaked, as he replied to his foe:

"Aye."

The dragon darted a quick glance at Bean who kept his face perfectly stoic. He alone caught the wink she gave him.

"Very well … Thou will, of course, permit the, um, faux allez?"

Hugh blinked, the first time he had since laying eyes on the dragon.

"The … I'm sorry. What—what am I permitting?"

"Faux allez, sir knight. Surely you are familiar with that most ancient and venerable custom? The one passed down from Saint Michael himself at the command of your Lord." She dipped her great head in a passable imitation of genuflecting. *"Jesus*

Christ, who decreed that in all battles betwixt our races, an honorable peace must first be sought before the first blood is shed."

Hugh gaped at the dragon, completely befuddled. Bean bit down on his tongue to keep from chuckling. She was a right clever dragon, that was for sure; and she surely knew the ways of young men, for she was playing this boy like a lute.

"Faux ... allez," Hugh whispered softly to himself.

The dragon assumed a lecturing pose.

"I'm sure you know the routine, Sir Hugh. But for the sake of your piper, I shall explicate. In the faux allez, each of the fighters, dragon and mortal, demonstrates their finest martial maneuvers, displays the fullness of their might, exhibits all their strength and skill in a single mock performance. Then, having witnessed first-hand their opponent's prowess, the combatants may adjudge for themselves whether their opponent would have had the power to slay them in combat—without the bother of actually slaying anyone. Should both combatants deem the other a worthy adversary, they may declare the challenge fully met without any loss to their honor."

"The faux allez ..." Hugh repeated.

Bean feared the lad wasn't quite grasping the line she was practically dangling in front of him.

"So," Bean ventured, "what your dragonship is saying is that you'll each put on a fighting show. And if you're both suitably impressed, then you can call off the fight. With honor."

"Just so." She nodded.

At last, comprehension broke through the cloudbank of young Hugh's confusion. "Yes!" he exclaimed all of a sudden. "Of course. The faux allez. A fighting show. I'm sure I've heard about that." His mood quickly perked. He straightened himself to his fullest height, tucked a fist into his hip, and declared he would gladly accept the ancient and well-known "faux allez" that the she-dragon had just invented for his sake. "So, um. Who should go first?"

She made a chiding expression.

"Of course, of course," he said hastily. "Ladies first."

The dragon nodded once and gestured for Hugh and Bean to stand back a ways, behind an outcrop of heavy rocks. Once the men were situated, she lifted her face towards the mountain's summit.

There was a blur of motion, a whoosh of air, and an explosion.

The dragon whirled about and whipped her tail and struck the peak of the mountain off, as clean as a butcher carving a flank. The ground tremored from the force of the blow. Great slabs of rock, some as big as boats, went hurtling through the air. She climbed up the ruined mountaintop, spread her wings, and flapped thrice, making a gale so powerful, Bean and Hugh had to grasp onto the nearby boulders to keep from being blown off the mountain. Her claws flashed. Her teeth snapped. She drew another breath and bellowed a roar so loud and so fell, Bean feared he would die from the sound of it.

It was as if all the ancient furies of the pagan gods had been unleashed. But the dragon had one last spectacle to show her human audience. The finale.

She paused to make sure Bean and Hugh had recovered themselves enough to pay attention. The dragon drew a deep breath that made a sound like bellows filling, and then she opened her jaws wide to the heavens.

A torrent of blinding, white fire shot into the sky. A column of light and heat that burst forth from the dragon's maw like a geyser. Up, up, higher and higher, it went all the way into the clouds. There the dragon's fire pooled and mingled with the sky, turning the gray canopy crimson. There was a murmur of thunder followed by bolts of blood red lightning that coursed down over the Black Cuillin Mountains like grasping fingers. A hellish storm, wrought by the inferno of a dragon's breath.

It made for quite a show.

When the last peal of thunder had faded away, the dragon slid back down to where Hugh and Bean were hiding. Smoke twirled about her body. Ash fell like snow over her head. She walked to the two carved columns as nonchalantly as if she had just returned from a market and sat down between them.

Cautiously, Bean and Hugh stepped out from behind the shelter of their rocks. For a long while, no one said anything. Bean brushed some of the ash from his shoulders and then, seeing that the dragon was waiting for their reaction, Bean clapped his hands in applause. It was a meager sound compared to what had just transpired, and Hugh's joining it didn't help much. Nevertheless, the dragon smiled at the compliment.

"*Thank you both.*" She turned to Hugh. "*Well, mortal. Are you sufficiently impressed with my power?*"

He had a hard time finding his voice. "G-good God, yes."

"*All right, then.*" She pointed a claw at Hugh. "*Now it's your turn. Show me your strength and skill, sir knight.*"

The boy looked to his right and then his left. After he found an open and relatively level patch of ground, he fixed his belt and, after murmuring something to himself, drew his blade. A feeble cry cracked in his throat:

"Strath Dubh!"

Then Hugh Lamont the Younger tramped about in a circle. He slashed his dirk through the air, slicing off a pretend foe's head. He stabbed a phantom enemy through its heart. He parried and turned away imaginary blows. Round and round he capered until he was huffing and soaked in sweat.

It was like watching a little boy in a grown man's body playing pretend with a sword. Bean could hear the dragon stifling her laughter. A puff of smoke escaped from her nostrils.

For his crescendo, Hugh shouted "Strath Dubh" once more and hopped up onto a nearby ledge. He jumped right back down, landing in a kneeling position with his squat little blade's point in the ground, a ridiculous pose he held for an awkwardly long while.

At last, he looked up and sheathed his sword.

"Well?"

The dragon seemed somewhat at a loss for words. "That was … Well, I've never seen the like."

"Me neither, m'lord." Bean clapped politely.

"*And were you impressed?*"

For the first time, Bean could sense the dragon was uncomfortable. For what Hugh had recounted before about dragons not being able to lie was, in fact, quite true. She scratched at some rocks and her eyes roved about, until they finally settled on Bean. To him, she replied, "*I was impressed with your performance.*"

"Excellent!" Hugh laughed.

"*Yes,*" she said hastily, "*so our affair is settled. No bloodshed. No moldering corpses. Honor's been satisfied.*" She motioned for the two of them to join her by the entrance to her lair. "*Now for the boons. My boon to you, Sir Hugh Lamont. You may each take of my horde what you can carry …*" She eyed them both. "*I don't expect that will cost me overmuch.*"

But Hugh was positively giddy. "Thank you! We will!"

Gauging from her expression, the youngster's reaction was not as polite as it should have been. Fortunately, Bean kept enough sense to ask the obvious question good manners dictated:

"And what boon would you like from my lord here?"

The glow in Hugh's cheeks ebbed ever so slightly. "Oh, right. I have to do something for you, too."

"*Yes. You do.*" As the wind moaned in the hollow of the mountain, the dragon leaned in close enough that Bean could feel the fire in her breath.

She dropped her voice low. Her eyes narrowed intently. *"Take what you can carry but tell no one of how you came by it. My boon is to be left alone. So don't come back here ever again … Unless you're invited."*

It was a fine June day in the valley when Mary MacFarlane was wedded to Hugh Lamont the Younger. From far and wide, villagers and farmhands and tradesmen and shepherds came to wish Sir Ian's daughter and Lord Hugh's son a long life of happiness. Old Hugh had thrown open his larders and bought enough casks to fill ten taverns. It was an especially large and merry crowd that had gathered beneath a clear summer sky at the manor. Flags and streamers and flowers filled a score of tables Lord Lamont had had specially made for the occasion.

The lord of Strath Dubh had come into some prosperity of late. A proper stone gate was fast arising around the perimeter of the old farmstead. And the drafty home he had lived in all his life would soon be relegated to servants' quarters while a real manor house of brick and timber and no less than four chimneys was being built. He had new oxen and more sheep than anyone could count and everyone in his house was wearing newly spun tartans. Where the gold had come from to pay for all this opulence, rumors ran rampant. A wealthy lowland uncle who had died without issue? Speculation in the wool market? Mary's dowry?

There was much talk, and even more argument, but most folk agreed the younger Hugh had played some part in this new-found wealth. He held his head higher lately, squared his shoulders more, like a young man who had sought and found his fortune. And now he had married a knight's daughter.

On the joyous day, Mary looked radiant, a storybook bride if ever there was one. She wore a snow-white dress accentuated with her new family's plaid thrown over a shoulder, a silver torque, and a brooch that bore Strath Dubh's newly christened sigil: St. Andrew's saltire with a rampant dragon in its center. Young Hugh's bride was gorgeous and gracious to everyone. At one table, she held a delicate discourse with her father's courtly relations; the next table over, she shared a ribald jape with her father-in-law's Highlanders that set them all roaring with laughter. Everyone counted young Hugh a lucky man.

There was music, too. Old Hugh Lamont had an English lutist roaming the tables, playing and singing with a voice of honey, as the first dishes were served. Later, when the fires were being lit and the first stars peeked through an indigo sky, a band of fifteen flutes, harps, shepherd pipes, shawms, and drums launched into a concert the likes of which the men and women of the valley had never heard. Loud and raucous and yet skillful in their art, these were performers fit for a lord—a true lord. A most glorious round of music for Mary and Hugh's celebration.

Only there was one musician missing.

There were no bagpipes at the wedding feast. For Bean Baird had taken leave to attend pressing business he claimed he had in the Cuillian Mountains. Though his absence vexed the elder Hugh greatly, the bridegroom knew enough of his piper's business that he lent him a pony, packed him food and whiskey for the journey, and bade him give his best regards to their mutual friend.

The first moon of June-time had Bean the piper retracing the very journey he had undertaken with Hugh Lamont that past winter. The warmer weather made the hike up the mountain a much less miserable undertaking than it had been before. His mount carried his supplies, as well as his bagpipes. When he came near to the top, he tied the pony off, brought out his pipes, and climbed the rest of the way.

At the summit, there was the she-dragon, waiting for Bean between those two heathen columns before her lair. Somehow, she seemed even greater, and more terrifying, than the first time he had met her. They exchanged greetings, Bean bowed low, and then the dragon got straight to the point:

"Start with that York reel. I was fond of that one ..."

So, Bean filled his pipe bag, tuned his drones, and played the York reel. After that, he went into the march medley he always used as a warmup. Then "King Malcolm's Lament." "Pitchfork in the Barley." "Orkney Boys." Every tune Bean had ever learned, and a few he had invented, he played up there at the top of the mountain, for an audience like no other. Sometimes, the she-dragon would clap along in time; other times, she would close her eyes and hum softly to herself; during the Highlanders' Last Stand, she stared straight at Bean, but her black eyes were somewhere far away.

For two and twenty years, Bean would repeat that journey up the nameless mountain in the Cuillians to give her dragonship a fine performance on his pipes. Every trip, he would bathe and shave and wear a clean tartan. For this was the bargain Bean Baird had struck with that bagpipe-loving dragon. Once a year, on the first full moon of June, he would give her a concert. Her "boon" of gold had been an advance to hire the piper for an annual performance. Bean the piper stayed true to his word and performed his end faithfully, year in and year out.

Until one wintry day in 1353, Bean woke up and felt a stiffness creeping through his chest. He picked up his pipes and set them under his arm to practice, as he had every morning, but he could not blow up the bag. No matter how hard he tried. A tight, coughing wheeze would seize his lungs every time he drew a deep breath.

He laid his pipes aside and never touched them again.

Three days later, Bean died in a chair in his cottage, his eyes fixed on his window, on the mountains beyond the valley.

———————

When the next June moon came, the dragon yawned and came out from her lair, eager to hear what new tunes her odd little piper would bring her this year. Only it was not Bean Baird she saw awaiting her, but a noble lord. He was richly dressed and bore himself like a hale warrior though his red hair and beard were tinged with the first snow of a man's middle years. At his side, stood a girl with strawberry blonde head and the fierce eyes of a hawk. A leathern case lay at her feet.

The dragon drew herself out of the hole in the mountain, and though the young girl uttered a gasp, she did not cringe behind her escort. The lord made a deep bow; the girl followed his example.

"Your dragonship," he greeted her.

"*Sir Hugh*," she replied. "*I did not expect to see you here, much less with …*"

"My daughter, Mary," he answered.

The young Mary stepped forward and dipped her head again.

"Mary Lamont, at your service."

She was surprisingly calm in the dragon's presence, even more so than her father, which the dragon found amusing. Still, a certain decorum needed to be maintained.

"I don't recall asking for your service, Mary Lamont. Nor inviting either of you to come see me."

She layered an ominous threat in her words, but also an invitation for Hugh to explain himself.

"No, good dragon," Hugh acknowledged, "you didn't. And for that I beg forgiveness for intruding upon your attention."

"Well, at least your manners have improved since our last encounter, Sir Hugh." The dragon waved a claw. *"But enough formality. What could bring you back to the place I enjoined you never to return?"*

He paused. The wind stirred in his hair. When he looked up at her, she caught a sparkle brimming in his eyes.

"There could be only one reason why I would presume to come here."

"Ah." The dragon sighed knowingly. *"I thought as much. Bean has gone on to that country to where all mortals must go. I am saddened."*

Though dragon eyes are not made for crying, nor their spirits for remorse, the darkness beneath this dragon's eyes flickered for a moment, as she reflected on the loss of Bean's company. No more bagpipe reels or marches. No more village gossip or farm-spun witticisms. No more Bean. The dragon shook her head, for she did not at all like the churn of these thoughts.

"It's the way of your kind, and there it is," she said, repeating one of Bean's favorite banalities. The dragon made to return to her lair. *"Thank you both for bringing me these tidings. Farewell …"*

"Wait, your dragonship."

It was the girl Mary who had spoken. The dragon reared her head over her shoulder and regarded the girl. She was frightfully bold.

"If I may show you something." Mary knelt down and opened the case at her feet.

When she had brought out what it contained, the dragon exclaimed, *"Are those bagpipes?"*

"Yes, ma'am," replied the girl, and she went to assemble the drone sticks and chanter to the bag. The woodgrain shone with a fresh polish, and the bag was covered in a deep blue cloth, and the fittings were silver ferrules with etched scrollwork. They seemed a much finer set of bagpipes than the dingy ones Bean used to play. While Mary adjusted the settings, Hugh explained:

"I know well," said he, "the debt I owe Bean … and you for sparing me from my challenge."

"You owe me nothing, knight."

"Bean never said outright what he had done," Hugh continued, "but I gathered he made a bargain with you. My daughter wishes to renew that bargain. For Bean's sake. She's a piper, too, you see."

The dragon considered the girl before her. Mary had the bagpipes up and at the ready on her shoulder. If they sounded half as splendid as they looked … But could this slender wisp of a creature summon the sound as Bean had? She seemed determined to try.

"*All right,*" said the dragon at last. "*Let's hear it, then.*"

Mary blew a deep breath, squeezed the bag beneath her arm, and struck in the pipes on her first try. She played a medley that sounded familiar to the dragon; familiar, but with some new embellishments gilded onto the music, some novel grace notes that hadn't been there before. It pleased the dragon. The girl played on without missing a note, and, quite without realizing it, the dragon's toe tapped right along in time. When Mary had finished, the dragon spoke up at once.

"*You were taught by Bean Baird, weren't you? Don't deny it.*"

"Aye," Mary replied proudly. "Most of what I know of piping, I learned at the knee of good old Bean. He was a great piper. One of the best. But I'm better still."

The dragon laughed. "*Are you now?*"

"Would you like to hear more?"

"*I would, Mary Lamont,*" said the dragon, "*Play for me this time each June. Play and count yourself blessed to keep company with a Scottish dragon. For that's a rare thing, better than gold. Aye, and there it is.*"

About Matthew C. Lucas

Matthew C. ("Matt") Lucas lives in Tampa with his wife, their two sons, dog, and axolotl. His works include the acclaimed historical fantasy series, *Yonder & Far* (Ellysian Press), fantasy novel, *Sword of the Godless* (Montag Press), epic fantasy novel, *The Mountain* (Montag Press), and several novellas and short stories that have appeared in various venues and anthologies. He's also not a half-bad bagpiper. You can learn more about Matt's doings at www.matthewclucas.com.

Dragon Drops

By Baden M Chant

"If pigs could fly we'd all need steel umbrellas" or so the old saying goes, so what about dragons? Dragons are dangerous, magical beasts, cunning and unpredictable in every way. Humans are earth-bound, unmagical, and mundane except, maybe, when we come into contact with dragons. Then anything might happen. We might transform, transcend, become something new. But is that a good thing? Are humans meant to be gods? Or is that only another way of going to hell?

Dragon Drops

by Baden M Chant

Frankie stepped out of the curtained alcove. It was deep in the Pile, the Society's ancient castle, in the darkest corner of the dankest chamber. The Society didn't believe in coddling apprentices.

She'd stashed her bag under the bed. It had been hard to pack without raising her mother's suspicions. *I hope I didn't leave anything important behind.*

Now, though, it was time to face the others. They were staring at her. All but the two or three who were deliberately not staring at her. Hildebrand was one of them. *Lucky for him.* She'd warned him to keep his distance. *I don't want the others thinking I followed him here. Thinking I'm one of those love-sick, mooning girls he always has at his heels. That would be unbearable.*

Frankie went over to the long table and sat down uninvited. The apprentices sniggered at this, but no one objected. They were all male, ranging from mere boys to young men. The only other female apprentice Frankie had ever heard of was now Bailiff to the Society, and a grandmother.

"Aren't you a bit old to go apprentice?" one of the younger boys asked after a moment's awkward silence.

Frankie replied with a tight smile and gripped her patience. "My mother wouldn't agree. I had to wait until I was old enough to indenture myself."

"But you have to apprentice six years. And journeyman eight! Why, you'll be an old lady by the time you're done!"

"You can do it all in three. As long as you're willing to stand boards."

"But you have to know the Book off by heart to stand!" he said, shocked anyone would try something so ridiculous. "The Book's as thick as me. Much better to serve time, everyone knows that."

"The rules allow the short way, and I mean to take it."

One of the older boys, a dark-haired youth with a narrow, sharp-featured face, gave a bark of laughter. "You think you can learn the Book in a year? You some kind of sodding genius?"

Frankie shook her head. "You don't understand. I've already learned the Book."

His eyes narrowed, "And where did you get a copy of the Book from, then?"

Frankie's smile grew tighter, but she didn't answer.

The dark-haired boy stared at her for a long moment and then turned and whispered something into the ear of the young man who was sitting next to him. He was old enough to have a reddish-blond beard, but he had a bovine look to him. It wasn't improved by the slow smile that spread across his face. "Even if you do it in three, you'll be an old maid, sure," he said, and then with a bigger grin, "Girls should be having babies your age, not going apprentice. Don't all girls want to have babies?"

Frankie's smile turned as fierce and wolfish as the blonde's was slow and grass-fed. "That's sharp. Shouldn't a man introduce himself before asking a question like that?"

"I'm Thomas," he said, seeming proud he knew his own name.

"I'm Frankie, and I don't want to have babies, Thomas. That's why I took the indenture."

"But you're a girl, girls have to have babies, otherwise…well?" He turned to the dark-haired youth for another prompt and was glared at for his trouble. He turned back. "Well, they do and all."

Frankie's smile grew fiercer yet. "But who is going to give them me? You?" At this, the other apprentices broke out sniggering again.

Frankie stood up and looked at Thomas until he stood as well. "Do you really think all girls have to have babies? Not a one good for anything else?"

"Sure. It's what's right. Everybody knows that," he said, turning to grin and wink at the table.

Frankie reached out and took hold of Thomas's tunic. Her smile softened. She pouted and pulled Thomas down as if for a kiss. The table went silent and slack jawed. A dagger appeared in Frankie's left hand, and she thrust the point forward until it needled Thomas's breeches. "Maybe I should turn you into a girl? Then you can have all the babies since you seem so worried the world's short of them!"

The apprentices jumped to their feet. A chair clattered to the ground. "Hold on now, it was just a bit of fun," one said. "We always haze the newcomers!"

"Hilarious. Can't you see me laughing?" Frankie said, pushing the dagger forward forcing Thomas up onto his tiptoes.

A heavy hand landed on Frankie's shoulder. "Ease off now, Frankie. Poor Thomas is a bit slow, but he always comes round in the end. I'm sure he'll mind his words now, won't you, Tom?" Hildebrand said.

"I will and all!" Thomas squawked, his calves beginning to quiver from the effort of keeping off the dagger point.

Frankie grunted and the blade vanished out of her hand. Thomas sagged back into his chair, sighing with relief.

"Do you know her then, Hildebrand?" one of the apprentices asked.

"From the cradle, you might say. Her mother stands coin-counter to my father, takes care of all his outside-Society business."

The dark-haired boy snorted. "No wonder she could get her hands on the Book."

Frankie grabbed Hildebrand's arm and dragged him back toward her little alcove.

"I told you not to tell anyone we knew each other," she whispered fiercely. "I don't want them thinking I got in by know who, or I signed because…"

"Because?"

"Because I'm in love with you like all those other stupid girls!"

"Aren't you, though?"

"You wish. I can't believe you couldn't keep it secret for one night! Now what are they going to think?"

"After that carry-on they'll think a she-devil's come among them." Hildebrand smiled down at her with his devastating, even-toothed grin. So warm, so beautiful, almost as warm and beautiful as his rich, chocolate-brown eyes. "If you wanted secrets kept, you shouldn't have gone and offered to castrate poor Tom when you'd only been indentured an hour."

Frankie chewed on that. "I was provoked."

"Provoked, were you? And so easily."

"Too hot to hand? Is that it? Frankie, the angry fierce girl? If only she'd had a father maybe she would have grown up proper!"

Hildebrand's smile grew warmer and deeper. "Oh, what a sad pity that would have been. A proper Frankie. I weep to think of it."

"Weep? You think it's funny. You're as bad as them."

"Never, Frankie, never that. I'll never be like them to you."

"And what do you mean by that?"

"Nothing, nothing. They are good lads. You shouldn't mind them so."

"Good lads, are they? The worst kind, then. Just you warn them. I've a hot hand and a hotter temper and if any of them thinks it'd be a fine lark to climb into my bed in the wee hours, he'll get what I offered that clod, Thomas!"

"Oh, they took that message to heart already. Be quiet and gentle as little lambs, they will. And more so now they know you, my friend."

"I don't need you propping me up. I can make my own way."

"True, sad as it is."

"Now what's that supposed to mean?"

But whatever Hildebrand might mean was drowned out by the wailing of the watchtower siren from up on High Hill. Hildebrand raised one perfect eyebrow. "Well, what a night this is turning out to be."

The journeyman hurried the apprentices through the dark streets. "Come on, you slugs. Look at them! Dragons flying right over the city! Can you believe it? A great migration! Must be. No stomping through the muddy, stinking countryside for drops this time. They'll be raining down on our front doorsteps more like! Move!"

Above them the great white moon was cut by a growing river of dark, winged silhouettes trailed by vortices of many-coloured sparks.

"Why are you here?" one of the boys grumbled, giving Frankie the side-eye. He was pulling an empty handcart down the steep, narrow streets after the journeyman. The cobbles made the wheels rattle and jolt. "Less people the better. Haven't even done one day's slog. Now you're on crew? I scrubbed and mopped a six-month before I ever got on crew."

"Don't worry, I've a nose for this work," Frankie said, too excited to care about his hostility.

"But an apprentice share is bollocks as is! Now you want to come and divvy it up even more?"

"I'll earn mine, rest easy on that."

"So what you said was true, about the Book and all?"

"Watch and see, eh?" Frankie said, standing on her tiptoes.

They'd come to a stop. A gaggle of people were blocking the street. The journeyman was shouting and trying to elbow his way forward. "Make a hole, will you!"

Frankie was only a dark-haired slip of a girl. There was no seeing over the crowds' heads for her, no matter how she stretched. Hildebrand, who had been driving the apprentices from the back, passed her without slowing. He'd seen something. *Of course he has, the stupid overgrown lummox.*

People who had ignored the journeyman parted before the long-striding Hildebrand like grass. On another day this would have irritated her, but now she took her chance to bob along in his wake.

They spilled out of the crowd to find a family of four standing before their badly damaged terrace. The roof was partially caved in, and half the wattle and daub facade had fallen into the street. A drop had hit the house and come to rest outside their front door. It sat there, a dark waist-high pile, sparking and hissing and spitting with magical potential.

"Jackpot!" shouted the journeyman. "Have you ever seen a drop so fresh in your life? What is it? Get the test kit out."

Frankie took a few steps closer.

"Well?" Hildebrand asked her.

"Mature black. Male, pretty sure. Yes, male. Look, you can tell by the reddish cast to the leptons. Look at it spark!"

The journeyman was watching her, hands on hips. "And who in the hell are you?"

"Frankie, apprentice. First day."

"First day? And you think you can identify a drop by eye?"

Frankie shrugged. "Run the test if you don't believe me."

The other apprentices were using a long-handled silver spoon to scoop the smallest portion of the drop into their test kit. The device buzzed. Clockwork wheels with depictions of dragons, colours, and ages whirled away and then aligned and locked with a ping. The journeyman grabbed it out of their hands. "Mature…unbelievable. Like she said, mature black male. Handle with care!"

Frankie, knowing that she was right, hadn't bothered paying any attention to the test. She was watching the family. They were beginning to glow. And the youngest boy's feet were not altogether touching the ground.

"Contamination!" Frankie screamed.

The mother looked bewildered. Her eyes went from the ruined house to her family, to the dropping and back again, round and round until she noticed something hot on her cheek. She wiped it off with a finger. The dragon excrement sat there dripping leptons and glowing red. Horrified at what she was doing but unable to stop herself, she put her finger to her mouth and sucked it clean.

"No!" Frankie screamed again. "Contamination! Contamination!"

The other apprentices were scrambling to get the watercart set up. It had a hand pump and a hose with a nozzle and mixing vessel attached. "Have you broken out the right grounder yet?" The journeyman was shouting. "Hurry it up, man!"

One of the apprentices thrust a ruby red vial into his hands. "Beithir blood! Tincture one thousand to one."

The journeyman took it. "Charging the mixer! Ready on the pump!"

Four of the apprentices grabbed the pump handles at the back of the cart, two to a side. Hildebrand was holding the hose. "Wax in your ears," he yelled, "cloaks up! And get those people away from here. She's going to turn!"

The crowd needed no encouragement. They were already fleeing in all directions. The mother's face was glowing with a dangerous red light. She hunched over and screamed in agony as dark black wings erupted from her back, glistening and feathered. "Wax your ears, Frankie, now!"

Frankie had been staring horrified and fascinated by the mother's transformation, but Hildebrand's familiar voice jolted her. She opened the little metal case in her kit, removed two big pinches of wax, pushed them into her ears, then drew up the hood of her dragon-leather cloak.

The mother was testing her wings. One flap, then two, and she was up and hovering. A tortured groan escaped her, rising and steadying into a sky-facing scream. It drew out and out until it became a single pure note. Silence fell, and then she began to sing.

The father was only mildly contaminated. All he needed was a dousing with properly tinctured grounder to set him right, but that also put him in danger. He took a step toward his wife, then two, dazzled by the sudden beauty of her song and still all too human to resist. That her teeth had transformed into fangs and her fingers, talons, was nothing to him compared to the sweet music of her voice. "Ah, so beautiful," he said, walking into her arms.

Even with the wax in her ears and her hood up Frankie still felt the lure. She wanted to draw nearer, to pull down her hood and unstop her ears, to get as close to that beautiful sound as she could. *Resist it!* But the father was defenceless. He looked overjoyed as his wife stooped down and ripped out his throat with her jagged teeth.

A moment later, a moment too late, the hose kicked in and doused the family. The harpy shied away from the water, screaming, dropping her prey, and sparking where the grounder touched her. Black wings beat against the air and she was up and gone into the night. "No, don't! It won't last! You'll fall. You'll fall!" Frankie yelled after her in vain. The woman was gone. She would fly on until the magic exhausted itself and then she would plunge down, down to her death.

"No! We could have saved her!"

"After what she's done it might be a mercy, Frankie," Hildebrand said, putting a comforting hand on her shoulder.

"Right. Let's police this up," the journeyman said as the apprentices pulled their hoods down and dug the wax out of their ears.

"What about them?" Frankie asked, pointing to the two wet and bedraggled children sitting on the cobbles crying.

The journeyman shrugged. "Orphanage?"

"Can't we do something?"

"Yes, we can get the drop out of here and into the vats before anyone else touches it. That is what we can do, so grab a sodding silver implement, apprentice. Time to shovel shit!"

———————————

"It's a strange life," Frankie told Hildebrand, sweating as they pushed the heavy cart back up the hill toward the Pile. All reclaimed droppings were stored there in a vaulted underground chamber lined with massive stone vats.

"What's this now?" Hildebrand asked, leaning one broad, perfectly tapered hand against the back of the cart and pushing it along effortlessly.

"The Society. Magic. Why are humans the only creatures who can use magic but have none but what we can take?" said Frankie putting her shoulder in and straining hard. "Dragon-leather cloaks to protect us. Dragon drop powered devices. Potions distilled from beast and herb."

"Scavengers are we, is that it? Can't be you're regretting the indenture already? Usually takes a week or two before the traditional mope sets in."

Frankie scorned this, "How could I regret it after all I went through to get in?"

"Give it time."

"Do you regret it?"

"It's the family trade, regretting is beside the point."

"Stop the cart!" The journeyman shouted. Frankie and Hildebrand looked up to see the ramp that led down to the vault was full of handcarts and crews waiting to bring in their spoils. "Looks like we've got a year's worth in a night," Hildebrand said.

"Isn't that a good thing?" Frankie replied.

"Is it, now? I wonder."

A boy weaved his way through the carts toward Hildebrand. "Found you, at last! There's trouble!"

"What, more?" Hildebrand asked.

"Alchemists! They're refusing to give up a drop. Said it fell in the Quarter, so they'll not give it us. Grand Master says to bring some likely lads."

"Does he, now? Well, feeling likely, Frankie?"

"I doubt I'm what your father had in mind."

"We can bring a few more."

Hildebrand went down the line and tapped a half-dozen of the bigger, stronger apprentices, including Thomas. He gave Frankie a nervous glance as he joined them. The group doubled back around High Hill, with its towered fortress and still wailing siren, toward the Alchemists Quarter.

A sudden darkness made Frankie look up. The migrating stream of dragons had swollen until it all but blotted out the full moon. Frankie felt an urge to grab for Hildebrand's hand. She pushed it down ruthlessly.

The Alchemists Quarter was a massive double square. The outer square housed offices, apothecaries, emporiums, boutiques, and living quarters. The inner was more like a fortress, but one designed to contain rather than repel. Alchemical experiments had a sad tendency to spectacular and unhelpful conclusions.

"You right? Sorry, I didn't think before bringing you here," Hildebrand said.

"I'm fine. I've wanted to come for a long time but never had the excuse. I think dad'd be happy I'm here. At long last!" Frankie said, straightening up.

"He might at that."

They passed through a narrow underbridge into the Clearance. It was a wide avenue, partially paved, partially turned over to gardens, between the inner and outer squares. On one side it was faced by lit windows and balconies crowded with gawkers, all looking up, on the other by a blank, black-faced basalt wall some five stories tall.

They saw some other Society men hurrying off to the right, so they followed and soon found themselves part of a sizeable standoff. Society on one side, Alchemists on the other, and between them a great silver drop, sparking and fizzing and full of icy light.

Hildebrand's father was there, the Grand Master of the Society. "You've no right to the drop, as you well know," he was saying. "It is we who have the license direct from the Corporate's own hand. The drop belongs to the Society."

The Alchemist, not the Lord High, but one of his lieutenants all in robes of purple and silver chained, was facing the Master, hands on hips. "The Society! Why do you insist on giving yourself such airs you...you coprophiliacs! You dunghill men. You dunnybrides. Why you're nothing but a pack of turd burglars!"

The Master turned red but held his anger admirably. "Be that as it may, the drop is ours. If you refuse it us, we shall have to fetch the Sergeant. He'll soon see who has the right of things."

The Alchemist snatched a glass vial from the folds of his robe and shook it until it glowed with ominous blue-black fire. "It fell on our property and we and we alone will say how it is disposed."

The Society men drew up their cloaks, loosened knives in their scabbards and brandished truncheons. The scene was balanced on the edge of an all-out brawl when Hildebrand's sudden laughter rang out. "I don't know what all this fuss is about. Why, we've had so many drops this night even a silver is hardly worth the shovelling."

The Alchemist looked at him. "What do you mean by that?"

"We've roads so choked with carts they can't even get down vault. The vats will be brimming before we're through. And here's you squabbling over a single drop, like it's the last any man will ever see."

The Alchemist stopped shaking his glass vial. The blue-black fire began to ebb. "Brimming?"

"Slopping over. So much so we'll have to sell far and wide to get anything like what we should. Plenty enough for all and for years to come, I don't doubt."

"It still fell on our land!"

"It's never going to be worth a visit from the Sergeant. Not after tonight. But for all that we've our rights to defend. Even if it were worthless we'd still have to make claim."

The Alchemist slipped his vial back into his robes. He looked at Hildebrand, still suspicious. "*If* what you say is true."

Hildebrand positioned himself between the two groups and smiled his most trustworthy smile. "How could it be otherwise? It's coming down like rain," he said, pointing up.

The Alchemist tilted his head back. His face turned white. "Watch out!"

Hildebrand looked up.

A golden drop, like a cloud of dewy thistledown, engulfed him.

Frankie screamed and ran towards him, but the Master grabbed her arm and pulled her back. "Think Frankie, you'll not save him charging in like a fool. What is it? Tell me!"

"Oh, it's a gold! A golden dragon! A female, all golds are. Can't you see? Oh, this is terrible. Hildebrand! Hildebrand!"

The Grand Master's face set grim. "Shovels! Shovels! Get him out. Quick!"

Some of the men had brought their carts. They retrieved silver shovels and heavy gloves, wrapped their cloaks tight about them, and began to dig. "Careful now, for your life's sake don't get any on you or your mates!"

They dug down through strange silken threads that clung and wrapped round their shovels and sparked alarmingly. At first bite the drop felt like wet wool, but wool that writhed and flicked with leptonic frisson. One man reeled away as the glittering fibres reached toward him like sinuous lines of golden lightning, but the others kept digging grimly, as though exhuming a grave.

"I see his boot!"

"Pull him out!"

The alchemists had watched all this nervously, but at the sight of Hildebrand being dragged free, they turned as one and fled. "Don't look, don't look. Get into the bunker!" Years of unfortunate contaminations had left them skittish as startled kittens.

The Society men rolled Hildebrand onto his back expecting to see a dead man. Even if the drop had not seemed as dense as usual or to have fallen as hard, to be struck like that by such a weight could only have snapped his neck. They gasped and fell back.

Far from dead, Hildebrand had emerged more beautiful and more full of life than before. His dark hair was now threaded through with gold, each half of his face was now a more perfect mirror of the other, his skin as pure and unblemished as the finest china, and his limbs and proportions subtly altered to a perfection beyond the birthright of any man.

To see him was to love him instantly. He was become as a god among men. His eyes flickered open, now grown deeper and more alive with light, and he stood and smiled upon the assembly.

Some tried to resist. They fell to their knees. Others hid their faces, but their eyes were drawn back to his light like filings to a lodestone. Hildebrand laughed with gentle good humour. "What is this, my friends? Stand to your feet."

Some tried and failed. Others fell flat to the ground, prostrate, worshipping.

To see him was to love him, and hopelessly. Frankie alone resisted.

She dragged her eyes away from Hildebrand's now gold-lit face and forced herself to walk toward the nearest water cart. *A bucket. I need a bucket. I won't love him. I won't. Not after I pushed him away all these years. I won't fall for him now because of some stupid magical contamination! I won't! I'll make him Hildebrand again. Stupid, stupid, Hildebrand. Only a blockhead like him could get himself shat on by a gold! Dope. Dummy. Dunce. Dolt. Dimwit. Dullard. Dumbarse. Drongo.* Step by step, insult by insult, she approached the cart.

Waves of love threatened to overwhelm her, but Frankie kept stoking the hot core of her anger to beat them back. She had more than enough fuel. A father dead before she was born. A mother who stubbornly opposed her ambitions. Hildebrand growing up so handsome no girl could resist him. *Stupid Hildebrand. Why hadn't he stayed gawky? What cursed fairy made him change into someone so ridiculously handsome? And now this? Idiot! Clod! Pain in the arse!*

She turned the spigot and filled her bucket with water, but the cart's kit had no grounder to match contamination from a gold. Frankie doubted there was anyone living who had even seen a golden drop before tonight. No one would come prepared for such an unlikely happening. But she knew what was needed. *How lucky I should have it handy.*

She leaned forward and let her tears drop into the bucket. Two splashes, three, a dozen. Angry tears, hurt tears, lonely tears – whatever they were they'd do. She sneered at herself. *A maiden's tears, how lovely.* And then her face grew more bitter still. *Don't lie to yourself.* She dragged the heavy bucket toward Hildebrand. *A mere maiden's tears won't do.* She put the bucket to her shoulder and then heaved the water toward Hildebrand. The water sparked and crackled as it fell on him, exploding into steam and drops that ran down his legs and sizzled as they hit the ground. The golden light dimmed and patches of normal colour appeared on Hildebrand's face. Frankie laughed bitterly. *The tears of a maiden in love but never kissed.* That's what the Book said. Only they could ground a gold. *How very convenient. You've lied to yourself all these years but there's the indisputable proof. You're as pathetic as all the rest. In love with the irresistible Hildebrand, you stupid fool.*

But her tears were not enough. As soon as the water drained away Hildebrand's glow brightened, redoubled. Now he was resplendent.

"Why do you resist it so, Frankie? When you love me. And I? I have loved you all my life. Come to me, and we will away together and forever."

"So, what if I love you!" Frankie said over her shoulder, trying to quell the way her heart leapt. *He loves me! No, not now. Don't think of it. Stay angry.* "So, what if you love me? What will that get me but a fat belly and a house full of squalling brats!"

"Will you deny our love?"

"I will!" Frankie said panting as she wiped her tears and mixed them into the bucket. "For now."

"For now?"

"If you stop this nonsense and come back to me as the real Hildebrand. Then I'll marry you, I promise. Once I'm Lord High Alchemist."

"You still wish to be a double master?"

"I'll be double master before I'm thirty! Just you watch me. A Master of the Society. A Master Alchemist. Both! And then I'll become the Lord High. You know I can do it."

Hildebrand laughed, "You'll be old and grey by then."

"Won't you love me if I'm old and grey?"

"Always."

"Then stop being stupid and wait. And when I'm Lord High and you're Grand Master, we'll have the biggest wedding this city has ever seen."

Frankie splashed another bucket of tear-tinctured water on Hildebrand. Her tears were coming freely now. She'd mixed in a hundred or more. Still, it was not enough. Hildebrand was becoming more a god and less a man every moment. Frankie's tear-tinctured buckets would never be enough. A bucket full of nothing but tears might not be enough.

"Do you hear?" Hildebrand asked her.

"What?"

"Music. I hear music. Is it? Ah, the music of the spheres. How I wish to see them, to grow closer, to become part of their song."

"No! Stay here, damn you. You'll not change, not leave, do you hear me! Not while I can stop you!"

But Hildebrand was becoming too bright to look upon. His skin was gold and his hair, alive with gold and silver light, floated about his head like wind-borne gossamer. His eyes turned upon her and they were golden and bright and fierce as a lion. "Come with me." It was an order. His hand held out to her, a demand.

Frankie shook her head, gritting her teeth and clenching her fists so hard her nails bit into her palms and made them bleed. "No, no! I want to be a double master. I want to be Lord High Alchemist, like my father would have been if he wasn't killed. I'll never go. I'll never marry you. Not until I've done it, do you hear me! So stay, stay here with me. I'll hurry. I'll do it as fast as I can! Then we can be happy. Then I'll go anywhere you like!"

Hildebrand looked at Frankie. A sad expression bathed his face in a beautiful melancholy, but his humanity was ebbing as the magic deepened its grip. The cares and interests of the mundane world were falling away from him one by one. "A pity. The things we would have seen. The joy we would have shared." He looked up. "I must away."

Hildebrand took a step, and another, and then he was walking on an invisible stair, one step and then the next, up and up.

Frankie ran at him, screaming, "No! No!" She leapt and wrapped his legs with her arms. The sudden terror that she would really lose him struck through her like a hundred spears of ice. Her tears streamed.

And where they fell they washed away the golden light. His feet began to sink back toward the ground.

"What are you doing, Frankie? Can't you hear the music? It is so beautiful. I must see it. I must join the infinite chorus!"

"No, you can't!"

"Why?"

"Because I can't go there with you! So you have to stay here. You have to marry me when I'm old and grey and smell like potions!"

"Come with me and you need never grow old."

"No! No, if I go with you —" a vision flooded Frankie's mind. A plain of wildflowers domed by crystal spheres spinning one over the other in a living motion as far from clockwork as a song was to a clanging bell. A beautiful girl walked there, with silver eyes and skin like moonlight and hair as dark as night, and it was her. Her hand was held by a young man all golden like the sun, gold of eye and gold of hair, and skin as lustrous as a thrice-polished crown, and it was Hildebrand. There was music there and scents of flowers and the pair were looking down, down to the ragged and squalid city where a young woman, her face twisted by tears, clasped the legs of a young man looking up, hand outstretched, reaching toward the vision of what they might be.

"No!" Frankie screamed, "That's not us. If I went, I wouldn't be myself anymore! Neither would you. You'll be some creature of magic who cared only about things I could never understand. I want Hildebrand. My Hildebrand. My dirty, stupid, stinky, human Hildebrand, not some glowing godling! We must stay ourselves!"

Hildebrand's hand reached up, up, straining, but there was something in him that forced his eyes down, down to the girl gripping his legs. She looked dull, and shadowed and drawn – weak and dirty, compared to the perfect vision above. And yet his hand stopped reaching up and dropped to the top of her head. It lay heavy there for a long moment.

Frankie waited for him to thrust her away, but instead he stroked her hair gently. His feet stopped surging upward and then floated slowly back to the ground. His hands drew Frankie up, and the last of the golden light faded as her tears washed his face and ran down his body melting wisps of silken gold and misting them away.

Hildebrand groaned as he returned once more to himself, perhaps in agony and loss, perhaps in relief. Frankie would never know or dare to ask.

They kissed; Frankie lifted off her feet in Hildebrand's embrace.

"You great stupid," Frankie said, burying her face in the nape of his neck.

"Yes," Hildebrand replied, "I'm all that."

About Baden M Chant

Baden M Chant currently resides in the caldera of a very extinct volcano with his partner and a menagerie of kids, dogs, cats and other wildlife. He's written for a number of Australian and international publications. His novella 'Access Denied' was nominated for an Aurealis Award. His novel 'Chimpman Zee' is available on Amazon. He blogs erratically at badenchant.com. Find him on x.com @badenchant, or on Bluesky @badenchant.bsky.social.

A Death of a Dragons

By Michael Vance

Death of Dragons is about what might happen when two apex species exist at the same time in the same place, and how the extinction of one seems inevitable. It attempts to capture the moment at which one such war ends, and how it might feel to watch a mighty opponent meet its end.

A Death of Dragons

By Michael Vance

It was in the season of flowers, with spring late arriving, that we followed the dying dragon up the mountainside. Nammah, ancient home of their kind. It towered over Avadon, so far below. The crags were black against the sky—burnt, I thought, appropriately enough. What battles must have been fought amongst their kind, I wondered, to have razed the landscape in this manner, as far as the eye could see?

I had seen one of them now, finally. Asmodeus, the king of them all, last of their kind. The black dragon of legend. His blood spattered the rocks of Nammah, and where it had struck the stone was pitted and scarred. Volcanic, as if scored by fire.

We could hear him, somewhere up above. That song they sing. It drives men mad with fear, but now there was a new note in it, some sorrow, as if Asmodeus knew he was dying. We used the song, and the blood, to track him up the mount.

I saw the woman, the witch from the south, going among the sleepers in the camp one night. She was looking for something, or someone, but spoke to no one, and she was still on my mind when I faded off to sleep.

The dragonsong floated through the camp like a lullaby, the song so soft now. I fell asleep listening to it, and I suspect that it is responsible for what happened next.

That night I dreamed of flying. I was scared, at first, as I took timid steps among the rocks. Whether I thought I was still on Nammah I don't recall now, but eventually my dreaming-self gathered the courage to step out over the void, and as I looked down, I felt my arms and legs thrashing against the air. But I did not drop. I can still recall my surprise as I stared down what seemed like miles to the valley below, as *something* kept me in the air. For some reason I did not question it long, did not turn back to the rocky ridge and safety. Instead, I pressed out further, into the wind, feeling the turbulence below, the blasts of air buffeting me. Further and further, I went, and when I looked back the mountain—*not* Nammah, I could see now— was already distant. It was not meant for me; I was intended to travel, to find my own home. It was the reason for flight, I thought. So, I flew.

I had never seen the earth in this way before. In fact, it did not resemble any land I knew at all—there were no great cities, none of our castles and farms or roads. Only land empty but for miles of trees and rivers and rock. So perfect, I thought, and I was grateful that my dreams had given me a look at this. The whole world was *mine*.

I woke troubled by it, wanting to return to the dream. Distantly, I noticed that the southern witch woman was walking among the party again, stooping and talking. I was too busy waking myself to think much of it until she was suddenly beside me, staring into my face.

"Your sleep was troubled?" she asked in a musical voice.

"No," I lied, not eager to speak with her.

She nodded and studied me. She had been beautiful once, I thought, but not any longer.

"You are Emeric, son of Roland. A Bandaran of the old line."

"I am." Fiercely this time—no lie was possible; pride would not allow it. She noted this and nodded. Sadly, it seemed. "Your father was killed at Charm." I nodded tightly. "Leaving you the last of your line." Another nod. "So for you, it is revenge." Our eyes locked, and there was no need to nod this time. She rose and walked off, apparently finished with me.

I found one of the rangers and asked about the dragon. She looked at me strangely but told me that he was not far now, that we would have him within the next couple of days, and that he now moved even more slowly than us. This was good, I thought at the time. Because I was eager for the hunt, for killing. For revenge, as the witch had said.

Asmodeus had killed my father at Charm, you see. It will be forgotten, by now, probably, but you must understand why I was there. It was one of the great battles of our time. Nija, the green dragon, died there, taking a thousand men and women with her before she screamed her last. Asmodeus had tried to protect her, while they finished her, and his wrath had been something to behold—or so I had been told. Because I was not there. My father had sent me on ahead to Mastema, where the ambush was already being prepared for Asmodeus himself. I had not been there when my father died, and I suspect he may have planned it that way. And though in my mind he died a hero's death, in truth I don't know even that. The dead were buried in a mass grave, their bodies unrecognizable after the dragon's fury. Lost forever, leaving us to make up our own stories.

Now I stared up the mountain, hatred filling me. The dragonsong, I noticed, had gone silent, and I prayed that Asmodeus had not died on the mountainside, alone and unpunished. Some part of me wanted to look him in the eye—wanted him to see me and know *why* he died. Of course, I knew that a beast like that could never truly understand such things, but *to me* it mattered. My father lay in a nameless grave, with only me to avenge him. That revenge, I swore, would be glorious indeed.

The camp moved in the early morning, men and horses struggling up the mountain almost before dawn. How many of them, I wondered, were here for the same reason as me? All of them, probably. The black dragon had laid waste to our kind like no other beast before him. Now all those who hunted him carried a personal hatred in their hearts. No one would return back down the mountain while he lived.

We hiked, and in the late afternoon the song returned. Faint at first, it was not the song they sing while hunting. This was quieter, just at the edge of perception, almost something you felt you could understand if you could only listen properly. Some of the others were bothered by it, and I heard cursing and superstitious talk from some of the men. I understood this, because wherever you came from, the dragonsong always meant death, and they did not like to hear it.

The witch passed me by while I prepared for sleep that night, looked at me strangely but did not speak. Why she was interested in me, I did not know. Nor did I care. If she stayed out of my way I had no conflict with her, whatever her interest.

Those dreams came again, and this time I began to understand.

I was myself still—yet I was not. It was me who flew over a pristine, perfect world, but as a watcher only. A ghost in someone else's memory, and I was beginning to see who that someone was. He hunted strange animals I had never seen before, over vast plains; I was with him when he made his first kill and shrieked his triumph to the sky. I watched the seasons roll away beneath him and realized that time was different for him—that in fact, it didn't matter to him at all, because it was no enemy. And so I noticed, though he did not, as the land changed, and a new creature came to the world below. Walking on two legs, he did not notice these ones until they formed small societies, built structures to announce themselves to his eyes. And then he saw only a new food source. Prey.

And he hunted.

I shuddered as I killed with him, felt his fangs rending them, and his claws tearing their soft forms to pieces. They were slow, these newcomers, easily frightened, and they made a disappointing foe. At first.

Because there was something different about the newcomers. And though they were nowhere near the most dangerous prey below, they *changed*. Their small huts became larger huts, and when their wood houses burned in dragonfire, they built with stone. And where before they had only been able to flee, soon they fought back. They hid, and set traps, fired airborne weapons from concealment, learned to hurl boulders through the air. They refused to obey the natural order, and soon he began to seek other prey.

And they multiplied. The wild herds were thinned by the two-legged hunters, and competing predators were hunted out of existence to make the world safe for them. Soon they were building mountains out of stones torn from the earth and had subdued their own herds of beasts. He quickly learned that they considered the beasts *theirs* now and would do battle to defend them. At first, he welcomed this, but they hunted him after that, and pursued him where before no creature in the land would have dared confront a dragon. He killed them when they came, but still they came; and he learned that though they died, their memories were long indeed.

Until one day he looked down and realized that his home was ruined. They had overrun the plain and changed even the landscape around them. And there were too many of them now for him to remove them all, though he considered that. But in the end, he took to the sky, his heart aching, and he shrieked out his song. He would remember. He would seek out his own kind, and sing of this to them, so that they would understand, and together they would overcome the two-legs and make the world the way it had been. The way it was meant to be.

But for now, he left. The skies were owned by dragons, the world was vast, and over every hill was another valley. It was not difficult to find a place where there were no two-legs. And soon, as he had hoped, he found his own kind. They were above him one day, a dozen adult dragons, and he called to them, heard them answer and knew they had seen him already. When they approached, he was not afraid, and he sang to them, stared at them in awe, and understood now that he himself was only a child. And that one day he would be like them …

I woke with my face wet, still overwhelmed with admiration for those great beasts. I touched my eyes and cheeks in astonishment, and then quickly wiped the evidence away: those tears were not mine.

The witch, of course, came again to visit me. Thea was her name, I now learned, and she was persistent.

"Your dreams still bother you," she said, kneeling down as I packed.

"No more than anyone's," I replied dully, unable to summon the effort for a lie.

"There are nightmares here," she said smoothly, with a look around that somehow failed to release me from her attention. "But you are sensitive to the song. I have seen your face as we get closer—you are barely in your own mind. Don't deny it," she said, anticipating my response.

"This song. What is it?" I was frightened now, and rightfully so.

She shook her head. "A song. Their language. It cannot be understood by our kind." I was about to argue that beasts did not have language. She saw; waited. I said nothing. "Asmodeus is the last of them. When he dies, they are no more. Ever. So his song is a heavy one, and there is a dark magic in it. I hear it, too. If it bothers you, perhaps I can help."

"I will survive the song, and the dragon," I told her.

"Perhaps the one," she replied, cryptically. "And should you survive, what will you do? After?"

It surprised me that she asked, but I made no attempt to lie at this point. "I will restore my family to its rightful place in the world. Once my father is avenged, I will move against the Kazamir family, until all our debts are paid. There will be blood spilled, you can be sure."

She nodded tightly, eyeing me. "After the dragon."

"After the dragon, yes. These things were put aside for the greater cause, but not forgotten, witch." It was a mark of my annoyance that I called her that to her face, but she did not react.

"As it must be, of course. One hatred must die to make way for the next. I suspect you will not be the only one making a choice like that, after Asmodeus has breathed his last. Who will men have to kill, once the dragons are no more?"

They called us to move then, and I forgot about the witch. It was cold on the mountainside, and clear as we moved onward. I thought about my father, for a time, until the dragonsong started up again. It distracted me horribly, and I struggled to listen as the rangers reported in. The others were excited, I noted distantly. The black dragon was close. Was it truly him in my dreams, I wondered? Or merely some part of my conscience, stirring my thoughts? The dragons were ancient, and had magic at their command, and somehow proximity to him had disturbed my dreams. I would resist, tonight, and not let him in, I decided. I would be stronger than the dragon.

This was laughable, of course. I see now how ludicrous my youthful ideas were. Asmodeus was dying on the mountain, and his song was bleeding out of him like a soul released, and for some reason I could hear him.

Hatred.

That is the word that memory conjures. I had thought that we hated *him*, we who had gathered to kill him on that mountain. But all of that was a leaf in the wind compared to his hatred for us. I was lost in it, when the dream came again, and forgot myself completely, and in that moment, I do believe that I *was* him, that he overcame and subsumed me entirely. And it was a terrifying thing to feel what was in his heart as he watched his kind die off.

They gathered together to defend themselves near the end—what was left of them. From all corners of the world they came, and I have forgotten some of the names now. But some of them will never be forgotten, I suspect: Thoth, the great gold demon from the south; Moloch, red and serpentine, the trickster and most intelligent among them. And Nija, the emerald monster from the east. It was this last one who so captivated Asmodeus, from the first. For though I recognized her, *he* had never seen her before, and I still recall that moment when he first laid eyes on her. She was larger than him then, and riding along in his mind I had to admit that she was beautiful, a creation that only God himself could have conceived. She felt Asmodeus watching her, and when she turned her massive head to regard the black dragon, her eyes were fire.

He lowered his wings and allowed her to circle above him and take his measure. I thought I could hear his heart hammering as he watched her circle, until finally she broke away and called him to join her, and he soared . . .

Love, I thought. First hatred, and now love. This surprised me. And I confess that, though I recognized her, I felt no hatred myself as I watched her lead him on to their conclave. Because he was right: she was beautiful. Even I could see it, and I knew there was some tragedy there, that she was gone from the world now.

Even as I thought this, I could feel his heart breaking, and the pain that was destroying the great black body. It was not our ambush that had killed him, I realized. It was the loss of the green dragon that had finally left him dying. I watched them fly into the setting sun together, and though he showed me no more, I knew how his story ended. One of us was crying as we watched her soar over the trees, the sun flashing off emerald scales. I was surrounded by song: from Nija and the other dragons within the dream, from Asmodeus as he sang a song of triumph back to them. But ultimately from within the dream itself, where I could hear the dragon singing a bitter farewell.

I opened my eyes, and I could still hear it—there was no interruption that time, from the dream to the waking world. And I felt like I could understand it all, now, and I turned my face away, in grief. I won't deny that. My hatred for him had died in the night, my hunger to kill and destroy, and I was sickened with myself to see that I was even there on the mount. But it was too late to turn back.

Thea the witch, of course, saw this and understood. She waited, and when I had half recovered myself, she joined me, squatted nearby as I lay motionless on blood-soaked rock.

"They say we will reach him within hours, today," she began. "He makes no attempt to flee." She looked at me, and we shared the same thought: he waits, because he knows that this is the end, and he has accepted death. "He may fight us, at the end, but he is horribly wounded, or we would never have caught him here. He will die today." And because some part of me could still remember *being* him, I pushed my face down against stone, and tried not to retch. "This is arrogance worthy of the gods, what we do here. To kill the last of their kind and end them forever."

"It was inevitable," I said, and she looked at me with some annoyance, not realizing that these thoughts were not mine. "We multiplied like locusts, and when they recognized the threat we posed, it was already too late for them. There were always too few of them—nature meant it that way. They reproduce so slowly, compared to us. It takes generations of our time just for their eggs to mature. They could never hope to restore their number, once we appeared in the world. This day was inevitable." She looked at me with disgust, and disappointment, and her eyes were cold when she stood.

"I hope that you will have a change of heart, when you understand," she said. "Seek me out, in Avadon, if you do. There are ways to leave this world, places to hide, if you decide that you need them after this." And then she was gone, leaving me to my last painful decision.

Should I have returned down the mountain that day? I could have. None would have prevented me leaving, or perhaps even noticed if I had, so focused were they on the task ahead. But I did not leave. The song was not over yet, and I knew that I had to stay and hear the end of it.

And what is there to record, of what happened next? Of that, I find it hard to say anything, though the images will remain burned into my memory forever. I suspect, though, that little needs to be said. There were epics being written about it, even in my time; it will have become legend, in yours. When there is nothing so beautiful left to destroy in the world, men will need to look back in envy on that day, and regret that they were not there to watch it die.

It was a terrible thing. Whatever you have heard, believe what I say here. There was no glory in it, and no heroes on the mountain that day. He was wounded, as we knew, but more terribly than we suspected. When we found him, he was almost dead already, and even the most bloodthirsty among us had to pause in awe at the sight of him. For he was ruined. The great wings were shattered and punched through like paper, and I could not understand how he had made it so far up the mountain like that. One foreleg had been torn away in our ambush at Mastema, and his blood had eaten the rock away entirely around the wound. The black scales were half missing, and through rents in his flesh we could see his bones exposed, and his bones shattered in turn. One of the eyes moved, though—he saw us. It was golden, with a sort of pupil at the center, and it moved, took us in as we entered the clearing. I think that he saw me in that moment, and when our eyes met, I wished that I was dead. Better to have died with my father, I felt, than to have come to take part in this.

From his mouth, or his nose, the song still struggled weakly to come out. It was faint now, a rattling, whistling hiss of death. There was no need to interpret the song, now. All could understand what it meant.

They fell on him with shouts. I don't recall who moved first, or if it was ordered, but once they had begun, they took to it with determination. I will say nothing of this. He was, as I said, already mostly gone, and this was just the end to it. Of all of them there on Nammah, only the witch and I did not take part. We watched though; God preserve me. *I* watched, because it was my duty now. I had seen him on that day when he first took to the air, and I watched until the song ended, and we all knew that he had left us.

And as the men celebrated their horrific triumph, and spoke of taking trophies, I turned away and, at last, began making my way back down the mountain. I was paid no notice, as I had expected, and even the witch let me go without comment. I felt no surprise when I heard the men begin to argue about treasure. It had always been rumored that the dragons kept vast hordes of gold and gems hidden in underground caves, but I knew that this was nonsense. *Is it?* Some part of my mind was not sure—there was something itching at me, even then, but I ignored it, and retreated to a world I thought I would recognize.

But I found that I could not quite leave.

There was a village, of sorts, at the bottom of Nammah. Not much, of course, because the dragons had always nested above, but there were tribes about, and so a place to trade was required. I stayed there, at the foot of the mountain, barely noticed among the small band of folk who made that place their home. I watched as the others slowly came down the mountain, headed back to wherever they had come from. Of Thea the witch, there was no sign, but then again, I made an effort not to show myself in those days.

No treasure had been found, of course, though it was months before the final seekers came down from Nammah empty handed. Soon, I knew, others would come, once word spread, and fools would seek the treasure probably for centuries. The less they found of it, the harder they would look, because that is the way with legends.

I don't know what drove me back up the mountain. *Something*, certainly, held me there once all the others had gone. Some memory that I felt certain was not even mine. I purchased a mule, and together of the two of us climbed Nammah. I knew my way now, but for some reason I did not return to the place where Asmodeus had fallen. Instead, my feet took another path, and I simply followed. The mule seemed resigned to it.

We reached a cave, or a fissure in the rocks, finally, and I tied the mule, telling him aloud that I would return. His ears flickered, and I was not sure he believed me. It was cold, when I entered the dark tunnel in the side of Nammah. Cold and dark, but I found my way somehow. Ever deeper I went, until at some point light returned, and I felt no surprise as I came upon a cavern hidden at the heart of the mountain. There were glowing orbs placed around that room, porcelain looking things held aloft in dragons' claws carved out of gold. They were ancient and fading, but they cast enough light to see by.

And so, we come to it at last. Now you understand how I came to find them, and how I knew what they were, and even perhaps why I took them.

The treasure.

There were four. Soft, and pale like ivory, they glowed slightly. I saw inky colors spreading below their surface, pulsing like blood. One was shot through with red, one with pale green, one gold, and one seemed lined with faint shadows. Black.

Eggs. The brood of the dragon Nija. Was Asmodeus the sire? I am not certain still, though I have my suspicions of course. He had known the eggs were there, hidden in the heart of Nammah; it was why he had chosen this place to die. And now I knew that he was not the last, as we had supposed.

I stared at them a long while, thinking. When I touched them, I could feel the life inside, and knew it felt me, also. And though they were not fragile, I knew it would be the work of a moment to smash them and so finish the work we had begun above. The dragons would be no more. And if I turned around and rode off down the mountain? What then? Would they hatch some day, and take the world by surprise with their return? And why, I wondered, was this responsibility *mine*.

But you know, of course, what I did. You know that I was unable to leave them there, or to destroy them. It took some work to safely pack them away—hide them—and then cart them off, away from Nammah and its legacy. But I accepted that. They were beautiful things, already, and I knew I would find a place to take them, somehow. And what to do with them then

. . .

Well.

Down on my knees in that cavern, I ran my hands over the silvery shells and felt the life stirring within. And softly, almost beneath my breath, I began to sing to them.

———————

That is nearly all of it. Some of the rest you might know. The eggs were taken down the mountain, and first to Avadon. I remembered something Thea had said to me: that she knew how to hide from this world. So, I found her. She was waiting for me, had expected and hoped that I would find her. So together we left with the eggs and travelled until we thought we had left humankind behind entirely. It was not enough, though. I was certain of this because I had seen the dragon's dreams, and knew that wherever we went, humans would one day follow, even if it took centuries. That our kind would spread like a plague, to cover the world entirely, because it was our destiny.

But this gave us time. Thea trained me, taught me magicks known to only a few. She felt that the dragon had chosen me, somehow. She herself had gone up Nammah planning to save Asmodeus but claims that her dreams had told that that was not her proper task. He had chosen me, she says, to save the eggs. Four dragons, instead of one. So that while men crowed in triumph, the eggs could be taken away in stealth, and live on. I am not convinced that she is correct—that he could have foretold what would happen, or if she is just explaining it based on what she knew had happened. The story works out well enough though, I suppose.

The eggs are behind me now, and they are stirring. Decades have passed since I took them, and until now I have had few misgivings about my decision. Thea has been dead many years, but she taught me how to open the ways to other places—other worlds. Doorways to somewhere that is nowhere. Worlds outside of time, like small bubbles in the fabric, where I can hide, and time will not touch me as long as we are sealed up there. When I look around me now, I see a small comfortable room, but it only appears that way because that is how I imagine it. This place is not completely real. My life has been lived, and my time is drawing short if I stay in the human world. I am old myself, now. And still the eggs are not yet hatched.

But their time is near. If I die before I finish this account, they will hatch one day, and the four will be loosed on the world again. Many will die, including the four dragons. Maybe they will multiply, and their numbers grow, and we will wage war on them again. But our kind is relentless, and one way or the other it will be the dragons who will die.

Thea sent the clues out—the clues that you must have found. Letters written to certain scholars, all across the world. Hints, pieces of the story, so that when I close the door, it may not all be lost forever. We—*they*—can be found again, by anyone who can decipher the clues, and has the capability of finding this place where I am now. So, they are gone, but perhaps not forever. The choice, you see, was never mine. It is *yours*, who holds this manuscript, and who has opened the way to find me here. You must decide what I could not. Are they gone forever, or do they one day return, to some new world that I cannot even imagine right now? Can we be safe from them, and them from us?

I pray that you choose wisely. And that one day there will be a world with a place for them.

And this is the difficult part now, for me. When I put down my pen this time, my part is over. I will speak the words to close the door to this place, sealing myself in the strange bubble. Thea says it will be like sleep, though she doubts that I will dream. But I will be frozen here, unable to wake myself, or ever leave. The eggs will be frozen too, unmoving outside of time while the world moves on. If it happens that we are never found, this is my end. We will wait here until the end of days, until time has run itself out. Even if we are discovered, you, reader, may choose not to wake me, or the dragons.

I may never know, in other words.

So, for now, my story ends. I am tired and sit here frightened in the eerie silence. It is time to lie down, now, and do what I came here to do. Close my eyes.

To dream.

And to wait.

About Michael Vance

Michael Vance is a resident of Ontario, Canada, where he lives with his wife and son. He has previously published fiction in On Spec magazine, BFS Horizons, and the Soul and Tesseracts anthologies. When not busy writing, he can be found driving his son to basketball practice.

Feeding the Dragon

By Dan Kemp

In the hills above a sleepy farming village, up past the upthrust cliffs known as the Rockwall, lies Dragon Valley. For years, the town drunk claimed his father robbed the cave at the valley's head, coming back with a sack of the dragon's gold and silver. Now Ingvar has the love of his life, the beautiful Ayleth on his mind, but needs coin to secure her hand in marriage. Rumors of the dragon's cavern and its riches tempt the young farmer, and his grandfather's sword is on the wall. Can Ingvar make it in and out of the valley alive without.... *Feeding the Dragon?*

Feeding the Dragon
By Dan Kemp

Like most teenaged males, Ingvar was in love. The object of his desire was Ayleth, a tall willowy blonde, just a year younger than he. They'd grown up closely, but not so closely as to ruin things with illusions of a brother-sister kinship. There had been little time to get too close. Ayleth was the oldest of four sisters and was busy with them, while the black pox had taken Ingvar's father and two of his five brothers in the horrible winter five years ago.

Losing his father had left him the man of the farm. It was a fertile patch of land with just the right amount of rain. In a good season he was moderately wealthy in grain, but to secure the hand of Ayleth, he would need a good bag of coin and he couldn't grow that. Hard currency was scarce out here in the border country. Most of what he grew was merely bartered at the market for what the farm needed.

But then there was Dragon Valley to the east, past where the good farming land of the river plains ended at jagged walls of upthrust granite, creating hopeless tangles of rock the farmers only ever got close to when chasing errant livestock. No one was sure if there was still a dragon in Dragon Valley. Not even the old-timers smoking their pipes and drinking ale from their carven cattle horns or fired-clay flagons on the tavern porch had actually seen it. Old Fezz, limping and worn from his six decades of farming and logging, would swear his father had seen it when he was young, but he only told the tale when deep in his cups. Once, when he had gone especially deep, the coins came out.

———————————

Ingvar remembered it well. It had been one of the first times he'd been permitted to join the old duffers on the tavern porch after a long day. Not in a chair, mind you, there were precious few of those, and there was a pecking order to them. Instead, the younger men were permitted to sit on one of the floor pillows made from old burlap grain sacks. They were to mostly listen while the old men held forth on the weather, planting, harvesting, or the occasional tale of the dead old gods. This time it had been about the dragon.

Old Fezz was a complicated one. He'd worked like a mule for all his years and had done quite well for himself. But his family seemed to do a little better than even that level of hard work would allow for. There were few secrets in the village, but Fezz's family's prosperity had always been one of them.

The old man had been drinking like a man possessed in that twilight hour, seeking to drown some nightmare. No one could tell what kind of nightmare until one of the younger men was complaining of having chased the wandering ram of his prized wool-sheep flock "up the rockwall, most of the way to Dragon Valley."

Another of the younger drinkers, feeling his ale, loudly asked "Why do they call it Dragon Valley if there ain't no dragon in it?" to no one in particular.

Fezz drained his old sewn-leather tankard and slammed it down on the cut-log side table. "There is a dragon in there! Don't speak of what you don't know, boy!"

Another of the old timers snorted with laughter, then hawked and spat off the side of the porch. "Fezz, you've been telling us that shit about your father and the bag of coins for sixty years now."

Fezz stood, swaying. Reaching into one of his belt pouches, he yelled "Explain this, then!"

The half-dozen coins were small things, no wider than the tip of a man's finger. No one could recognize the likeness of the long-dead king on them, or the language the marks were in, but in the failing sunlight, even those country folk who saw very little of it still knew the gleam of silver. It was a good thing the locals believed the gods had died off, since several of their names were taken in vain by voices loud and hushed.

"Sorry, old friend," said one.

"I'm sorry, Fezz," another replied.

Fezz waved them off. "It's all right. I've kept the secret all these years like my father told me, but if doesn't matter much. All I had were daughters and they're married off now. None of my blood are going to do what my father did and what I didn't."

Ingvar caught himself asking "Which was?"

The last of the twilight faded. Fezz waved for a refill, but only when the serving wench had moved on with her great earthenware ale pitcher did he continue. "As I have sometimes said after a drink too many, Father went into Dragon Valley, and he came back with a bag of coin."

One of the other old-timers snorted. "So that's how he got that big well dug that spring."

Fezz nodded. "And he couldn't pay for it in silver or gold, since that would give the game away. He bought trade goods from a merchant caravan then traded those off to the hands that helped in the work. I was too young to understand it then, but in time I saw what he was up to."

"Which was?"

"Hiding both the fact we had coin and more importantly, where he got it. It's no secret we're all poor out here. There's plenty of good land and grain to go around, but we mostly barter amongst ourselves. Firewood for wheat or salt pork, a blacksmith job for a deer haunch or two, then perhaps the labor of one friend now exchanged for the labor of another friend later."

Everyone present nodded. While few ever had the philosophical bent to explain their way of life, it was simple enough when Fezz laid it all out. It was how things had always been in the villages along the river, even if their town was newer than most, barely fifty years old when one two days' walk to the southwest was five hundred...

"Father always believed in the dragon. He said he'd seen it in flight several times when he was young, back when the family still ran sheep and like Hvarl here, chased one to the rockwall occasionally."

"Aye," a voice in the dark agreed, "and my father said your father was full of shit too."

Fezz nodded. "That's because your father didn't know the rockwall. He, like you do now, grew wheat and potatoes, Ulric, and those don't run away from you in a blind panic when they don't like a scent on the wind."

Everyone had a good chuckle at that. In time, *chasing a potato* became a local colloquialism for a fool's task.

"My father, like many of your fathers or grandfathers, had been a soldier back in the war that set Carolus on the throne. As a soldier of the victorious side, Father had been gifted the land he'd farmed until his death, the same land grants which birthed this village, mind you, and that gave him no small experience of mortal danger. He had still held onto his sword. One afternoon, when the sun was right, he saw the dragon set down to land. There's a cave where the rock splits at the head of the valley, and it crawled in."

Another commented "Not that I know shit about killing dragons, but I have hunted bear, and in a cave with spears is better than in the open."

Fezz nodded. "That was what Father thought. He took two fresh spears and his old sword, figuring to catch it asleep and unaware."

"Did he?" Ingvar asked.

Fezz shrugged. "I don't know, and I don't know anyone who does. Father told the story of going, and he came back with a bag containing maybe ten pounds of coin. Years later, Mother told me his sword was missing when he came home. He never did claim to have actually killed it, at least not to me or anyone who told me."

"Did you go back for more coin?"

Shaking his head, Fezz shivered. "Father laid a geas on me when I came of age never to approach the rockwall. That was one reason we stopped running sheep and got into cattle. Those won't climb into the boulders."

"If he had killed the dragon, why would it matter if you went back?"

Another voice broke in. "Blood-curse, maybe?"

"Maybe he just didn't want you taking the risk that it did live."

Drinking a little more, Fezz waved for silence before continuing. "I have obeyed that geas Father laid on me. Now I'm too old to try. I've never seen the beast, but I know it was there, and my family tasted of its treasure to prove it. Let no one ever say there isn't a dragon in Dragon Valley." He belched, then stood with a stagger. "Now I'm going to stumble off and piss, then see if I can't find my way to my bed." He then sat back down. "All right, that was a bad idea."

One of his old friends, Ormond the blacksmith, stood up, and then helped Fezz back to his feet. "Let's go, you old wanker. You'll never make it the two miles out to your place, so you can sleep it off next to the fire at mine." The pair wandered off into the dark, breaking the spell of the evening's gathering. The others soon made their farewells and departed.

Ingvar fairly wiggled with lightning bursts of thought. Either the dragon was dead in that cave, leaving the hoarded treasure unguarded, or it was still alive and could be hunted like any other beast. If Fortune truly smiled, the dragon would be gone doing whatever dragons do and simple theft would suffice. Any way he sliced it, there was gold for the taking up there past the rockwall, not even a full day's hike. And he needed that gold to get Ayleth's hand in marriage.

Ingvar never met his grandfather, at least not that he could remember. The old man's war wounds had killed him in less than his full span of years. His gravestone was out by one of the big oaks past the tool shed. That was fitting, as some of the steel around the place had come back from the wars with him. Old spear tips made up the teeth of the plow frame, the axe hadn't originally been intended for trees, and so on. But inside the house, in his mother's room, his grandfather's sword still hung on the wall as a memorial of his former life and the service to a distant throne that had quite honestly forgotten about him.

Ingvar needed a sword to kill the dragon and get the coins he'd need to wed Ayleth. His grandfather had provided one. Now it was just a matter of finding the lair and stabbing the beast. Ingvar had raised and killed pigs. He'd aided other farms with sheep or cattle. In the fall after the harvest, he'd hunted deer as he'd been taught to. He had spilled blood before. This would be much the same, he told himself, just a little bigger.

Talking with Mother about his plan would be foolish, but the black pox that had taken her husband and two of her sons had left her rather frail. She rarely left her room except on nice days when she moved to sit on the porch instead. If he wanted the sword, he had to go through her. The prospect of facing the dragon unnerved him less.

He entered her room. "Mother, I need Grandfather's sword," he blurted nervously.

She looked up from her knitting and smiled. "You aren't going to go getting in a fight at the tavern, are you?"

Ingvar sighed. "Mother, I was twelve when that happened."

"Yes, and you and Hvarl beat each other bloody with sticks instead when you couldn't get either families' old swords. It's been cleaned and oiled. What do you want it for, then?"

The idea of lying didn't occur to him at that moment. "I'm going up to the rockwall, going to look in the cave in Dragon Valley, and perhaps stab a sleeping dragon with it so I can have enough coin to marry Ayleth and give you a grandson."

His mother slouched back in her chair. "You've mooned over her since you were old enough to realize that girls were different. But there is no dragon in Dragon Valley."

Ingvar shrugged. "Then I'll be safe, and the sword will be too."

She shook her head, not as a no, but in thought. Finally, she spoke again. "If I tell you no, you'll just go up there with a spear or something worse like a pruning hook."

"It will be all right, Mother. It's probably an empty cave."

She sighed. "No cave is empty. They all have some nightmare in it."

Ingvar rose with the sun, strapping the sword on. He hoped his father and grandfather would be proud of him as he made the slow easy walk to the rockwall, then journeyed upward into the jagged hills. So long as he headed upward, he knew he would hit the valley easily enough. Then the cave at the valley's head should be easy enough to find.

It was midday when he reached it. The cave looked narrower than he would have thought possible for a large beast to call home. Maybe that meant it was a smaller dragon, he told himself. Maybe there was no dragon, and it was all a waste of time and he'd never win Ayleth's hand.

He cursed as he moved further inward. He should have brought a torch. He should have brought a couple spears. Soon he could see almost nothing and was holding onto the right-hand cave wall as to not become hopelessly lost in the underground dark. There was a sense of a vast empty darkness off to his left. He tapped forward with each step, warily feeling for sinkholes or drop-offs.

Then the darkness wasn't so empty.

"Oh, wonderful. Another mortal who thinks he's a dragonslayer." The impossibly deep voice came from over his head in the echoing darkness. A row of torches along the wall sprung to life, illuminating the cavern.

As Ingvar turned, he was confronted by at least fifteen tons of muscle clad in gleaming dark red scales. Shining yellow eyes contemplated him from thirty feet above his head, and much the same as cats contemplate mice.

"That three feet of scrap iron you're holding won't get the job done, boy," the dragon said. He held up one taloned forefoot. Each talon was the size of Ingvar's blade. As the dragon chuckled, a spurt of flame the size of a campfire escaped his nostril.

Ingvar realized he'd been a fool, and that he was going to die without ever seeing his family again, let alone his beloved Ayleth. As the mindless terror hit, he felt his bladder let go. The dragon looked at the fresh puddle dripping from Ingvar's trousers and sneered. "I just had the floors done, too."

The dragon spoke a few words of magic that hurt Ingvar's ears, and with a *pop* of shifting air, the dragon changed shape. In human form, he was tall and broadly built, clad in a blood-red shirt and black pants,

Ingvar stammered. "Ma- ma- magic?"

The not-man sighed. "I'm a dragon, you fool. We are the eldest of the various magic-using kindreds. The elves are latecomers, and most humans are incompetent dabblers at best."

Ingvar was confused. "Elves are real?" That wasn't the only thing that confused Ingvar. Was the creature he spoke with a dragon that looked like a man, or was he a man who could turn into a dragon? Ingvar didn't know.

Whatever 'he' really was, he merely sighed derisively. "Shut up, human."

Ingvar shut up.

The man-dragon continued. "I find this form to be easier indoors. Over the years as I have grown and my collection has piled up, I simply don't have the room to spread my wings or stretch my claws properly in here when I'm awake. If it did come to a fight in here, not that you're going to be much of one, my flames would be terrible for the furniture and artwork." He pointed toward the nearest wall where a variety of framed paintings hung." I like my collection and I certainly wouldn't ruin them merely to make a cinder of the likes of you." Past the wall of art, a side alcove sufficient to hold a company of soldiers was instead piled thickly with gold and silver coins, though flattened like a dog's bed. Maybe the stories were true, and dragons did sleep on coin. Ingvar's heart soared. He only needed a little of it…

The dragon-man snapped his fingers again, and an ornate gold-hilted broadsword appeared around 'his' waist, hanging from a belt of rich black saddle leather in a delicately tooled scabbard. The man-dragon drew the sword and held it up, admiring it in the torchlight as any human warrior would. The ancient watered-steel blade was deeply graven with runes, hinting at mysterious lineage and perhaps latent power. "Quite a blade, isn't it? I… *obtained* it, shall we say, from another of you little bastards who came to rob me, maybe three of your centuries ago. He clanked in here wearing shining armor and spouting ridiculous rhetoric about justice and righteousness. He didn't even have poverty as an excuse. Robbery is at least a reason to come bother me, as I'm sure it is your reason. You look like the last few peasants who crept in here dreaming of coin. Not this fool. Instead, he was merely in it for the glory of killing one of my kind. Disrespectful, really. His skull sits on one of my bookshelves holding candles these days."

Ingvar didn't want his body parts to serve forever as a candle holder. That was somehow even more terrifying than ending up as dragon shit.

His opponent had returned his attention to his sword. "I liked this sword so much that I studied its use. Swords can be subtle things, and I learned to appreciate the art of the blade. I also spent time perfecting this guise. Once

I felt confident in my skill, I carried it on numerous…*adventures.* I went out once a year for a month or two at a time for decades. Ironic, really. What better way to instigate humans with delusions of heroism to carry on little schemes that suited my purposes than to appear as one of them?"

Ingvar's appreciation for dragonkind had merely been folklorish thoughts of wings and teeth and flame. Somehow the notion of dragons walking among man as manipulators and murderers was far more terrifying.

"Certainly, I could destroy a small army by myself if I tried. That's a lot of arrows though, and not every spot of my hide is completely proof. It's like being chewed on by insects. It won't really hurt you badly, but it's unpleasant." The man-dragon relaxed his stance, and looked at Ingvar with a piercing, appraising gaze. "With that experience behind me, I have come to appreciate you murderous little monkeys in ways few of my kind do. No matter how stupid most of you are, you do have drive, and some of you even have clarity of vision."

While the dragon-man spoke, Ingvar calculated his chances. He'd had no chance against the dragon in his true form, but this? This was just a man, and all men could be slain. All he needed to do was just wound him enough to bag up some coins and make his escape. Just a few pounds of the dragon's hoard could set him and Ayleth up for life, and maybe even stake his younger brothers to adjoining lands of their own one day…

The dragon-man looked at Ingvar as if he could see the wheels spinning in his brain. He shook his head in warning. "Oh, no, don't even think it, boy."

With a scream of terrified fury and his grandfather's sword held high, Ingvar charged his foe. In a flash, the man-dragon sidestepped and with the flat of his own ancient trophy blade, he flicked Ingvar hard across the wrists. Bones cracked, the fury transforming to pain. His sword clattered to the floor as his hands became useless. The dragon-man sighed. "You thought it. Too much drive, not enough clarity of vision."

Sinking to his knees, Ingvar looked at the dragon-man through tears of agony, cradling shattered forearms. The nightmarishly keen edge of the relic blade lowered to kiss the side of Ingvar's neck. The man-dragon's chuckle made things far worse. The creature was enjoying Ingvar's agony. "It has been a long, long time since one of you little bastards have made the trip out here. Even longer since I got to use my favorite toy here, and I confess I have enjoyed the entertainment. So, I'll make you an offer you can't refuse, *boy.*"

Ingvar was terrified and in pain. He had no idea why he was still alive, let alone why the dragon was still talking to him.

"Here's your offer. Refuse it and you're ashes." The dragon-man tossed a decent-sized canvas sack on the floor. It clinked as it hit the stone floor.

Ingvar had no idea what was going on but resolved to be polite. "I don't understand, sire."

The man-dragon sighed, a tiny curl of smoke escaping. "First, I'm not your sire, boy, but then you couldn't pronounce my true name either. Your mouth's not built for the language and your ears aren't good enough. Now do your hands work?"

Ingvar tried, but his fingers wouldn't do what he wanted, and the rope tying the sack closed defeated him. "No, sir."

The dragon-man sighed. "'Sire' now rather than 'sire,' I see. Well, for a shit-smelling farm bumpkin, you do try having fair manners. I've got to give you that much." He reached down, retrieved the bag, and untied it. Reaching in, he pulled out a thick glass bottle of perhaps half a pint. "Here, shake it up then take a good swallow off the top."

Ingvar tried and dropped it, his hands useless. The heavy glass withstood the fall to the stone floor, but the dragon still grumbled in some unfamiliar but probably human tongue. He picked the bottle up, shook it, and then uncorked it before handing it to Ingvar with a surprising gentleness.

Fumbling a bit, Ingvar drank. The taste was sweet and somehow reminded him of how lightning-laden storm clouds felt before the first flash. Swallowing, he looked at the man-dragon. "What does that- *oh!*" He only just barely set the bottle down without spilling it as the fire began in his blood.

For a moment, the pain of his shattered wrists was forgotten, lost in a whole new burning feeling as the bones straightened. Jagged ends found each other and reknit. What would have taken months after a trip to what passed for the local healer took seconds, but dead gods above, it *hurt!* Ingvar moaned as the flames within him melted bones together and a torn tendon he hadn't known about fused back in place.

The dragon-man shrugged. "Give it a little time. You'll be better than new in a couple minutes. The pain you feel meanwhile is the price of being able to work your fields again this season, so you don't starve this winter."

Ingvar panted from the exertion of it all. "You didn't have to break my arms, sir."

The man-dragon smirked. "No, boy, I didn't. I could have cut them off instead, or merely taken your head, little human. Maybe I should have remained in my true form and just stepped on you. But," he sighed, looking about, "I did just have the floors done."

"Thank you for not killing me."

The dragon-man sighed again. "Shut up about it, boy, or you'll make me reconsider. Now, as for the bag. I have no idea what the shelf life is for a healing potion, but you have more left in the bottle for a future emergency. There're also some several pounds of gold and silver coins. I didn't bother weighing because, to be blunt, I don't care enough to be exact. Could be five pounds, could be ten or even more. Pay off your farm or whatever, then marry some peasant wench and have little baby peasants. Your sword, now it stays here in my collection as my trophy."

Ingvar thought of his mother. "It was my grandfather's."

The dragon-man sneered. "That's very nice. I also don't care. That's the price of trying me and failing in the attempt."

Ingvar looked at the sword on the floor, and figured his mother would rather have him back alive and siring grandchildren than to have him in a dragon's belly and her father's blade still hanging on the wall. He nodded in silent acquiescence.

The man-dragon picked it up, looking at it with the eye of an expert appraiser. "Carolean-pattern foot officer's sword. Rather common in this part of the country for obvious reasons, so I have six or seven of these. It's in excellent condition though, so I'm quite glad to have it anyway. It will make a lovely souvenir of our time together, boy."

Ingvar nodded.

"I'll take the scabbard too. The original brown leather versions are scarce. Most were dyed black when the uniform regulations changed."

Ingvar nodded in resignation and undid his sword belt.

"Now, here's the hook in the bait, little fish. I'm letting you go. If I ever smell your blood near my gate again, I shall then incinerate you, and slowly, but it will not stop there. I shall fly to your little flyspeck of a village where I will then hunt down your entire bloodline with truly artistic abandon. And that doesn't mean your little brats yet unborn can come try me either. Your family gets one free pass, and you just used it. I'll smell your blood in your great-grandchildren yet unborn."

Ingvar stared back at the dragon, his eyes confused and voice shaky. "Why?"

"Because by your return, you will have then spat upon my gesture of magnanimity. I can't have that now, can I?"

"I'm still wondering why you're letting me live and not eating me."

The dragon-man snorted. "Why? Uncooked man-flesh tastes terrible, and it's arguably worse cooked. Believe me, I did try it several ways. I just don't like it."

The notion of a dragon who didn't like the taste of people reminded him of that one odd old man in town who insisted vegetables were healthier than meat. He supposed every species had its odd duck.

"Again, it's mostly the taste," the man-dragon sighed. "Your kind eats a weird and varied diet, so the flavor of human meat is just… off. But you're mostly bone, so you're not very filling. Every now and then one of the others would eat an entire village before the winter hibernation, but if you empty out a town it takes forever for it to refill and then some nobleman is just as likely to send his army after you rather than letting you sleep for a season. Some of our more savage kin enjoy that sort of thing, much younger reds, maybe blacks or greens, but I personally find it too much work to bother."

"If people taste bad, what do you eat then?" Ingvar asked.

He snorted. "Trying to become a scholar of dragon-lore now that you've survived more than a moment in my presence, boy?"

Ingvar nodded respectfully. "I was wondering why I've not been eaten, yes, sir."

"Plains bison are a favorite, really. Get out of this valley, fly an hour or two easterly to the other side of these mountains, and there are enough of them to darken the land. Sure, there's bone in them, but once dressed out, each one's still half a ton or more of rich red meat at a sitting, Meal fit for a king, I tell you. Tenderloin, haunch, all it needs is a slow touch of flame and it's perfect. Maybe a little salt if I'm in human form. Things do taste a little different when I change my shape."

The dragon-man continued. "But never mind food for the moment, your kind provides other delights. The lingering fear of those who run is delightfully delicious. Every now and then I have to let one of you monkeys leave my domain in pants-pissing fear to spread the stories and terrify the rest of you. It keeps the rest of you at a distance."

"Why live so close to humans then if you don't eat us and we're an annoyance?"

"Business. Your kind, if not you specifically, have money and I want it. I'm no gold miner."

"Business? I don't understand, sir."

The man-dragon snapped a finger and one of the antique chairs slid across the polished stone floor to him. Flipping his sword belt forward, he casually sat. "I collect twenty percent off any passing merchant caravans as a... fire insurance payment. I also receive regular tribute payments from certain towns. Not yours, I mean the big ones to the north and the east that get the caravan traffic. There's no money in yours."

Ingvar had to admit the dragon had a point there.

"Then there's other opportunities to turn a shilling. One town, rather than gold, believed too much of the folklore and tried buying me off with a particularly lovely young lady of high blood and promised virtue. It might have worked with some of my kind, but again, I don't like the taste of human meat. Instead, I placed her with a noble house elsewhere as a bride, and that for a substantial fee. They had a firstborn son who wasn't especially good-looking, and they paid well in gold to get that one married off. More than the first town should have paid me, really."

Ingvar found all this horribly disconcerting.

The dragon sighed. "Story time is over. Get thee gone and stay there. Know that the lair of, damn, you can't pronounce that... call me Pyros then, is forever forbidden to you and your bloodline on pain of extermination. Run along now." The air popped again, as the man-dragon shifted forms back to dragon-dragon. Fifteen tons of nightmare stared at him with glowing yellow eyes and a toothy grin. In his impossibly deep beast-voice, Pyros bellowed "RUN, BOY! RUN!"

That was more than Ingvar's already overtaxed courage could handle, and he ran from the cave, clutching his canvas sack of loot and screaming incoherently. Behind him, the dragon laughed, and laughed... a sound that would haunt his dreams for decades yet to come.

Ingvar ran, spurred by terror, until his legs turned to straw from fatigue. Even then, he didn't stop. The walk home seemed to go far faster than the journey to Dragon Valley had. What seemed to take half a day took much less as he forced his way through the dark, hoping for the hearth-fire of home to take away the thought of dragon-flame. He suspected he'd never look at the hearth the same way again. Visions of flame and tooth crept in every time fatigue closed his eyes. He'd stumble and continue. It wasn't far.

It wasn't far.

It wouldn't be much further.

———————

Ingvar stumbled back into the village before dawn. Taking some of the larger gold coins and secreting them in his belt pouch, he hid the sack in his barn before walking onward to Ayleth's family's farm two miles further. He arrived at their door in time to smell breakfast cooking with their chimney smoke.

Ayleth's father opened the door when Ingvar knocked. He tried to appear stern, but a kindly smile snuck in. "What do you want, Ingvar?"

Ingvar went to one knee. "Sir, I have come to ask for Ayleth's hand in marriage. I have secured the prospects to do so properly."

The older man sighed. "I had a feeling this day would come. I appreciate you speaking to me first but let us see what she thinks about this." He turned back into their house of heavy logs and called "Ayleth? Ingvar is here to ask a question!"

She came to the door in a long dress of dark green, wiping her hands on a towel. When she saw Ingvar kneeling, she smiled warmly, but looking back out into the distance, both her face and her father's face went blank with wonderment that hadn't yet turned to terror. "Dead gods above...," her father said.

Ayleth pointed out above the trees. "Is that a... *dragon?*" she squeaked.

Ingvar turned his head just in time to see a flash of distant dark red glinting in the morning sun before vanishing over the horizon.

———————

Two years later, Ingvar was sitting on his own porch enjoying the night breeze. Ayleth had dozed off hours ago, and the baby was finally asleep. He had caught a second wind and was debating walking the half mile down to see what was going on at the tavern. Instead, a figure came striding boldly through the night. As it neared, Ingvar's heart leapt into his throat and his stomach churned. It was a tall man he knew well, still clad in a blood red shirt, black trousers, and with that gold-hilted broadsword strapped around 'his' waist. "Good evening, boy. How's the family?" he asked with a terrifying grin.

Ingvar stammered in terror, half-bowing. "Well, thank you sir. Three of us now."

Pyros the man-dragon smirked. "Glad to hear it. Don't worry about inviting me in. I know the lateness of the hour and I have other places to be quickly. But I'm about to make you another offer, boy."

Swallowing hard, Ingvar considered his words, and answered "I'm listening…"

Reaching into a belt pouch, Pyros flipped a large gold coin to Ingvar. "I'm maintaining my lease on your life, little burglar, and more broadly the lives of your loved ones as well. You continue to breathe at my sufferance. So, with that in mind, I left something in that empty cattle pen of yours."

Ingvar merely stared at him. On the wind came a grunting and snorting, like an enormous hog rather than a cow.

"Remember when I told you about the plains bison?"

Ingvar nodded. "Yes, sir."

"I'll be passing back through tomorrow or perhaps the day after. I'll be in a hurry and will definitely have quite an appetite, so I left myself a bit of lunch in your cattle pen since you aren't using it. Still on the hoof, and not very happy about being carried fifty leagues or so over the mountains in my rear talons, so I'd let them calm down for a bit."

"There's a… bison in my cattle pen?"

"No, there's *bison*, plural. One just might not do it for me, you know. Now they're quite ill-tempered beasts. Do not mistake them for merely fluffy cows or they might kill you as surely as I could have. I still might kill you if you lose my meal," Pyros smirked sadistically.

Ingvar couldn't speak a response to that. His only noise was a sort of distressed moaning.

Instead, Pyros laughed. "Oh, come now. Be cheerful, lad. How many men can say they fed a dragon and lived to tell the tale? If I'm of good cheer, I might even save you some tenderloin. You'll love it."

Ingvar fainted. Pyros merely smirked and laughed as he walked back into the darkness. He had business elsewhere.

About Dan Kemp

Finishing at Ole Miss in 1998, Dan spent the next decade in infantry assignments in South Korea and the 101st Airborne. That lasted as long as his knees and his back held out. A master's in military history (Norwich

University '12) and a somewhat turbulent personal life after the Army inspired what became the *Athenaeum Inc* trilogy about the shadowy and violent world of military-intelligence contracting (*Door Number Three, Doubling Down* and 2025's *Triple Play*). Meanwhile he slung out a variety of short stories. These have been on everything from intelligent combat machines and the sinking of the *Bismarck* to the feeding of dragons. He lives in the Tennessee hills south of Fort Campbell with a few dogs, a few too many cats, and a little bit of a weapons collection.

Dan Kemp

Altitude

By Eddie Spohn

When a pair of dragons settles on a nearby mountain peak, Earl Dunreid knows he has a problem. He is not particularly wealthy or well liked by his relative the king, and his band of knights, motivated more by greed than honor, are not impressed by the meager bounty he's offered for the extermination of the deadly new residents. When the dragons begin killing villagers, Dunreid is forced to up the ante and make an offer no knight can refuse: his daughter Sasha's hand in marriage.

Lady Sasha is not so enthusiastic about the idea. She and a peasant boy named Lawrence have fallen in love. When Lawrence hears of the earl's offer, he sees the one chance to be with his love, his lack of knighthood be damned.

But first there is a dangerous mountain to climb and a group of real knights to contend with along the way.

And dragons do not take kindly to threats.

Eddie Spohn

Altitude

By Eddie Spohn

Spring had come to the Southern Continent, bringing with it warmer weather and the influx of dragons migrating back from the North. For the yearlings it was a period of great activity; this was when young dragons paired off with their life partners. Females stood back as the males displayed their breeding colors and fought with each other to establish dominance and gain favor in the eyes of potential mates. These scuffles were for the most part symbolic and usually resulted in minor scratches and injured pride. Sometimes they turned deadly.

One of the yearling females was the object of a good deal of attention from the frisky males. She was stocky and full bodied, the greenish-blue iridescence of her scaling glittering in the daylight like points of fire. She shimmered with every move; the undulations of her finely muscled tail drove her suitors to a frenzy. Clusters of males performed aerial acrobatics and tore at one another in midair with a severity none of the other females were treated to. She watched casually from a perch on a sun-warmed boulder, the surrounding landscape still streaked with tenacious patches of snow, the distant sea a roaring sheet of misty steel.

Her bright red eyes took in the mortal combat happening before her. Suitors killed one another as claws found integral gaps in protective armor and severed major arteries, sending those in the air shrieking and spewing blue blood as they plummeted to the rocky ground. Others, instead of the ritual steam blasts, released defensive streams of real fire at opponents, the kind only reserved for mortal enemies, blinding or crippling or cooking targets to smoking cinders within their protective armor plating.

The adults did nothing to intervene in the carnage. It was a sometimes-unfortunate part of the mating display, and their parental instincts were over with after the first year. If one of their progeny died attempting to gain a mate, the event was barely acknowledged unless prey were scarce. During times of famine, even family was on the menu.

There was one male who was detached from the violence. He too had his eyes on the shimmering she-dragon, the gemstone studded beauty. He was on the ground, doing a solo dance, the ritualized head bobbing accompanied by the flaring of his multicolored gills. He used the muscles closest to his skin to manipulate his scales, flicking sheets of them from side to side so that they caught the sun and created a scintillating display of reds and oranges and greens. It was attracting the attention of other females, and he moved away from them, keeping near to the object of his desire and making it clear to the others to look elsewhere.

His display finally did catch her ruby eyes and held them. His dance increased in complexity and fervor, equal in ferocity to those of the males killing themselves in mortal combat. The dance was meant to show off his strength, the length of his claws, the width of his chest. His glimmering colors and clear green eyes were indicators of good health. He shot a burst of steam far into the air to show his lung capacity and ability to defend her and any offspring. He spread his wings to show their span and thickness.

She continued to watch him, then roused herself and moved off the stone to get closer to him. They approached one another, heads lowered, sniffed at the pheromone ducts under each other's wings. She found his scent appealing; the cinnamon-like odor of virility and strength.

She lowered her head and gave a low growl of approval. They stood up on their clawed feet, armored chests together, and wrapped wings around one another, braiding the lengths of their necks together until their faces were side by side.

They were now a pair.

They flew off a short distance to find a suitable place to mate. They found a deserted fjord, with plenty of caves to protect them from the still cool sea winds. The location was a desirable one, and the male had many fights with others attempting to encroach on his territory. This time it was not steam he released from his nostrils, and he was fresh and strong, and the attempted invasions soon ceased. Their mating occurred in the darkest hour of their first night together, a feverish intertwining that could just as easily have passed for the same mortal combat which killed so many males during the day. But it always ended in them lying breathlessly intertwined, growling in low tones as contented ribbons of steam rose from their nostrils and gills. It was a sound heard everywhere on the continent.

They hunted together that spring and summer, plucking large creatures from a sea teeming with life. The she-dragon was gravid, her belly filled with developing eggs that would not be mature until the flight up north. She ate copious amounts of prey items as she slowly, very slowly, began to swell. She could feel the hundreds of still small eggs within her, each one a part of her and yet another, and she knew that not all of them would see the outside world. Life was brutal even within the womb. Her body, by some selective process, would reabsorb the weaker embryos in order to feed the few strongest.

Late in the fall, after a brutally hot summer, when the nights grew cold with approaching winter and the fierce winds returned, the mated pairs flew off, following invisible magnetic fields to the northern birthing grounds.

––––––––––

Lawrence was out in the far corner of the fields, turning the earth with an iron spade in preparation for the spring planting of barley. The day was unusually warm for this time of year, and he was shirtless and soaked with perspiration after hours of the back breaking labor; the sweat flowed in rivulets down his flesh, cutting lines in the coating of raised dust sticking to him.

He looked back in the direction of the hut, where his younger brother, Bradley, was digging as well. The two of them were having a contest to see who could do the most before their father returned from his errand, helping out another of the farmers to patch his sod roof. Lawrence had gone with his father a few times and knew that such occasions were an excuse for the older men to get together and swig some rough fermented mead. He did not like the stuff himself.

Lawrence was winning the contest. It was solely for the old man's approval, as they had nothing material to win. His brother sensed his gaze and paused in his work to give a weary smile. "Hope Dad's enjoying his self," he called out to Lawrence, who put a finger on his own lips to signal the younger man to keep quiet.

"What was that?" their sister asked, watching them from the doorless entry of the hut.

They ignored her and resumed digging. The families of their neighbors were also out in the adjoining fields, doing the laborious prep work for the harvest of grain that would keep them alive next winter.

Winter was a harsh time here in the North. There was always the risk of freezing to death or starvation. Fending off the latter depended heavily on the bounty of their warm weather harvests. The manor lord always got his fixed share of the harvest first, and it was due regardless of how the crops did. Whatever was left belonged to the farmers working the leased land.

The locals had come through this last winter with only a few of the oldest serfs passing on. That was all a memory now, chased away by the spring sun, a bright orange sphere of promise.

Lawrence had just broken up a large clod of the dry earth when he saw a brilliant white shape out of the corner of his eye. There, along a patch of woods bordering the nearby creek, stood a young woman with long hair that gleamed in the sun like fine strands of gold. She watched him with interest, a tight smile on her ruby painted lips. Lawrence paused and looked back at her. He had never seen her before. He raised a hand in a casual wave and she returned it, her smile widening.

She took the gesture as an invitation and strode over to him, moving gracefully, head held high in a confidence Lawrence had never seen in any of the local girls, who by the age of this woman were already showing the first bit of a slouch or grace robbing injury from the hard labor of peasant life.

"I've been watching you," she said with admiration. "You are a strong and hard worker."

"Thank you," Lawrence said, suddenly conscious of the dust covering him. He thought to retrieve his shirt and wipe himself off; the garment was too far away, draped across a length of wooden fencing. The girl, unlike him, was immaculate. Her dress was of fine material and clean, as was her porcelain toned skin and golden hair. Wisps of fragrant oils radiated from her.

Her green eyes were sad, though, and puffy from crying. They held his stare and Lawrence saw in them things that made his heart flutter madly. "What is your name?" he asked her.

"Sasha," she said.

"I'm Lawrence. I've never seen you before."

She pointed to the manor lord's castle. Not quite fit for a king but befitting the master of this little wedge of the empire. "You live there?" Lawrence asked.

"Yes," she said.

He imagined her to be some caretaker's daughter, sneaking out for a walk. "You were crying. Why?"

Sasha looked down at her feet. Her white leather shoes were coated in dust, the only part of her with any blemish. She answered his question in a weary voice. "Because soon I must become a wife and leave here."

No, Lawrence thought. He wanted to tell her that could not be, he would miss her, that if she stayed he would build the two of them the finest sod house she'd ever seen. The white dress and manor home brought him back to reality. What kind of silly nonsense was he thinking? She was not nobility but was still on a social echelon mountains above him.

"You won't be happy being a wife?" Lawrence asked her.

"I would," she said. "If it was to a husband I truly loved," and her eyes saw deep into his soul.

The two of them had been transfixed in that way of people making a real connection; it was as if the outside world had fallen away and there was only the two of them. Neither of them heard the thumping of horses' hooves until the animals were neighing and tearing up the earth around them, a pair of muscular steeds ridden by knights in gleaming armor.

"Lady Sasha!" a deep voice boomed. One of the knights was levelling a long sword at Lawrence's throat. "Has he dared touch you? I will cut him down right here."

"No," Sasha told him curtly.

The other knight dismounted and gave her a slight bow. "M'lady, your father is most worried about you. You cannot be wandering outside the manor amongst the commoners."

Sasha looked with sad longing upon Lawrence. The knight which had dismounted guided her towards his steed, helping her up onto the saddle, then leading the horse away on foot. Sasha glanced back at Lawrence, her eyes saying all the things she could not.

The knight with the sword to Lawrence's throat flipped open the face protector of his helmet. He was a middle-aged man with a battle scar diagonally crossing his face. He saw Sasha's parting look at this commoner and his cheeks reddened. "I should kill you right here for even getting close to her," he said in a level voice that brought to mind dark nights in the dead of winter. "You would do well to send her immediately home should she sneak out again in the future."

"Perhaps you would do well to keep a better eye on her," Lawrence said, meeting the knight's stare with a cold one of his own.

The knight tensed and the arm holding the sword shook with barely contained energy. He finally won some inner battle over his desire to kill this peasant upstart. He re-sheathed his sword and gave the horse a sharp kick to the flanks to get it moving.

Lawrence watched the knights on their way back to the manor, crossing without concern the worked gardens of the peasants, none of which dared to raise a voice of protest.

———————

The glimmering she-dragon and her mate found a suitable nesting spot on a ledge midway up a mountain peak uninhabited by others of their kind. She had, immediately upon landing, used her diamond hard talons to dig a bowl-shaped depression in the living stone of the mountain. She settled into this, waiting for her cargo of eggs to drop.

The mountain had a robust population of wooly mountain goats, which, for all their agility and speed, had no hope of escaping the talons of the male, who did the hunting while the she-dragon tended to the nest. She was ravenous at this point in gestation, and the male brought back to her a steady stream of twitching food items.

Their nesting spot had a panoramic view of the valley below. Stretched out along the fertile lowlands was the castle of the manor lord, and the cultivated fields of his town of serfs. With their keen vision, the dragons clearly noted the movements of the inhabitants. When the wind was right, it carried up to their nostrils the scent of the villagers. Food security for when the babies came, and the supply of goats ran out.

———————

The Earl of Dunreid, lord of the manor, knew he had a problem now. There had not been a dragon in this part of the kingdom since before his birth, but the story of *that* legendary breeding pair was written down in the moldering pages of the Chronicles. The book told of how the village was nearly decimated until the king sent his best knights to dispatch the pests. The dragon extermination came at the cost of nearly a hundred of his best men.

This was back when the manor was ruled by a different earl under a different king. Dunreid knew there would be no such rescue these days. If the reports of messengers were to be believed, the war with the Orassian Empire was consuming most of the military, and because of that there were more dragons than ever in the southerly parts of the kingdom. The king's priority would be to use any available personnel to protect those regions. That was where the iron was mined, and the large weapons foundries operated. There were gems to be had and large cities full of commerce and industry. The literal beating heart of the realm.

Earl Dunreid, a distant relative who the king did not like much to begin with, had only a small manor which produced a scant bit of produce. He relied on a small group of modestly paid knights for protection. They were soldiers for hire, mercenaries, and not members of the king's official troops.

When Dunreid brought up the issue of dispatching the dragons, the group of knights flatly refused. It was not in their obligation to perform such a dangerous task. And why worry about it? they asked him. The dragons were in the distance, not causing any problems.

Dunreid, as one of the few literate people in the region, knew from the Chronicles that *that* would change.

It did.

The male dragon swooped down one morning and flew away with two of the serfs impaled in its claws.

The earl's finances were low, and the knights refused the highest monetary reward he could offer. It was then that an idea occurred to him, and he offered up the most valuable prize, and one that included a chance to be part of royalty (however distant and low on the hierarchy).

The announcement was made that his daughter Sasha would wed the knight who brought back a dragon's horn. But there were two dragons, and what if two knights returned, each with a horn? Well then, any ties of that sort would be resolved with a little joust.

Lawrence was an adept archer. He had a bow made of hickory wood and strung with a length of deer tendon. He had a quiver of deerskin and arrows of hickory sharpened to vicious points. He had crafted all of it. When time permitted, he and the other farmers would set up wood stump targets and shoot at them from various distances. It was a friendly competition to the others, but Lawrence dreamed of being an archer in the king's army. If the war kept on, conscripts would soon be called from the outer regions of the realm. He wanted to be ready. He wanted to be the *best*.

"Why would you *want* to shoot arrows for the king?" the other boys often asked him.

"Because soldiers travel and have adventure," was Lawrence's answer.

"Yeah, peasants get sent out first to be human shields. And the King's soldiers die with frostbitten toes."

"You don't know that," Lawrence argued, but he only had to look around to know it was probably true. He and the others were just farm animals to the royalty, living tools providing a service. No thought was given to their wellbeing. There was no hope of distinction or that hard work would somehow elevate you to a higher station in life.

Still he dreamt of a soldier's adventure, catching the eye of some superior during a dangerous battle and being rewarded for his bravery, perhaps even becoming a knight.

News of the details surrounding Sasha's impending betrothal spread throughout the manor, as these things tend to do. "I want to go," Lawrence said.

"Stop talking nonsense," his father told him. "The Earl's not going to give his daughter to one of us. Killing dragons is a knight's job, not a farmer's."

But this farmer loves Sasha, he thought, his blood boiling with desire. He pointed something out to his father. "The dragon took our neighbors. Two of us."

"It is not our place to hunt them down," his father repeated. "We are farmers. That is our job, and how we pay for our land. Part of that payment includes our protection. If something were to happen to our crops while we were out gallivanting the countryside, then *all* of us suffer."

Lawrence wondered how his father would have reacted had the victims of the dragons been members of the immediate family. Would he have taken it so calmly and left revenge in the hands of the knights? Lawrence prayed not and wondered when life on the manor had stolen his father's vigor and manhood. *It'll never happen to me,* he vowed.

He knew what he had to do.

Lawrence crept out of the sod dwelling at midnight. Farmers slept soundly and deeply, but even so he was very careful about how he exited. He had the bow and quiver full of arrows slung over his back. Around his waist was a pig's bladder of water and a leather sack containing a half loaf of bread and some radishes. He made his way between cultivated lots, following the dim yellow lines of footpaths worn down to underlying sand. The sky was brilliant with the flickering diamond chips of stars. The night was typical for a northern spring, cool but not uncomfortable.

He had a good feeling in his bones. He couldn't wait to see the expression on the earl's face when he came to the manor house bearing the dragon horns. *I can get used to being a royal*, he thought with the naïve confidence of one who had yet to see how life really worked.

He headed out past the last of the cultivated fields. This is where the dragon had swooped down and carried the elder Mcgintry and his only son to a nest on the nearby mountain peak. The two were taken before the watching eyes of wife and mother. *And father says it is not the job of farmers to hunt down the dragons. He says leave it to the knights.*

The thought angered Lawrence and put fire in his steps. He strode along at a steady pace, his eyes now accustomed to the dark. The world was all greys and blacks except for the yellow streaks of sandy trails. He entered a path in the woods and crossed the stream on a rickety wooden bridge, headed towards the outline of the mountains, jagged spikes of onyx against the glittering star-dusted sky. The dragons were up there, on the highest peak, according to the witnesses of the Mcgintry abductions.

No, it is not a kidnapping. They were taken as food.

But you'll pay for this meal, Lawrence vowed. He strode through the lowland oak forest, catching glimpses of the mountain peak through the mostly bare branches. The buds were only just beginning to break, extending frilly strands of newborn leaves that were black shadows, shaped like talons, like *dragon* claws.

But he knew the ones on an actual dragon would be *much* bigger.

They won't get the chance to use them, Lawrence told himself. *I'm going to put an arrow right between their breastplates.*

He'd heard, in the many tales told on the manor, that *that* was the easiest way to kill a dragon, by stabbing it in the seam running down the anterior plating, from throat to hind legs. A shot to the eyes could possibly blind them as well. But the honorable way to kill one, the way the knights first class of legend did it, was the tiny triangle of exposed flesh between the eyes which presents itself when the dragon's gills are extended. This was most dangerous, as the gills were extended only as the dragon was about to release a burst of fire, and to get a shot one had to be facing the creature head on (meaning the intended target of its fiery blast). Who got the best of who – dead dragon or fried hunter—in this case was a question of milliseconds.

Lawrence ran these scenarios through his head to the best of his naïve imaginings. He could not bring himself to be afraid; this quest was merely a steppingstone to another, much desired scenario involving Sasha. Such visions kept him warm through the rest of the lowland forest.

It was still night when the forest thinned out and the ground became rocky and strewn with boulders. The trees were replaced by sparse vegetation; spiny, low-lying bushes popped up between the rocks. The tips of their foliage was needle sharp and pricked his skin painfully, and from this point on he made his way more carefully. The ground was beginning a steep incline; he was at the bae of the mountain, and it dominated his view. He now had to look directly upwards to see his destination.

Lawrence began the climb, calf muscles and legs burning with the effort of it. After some time, the sky to the east turned purple, then lavender. Details of the terrain around him came into a light blue focus as the first sliver of sun peeked over the rim of the horizon.

The she-dragon was curled about her clutch of eggs. Her mate was lying on his side, parallel to her, breastplates pressed against her spiny back , his six hearts thumping a soothing beat. The dragons slept and dreamed: she of the day when the first baby burst free of its confines and called out to be fed; he of fighting off other males competing for the privilege of mating with his bejeweled partner.

In there among the dreams were detected sensations not the mere fabrications of sleeping minds. The occasional clang of metal against stone; hushed whispers that were not the exhalations of either dragon partner; the rapid thump of alien heartbeats; the smell of warm blood as yet unshed and the stink peculiar to unwashed mammalian bodies.

These external stimuli reached a point that woke the sleeping dragons. They raised their drowsy heads, scanning the surroundings now lit by the very first traces of dawn light.

There were three knights surrounding the nest. They had been creeping up upon it in an attempt to get close enough to strike. Despite the need for stealth while they did so, they were busy scolding one another in feverish whispers about which of them had the right to make the kill.

The male dragon instantly flared his gills and let out a streamer of fire that caught the closest knight to him. The man screamed within the jet of plasma-orange around a center of blue- and his armor began to glow and drip away as he collapsed into a smoking mess.

A knight had gotten within striking distance of the she-dragon, and he swung his broad sword as she lifted her head. The sword struck her armor with a sparking clang and bounced harmlessly off. Because of the sword's weight, the knight could not choke back on the swing and the blade continued its downward arc; the she-dragon was now lifting herself up on her front legs, briefly leaving the clutch of eggs exposed, and the sword broke two of them. The prematurely breached embryonic dragons churned within the spilled amnion and let out their death mewls.

The knight who'd broken the eggs hefted his sword again, intending to thrust upward into the she-dragon's chest. The she-dragon, looking down at him, flared her gills and breathed out a blast of searing plasma. The knight's last thought before pain made thought impossible was, *These things are a lot bigger than I thought.*

The male took out the remaining knight, turning him into a glob of molten magma. Then he stood erect on his back legs and began patrolling the area for other enemies.

The she-dragon remained with the nest to guard the remaining undamaged pair of eggs. After checking them to be sure they were intact (they were), she sniffed at the gooey piles of amnion from the ruptured ones, nudging the motionless embryos with the tip of her nose. She grunted, searching for a response, and got none.

She roared and sent a blast of fire skyward.

Lawrence was halfway up the mountain, leaning forward against the steep angle of the boulder strewn surface. Millions of years of weathering, along with the fracturing action of lichens and plant roots, had created a thin coating of mineral soil in between the many stone outcroppings. Sometimes a too powerful flexing of his calves pushed through to the stone below and he nearly lost his footing. He guessed that once he started the trip down in such a fashion, there would be no stopping him, and he'd be a mashed-up lump of pulp by the time he reached ground level. Conifer trees grew here, pyramids of blue-green needles stretching skyward. Shaggy mountain goats bleated as they hopped over boulders and ascended vertical surfaces with gravity defying abandon.

Shut up! he wanted to scream at the goats. He had no idea how far up the dragons might be (or if they were even on *this* side of the mountain); the damn bleating of the animals would give away his attempts at a stealthy attack. A short distance ahead and above, something stepped out from behind a jagged outcropping. Lawrence thought it was another goat.

It wasn't. The knight from the manor, who'd held the sword at his throat, was leaning back against gravity, the heavy sword by his side. The face shield of his helmet was up to expose his amused expression. "Well, well, well, what have we here?" he mocked. "A farm boy on a knight's errand?" He began to inch carefully forward.

Lawrence unslung his bow and slid an arrow from the quiver at his back.

The knight paused to laugh. "Don't be silly, boy. Your little toy won't do you any good. Don't you see I'm wearing *armor?* And," he added, "I have the high ground. So, what I would suggest to you is that you turn around and go back home to your mother and father while you still can."

Lawrence strung the arrow. He was sure he could plant it in the pale oval from which the knight glared out at him.

"You're not going to ruin this for me, boy," the knight hissed. He had separated from the others and hung back, calculating that in their bickering haste they would be torched, and he could sneak up alone to finish the dragons. "I cannot allow you to pass and destroy my advantage." He began a slide to bridge the gap between him and Lawrence, raising the sword high overhead for a killing swipe.

At the same moment, there were several flashes of bright light a few hundred feet up the mountain. The figure of the male dragon was vast and shimmering in the early morning sun, its eyes glowing like molten emeralds as it swooped down the mountainside towards them. The knight was still sliding forward but he saw the reflection in Lawrence's eyes of the beast at his back, and as the shadow of it fell over him, the dragon let loose a stream of liquid blue fire. Lawrence rolled to the left, ducking behind an outcropping as the stream of fire whipped past, carrying with it a bubbling mass of metal and charred flesh. A wave of heat washed over Lawrence and baked his skin red with first degree burns.

The male dragon flew past and then banked for another run, looking directly at Lawrence. There was no escaping, there was no chance except to take a chance, and Lawrence took quick aim for his moment of truth, his eyes locked with the dragon's. The gill plates at the side of its head flared outward, pulling apart the meeting place of three sections of armor between the dragon's eyes, exposing a small pink triangle.

Lawrence let the arrow fly and it sank into that gap in the armor. The first tendrils of smoke were coming from the dragon's mouth, which was open and flashing with the start of the combustion cycle. But instead of releasing fire the male dragon shrieked and crashed on the rocks, torn and bloody and brain dead by the time its tumbling form came to a stop just feet from Lawrence, who was crouched down with his eyes closed and ready to die.

Just after the she-dragon vented her fury at the sky, the last remaining knight attacked. He had hidden behind some rocks and crept upon the nest when the male left. This knight had a staff, with a long wooden handle tipped with a curved, meter long blade tempered and specially sharpened for this purpose. He went for the pectoral seam in the she-dragon's armor, that thin line between the rows of shiny chiton, exposed now that she was standing upright.

He jabbed at the target and the tip of the blade punctured her, not deep or fatal, just enough to cause some pain, and before the knight could thrust any deeper, the she-dragon shifted position sharply and snapped the tip off, leaving the point of metal lodged in her flesh. She swung a taloned hand at the knight, splintering the handle of the staff and sending him flying down one side of the mountain.

To her dismay, one of the remaining eggs had burst during this last struggle, the premature dragonet shivering out its life in a pool of amnion , not developed enough to survive the outside world just yet.

Cutting off her sorrow, the death cry of her mate and companion rolled up from the lower altitudes and even though the sound said it all, that it was too late, the she-dragon could not keep from going to his aid.

Lawrence heard the flapping of great wings as the she-dragon now bore down on him, dragged from the nest by the death cry of her mate. Lawrence had no hope of stopping *her*, the attack was so swift. As he locked eyes with this new dragon, and the first streaks of plasma blue flame rushed his way, he could not help thinking how beautiful she was.

The immediate threat neutralized, the she-dragon flew back up to the nest, scooped the remaining egg in her talons, and flew off. She headed further north, passing over many villages, sometimes being shot at by crossbows and arrows, which bounced harmlessly off her armor. In return she would strafe them with fire, pouring all her rage into the act, bringing the temperature of the exhalation to levels so high she was in danger of self combusting. She knew that nowhere was safe for her kind if it was near these strange beings, who had no natural weapons but could manufacture them from materials in the environment.

She knew she had to find a place away from *them*.

She found it, in a place of snow and mountains, where there were none of *them* but plenty of other prey. She found an isolated mountain and formed a nest in the snow. The she-dragon herself could survive these cold temperatures, but she did not know if the precious cargo would, for this was farther north than any dragon had ever gone. She stayed there, covering the egg with her body, providing warmth for many weeks, far past the normal gestation period. She checked frequently, expecting the embryo to have died, but it clung to life, developing much slower in the cooler temps.

One day she felt the miraculous first rustlings beneath her. She lifted her belly to watch as the baby pecked a hole in the shell with its egg tooth and then broke through, its head stretched out and giving a healthy mewl, full of vigor and life and eager to receive its first meal of regurgitated and predigested meat.

A baby she-dragon, as lustrous and beautiful as her mother, with the feistiness of the father who had died to protect her.

As for Lawrence, he did not die, contrary to what you may have been led to believe. Just as that stream of fire had been heading his way, he'd found a depression in the ground just deep enough to keep him from being roasted.

He returned to the manor, red as a lobster (not that any of the manor folk knew what a lobster was) bearing the cut off horn of the male dragon.

Sasha was relieved to see him (she'd been having nightmares about a life wed to one of the other knights), and her father at first reneged on his deal, claiming the marriage was only promised to knights, but after Sasha pled with him, and the earl saw what it meant to her, he made Lawrence an honorary knight due to his bravery, thereby meeting the requirements for the wedding to take place.

I'd love to say everyone lived happily ever after, but we all know that's bullshit. They were happy for the moment, though, and this moment is the only thing any of us really have.

About Eddie Spohn

Eddie Spohn is a writer from Long Island, New York. He paints houses to keep homelessness and starvation at bay. He is happiest at the beach scribbling in his notebook. The first draft of Altitude, the story in this anthology, was written at Smith's Point, New York, part of the Fire Island National Seashore. If you're ever there watching the sunrise, as Eddie has done many times, you'll find it easy to believe in magic...

Love...

And dragons.

The Dragon and the Horse

By Parker McIntosh

Byzanthum the young dragon, sent away from his nest, strikes out in the world to make a name for himself. But being a dragon isn't as easy as his mother has made it look. Through gullibility and inattentiveness, he finds himself trapped, and must rely on his instincts if he hopes to survive, let alone become a legend in his own right.

Parker McIntosh

The Dragon and the Horse
By Parker McIntosh

There comes a time in every young dragon's life when they must leave the nest and find their own hoard. For Byzanthum's mother, that time couldn't come quickly enough.

Byzanthum was as cute as any hatchling. His emerald-green scales shimmered in the milky albumin of his broken eggshell. She doted on his little squawks and the puffs of smoke he sent at the chickens she fed him, their heads snapped off so that he could practice hunting their death-rattle sprints. But he grew clingy. Byzanthum was her first hatchling and, as dragons only procreated once every hundred years or so, she'd never known another mother dragon. He clung to her belly scales for weeks at a time, the claws at the tips of his wings dug into her stomach leaving aching sores that took months to heal. She told herself it was cute. Until he grew bigger, and his clutching made it impossible to fly. He wanted to follow her everywhere. His cries achieved a sonorous, petulant quality that made her wince whenever she heard him.

"Why are you leaving?" he cried whenever she left to hunt. "When will you be back?"

She started flying farther afield to give herself more time without him and she found herself relishing the days when game was scarce, and she had to stay away overnight. On those days, she could hear Byzanthum's cries from miles away as she returned, and they made her shudder.

But she was his mother. She remembered when she left her own nest, of her own volition. She'd gone on a test flight, found a sheep in a field, killed and eaten it. As she picked the wool from her teeth with a rib bone, she realized she didn't need her own mother anymore, and flew on and away. She kept waiting for Byzanthum to have that same realization. As he grew older, and larger, he just clung to her more tightly.

It was not a sustainable situation. Byzanthum's mother kept her hoard in the extinct crater of a small volcano. Most of the crater's rocky floor was covered in gold coins and gems. Her body's length stretched around the entire crater so that she could nestle herself comfortably atop her treasure. Byzanthum was still only a fraction of her size, but the room he took cramped her. They were like two cats trying to sit in the same box. She mentioned, for the umpteenth time, that he should consider finding his own lair. Secure his own treasure.

"But mother, you have so much treasure here. Why can't we share it. With the both of us defending it, no one would dare try to steal it from you."

If Byzanthum wanted to stay, this was not the argument to make. The threat to even a single coin of her treasure snapped maternal instinct. Tongues of flame licked her chin and she rose to her full height, the crest of her horns reaching up over the lips of the crater. She spread her wings, a great sail that blotted out the sun. And she roared. She howled at him. Her claws rent chalices and soldered coins together. Byzanthum fled.

Byzanthum's first sullen flight as an independent dragon was a long one. He was angry at his mother for rejecting him and sought to put as many miles as he could between them. As he travelled farther away and the landscape changed from the smoky volcanic range of his youth to greener and brighter pastures, Byzanthum's anger turned to unease. He wasn't familiar with the topography. He was used to shooting flames at rock until it melted, but it looked like even a small puff might ignite the entire landscape. He wondered if there were any dragons that lived there at all. He was about to turn around, thinking he could settle just a few mountains away from his mother's volcano and hope she would eventually regret sending him away, when he saw something glint through the trees far below. Like a crow, he was drawn to the shine of potential treasures. Byzanthum's dragon instincts kicked in, and he flew lower to investigate.

The knight was in a full suit of silver armor. A crimson cape that matched his horse's regalia fluttered behind him. An indigo flag fluttered from the tip of his lance. Byzanthum landed in the road ahead of him and the knight's horse, well trained, stopped a safe distance away.

"A dragon!" the knight said to nobody in particular. Byzanthum stared at his armor, wondering if it was just polished steel or real silver. Silver seemed unlikely, but he salivated at the prospect. Gold would have been better, but silver would do. He realized how much he missed the feeling of treasure spilling through his claws.

"Give me your armor and I'll let you live," Byzanthum roared, but his voice cracked and the spout of flame he meant to shoot menacingly in the air sparked out and he coughed out a cloud of smoke.

"I'll give you my lance!"

The knight spurred the horse. His horse didn't need to be prompted twice. She whinnied a more threatening growl than Byzanthum's roar and charged. The knight lowered his lance and the flag whipped back flush with the pole.

Byzanthum watched the horse approach curiously. He didn't understand why the knight would charge so recklessly to his death. The horse and knight together were just a little smaller than Byzanthum's adolescent body, but they were clunky. They approached at a gallop and wouldn't be able to turn easily.

Byzanthum waited until they were just a few yards away before he leapt into the air. He grabbed the lance between his foreclaws, miscalculating his own timing so that the lance pricked his belly scales, and surged into the air. He had only intended to disarm the soldier, but he didn't realize the knight was attached to it. The knight's body, caught with his feet in the stirrups and the lance bound to his arm, stretched and split in two with a bloody pop. Byzanthum felt the chainmail rending and was jerked back to the ground. He only just missed impaling himself on the lance that was still attached to the knight's lifeless torso. The horse galloped on with the knight's bodiless legs flopping in time with each stride.

After a moment to catch his breath, Byzanthum took stock of his victory. The prick to his stomach was no worse than the sores his mother used to get on her stomach, and he wondered if each of those represented a close call with a knight's lance. He wished that he had asked her more about surviving outside the nest.

Byzanthum was disappointed to find the knight's armor was just steel, and poor steel at that. It frayed and tore easily in his claws. He was happy to discover two rings, one copper and one gold, once he removed the lance and gauntlets from the knight's hands.

"My first piece of gold," he murmured.

Byzanthum stared so intently at the gold ring that he didn't notice the horse return until it was almost upon him. He tried to make up for his inattentiveness with bluster while quickly secreting the gold ring beneath a scale.

"Bold of you to return. I suppose you'll make a decent meal." Smoke wafted from his nostrils.

The horse didn't look impressed by his words or demeanor. "I wonder if you could remove the rest of my old master. It's quite awkward to run like this."

Byzanthum didn't know what to do. He could have killed and eaten the horse easily if he wanted to, but the horse didn't look scared at all. If anything, she looked bored.

"There's a jeweled dagger on his hip and a small pouch of coins, if that's what you're after."

That settled it. Byzanthum unclasped the saddle and bridle and the knight's legs fell from the horse. He removed a sword, which was a plain, ugly bit of iron, and the dagger, which was plated in gold and inlaid with an emerald that matched his scales beautifully. He realized he wasn't paying attention to the horse, who should by all rights have been his enemy, and snapped his face back up to her. The horse gave a snort but otherwise did nothing.

"I suppose you're planning on staying, then," the horse said. "Taking up residence somewhere and terrifying these parts?"

"I haven't decided yet," Byzanthum said. He opened his mouth but found that he didn't have anything else to say. He didn't know anything about setting up a new lair. Would he have to build it himself? His mother's lair was inside an extinct volcano, but he hadn't seen any volcanoes, alive or extinct, for miles and miles of flying. The ground around him was grassy and soft. The forests didn't offer any protection. It didn't appear to be a place suitable for a dragon to live. He was about to say so when the horse continued.

"There is a castle not far from here. My former master's castle, that is. It's not much more than a tower and a few buildings, but it would provide some shelter and a place to store your treasure."

That sounded perfect. The horse seemed to know more about what a dragon needed than Byzanthum did, but he didn't want to give away his ignorance. He pretended to consider.

"You'd want me to live at the castle? After I ripped your master in two?"

The horse stomped the ground and tossed her head. "He was a brute. Always spurring me harder than he needed to, feeding me less than I wanted, making me carry more than was comfortable. Not very intelligent either. He never kept track of tithes and taxes on the fields surrounding the castle, so he was always in need of money, always going off to war. That's where we were headed when you interrupted him. Off to offer services to the King far to the south. I'm sure you would do a better job of managing the castle than he did."

Byzanthum wasn't sure at all that he would be able to. He barely knew how to be a dragon alone out of the nest. He didn't know anything about managing a castle's grounds.

"I'm sure the people in the castle would object to a dragon," he said, trying to cover his discomfort at the prospect of managing an estate. "The guards, the queen, the stableboys, they would all run screaming when I landed on the ramparts."

"The knight didn't have a wife. The guards might run away but a terrifying dragon like yourself wouldn't have use for guards anyway. If I spoke with them, the stableboys and people of the surrounding area would stay. You'd need them to sell goods at market to grow your treasure hoard."

"Why would you help me like that?" Byzanthum asked, but he didn't hear the answer. As soon as the horse mentioned a growing hoard of treasure, he was enamored.

The horse advanced ahead of Byzanthum to warn the stableboys and the people she expected to stay and when Byzanthum arrived, he found the castle nearly abandoned. The guards, not as foolhardy as their master, ran off as soon as they heard the word dragon.

The castle was a pitiful three-story building that sat atop a small bluff overlooking fields and forest. A series of one-story buildings created a small square which were all encased in a low stone wall. Byzanthum thought that his mother would have needed to curl her length twice around the interior walls to comfortably lay down, but it was more than enough room for him.

The infamy of an estate taken over by a dragon ranged wide across the land and Byzanthum found it an easy and prosperous home. The horse, Bruta, proved to be an excellent steward. And once she explained the system of taxes and tithes, Byzanthum found himself very capable of keeping track of what treasures were owed, and even more effective at extracting them. No one was willing to stiff a dragon.

In return, the people who chose to live in the castle and the surrounding area were free from marauders. Wolves and bears left the woods, leaving livestock safe. Crime plummeted and the King's tax collectors stayed far away. The people were wary of Byzanthum when he chose to show himself, but that was rare. He preferred to stay in the square, organizing his growing hoard of treasure in the tower, and let Bruta handle the day-to-day estate dealings. He only emerged to hunt, which he most often did at night, or to deal with heroes and knights.

The King seemed to prefer pretending that Byzanthum didn't exist as long as he stayed in his far-flung estate and didn't bother the nearby landowners aside from poaching the odd sheep. But self-motivated heroes and knights began to appear at his doorstep, challenging him. It was never a real contest, but they were indefatigable. Regardless of how many he burned, ripped apart, or devoured, there was always another challenger ready to try and kill him.

"There's another hero. This one with a whole slew of knights and a few archers." Bruta had just returned from a merchant trip south where the estate's goods had been sold.

"Another one?" Byzanthum asked. He took the chest of copper coins from her cart. They didn't sparkle like gold ones, but he was amassing quite the hoard of them. He poured them out onto the pile he was forming around the base of the tower. He wanted a mountain big enough to cover himself in. Gold would have been better, but if he wanted gold, he needed to go out and maraud for it. And that would bring even more knights. "Did you get a good count? Last time there were ten lancers and they almost corralled me on the ground before I could burn enough of them to break free."

"Five lancers. Plus, the archers I mentioned."

"The archers don't bother me," Byzanthum shrugged. "Their arrows can't even pierce my wing membrane. It's the lancers with those new enforced tips that have been driving me crazy. Five shouldn't be a problem."

"Interesting," Bruta said. "What are you doing over here?" She tossed her head at the growing pile of copper coins around the tower.

"I'm too big to get in and out of the tower easily. Back in my mother's lair we spread the treasure all over the place. You could, well, it was easier to look at." He didn't want to admit he missed being able to dive in and out of mountains of gold.

Bruta whinnied. "That sounds lovely. But if you leave it all out in the open like this, it will tarnish when it rains."

"Rains?" Byzanthum looked up. "It almost never rained up north. It rains here?"

Bruta nodded. "Torrentially. You'll want to get your treasure safely inside. Unless," she paused.

"Unless what?" Byzanthum was already in a panic, using his claws and tail to shovel waves of copper coins into the door and first-floor windows of the tower. The prospect of any damage to his treasure clutched his heart.

Bruta looked up and considered the sky. She trotted around the perimeter of the square, and Byzanthum began to suspect she was intentionally stringing him along. He looked back up at the sky, searching for anything like a rain cloud, and saw nothing.

"Yes, I think that would work," Bruta said, returning to Byzanthum. His suspicions vanished. "We could hire builders to connect the roofs of the buildings to the top of the tower. It would protect the treasure, and you, from the elements."

"But how would I get in and out if I can't just fly into the courtyard?"

Bruta considered this as well and trotted over to the gates. "If we demolished one of these buildings, the gate could be widened. It would take a while, but-"

Byzanthum interrupted her by spitting a bout of fire at the building. He tore at the stone foundations and burned the walls until the roof collapsed in a heap of rubble.

Bruta looked at him and snorted. "I suppose that would work as well."

"Build the roof," Byzanthum said. He already regretted burning down the building. It made the castle look shabby, and just when he was starting to feel proud of his growing hoard. "I'm going to handle the hero." He took two bounds and leaped into the air. The hero and his knights were about to bear the unfair brunt of his frustration.

———

Byzanthum stayed away from the castle as much as he could during the construction of the roof. It pained him to see his hoard covered up, plank by plank. It also pained him to pay the workers who built the roof, though he instructed Bruta to make those payments from the taxes and tithes the workers would have owed to him. He couldn't bear the idea of actually handing over any of his treasure, even if it was mostly just copper coins.

One day he returned from a hunt in a nearby kingdom, having feasted on three rams and marauding a chest of fine linens from a farmer's hut, and found his castle completely covered. The slight glow of his treasure carpeting the square was swallowed up by a dull, ugly roof. He landed outside the square and sauntered through the still charred remains of the gate.

"Are you not pleased with the roof?" Bruta asked, noting Byzanthum's sour mood. "I've never known builders to work so quickly and with such precision. They even double shingled and treated the planks. The stones of the castle will wear away before the roof comes down."

"It's fine," Byzanthum said. He tossed the chest of linens through a window of the tower and flinched when he heard the fine woodwork splinter. "It just doesn't glow the same way it used to."

"We can fix that. I was going to tell you our plan is to bring torches in. We'll get the place perpetually lit. You'll see the glow through the gate from miles away."

The idea of a glowing entrance to his secret hoard cheered Byzanthum up and he curled himself up and prepared to fall asleep. His stomach was full, and he wanted to rest, but Bruta didn't leave. She stomped her feet and tossed her head.

"Is there anything else?" Byzanthum asked.

Bruta shifted her eyes and looked around like she was waiting for something.

"Are you looking for a pat on the back? Tell the stableboy I've ordered him to give you a full brush down. Now leave me to rest."

"It isn't that." Bruta sneezed and raised her voice. "I just said you'd be able to see the glow through the gate from miles away."

Byzanthum had a brief moment to puzzle over why Bruta would repeat herself when there was a terrible clash from outside the square. Dozens of knights in full armor, all bearing sharp, needlelike lances, rushed into the room.

"Oh no," Bruta said after the last of the knights appeared and took position around the gate. Her voice didn't sound worried. She sounded gleeful. "It looks like we're under attack."

"I can see that, Bruta," Byzanthum said. He reared up on his hind legs and his head smashed into the slope of the roof. To stand up to his full height he would have to move closer to the center of the square, and closer to the lances. He shot a quick bout of flame at the knights, prompting them to step back, and he moved forward. "How did they get here so quickly without any of our watch noticing? I would have noticed a group of this size on my flight in.

Byzanthum looked up from the knights and saw Bruta's nostrils flare a sneer at him. Behind her, people who lived in the surrounding area crowded around. They didn't look surprised to see the knights. They looked like they were ready to watch a battle.

I'll kill them all, Byzanthum thought. *They'll all burn in-*

Byzanthum's thoughts were interrupted by the first advancing knight's lance tip stabbing into his shoulder. He roared in pain and shot a flame at the knight, who cowered back behind a heavy shield. Another knight advanced. Byzanthum shot fire at him too, but he hid behind a shield as well. Slowly, the knights and their lances inched closer.

It quickly became clear that Byzanthum was outmatched. There were too many knights to fight, too many lances to deal with. The knights seemed to have somehow learned from their late compatriots how best to attack a dragon, and it only took one look at Bruta's sneering eyes to know who had given away his secrets.

Byzanthum sent a fireball at the crouched knights and leapt into the air. He could come back and get revenge whenever he wanted but he just needed to get away from them. He wasn't thinking about anything but getting away and forgot about the roof. His head cracked into the wood again and he felt his wings crumple against the thick, reinforced wooden beams. He fell to the floor in a roar of pain. He knew in an instant that he wasn't seriously injured, but he also knew that he was in trouble. The knights were on him in an instant. Their lances pricked him, few finding purchase beneath his rough scales, but each of them a searing threat.

Part of Byzanthum wanted to curl up into a ball and just let his doom come to him. This dragon business was too much. He hated how reliant he was on the horse. He hated the slow accumulation of tarnished copper coins. More than anything, he missed the comfort of his mother's lair. The warm gold reflecting like green fire in the emerald of his scales.

A lance stabbed deep into Byzanthum's arm and shook him brutally from his wishing. He roared a petulant, pathetic roar, not even worthy of a cat. And then he heard a nicker. A chortling whinny. He searched the room desperately and found Bruta, rearing up on her hind legs and laughing. Byzanthum felt rage rising. He was a dragon. She was a horse. She dared to laugh at him? He'd dismembered her master and taken ownership of his castle.

The next lance, Byzanthum caught in his foreclaws and ripped from the knight. He hoped to have split the man, like the first knight, but this one knew better than to attach himself to his weapon. The wood of the lance exploded in a pulse of splinters. Quicker than he'd ever moved before he reached out and grabbed the knight's still extended arm and pulled him close. He felt the knight's shoulder pop out of its socket, felt the stink of the man's fear suddenly waft from his armor. He took the knight's helmet between his jaws and ripped it off.

The knights quieted and backed away. Bruta fell back onto all fours and looked uncertainly at the proceedings.

Byzanthum roared. Not a tinny, fledgling roar, but a roar that shook the new timber of the castle and shattered its windows.

The knights looked at each other and reformed the line of lances. Byzanthum wasn't afraid. They attacked and he pulled them one by one to their end. He knew there were still too many to handle on his own. He glanced up, thinking he might smash through the roof, but gave the idea up immediately. The roof was a trap. Its shingles were made of stone and fireproof. He couldn't get out that way. He stepped forward into the middle of the square, near the tower, where the roof was highest. He breathed in and summoned the biggest geyser of flame he had ever blown and strafed the knights. They shielded themselves as they had before, just as he expected. Just as his flame ran out, Byzanthum dropped to all fours and rushed at the knights. He opened his mouth and roared.

Saliva flew from his mouth and dripped from his teeth. His scales were alive in flame and his eyes glowed red and green. The knights, stunned at the charge, leaped out of the way. Byzanthum burst out of the castle and into the air. He didn't look back to see if they were watching him. He just wanted to get away.

───────────────

For a long time, Byzanthum just flew. Hard and fast, pumping his wings with fury and diving into thermal currents like a plummeting falcon divebombing fluttering prey. He flew without a care of direction. To be away was enough.

Eventually, Byzanthum noticed a change in the landscape below. The soft green hills of pasture and forest gave way to harsher black volcanic rock. He recognized jagged peaks and was filled with a piercing homesickness that struck him like a lance in his stomach. He adjusted his course.

Byzanthum's mother's crater looked exactly as he remembered it. If his longing and imagination had increased the quantity of her gold, in his absence she'd acquired it. The glow of treasure hung above the crater like a halo and Byzanthum couldn't stay away. He circled the crater twice, high above and glanced down through thin gray clouds, but didn't see his mother. He thought he might surprise her when she returned. He spiraled down and landed with a clatter of golden coins.

As soon as Byzanthum's claws touched the ground the world around him erupted into an inferno of twisting and roaring flames. He crouched low and backed away. He looked for a way to leap into the air to escape but the entire opening of the crater was covered in a ceiling of fire. He didn't know what was happening. He recognized dragon fire but hadn't noticed a dragon nearby. Had his mother's home been usurped?

"You would dare make an attempt on my gold?"

The voice bellowed, deep and guttural and, thankfully, familiar. Byzanthum cleared his throat but maintained as subservient a position as he could.

"Mother," he called. "Mother, I've come to visit you."

The intensity of the inferno raging around Byzanthum lessened. The heat stopped buffeting his back and wings and then the fire disappeared. The shocking blue of the sky suddenly visible again surprised Byzanthum. For a few interminable moments, the world had been made of fire unlike any he had seen.

"What are you doing here?"

Byzanthum's mother stood amid a pile of gold she'd been buried under. It was why her hoard looked so impressive, and why Byzanthum hadn't seen her. Smoke leaked out of her nostrils. She didn't approach him in the warm embrace of parenthood that he'd expected.

"I came to see you," he said. "I, well, I missed you."

Still, she didn't move. She looked at him, eyes glowing red and narrowed to slits. Finally, she huffed, as if accepting that yes, this was her son. "That is," she paused and coughed, "unusual. I haven't seen my own mother since I left the nest, eons ago. When a dragon sees another, it is typical to fly away. When you find a hoard, you leave it be unless you are prepared to fight for it."

"I didn't know," Byzanthum said. He felt numb. Scolded. "I guess there's a lot about being a dragon I don't know. I wish you'd told me more before making me leave."

His mother sighed, sending a frustrated billow smoke out over the mouth of the crater. "You should have known. No one needed to tell me."

Byzanthum hung his head in shame. He felt embarrassed by the horse and the people from his castle. And now he felt embarrassed in the one place he'd ever felt at home. He prepared himself to leave, lonely, and unanswered, but when he looked up his mother's steely gaze had softened.

"I suppose no one told me it had to be that way either. Come on. Tell me what's bothering you." She raised an enveloping wing and pulled Byzanthum to her flank.

He told her everything that had happened to him since leaving her side. She snorted with laughter at the dismembered knight who had charged so brazenly. But she was not impressed by his taking over of the castle, and the horse's handling of his affairs. When he told her about the deception, the roof, the knights and their lances, he felt the heat rising in her scales and saw coals shimmering at the base of the smoke pouring out of her angry nostrils.

"I didn't know where else to go," he said. "I just flew and flew and then I was back here."

His mother didn't say anything for a long while, and weariness started to take over. Byzanthum's wings were heavy, his body prickled all over from the knights' lances. He felt warm and safe and at home for the first time in a long time. His eyes drooped and then closed.

"You failed because you were not acting like a dragon. You were acting like a human." Byzanthum's eyes shot open. He didn't realize how much of an insult this was until he felt the revulsion burning through his limbs. He felt a little like when Bruta had laughed at him, and he recoiled. His mother continued. "You took possession of a castle and let others run it for you. Dragons are solitary by nature. By abdicating your control, you made yourself weak. You didn't build your treasure hoard by plunder and force; you accumulated it by tax."

"I had a good hoard started," Byzanthum protested. "I filled the square with coins."

"Gold coins?" his mother asked.

"Copper," he said. "But there were mounds and mounds of it." There was no harm in exaggerating a bit now. The coin would be long dispersed to the knights who had chased him away. He imagined Bruta got a shiny new leather saddle out of the deal, too.

"Did it feel anything like the gold here?"

Byzanthum looked around, felt the warm bask of the gold, the sharp scent of silver, and the giddy pleasure of jewels, and knew she was right.

"Did you take any gold at all?" she asked, quietly.

"A little," he said. He found he could remember each and every speck of gold, silver, and precious gem that had dotted the predominantly copper hoard. "And there's this." He pulled out the little golden ring, the first piece of treasure he'd ever taken. It was bent and scuffed, but he could feel its purity. It was all he had left of his years away. The only thing he had to show for all that time.

"You took this from the knight?" his mother asked. Byzanthum nodded. "Then it is more precious for you than any of the treasure here."

Byzanthum scoffed but found that she was right. He wouldn't have traded that ring for anything in his mother's crater.

"You took that in the right way. Let it be a lesson. Don't settle down and allow yourself to become complacent and reliant on other creatures. You are the King of whatever kingdom you set. If someone would take it from you, they will have to do so by force. Build your hoard of gold and defend it with your last burning ember. Now go."

She shifted, dislodging Byzanthum from his place against her side. The abruptness of her change stunned him. He sputtered. "Can't I stay here for just one night? I'm tired from the fight and the journey."

"No. It would be inappropriate. When I saw you flying here like a honing pigeon from miles away, I didn't recognize you as my son. I saw a dragon. A threat. You knew about my hoard and were coming to take it. I've suppressed that jealousy, but I won't be able to forever. You have to go."

Byzanthum wanted to protest but knew his mother was right. He dreamed of basking in the glow of the surrounding treasure and was more than a little drunk on the idea of stretching out on top of it and burying himself beneath it. He nodded his head, thanked his mother, and jumped into the sky.

Byzanthum's flight was long and uncomfortable. He crossed the volcanic ranges, sometimes flying through the night, sometimes sleeping on exposed, frigid mountaintops. He ate wild game when he could find it. More often, he went hungry. Occasionally, he saw dragon-sign. Caves set into the faces of inaccessible cliff faces that glowed with the promise of hidden gold, or the charred remains of small bands of knights. When he saw these, he changed direction and averted his eyes. He didn't want to raise the ire of an older, more accomplished dragon. Or to be tempted by their treasure.

Far over the mountains and into the foothills, Byzanthum found another castle. It was remote. An old keep with an open square, minimally inhabited. He circled the castle high and out of sight for days, looking for signs that another dragon lived nearby, and saw none.

When he attacked, he did so mercilessly. There weren't many armed men guarding the castle and the people who lived in the surrounding village didn't need another reason to leave the remote area. Those who escaped the fury of his inferno fled with little resistance, and Byzanthum never saw them again. But he didn't stop there. He burned the land around the castle until it was black, inhospitable, pumice. He tore the castle gates down so that the only entrance was from above. He clawed and burned his way into the keep, making a cave-like structure out of the castle where he could safely hoard his treasure away from the elements and the prying eyes of would-be thieves.

The outpost developed a reputation, but a different kind of reputation than Byzanthum's first home. It was inhospitable. A dangerous place that people warned each other about. Bands of knights didn't immediately come to try and displace the invading dragon. There were no stories from villagers at the market about how their lord had been brutally murdered by a dragon who they now found themselves working for. The few stories that existed were of ceaseless fire and bloody claws.

There were also no nearby villages to terrorize, no farmers who could complain of missing sheep or cattle. Byzanthum flew far and wide to find food. And farther still to plunder. He chose his quarry at random. He never attacked kingdoms that shared a border, so that stories of his attacks would take longer to fester. He waited years before attacking a castle again, sometimes leapfrogging the reign of a king so that the ruler might have forgotten that a dragon had ever stolen their gold.

Byzanthum's treasure hoard grew. Not with copper coins or worthless trinkets. Gold that glowed with the warmth of dragon fire and jewels that glittered almost as brightly as his scales filled his keep until he could bury his growing body beneath them. He slept for weeks at a time under that blanket of treasure.

There were those few foolhardy knights and heroes who decided they would test their mettle against the dragon of the hinterlands. It always took them a long time to find him. The outpost, once abandoned, was forgotten in less than a generation. The road leading to it scabbed over with weeds and the trickery of the mountain passes claimed the lives of more knights than even Byzanthum.

Byzanthum was surprised then to wake from a golden slumber to a familiar clip-clopping of hooves on rock. He felt his heart quicken with an old adolescent fear that was quickly overcome by rage. He lifted his now considerable heft, shook loose coins and jewels from his scales and wings, and emerged from the keep.

When Byzanthum looked down from the ramparts of the castle, he began to laugh. Not the squeaky, immature laugh of a young, horse-sized dragon, but the bellowing roar of a fearsome monster. His voice echoed in the canyons of the mountains nearby and set off an avalanche on the high slopes.

A small contingent of knights stood at the edge of the burned fields. Their horses refused to step from the desolate road onto the ruined earth surrounding the castle. The knights appeared to have been deliberating this development when Byzanthum started laughing. They were frozen in a little huddle and all of them were staring at him. Off to one side, unsaddled but covered in a rich, colorful blanket, was Bruta. She had a lot of grays in her mane that gave her a distinguished aura.

"Where's the trick?" Byzanthum said softly to himself. There were a few dozen knights, one with a great, jeweled sword that shone so brightly that it appeared to glow. The rest of them held lances. It was a pitiful band to try and kill an adult dragon, and Byzanthum wondered if Bruta really thought he would be as easy to deal with as the last time she'd betrayed him. But he waited patiently to see if another stone might turn over.

"What are you doing here?" Byzanthum roared. He appreciated the shock on the faces of the knights and began to think that they may have underestimated their prey.

The knight holding the impressive sword took a step forward. "We are the knights-"

"Yes, I can see you are knights. What are knights doing at the gates of my castle?"

"This is not your castle," the knight said.

"Is it not?" Byzanthum turned his long neck from side to side, pretending to search. "I don't see anyone else laying claim to it. Whose castle is it?"

"It belongs to the people of Hinteroden."

Byzanthum had no idea where the kingdom of Hinteroden was, but then the names of the kingdoms seemed to change with the seasons. He never bothered to try and keep up with human politics. The knight continued.

"Stories of your marauding have displeased our King. You will rue the day you hatched, lizard." The knight pointed the sword at Byzanthum and gave it several threatening swirls.

There had been a time in Byzanthum's life when this kind of jibe might have sent him into a rage. But he was older and better practiced. Also, the sword intrigued him. He could smell the gold, ruby, and sapphire encrusting the hilt. But even the blade appeared to be made up of some strange combination of rare metals.

"I can see you're admiring my blade," the knight said. He held it aloft and all of the knights paused to admire it. "It is the lost blade of Hinteroden. Forged of the-"

"It will make a nice addition to my hoard," Byzanthum said.

"It will make a mince of your-"

Byzanthum leapt from the rampart and into the air, cutting off whatever the knight was going to say. He'd seen and heard enough from the knights. They weren't moving into any tricky formation. There was no movement in the nearby mountains that might indicate another, larger, contingent of knights. There was just this pitiful band and the misguided horse who brought them to him.

Byzanthum soared high into the sunlight and then dove down with the sun at his back. The first dozen knights lifted their lances too late, and he dealt them a mortal gush of fire that made melted cairns of their armor. He flew away before the rest of the knights could react. The rest of the knights attempted to hide behind their fire-resistant shields, but Byzanthum flew down and landed amidst them. He struck out with his tail and ripped bodies apart with his claws. He even made a show of swallowing two less armored knights whole.

When Byzanthum looked up from his killing field he saw one knight left, the one with the sword. He was standing far away, staring blankly at Byzanthum, as if he couldn't comprehend the speed at which the dragon dispatched an entire contingent of knights. He realized Byzanthum was looking at him and he jerked his body. He stepped back and dropped the sword to the ground. He turned around and ran, but his horse had already fled. There was only Bruta left. She still stood off to the side and out of the action. She pawed her hoofs and tossed her head at the knight, but he jumped up onto her blanket. He grabbed her ears and kicked her haunches. She started to run.

Bruta made it all of ten paces before Byzanthum was upon her. He flew low, just behind her haunches and tickled her with little sparks of flame. The knight bent low over her neck and Byzanthum could smell the man's sweat stinking through his armor. He glided above them, silently, and waited. The knight turned back to look and just as he raised his head Byzanthum snapped down and snipped his head off. The knight's body bounced on Bruta's back and fell sideways. Its feet tangled in the blanket and wouldn't come loose. Byzanthum landed and after a few awkward strides Bruta came to a halt.

"I suppose that's the end of it then," Bruta said. She lifted her nose up and closed her eyes. "Go on. Get it over with."

Byzanthum considered the horse carefully. He'd dreamed about this moment. Tearing the horse limb from limb. He'd considered flying south and searching out his old home to see if she was still there but ignored the impulse. He thought her long dead, anyway. There couldn't be many horses as old as Bruta must have been.

"Why did you come here?" he asked.

Bruta's neck dropped, her eyes opened, and then she bowed her head to the ground. "To maintain my independence. It was stupid, I know. There was no chance you'd still be the stingy little whelp you were the last I saw you, but they wouldn't listen to me."

"Independence? What do you mean?"

"After I orchestrated your removal from the tower, I became a celebrity. They fed me at inns, stableboys brushed me whenever I asked, and no one ever rode me again. I never had to deal with spurs in my haunches or a bit between my teeth. But humans have a short memory. It wasn't long before someone tried to saddle and break me. So, I sought out other dragons."

"You hunted dragons?"

"Sought them out," Bruta said. She tossed her head and snorted. "I suppose it was hunting them. Young dragons, like you were. Dragons who didn't know their place in the world who were pestering kingdoms. With the information I had after the encounter with you, it was easy to organize forces to expel them, or sometimes trick them, like I did to you.

"But there were only so many young dragons encroaching on the land of humans. Before long, I had to sell my services to bands of knights and heroes trying to make a name for themselves. They traveled out into the hinterlands, seeking treasure and glory. The dragons they fought were…formidable. They were rarely successful."

Byzanthum snorted a quick spout of flame at the idea of a band of knights attacking his mother's crater. A whole army wouldn't have stood a chance.

"But you always got away," he said.

"Like I said, humans have a short memory. I didn't. I remembered how easy it was for you to dispatch entire bands of knights that were ill-prepared when you were a whelp. It stood to reason that an adult dragon would be unapproachable, so as they approached armed with all the knowledge I had, I kept my distance."

"What was different this time?" Byzanthum sneered. "Why get so close and take the risk?"

"I recognized you."

"You thought I'd make an easy target?" Byzanthum saw red. He felt heat rising in his gullet and knew he'd need to expel it soon, either at the horse or in the air. He wasn't sure yet whether a quick inferno was a suitable death for Bruta.

"I couldn't believe it was you," Bruta said. She lowered her head and shook it. "I'm an old horse, Byzanthum. I don't have many years left. When I found my way to Hinteroden, I thought my dragon hunting years were over. I thought I wouldn't have to keep proving myself, but they were talking about putting me in front of a plow, or having children learn to ride on me. I couldn't stand the thought of little children pulling my mane, poking my eyes, and forgetting to brush me down. Pulling a plow would have killed me. Sharing my knowledge and leading those expeditions was the only way to avoid the whip and saddle. I'd rather die than submit again."

Byzanthum's fire died down. He couldn't imagine being under someone else's thumb. During his time as lord of the tower, he never felt completely autonomous, and understood how Bruta could have felt that way, too.

"How did you find me?" he asked. His voice was lower. Still imposing but not threatening to spit fire just yet.

"Chance," Bruta said. She laughed. "There were a few stories about a dragon plundering castles and keeps in this country, but they never struck the same place twice. And the stories were never the same. Sometimes the dragon was as big as a house, sometimes so big their bulk blotted out the sky. I figured some of that was embellishment, but they were all the same in one respect. The dragon had emerald scales. I heard that and I wondered, but I didn't believe I'd ever actually see you again.

"After we wasted months tracking news of dragon sightings and never seeing you once, the knights wanted to come out here, beyond the edge of civilization, to try and find your home. I was hesitant, but they persisted. After my old incursions into the Hinterlands, I had an idea of the type of terrain your kind likes to nest in. And when one of the old knights remembered a story about an old hunting lodge with a tower, well, it seemed to be a good place to look."

Byzanthum narrowed his eyes. "You are shrewder than any human I've encountered. Most of the knights that find me here are just lucky. They would have done well to have listened to you better and left me alone in the first place."

"Obviously." Bruta tossed her head at the corpses littering the ground behind Byzanthum. He looked at them blankly, and then laughed. He laughed so hard he shot happy fire into the sky. When he finally got control of himself again, Bruta was staring at him. She almost looked bored. "Let's get it over with," she said.

Byzanthum waited until he saw a little quivering uncertainty enter Bruta's eyes before answering. He didn't want to kill the horse anymore.

"There's an old barn on the side of castle, here. It's empty and drafty. There aren't any stableboys to brush you down. And the only food you'll find is in an overgrown meadow, a few miles away. It's yours, if you want it."

"I'll be no one's beast of burden, human or otherwise," Bruta said. "I'm old and nearly broken, but I have too much pride for that. If you want some kind of arrangement where I run your castle for you, you better just kill me now, because I'll always be looking for a way to do you in."

Byzanthum chuckled. "I wouldn't expect anything from you, even your company. If you choose to leave, leave. If you choose to stay, stay. I'm offering you a place to live out your life unencumbered. It won't be comfortable, but you won't answer to anyone."

Bruta looked about to speak but Byzanthum cut her off. "I will warn you though. If you choose to leave and you lead another army back to vanquish me, I will kill them all and your death will be unspeakably painful. If you choose to stay, I will be watching you. I won't ask anything of you, just know that I don't trust you. Those are my terms."

Bruta considered, snorted, looked up and nodded her head. She gestured at the bodies of the knights around him. "I suppose I should help you clean up this mess."

Byzanthum blew a plume of smoke. "I'm quite capable of handling this. I won't have to hunt for weeks. Go get yourself settled and see if the barn agrees with you."

Bruta trotted away like she made deals with dragons every day. Byzanthum shook his head in disbelief. She was already acting like she was doing him a favor by staying.

Bruta lived at the castle for another six years before she died of old age. By the end, her whole coat turned snow-colored gray and Byzanthum pondered often how old she was, though he never asked. They didn't speak much to each other in those years. Bruta trotted off to the meadow every morning and back every evening. When she died, Byzanthum couldn't bring himself to eat her. He built a pyre and burned her corpse and found that a tightly wound muscle in his back finally relaxed. He'd expected some form of treachery the entire time she lived with him. But he was wrong. She just wanted to live out her golden years without a bit in her mouth.

About Parker McIntosh

Parker McIntosh's work has appeared or is forthcoming with Penumbric Speculative Fiction Magazine, The Toronto Journal, The Flexible Persona, among other publications. He lives in Southern Oregon with his wife and small dog, and when not writing works in financial services.

The Fellowship of the Unlikely

By Kenneth E. Givens II

The University of Promise has a missing professor, a dragonborn who went on a research trip to find dragons. Now, they have tasked their leading research student to assemble a team of adventurers to brave the wild and bring him back. The unlikely fellowship is formed over an ale at a tavern of ill-repute, and from that point on the group follows a treacherous trail through the countryside with evil lurking at every turn. A conniving thief who has no shame, an all-too-serious mercenary who prefers to talk with his blade, an old mage with little wisdom and even less magic, and a coddled researcher who has never ventured beyond the University gates all set out with different goals in mind but the same wild curiosity urging them forward: are dragons real?

The Fellowship of the Unlikely

By Kenneth E. Givens II

"Welcome to the Earlisque Tavern. We have ale, watered wine, or flavored and unflavored sugar spirits." The barkeep asked in Azhuran as he threw a towel over his shoulder.

"Umm, I will take watered wine, please." Viktor stammered out as he wiped sweat from his brow. He had never been to a bar before, and he hoped he would never go to another in the future, at least not one as dirty and dimly lit as this one. Or, as loud.

"Grab a table and I will bring it over in a minute. You want food? We have minced pie."

"Minced meat pie?"

"Minced pie. Take it or leave it."

"I will leave it."

"Suit yourself." The barkeep finished as he turned away to presumably find a glass for his watered wine.

Viktor turned from the bar and surveyed the room. There were men and women of every race, clothed for every occasion. Well, almost every occasion. He did not see anyone else dressed like him, starched wool pants, tucked in silk shirt, and a striped jacket. As a researcher from the great University of Promise in Northos, at the fork in the river near the city of Whitewater, he was sheltered from the world around him. That was the case no more.

He meandered over to a booth in the corner, slightly partitioned off from the rest of the bar by a huge stuffed bear that was posed on two feet, wedged between the second level's floor joists. He had clear sight on the front door, while also remaining inconspicuous, or so he thought.

"There ye are. The watered wine is two scratch but I can give you a deal on the room for the night and round it up to a fifth in total."

"A fifth? A room in town doesn't go for half that, with watered wine usually going at two for a scratch, not vice versa. I know I do not look as rough and tumble as your usual crowd, but I am well versed in the economics around Northos. I could share with all these patrons that you're gouging them for more than what they are getting."

"Easy, easy. I will give you the watered wine for a scratch, not two for one. But I will concede on the room and offer it to you at the going rate of four scratch. Fair?"

"Fair." Viktor rooted around in his bag and pulled out a large coin purse. Several heads turned at the sound of jingling coins, but Viktor did not notice. He pulled out six scratch and deposited them in the hand of the barkeep. "Keep the change. Please check on me every so often as I have a group who shall be joining me soon." He pulled out his pocket watch, glimmering gold even in the dimly lit bar, drawing more eyes from the onlookers.

"Aye, sir." The barkeep leaned in to add, "You may want to be careful flashing such a large purse in a place such as this. The gold trinket too. I don't want no trouble, but you may be asking for an unwanted visitor or two if you understand my meaning." He finished while nodding around the room at the prying eyes.

"Aye." Viktor said as he audibly gulped. The room was filled with soldiers, mercenaries, farmers, and a lot of other tough, weathered, hardworking individuals who most likely never saw half so much in their lifetimes as Viktor had in his purse. He hoped his group arrived soon, as he sat in the booth fidgeting with his striped jacket, matching the fashion in Whitewater but standing out in the packed bar.

The door opened and a man strode in, standing two or three heads taller than any man in the room, with shoulders as broad as an ox. He wore a dark green jacket that ran to his polished steel shin guards, with a cowl that he now pulled down to his shoulders, revealing a tan face covered in runic tattoos, a scar from his left ear to the top of his lip, blonde hair pulled back in to a ponytail with the sides of his head shaved, and a goatee that ended with two braids near the center of his chest. He scanned the room until his eyes fell on Viktor, and then he walked the short distance over to the booth without breaking eye contact.

"You Viktor from Whitestone?" He said in a deep, raspy voice that reminded Viktor of the sound you got by rubbing two stones together. He spoke Northosian but the accent was very thick and if Viktor was not a native of Northos, he was unsure if he would even be able to understand.

"Aye, and you must be Drag from Northos?" The man grunted his agreement, removed his jacket uncovering more of his steel armor, positioned his sheathed sword with his hand on the pommel, and sat in the booth opposite of Viktor. "What part of Northos?"

"Between the Beyond and the Sea of Death. We don't have towns like you rich folk."

"Oh, I am far from rich."

"You are offering me more than my entire clan made from raids last summer to join whatever this is."

"Viktor?" A woman had snuck up on them both and now peered out from behind the bear. She spoke Azhuran which seemed to thoroughly confuse the large Northosian, as he stared angrily between the two of them as if they were making a jape at his expense. Black stubble covered her head where hair should have flowed freely, and she had metal rings dangling from her nose, two more from her lips, which themselves were painted black in contrast to her pale-as-snow skin. She wore a leather jerkin, but looked to have no undershirt, and some colorfully striped pantaloons.

"Yes, and you must be Mae Raven."

"Yes, but I go by Grin." She smiled, showing off two gold incisors that seemed to be enlarged as if to look like a vampire. Viktor had no clue as to why someone would want to look the part of a vampire for fear of being beheaded, but to each their own he always said.

"Grin it is. This is Drag, but he only speaks Northosian." At the mention of his name, he pounded fists into the table. "I was only telling her that you speak Northosian. Her name is Grin." Viktor noted in Northosian to which the big man nodded but looked no less pissed about the language barrier.

"I speak Northosian but not good." She added slowly as if she had to think of each word. Viktor was thankful that she spoke Northosian because the final addition to their party would also be able to speak as a native. "So, what have I missed?"

"Nothing. We are waiting for the full party to arrive before we discuss business." Viktor said as he waved the barkeep over. "We have one more person coming."

The door opened again, and an average looking man stumbled in, wearing a leather cuirass with matching vambraces, and leather boots. He did not have a cloak, but he did not seem wet from the rain outside. He walked with a limp and used a white staff as a walking stick, but he still had the audacity to wear a bastard sword at his hip. He fit the description of Mort, who was the last to join the group.

"What would you two like to drink? We have ale, watered wine, or flavored and unflavored sugar spirits." The barkeep asked and Viktor relayed to Drag.

"I will have flavored sugar spirits." Grin ordered, living up to her nickname as she smiled at the Barkeep.

"He will have ale and I will have another watered wine, please. And here is our final guest." He added as Mort slid into the booth as if he already intimately knew each of the unlikely trio.

"I will have a water, with lemon, good sir." Mort uttered without a glance at the barkeep.

"Is all of this going on your tab?" He indicated to Viktor who curtly nodded.

"Mort?" Viktor asked.

"Who else would I be?" Mort responded in Northosian, and though Viktor wanted to laugh, the seriousness on Mort's face made him think he shouldn't.

"Well, now that we are all here in Earlisque, I wanted to thank you all for responding to my summons. I have been tasked by the University of Promise in Northos to travel into the Darker Realms to find two things: my former professor, Dr. Sharkub, and the thing she went searching for, a dragon."

"Dragons don't exist." Grin noted as she crossed her arms in frustration. "I traveled here all the way from the Aurum Empire and had to take three different ships. That cost me nearly half a crown. All because you promised reimbursement, and a full crown upon arrival. Then, five more crowns upon completion of the contract, plus reimbursement for our return journey. And now, you tell us we hunt the impossible. Dragons went extinct forever ago, if they ever existed to begin with, and how do you complete a contract based on a fib of a target?"

Drag looked frustrated but said nothing. Mort looked like he was not even paying attention to the conversation at hand, picking dirt from under his well-manicured fingernails.

"Yes, yes. I have your crowns here and will pay you for the trip, but I need you all for the contract. Honestly, I hoped for more respondents but received none. Fate is a fickle thing, and it has thrust us together for this task." Viktor slid them each a crown and a silver, equal to half a crown, as promised. Drag and Grin bit their coins to confirm they were real before depositing them into hidden purses. Mort left his on the table without a care in the world.

"You really should not flash that much money in here." Grin noted as she cast wearisome eyes around the room.

"Yes, the barkeep offered the same advice." Viktor pulled out another four scratch to hand to the barkeep. "Speaking of the barkeep, here he is."

"An ale, a flavored sugar spirit, and a water with lemon."

"Here you go. I would also like another room, but this should cover most of it. I will give you another four scratch in the morning as long as we are left alone for the evening." The barkeep nodded and smiled this time when he pocketed the coins before heading back to the bar.

"So, we venture into the great unknown, to find dragons and a lost traveler? When do we leave?" Mort spoke matter-of-factly.

"On the morrow. Here are your contracts, signed by the University and backed by the Aurum Bank in case I do not make it back but any of you do. Please note that my safe return comes with twice the profit, so it would be short-sighted to kill me and trek back to the University to claim your prize."

"It seems we have two rooms for the night, but I recommend one of us stays with you, Viktor, after you waved all those coins around for everyone to see. I don't doubt someone will attempt to separate you from that purse." Grin said, voice low as she looked around the room. "There are a lot of killers in this room. Good thing we have this broad hunk of meat." She indicated towards Drag as she spoke. He grunted and drained his ale.

"Let's go." He muttered.

The barkeep led them past staring eyes, up the stairs, to the rooms at the end of the hall on the top floor. Grin got the smaller of the two rooms to herself, and the odd trio took the larger room that came with two beds and a hastily made floor bed of potato sacks, some loose straw, and a few lumpy pillows, stained through with who knew what. It smelled of cat piss and the air was thick. Without asking, the large Northosian took to the floor after Mort aided him in removing his armor, no words exchanged. Viktor took his jacket off and lay in one of the beds, closed his eyes, and nearly fell asleep before rustling at the door made him sit up. Mort was carving something in the wood by the door. The Northosian warrior looked on in curiosity as well but said nothing.

"What are you doing, Mort?"

"Protecting us all. A small runic spell to prevent unwanted guests from crossing the threshold, unless we break the spell first." As he turned from the door, a glowing sigil was carved into the door beside the knob, another on the wall beside the door, an exact mirror to the first.

"A spell? You're a mage?"

"No, no, no." He said with his hands up in protest. "That wouldn't pay in this day and age. What, with mages being hunted to extinction and all. No, I am something else entirely. But all you need to know for the time being is that I can cast spells, but only using runes. I have tried spell casting through the Source but it rarely works to my benefit and seems to have a dark mind of its own. You can see my irises are still black as night, no blue or green or red, all tell-tale signs of mages." He shrugged before walking over and collapsing in the bed opposite Viktor. He was snoring before his head hit the pillow.

———————

A loud crash threw Viktor into motion without knowing where he was at, let alone what he was to do. He stared wild-eyed at the door, which was shattered, but it looked like it had shattered outwardly into the hall, as shards of wood were protruding from walls, the floor, and the face, arms, and chests of several screaming men. The hallway was alive with nearly half a dozen bar patrons, only three of which seemed injured, the others in shock of what had happened.

In their confusion, Drag was up, long dagger in his right hand and short dagger, reverse grip in his left. Mort grinned casually as he stood and drew a bastard sword from his bag. Viktor did not have anything but a small ceremonial knife that he was not sure would even hold up in a real fight. He drew the bronze blade anyways and cowered behind Drag, who charged into the fray.

The three injured foes were left to die their slow deaths. Drag swept the blades from side to side as he advanced on the uninjured three remaining foes. They snapped into it but Drag made quick work of the first. In the tight quarters of the hallway, the soldier's long sword was a severe disadvantage and in three quick maneuvers Drag had left him without a sword, or sword arm for that matter, as he tried to push his own guts back into his stomach cavity. The other two soldiers threw down their swords and ran for the stairs with Drag giving chase, but only so far as the top of the stairs.

Grin peaked out of her room, smiled, and shut the door again. She returned moments later with her pack of supplies. Mort calmly slit the throats of the three injured men to put them out of their misery as he put it to Viktor. The alarming part to Viktor was the calmness of the movements as if Mort was carrying out a predestined task that needed to be done but there was no rush since it was going to be done regardless.

"Ok, boss. Where to first?" Grin asked.

"We are leaving?"

"Of course we are. Did you not see those two run away? They will be back with more people, trust me. And we want to be long gone by then."

"Ok, well, I had a boat on retainer to take us upriver to a small city where

Dr. Sharkub was last seen. It is a quicker ride by horseback but less comfortable, and still nearly three weeks of riding."

"Well, a horse isn't going to ride itself. Come on." Mort added as he began descending the stairs.

Viktor was uncomfortable with the arrangement, so he left a hastily scrawled note with four pieces, one for each horse, and the total equivalent of forty scratch. It was more than the going rate for a horse, so he hoped this counted as a purchase and not thievery, though it felt a whole lot more like the latter. They were well into the start of their journey before the sun peaked above the horizon up ahead of them and well to the right. They were heading North, and they would not see anything but plains ahead of them and forests to the right for the first week at least, and then the landscape should change to hills and plains for the remainder of the trip, at least according to the University maps Viktor had brought with him for aid. There were not any documented settlements or cities between Earlisque and the city of Bleakshire.

They had provisions enough to keep them fed for the trip, if they rationed well, and they rode close enough to the river that water was not an issue. However, whenever they got close enough to the river to fetch water, Grin insisted on grabbing it for everyone to keep the group's horse tracks away from the water for fear of being followed by the group from Earlisque.

The saddle soreness became unbearable after two days of walking and trotting for Viktor. He had Mort help apply soothing cream from his stock of supplies, and though Mort took the event about as seriously as he took anything else, it was the most embarrassing moment in Viktor's short life. They rode from sunup to sundown with brief breaks to eat, refill water bottles, and piss or shit. The winds were calm during the day but were bad at night, even in the canvas tent that fit all four of the travelers. They took turns on watch throughout each night and only lit fires for lunch if they had caught something to eat. Grin was a terrific shot with a bow, and a pretty decent scout. Mort collected plants along the way for balms or poultices but outside of Grin talking about what she scouted, or a few words exchanged when switching for watch duty, nobody talked. Viktor had to note in his logbook that this had to be the most unlikely group of paid muscle anyone had ever assembled.

The plains opened after a week, just as the maps had indicated. Grin eased off her concerns after the first week ended with no run-ins with any living being, human or animal. This was especially important as no one had taken a bath since the journey began. Grin scouted out the area before they tied their horses to trees and began to disrobe. Viktor had to admit to himself that he had not thought twice about the fact that Grin was a woman amongst men, but she did not seem to care either. They all dipped butt naked into the icy water and used their hands to scrub off loose dirt. Though Viktor could not look at his own rear end, he could feel the bruises on the insides of this thighs and the back of his ass. No one else looked worse for wear.

A twig snapping off in the woods ended their childlike appreciation for the cold water. Grin ducked under the water and disappeared, while Drag attempted to sprint from the hip deep water, splashing about and creating the loudest commotion possible. Mort made no move, but Viktor took Drag's lead.

"Halt!" A scratchy, squeak of a voice declared in Azhuran.

Viktor turned to lock eyes with a robust Orc, with yellowing skin and a balding head, no weapons in hand, pointing his finger at Viktor and Drag, who was still splashing about.

"We don't want any trouble. We are just headed to Bleakshire."

"Bleakshire, eh? Well, you have to pay the toll to get to Bleakshire."

"The toll?"

"Yeah, nobody told you? These lands belong to me. And I say there is a toll, so there is a toll."

"And you are?"

"Azuk. Now, where is that woman that was with you?"

Viktor looked around. Mort was still standing where he was when the orc arrived, and Drag was now staring down two men, rather small by comparison, but they were armed. Grin was nowhere to be seen.

"I honestly don't know."

"Sevuk!" He shouted and one of the men eying Drag responded. "Go find the woman. Kill her if you must, but if you bring her back alive, you get a go at her second only to me."

"You said a toll, nothing more!" Viktor groaned.

"We never agreed to terms. Here is the deal. We get to keep your horses, your supplies, and the girl. In return, we let you keep your lives and your clothes."

"Whoa, whoa, whoa. That is not fair."

"Who said anything about fair."

"Well, there are three of us and three of you. What if I were to say we take our odds?"

"I would say there are a half dozen archers staring you and your group down now. But go ahead, make my day. If I kill you, we get to keep your clothes too."

"Fate is a fickle thing, and it has thrust us together." Viktor mumbled to no one in particular. "Go Drag!" He finished in Northosian, hoping the Orcs did not speak the language.

Drag grabbed hold of the business end of the blade in his face, pulling the orc off balance and into the water, putting his full weight onto the bandit's back and taking them both under. A few arrows peppered the water around them, one taking Viktor in the upper arm and one just nicking his forehead. Mort had barely moved, as if he knew the arrows were not going to hit him, but he marched towards the bandit leader, Azuk, not towards their weapons or clothes.

Drag came up finally and was brandishing a sword, taking off in the same direction as Mort, leaving the lifeless body to float on the surface of the water. Azuk surprised everyone when he retreated, and no more arrows came forth from the trees. Viktor made it to the weapons and horses in time to hear a loud shrill, and then utter silence. He drew his ornamental dagger for the second time, and put his back against a tree for cover, hoping he would yet again get away from a skirmish without having to fight.

After what seemed like hours but was more than likely only minutes, both Mort and Drag stumbled out of the water, unmarked, but carrying objects in both hands. They dropped what ended up totaling five heads on the ground, in addition to a supply bag from each shoulder. The heads were of two orcs, one of them looked similar enough to Azuk, and three humans. Viktor retched.

"They put up no fight. I kill them fast and easy while they ran." Drag spoke in choppy sentences.

"It looked like we got them all, but we should be moving along lest we want to draw unwanted attention or revengeful bandits."

"What about Grin?"

"She has been in the tree above you since I left the water on the opposite bank." Mort responded, as the young woman dropped from the branches above, laughing at the surprised look on Viktor's face.

"Sorry, Viktor. I did not want to give away our position." She punched him jokingly on the shoulder which made him wince. She had not noticed the arrow sticking out the front of his upper arm. "Oh, we need to take that out and clean the wound. Bandits are notorious for not cleaning their weapons which can easily lead to pale fever. Come here."

She pulled him away from the other two men who were already dressing as they distributed their haul from the bandits into bags strapped to each horse. He only now became fully aware that they were both still naked and he immediately put both of his hands in front of his crotch to block the majority of her view, and he diverted his eyes in an attempt to make her less uncomfortable with the situation.

"Oh, don't be bashful now. I saw that thing flopping around as you ran for your life to the cover of those trees."

He could not tell if he was blushing, nor did his olive complexion allow for the reddening of his cheeks to be as pronounced as her ghostly skin might, but he believed there was no way he had ever been as embarrassed in a moment as he was then and there. He almost returned to the horses, regardless of the arrow.

"Ok, I will stop making you uncomfortable. But it is truly fun, ya know." She said but once he looked her in the eye, she bit her lip and strummed her forefinger across her left nipple, laughing at his uncomfortable reaction. "Ok, ok. I promise to stop now."

He decidedly closed his eyes and refused to open them until she was done. She placed a stick in his mouth and told him to bite down. It may have been the only thing that prevented him from passing out as she pulled the arrow out of his arm. He spit the stick out and bent over to catch his breath, then she hit the wound with some sort of spirit she had found on the bandit leader. The burn was excruciating but far less so than what she did later that night when they were miles away at a new campsite. Before the sun dipped below the horizon, while Viktor helped Mort set up the tent, as much as he could help with one arm, Drag grabbed him around the shoulders and lifted him off the ground. Grin snuck up behind him and shoved the red-hot tip of a blade into the arrow wound. This time, he did pass out.

The rest of the week went back to silence amongst the group. The spirits kept the wound clean and Viktor did not succumb to the pale fever. They were able to hunt easily in the open plains, and they made good time by all accounts. When they could finally see the buildings of Bleakshire in the distance by use of the looking glass Viktor brought, they sat and discussed their plan.

"Viktor, tell us more about Dr. Sharkub." Grin asked first.

"He was a professor of history at the University. His favorite topic was dragons, but he also taught several subject courses including geography, cartography, ship building and sailing, as well as providing his leadership on the Azhuran dig site of Nymilaith, the only ever documented dragon."

"Nymilaith was supposedly dug up two hundred years ago." Grin said, clearly losing patience.

"Dr. Sharkub is a Dragonborn. He was born nearly three hundred years ago. Also, Nymilaith is real. His bones are on display at the University but only students and faculty are allowed to know about it. One of our best kept secrets."

"Wait, wait, wait. Dr. Sharkub is a Dragonborn? Aren't they extinct?" Grin asked again, Mort lounging lazily on a log, never one for conversation, and Drag was attempting to follow the conversation, but he seemed to have lost interest as well.

"Nearly extinct. I know of only four, including Dr. Sharkub." Viktor thumbed through his notebook as he spoke, but Grin sat back, flabbergasted by his response.

"So, your professor came all this way to Bleakshire. Why?"

"He read a text that said a Dragonborn living in Bleakshire had ventured off into the forest north of the city and never returned. He believed the Dragonborn metamorphose into a dragon and never returned to civilization. This happened only fifty or so years ago and several sightings of a dragon have been spread around since then, all pointing to this city as the jumping off point."

"What's your plan?"

"We go into the city, ask around about Dragonborn and dragon sightings in the last few weeks. We chase down any leads, and if all else fails, we head north. There is a lake there according to the map, and just across the lake is a small, abandoned castle built into the side of a mountain. According to the texts, there are caves near the castle and some large enough to house a dragon."

"What if we do not find anything there? Will we be paid and cut loose, or will we be forced to hunt endlessly for a figment of one's imagination?" She looked up and met his eyes. They seemed full of dashed hopes. "No offence." She added, but it did nothing to change the emotions written on his face.

"I ask for one morning in the city, an afternoon hike to the castle, and one full day of exploring. After that, I promise to cut you all loose."

"Well, what else would we do." Mort chimed in much the same way he had for the majority of the previous three weeks, late with little or nothing to add. But the man was almost always first on his horse and first moving in the direction of their next objective.

The city was smaller than it had looked in the looking glass. The buildings were more like sheds or lean-to's, made from leftover materials and even trash in a few instances. The people were not poor in the conventional sense as they had no monetary system and instead relied on the bartering system, but their way of life was well below the means of a peasant in all the cities Viktor had ever been. They also very rarely had guests, let alone four. They huddled around the group as they entered the city and they began trying to barter for the weapons, the food, and the water. Even when they were told no, they continued to pick at their packs and agitate the horses before finally, Drag drew his sword and shouted.

"I am Embelaweh, the leader of Bleakshire." A thin, pasty white man with a wispy white beard and the only hair on his head was a patch above each ear. His ribs were visible, and he had a way of talking where he whistled at the end of each word, and it seemed like each breath could very well be his last. "I welcome you all to our city. Where are you fine folks travelling from, and why are you here?"

"I am Viktor. These people are Drag, Grin, and Mort. We come all the way from Northos and the Aurum Empire in search of Dr. Sharkub. He was a Dragonborn visiting here not six months past. Have your seen a Dragonborn that recently?" Embelaweh looked around uncomfortably before locking eyes with Viktor.

"We know this man that you speak of, but we do not wish to have any part of it." The group began dispersing back to the hovels from which they came.

"Wait, what happened?" Viktor jumped off his horse and passed the reigns to Grin as he followed the starving man. "Please, tell me. Good or bad. That man was very close to me, and I just want to find him."

"Take the road north. It will end at the great lake. Cross the lake and enter the castle, but do not go unprepared. You will find your professor there, but I assure you, he is not the same man you knew." He turned and looked at the entire group before adding, "You have all been warned." He finished with a coughing fit before pushing Viktor's hand away and power walking away.

"There you have it. We will find Dr. Sharkub in the castle. Looks like we should head that way."

"What else would we do." Mart said as his horse trotted off to the north, coining the same phrase for what seemed like the fiftieth time in only a matter of weeks.

"Yeah, what else would we do." Viktor muttered as he pulled himself back onto his horse.

———————

The lake was somehow both smaller and bigger than expected. It was smaller based on where the mind wondered when someone called it a great lake but, in a sense, it was also larger when one had to think of ways to cross it with gear. The castle loomed on the other side, not twenty strides from the lake, but there were stains on the castle walls where the water line must have been at one time or another, making it a clearly defensible castle. It made Viktor consider why it was abandoned.

"I see no way across with our packs. They will weigh the horses down too much." Viktor shared with the group. Drag was sitting in the grass by the lake, as if he was on a picnic, and not on a paid expedition. Grin was fumbling through her packs for what she needed to take with her. Mort simply tied up his horse, grabbed his small sack, and began walking into the water. "Hey, Mort, wait." He took no heed to the command.

Viktor followed him, and as Viktor passed Drag, he stood and began stripping his armor. Grin removed all of her clothes, eyed Viktor and giggled, before she wrapped the clothes in her waterproof lamb stomach bag. She followed Viktor into the water, swimming closer to him than he preferred. Drag finally entered the water, holding his sheathed blade above the water to avoid it getting wet. Viktor did not know how deep the lake was but about halfway across, he could tell the temperature of the water was much cooler, indicating to him that the lake was fairly deep here.

Making it to the other side, somewhat out of breath, but altogether unscathed was the first bit of good luck the unlikely fellowship had thus far on the journey. Grin clothed herself but not before flaunting her body in front of Viktor by acting like she needed to stretch in that exact moment.

Viktor walked over to Mort and tried to get a read on what he thought they should do next.

"I think we should try calling out for Dr. Sharkub once we enter the castle. What do you think?" Viktor asked Mort.

"Well, what else would we do?" He answered with a question, which yet again did nothing to help Viktor make a decision. Viktor decided to just go with it, so he led them up the front doors, made of large oak boards and tied together with wrought iron, rusted with time, but not hundreds of years. They looked no older than the doors to the University which had been replaced when Viktor had first enrolled several years back, but not hundreds, let alone tens of years.

He pushed and doors opened into a large foyer only lit by the dying sunlight. Leaves were all over the floor, from years of seasonal cycles. There were no clear footprints so it would have been an absolute guess as to when the last person passed the threshold to the castle. Suits of armor, rusted and in some cases disintegrated, lined the walls of the circular foyer, carved stone stairs leading to the upper floors of the castle. Drag grabbed some metal torches from sconces on the wall and stuffed each with oil-soaked cloth for each person in the party, before lighting them in turn.

"Where would you like us to start?" Grin asked.

"Let's split up. Drag, you take the main floor. Grin, you take the second floor and work your way up. I will start at the top and work my way down. Mort, you take the basement." He locked eyes with each in order as he assigned tasks. They each nodded and walked away, towards their tasks.

The first floor reminded Drag of wastefulness. Nothing in the hall glorified weapons or war, not even the suits of armor. No respectable soldier would dress in steel so thick and bulky. It just makes you a slow target. There was a room with shattered glass cases that once held valuables, Drag assumed. Another room had floor to ceiling shelves packed tight with all varieties of colored books. The last large room had some sort of tools laying around, along with plenty of seating to one side of the room. It must have been used for physical sport, but which one, Drag did not know, nor did he care. Back to the foyer.

The second floor was just two large empty dining halls. Grin had wiped the cobwebs off of a few paintings, but she saw nothing of value that she could haul easily back to the Aurum Empire. She jogged up to the third floor and again fell short of finding something of value. Sitting areas with foot bowls, she could only guess what they were for, and terribly damaged furniture. The fourth floor showed a glimmer of hope, bedrooms. She searched under beds, in drawers, and tried to find every nook and cranny for long lost jewels, but to no avail. The fifth floor produced more bedrooms of the same quality as below.

Viktor was sweating and breathing hard by the time he reached the twelfth floor. There was one large circular room with arrow slits in every direction. He quickly began calling out for Dr. Sharkub but he had little hope of finding him up here, at least not alive. The stairs were so dusty that he left a clear trail, but there were no disturbances in the dust from any of the floors when he walked past them. The eleventh floor, tenth floor, ninth floor, and eighth floors all had rooms filled with cobwebs and dust. The architecture was phenomenal for how old the castle was but in general, with some cleaning it could have passed for a magnificent castle even by the current standards.

The cold air of the basement was inviting. It reminded Mort of death's cold embrace, both meaningful, and meaningless. The smell gave away the beast before Mort laid eyes on it, but then again, Mort knew the creature would be down here. Now, to find a way to help the group find the creature without telling them more than they should know. He meandered quietly back up to the foyer and sat down, waiting for Drag, Grin, and Viktor to finally arrive.

Drag showed up first, after scanning the first floor. He sat on a bench opposite Mort and pulled out his pipe. It took quite some time before Grin and Viktor showed up together, with the latter wiping his forehead free of sweat with his handkerchief.

"Any sign of anything out of place?" Viktor asked Drag and Mort.

"No, just a waste of a good castle." Drag responded.

"The dragon is in the basement." Mort responded monotonously.

"Why didn't you say so Mort?" Drag demanded, dropping the pipe while rising from the bench.

"I was waiting for the group. She is sleeping."

"She? How do you know it is a female?" Viktor asked, but his voice had dropped to a near whisper.

"I believe it is Dr. Sharkub. She was a female, no?"

"You believe it is Dr. Sharkub? Wait, what?" Viktor was rubbing his forehead as if that would cause everything to make sense. "Dr. Sharkub is not a dragon."

"She was a Dragonborn. We know they turn into dragons after a metamorphosis period."

"No, that is just a myth," Grin finally chimed in.

"Yes, just a myth. Even I know that," Drag added.

Without another word, Mort grabbed Viktor's arm and led him towards the stairs into the basement. Drag let Grin follow first so he could bring up the rear. Torchlight worked well enough but the total darkness surrounding them in the basement played tricks on the eyes. The steps led down to a large opening but without light in the space, it was impossible to see how large a room they had entered.

"Smells like piss." Drag whispered.

"That is clue number one. For clue number two, stop moving and just listen." Mort whispered from the front of the group.

Drag could hear the raspy breath of Viktor, but also something deeper. Not quite a snore but along the lines of a deep breath and a snore. It was a beast for sure, but a dragon, there was no telling.

"What do we do?" Grin asked.

"We need someone to sneak over to the dragon, and confirm it is a dragon. See how big it is, and whether it is something we could take on with our current group by torchlight." Viktor responded.

"I am not very sneaky." Drag responded almost a little too loudly, which Grin told him with the look on her face and the finger on her mouth. They were huddled up in a circle with the torchlight bright enough to see everyone's facial features.

"It sure as shit will not be me." Grin added, but as she looked around the group, everyone's faces prominently disagreed. "Why me?"

"You were selected as the sneak. When I sent you letters, you responded by saying you broke into the Aurum Bank just to prove you could do it."

"That was a bit of an exaggeration. I broke into a bank in Aurum, but not the Aurum Bank."

"Enough. I will go, but Viktor is coming with me." Mort grabbed Viktor again and yanked him calmly to follow while crouched. He took Viktor's torch and left his own with Drag.

"Fate is a fickle thing." Viktor said to himself, voice shaking in his own ears.

They moved slowly towards the breathing sound, the sound growing deeper and louder with every step. Every few steps, Viktor would look back over his shoulder to see how far back Drag and Grin were, until finally, they were dots in the distance.

Viktor stopped abruptly as Mort's hand landed on his chest. He leaned over and placed his finger across his lips to let Viktor know they were close and not to speak. Viktor was so nervous he held onto Mort's arm as they made their final approach. The torch light illuminated the stone wall in front of them, and even though it looked like white stone in lieu of the natural gray stone they had seen elsewhere in the castle, Viktor explained it away in his mind as being the basement, where the least amount of attention was paid to finishes. Mort looked back at him with his eyes no wider than usual, but the furrow in his brows was different. He was jabbing his finger in the direction from where they came and he began to walk back.

"Wait, we reached the far wall, but the animal has to be close, I can hear it." Viktor had grabbed Mort's arm again when he noticed something odd about the stone wall. It was moving.

"Run, you fool!"

The basement filled with a roar that echoed about, piercing Viktor's ears. He was running to keep up with the torch light in front of him, but Mort was pulling away from him and fast. The room was suddenly aglow with a blinding white light from behind him. In that moment, Viktor saw Grin and Drag waving them towards the stairs, Mort halfway between them and him, and as he shielded his eyes and looked over his shoulder, he saw a dragon. The flames were so hot he could feel them, even though the dragon was waving its head back and forth, and they were not aimed directly at him. Its wings were tucked up against its sides, out of the way of its four galloping short legs. Viktor ran as fast as his legs would take him, but he knew it was too late.

Mort reached the bottom of the stairs and pushed Grin and Drag to move up the stairs. They reached the landing just as flames filled the stairwell. Drag tackled Grin to the floor in the foyer and Mort dove beside them, rolling to put the flames on the edge of his cloak out. Both Drag and Grin had smoke coming from their armor but no flames.

"The dragon is too big to come up the stairs, but it has to be feeding somehow, so I am sure it has a way to exit the basement. We should not leave until morning." Mort commented calmly, as if he had not just almost burnt to a crisp.

"What about Viktor?" Grin asked.

"Viktor has undoubtedly perished. There is naught for us to do about that, unfortunately."

"At least we have our contracts. No one will believe we saw a dragon." Grin commented, as much to herself as the rest of the group.

"I will return with warriors. We will cage this beast and that will be more than this paper is worth." Drag responded, greed in his eyes.

Mort knew the truth of it though.

"Welcome to the Earlisque Tavern. We have ale, watered wine, or flavored and unflavored sugar spirits." The barkeep asked in Azhuran as he placed his hands on the bar and leaned in to hear.

"I hear the adventurers who found that dragon outside of Bleakshire passed through this very tavern?"

"I am trying to run a business here. Now, do you want something or not?"

"I want to hear about thee travelers." The man placed a crown on the bar and slid it across the barkeep who pocketed it quickly.

"Yea, they came through here nearly six months past. The researcher fella had a purse that could have bought this town. He was met with a large Northosian, a pole thin Azhuran, and some daft old man who didn't stand out really. Only the old man ever returned through here and truth be told, I didn't even see him return personally. My sister works down at the docks and said someone told her that he boarded a ship setting sail to the Aurum Empire. Apparently, he had a contract with the Aurum Bank through the University of Promise in Northos."

"What happened to the other three?"

"No one knows for sure. The stories I have heard say one of two things happened to that researcher kid. He was either killed by the group to get more money which don't make sense to me, or he was killed by the dragon, which I think is more likely. As for the other two, the Northosian paid about a dozen warriors from Bleakshire to try and kill the damned beast. The leader from Bleakshire confirms he sent most of their fighters, but none returned. The grass between the lake and the castle was scorched so they did not look around for bodies. And the girl, well, she disappeared. Some say she ran off with everyone's money. Some say she tried to get as far away from what she saw as she could. Me, well I think she did a little bit of both."

"Any more guides taking trips up towards Bleakshire these days?"

"Aye, just the one guide. She guarantees you see a dragon or your money back."

"Really?"

"Yeah, but beware. I haven't seen the first traveler return from her trips. Likely, she stabs them in the back and robs them as soon as they are out of sight from the city gates."

"I wouldn't say that." A woman chimed in, sitting just a few spots down. Her black cropped hair framed her face. And matched the paint she had on her lips. She had metal rings dangling from her nose and lips. A dark dragon tattoo on her pale upper arm snaked out from under her leather jerkin. "There are certain hazards that come with hunting a dragon." She smiled, showing off two gold incisors.

About Kenneth E. Givens II

Kenneth was born and raised in Grovetown, GA before he went on to major in Civil Engineering at Georgia Southern University. Upon graduation, he travelled the US, quickly making a name for himself as a Project Manager for heavy industrial and manufacturing construction projects. He travels less now and currently resides in Columbia, SC with his wife since 2017, Tabitha, and their cat, Arya of House Stark. Kenneth spends his time in the community serving on several non-profit boards, assisting his lifelong friend in running their own non-profit, serving as President of his neighborhood HOA, and playing in several adult sports leagues, too many if you were to ask his wife. Kenneth attempts to write daily but he is also a voracious reader and can oftentimes be found in his favorite room at home, the library, reading in his bean bag chair while enjoying a dram from his Scotch collection.

The Jotunni: The Zombie Dragon

By Nathan Pedde

Greyfell Julson, pilot of a fifteen-foot-tall Jotunni mecha, and mercenary with the airship Folkestone, hunts for monsters and bounties. Holding many titles, accomplishments, and accolades — none of which will save him if a madman reanimates the evil dragon, Lohikaarme-ajdaho.

The ruined temple complex of Drachen Hills stirs and rumbles with undead life. Necromancer and Count Parthalan Reis desires enough wealth and power to defeat his illegitimate brother, the Duke. His plan, raise an army of the dead with the great dragon's corpse as his mount.

The dragon has other plans, as the ancient beast ruled the world eons before. He will rule once more unless Greyfell can stop the mad Count before he completes his rite. The necromancer and madman must not awaken the ancient evil. He should leave it alone where it lies — if he had more brains than ambition.

Nathan Pedde

THE JOTUNNI: THE ZOMBIE DRAGON
By Nathan Pedde

"Dragon, Drachen, Ajagar, Ikiyoka, Dregana. Multiple names for the same mythical beast. Created from pure hate three thousand years ago, they are now extinct. The last mythical beast, Lohikaarme-ajdaho, lays buried at the Drachen Hills Temple Complex, where it rests under its mound. Proto humans used to worship it."

Neddy Bonnet, *Mythical Races of Medgaea.*

———————

Earl Greyfell Julson of House Iskold tossed and turned in his sleep. He was the third son of the Jarl Jule Asgeirson of Kaldai. Having left home at twenty-two, he was now thirty-six. He had no intention of heading home before he earned his fortune—which he spent it as fast as he earned it.

His dream was chaotic and haphazard, with him being chased by a large skull with a snout and reptilian teeth. He never remembered his dreams, except this was different. He couldn't comprehend the hidden meaning.

He ran down a long hallway with stone walls lining either side. He hunted for a place to hide, while the skull followed behind. Red flames burned from its eyes as its teeth chomped, chasing after. No matter what he did, the sheer white severed head chased him. It was like it match his speed.

"I should wake up."

He understood it was a dream, except it helped nothing. The skull was massive, and the primitive side of his brain told him it was real. He had seen nothing that could have a skull that size. It was large enough that if it were to open its mouth, he could stand at its teeth and his head wouldn't hit the top teeth. The word Drachen reverberated around the hills.

Greyfell discovered he stood at the top of a hill surrounded by a forest. The skull was nowhere to be found. It vanished because of being his dream. He scanned his surroundings, wondering what else his dream would bring.

Except nothing else came. He had never seen the hilltop before. Strange stone structures spread around him. They were eight obelisks standing at the base of the hill. He couldn't understand the pictograph writing, but the depiction of a winged beast predominated across each.

Greyfell jerked awake as the airship *Folkestone* bounced across the sky of Midgaea. The turbulence woke him from the nightmare, something which never happened. For over six years, he traveled throughout the known world. After the first month, he experienced no issues with the ship's pitch and roll. It differed from a sailing kind, which had a steady rhythm to its motion. An airship bounced along in a haphazard method.

Sweat dripped from his head, sticking his shirt to his chest and hair to his scalp. He stripped the damp clothing off him, letting it fall to the ground. Wearing nothing but a pair of shorts, Greyfell left the room. His long nose jutted out from his face. He wore his red hair in a single long braid with shaved sides. It was a style from his homeland back home in the far north.

Greyfell pulled on a pair of pants and a clean shirt. They weren't anything fancy, but he didn't need one. He had never enjoyed the trappings of luxury, like his many brothers did. Growing up, he'd rather wear linen or wool rather than silk.

With his boots tied, he grabbed a handle along the corridor as the *Folkestone* bounced and dipped. It was everything he could do to not flatten himself across the deck. The airship was custom refitted from an older cargo transport design. It used to transport heavy bulk cargo, though small in quantity. Like all airships, it used massive, crystal-infused Ran Setu stones to help keep it aloft. Now the craft had an expanded crew capacity with the ability to hold five jotunni suits. They only had one - his. Using the structures of the cargo hold, they built the *Folkestone* surrounding it. It resembled an odd bird of prey than anything.

Greyfell wandered through the empty corridors, past the crew quarters, to the mess hall. It was a tight room with tables and chairs filling every square foot. It had enough space for everyone to eat, but not for extra crew members.

A window led into the tiny kitchen or galley occupied by a lone crew member. Although the man had a name, he hadn't heard it in months because everyone called him Cookie. Ager Nino stood a head shorter than himself. The cook, from an unfamiliar desert nation, had darker skin than him. When asked, he'd never give him a straight answer. He'd whip his bald head with a rag and scowl at him.

"Is there grub yet?" Greyfell asked.

"What do you think, Utri?" Cookie replied, using a slang term in his own language.

"I think that you're a miracle worker."

Cookie handed him a small clay cup the size of his hand. "You look like shit. Here, take this. Leave me alone for a few hours."

Greyfell took the cup and glanced at it. The cold dark liquid spoke of a hot delicious past for the java. Now it was sadness in a cup.

"Thanks."

"And button your shirt up. Are you twelve?"

He left the mess hall, sipping at the dark liquid. It wasn't anything to be proud of, but he'd drink it. He had worse in the past.

Greyfell's dream still haunted him. It was like a shadow hovering over his head. He took another sip of his cold java, but it didn't help.

He stepped into the hangar and stopped. It was in a state of chaos, which wasn't surprising. They used most of the port side for general cargo, despite the hangar being refitted to hold five of the massive jotunni. Crates and skids lay piled along the walls and ceiling, which the crew had secured with straps. Along a nearby wall, with the hanger ramp on the opposite, hung Greyfell's jotunni, the *Talisman*. The crew disassembled it to repair the machine.

A jotunni was a fifteen-foot-tall bipedal armor where the pilot, or knight, operated it from inside its torso. Powered by massive apparatuses of thirty-two separate crystals, the suit ran on magic and runes. His machine resembled a knight of old, like the ones seen lining the halls of some king.

The torso hung on a hoist with heavy chains, keeping it in the air. The team removed every piece of armor from the superstructure below. They spread the pieces of armor across the deck of the hangar. The crew had removed its legs and laid them beside it. It looked like someone had peeled the skin from the machine, leaving the skeleton alone.

Two hammers, one a massive two-handed behemoth six feet long, and the other a smaller four-foot-long version, lay on the deck. His last weapon, a single-handed mace, lay close by. Regardless of the enemy they faced, artists depicted heroes of old carrying swords. In the real world, they used weapons capable of breaking through the turtle-shell-like armor of the jotunni. A heavy hammer could deliver a blow that could crush the plumed helmet and the fragile skull underneath, whereas the metal armor could turn a sword's edge.

Alfarinn Hellandson, second son of Earl Helland Baegisason of Lillebe and his cousin, stood before the disassembled suit. Alf surpassed Greyfell's height by a head, and he surpassed nearly everyone else. His cousin's shoulders were broader, with a small potbelly. Alf was also the artificer engineer whose job was to keep the jotunni in working order. He wore a long brown leather jacket with the tools lining the pockets. He kept his hair cropped short lest it were to get caught in gears and pulleys. Alf raised his hands above his head, chanting a few words in a low voice. On his arms were runic tattoos marking him as an artificer engineer.

Laying in the middle of the decking was the crystal apparatus. It was the power source for the jotunni and different versions of the device powered various other machines. Its heavy armored shell lay face down, showing the glass-encased innards. An apparatus comprised thirty-two different crystals with each encased in separate glass enclosures. Each either attracted or repelled each, giving a push-pull which generated the magical energy. It was large enough to cover the *Talisman's* entire back like a knapsack.

Greyfell wandered to the device, mesmerized by the crystals.

"Don't get any closer," Alf said. "Need I remind you of what happens if a single crystal touches another?"

"Yeah, yeah," Greyfell said. "That's childhood knowledge. I've only seen small crystals pop. Never something that big."

"It's massive. If that were to explode, it would turn the *Folkestone* into kindling. It could level small towns."

"Alright. I'll step away from the death device." Greyfell walked away from the device toward a small table in a corner, sipping at his java.

"You should be sleeping."

"Not happening tonight. It's hard right before a mission."

"Then be quiet. Now that we have fixed this steel death trap, we need to put it back together. Or else you're fighting without it."

Greyfell glanced at a ladder leading to the access point into the upper deck of the *Folkestone*. He climbed it and opened the hatch. Wind ripped at his face and clothes, trying to rip them from him or him off the ship. The top of the airship stretched flat with two sails forward of the three propellers along the aft.

Glancing at the night sky, he was disappointed by the lack of stars. Not that there was cloud cover to hamper his view. The planet Hesiod was in his way. Midgaea, the planetoid Greyfell dwelled on, orbited the gas giant. Both orbited the star, the ancients named Aether. The oranges, browns, and yellows refracted light from the star brightening up the night sky. It wasn't anything like having the sun blasting the darkness away, but it helped.

Greyfell stepped from the ladder back into the hangar. He turned from the rungs to find Alf standing in his way. A scowl lay plastered across his face.

"What?" Greyfell asked.

"What are we doing?" Alf asked.

"Working as mercenaries."

"No shit, you vain, rump-fed lout. But why are we still out here? Isn't it time to go home?"

"Do you have enough money?"

"Several times over."

Gordics like Greyfell and Alf left home for a coming-of-age ritual. Back in the ancient past, his ancestors would venture out on their longship to accumulate enough wealth to start their lives. Greyfell's father made him Earl of Haumdal — an empty title — then sent him on his mission. He didn't announce the fact that he was an earl to the crew. They all thought he was one of them.

"Home sick?"

"Perhaps."

"Then go," Greyfell said. "Once this mission is complete, have the captain drop you at the next port of call."

"Do you have enough money?"

"Not anywhere close."

Alf rubbed at his forehead. "Stop spending it on booze and women."

"I'm not. But the moment I return, my brothers will send assassins. I need enough money to fend them off."

"So, you don't spend all your money at taverns and brothels?"

"Taverns, yes. Brothels, no."

"We'll talk once this mission is done," Alf said, leaving Greyfell to stand along in the hangar.

———————

Hours passed as Greyfell stared out at Hesiod before he headed back inside. He enjoyed the crisp night air with the silence that it brought. Except traveling meant the wind rocked by him as if he was in a storm.

Heading inside, he ended up standing at a desk in Captain Mikella's office. She sat on a massive chair covered in rich furs. In front of her was a small oak desk covered with parchments. Flags, paintings, and a piece of a tapestry covered the walls. These were loot gathered over decades.

Mikella was the daughter of a former merchant who gave her the crumbs of his wealth before creditors took the rest. She was as tall as Greyfell, with long black hair and a smaller face. She wore dark pants, a green silk shirt, with waistcoat and a floppy hat. Strapped to her waist was a cutlass. It was a plain but serviceable weapon with no fancy decoration.

They went over maps and rumors. She said the plan was solid, except he went over every scrap of information he had. It wasn't much. They talked to three farmers and a merchant.

"Who's the target?" Greyfell asked.

Mikella gave him a flat stare. "You and your questions."

"I'm the one in the jotunni fighting whatever. I want to know what challenges I'll face.

"You ask a lot of questions for a Gordic."

"Perhaps if Siaurians would ask questions, listen to the answers, maybe the empire wouldn't be in strife."

Mikella narrowed her eyes. It was an old argument they had for all the time they worked together. Historically, Gordics made their money by raiding the Great Siaurian Empire or serving in its armies as mercenaries. It had created a rivalry between the two peoples.

"Parthalan Reis," Mikella replied.

"Who?"

"More like Count Parthalan Reis of the House Reis."

"Again. Never heard of him."

"He's the Count of Transylvan, vassal of Duke Bartholemy Reis of Carphta." Mikella made it sound like the fancy titles should mean something to him - it didn't.

"We're in the Great Siaurian Empire," Greyfell replied. "There's a few dozen dukes, and hundreds of counts. All of which are murdering, and inheriting titles like a gambler plays dice. I don't know any of their names."

"Minor nobleman," Mikella said. "Word is that he's become a necromancer or warlock. His brother, Duke Bartholemy, is paying us to bring him back in chains."

"Right. What's the mission?"

"We've tracked him to Drachen Hills, where reports suggest he's trying to raise an undead army."

"Drachen? That name sounds familiar."

"Ancient temple complex built three thousand years before. It crumbled into ruins with a few villages around it by similar names. Then the Battle of Drachen, twenty years ago."

"No. That's not it. Anyways, we go in, club him then drag him back in chains. Why do we need the *Talisman?*"

"Want to fight undead with a sword?"

Greyfell rubbed at his nose. "Until a week ago, I didn't think the undead existed. They were stories to scare children and the gullible."

"I didn't either, yet here we are."

"Why aren't we getting normal jobs anymore?"

"It's better work than picking fights with cheating noblemen or stomping some peasant revolt."

She wasn't wrong. He'd take stomping on a skeleton over a fifteen-foot-tall metal monster any day.

Greyfell picked up a scrap of paper - a list of assets the Count owned at the time he went rogue. On it was a list of farms, its animals, to an inventory of its weapons.

"What's this here? Skullcrusher? Hunting dog?"

"Do you know anyone who names a pet that?"

"I would. Be a great big mastiff. Perhaps a poodle, which would be funny."

"It's a jotunni," Mikella said.

"Great. And I see there's three draug."

With a jotunni fifteen-feet tall and expensive, a suit of draug was much cheaper. It was a man-sized suit of armor powered using a miniature version of the crystal apparatus. They were as annoying as wasps. Easy to deal with in small numbers, but impossible once they swarmed.

"That's why you're going in the Talisman."

Greyfell moved the papers around, staring at a map with the name Drachen on it. "I heard the old temple was a dragon cult. They worship its tomb and prophesied the rebirth of their reptilian god."

"Hence the name, Drachen."

"Think there's any dragon corpses in them hills?"

"Will three thousand years leave its bones intact? That's how long ago someone sighted the last dragon?"

Greyfell nodded, as she had a point. Most bodies decomposed in a few dozen years, let alone three thousand. Crushing skeletons into dust would be hard enough.

"We'll put you in five miles from the old temple mounds," Mikella said. "You'll walk from there."

"Why not right in the complex?"

"With our luck, if he's learning the dark arts, then he may have some way to threaten the *Folkestone*. I won't risk the ship."

"Understood."

"We'll be three minutes away if we're needed."

Greyfell rubbed at the bridge of his nose as a headache started to build and fester.

———————————

Greyfell hung in *Talisman's* harness with its straps and cables connecting him to the machine. When he had first donned the suit all those years ago, it felt claustrophobic. As if he climbed into his own coffin. Considering he had to pull the corpse of the previous pilot out, it was fitting.

It became a second home - spending time with an old friend. It was the same when he fought with the Iron Wolves back home. His armor back then was the same. It was as if he had amputated a limb when he left.

"You ready?" Mikella asked.

Her words echoed, hollow through a set of three crystals attached to the suit by his ear. They were the tubeless-phone. In the *Folkestone*, the captain sent messages across the ship by talking through a complex set of brass tubes. This allowed her orders to pass to the various departments. This wasn't possible in a walking jotunni. An artificer engineer installed a tubeless version to allow communication.

"As good as I'll ever be," Greyfell said, maneuvering the *Talisman*.

With his visor open, he walked across the deck toward the ramp with Alf directing him. The massive machine and tight hanger could fatally harm an unaware crew member with a misstep.

Greyfell stepped to the ramp in its horizontal position. With the *Folkestone's* tail above the exit, it was as if he would exit from the crafts behind - a fact which humored him. He grabbed hold of a cable and slipped his foot through a stirrup. He hung a hundred feet above a clearing in the trees. Mikella desired to place him on the ground allowing him to walk out, except the clearing was too narrow for the airship. He needed to be connected with a cable. It was a simple process, which was complicated by the fact he was in a fifteen-foot-tall machine.

"Three minutes, *Talisman*," Mikella said.

"Aknowledged."

The dark canopy of pine trees flew close by underneath him. From his vantage point. It was like he flew by on his own, like a bird. Despite feeling like a bird's dropping, he stubbornly held on.

Then the *Folkestone* stopped and hovered. The captain's assessment of the clearing size was correct. The airship would need five more feet in every direction to fit.

Behind Greyfell, Alf stood at the edge of the ramp, waving his arms. It was the signal to hold on. The ramp dropped and Greyfell dangled by the cable. It was all he could do to keep hold. Then he descended into the clearing below.

Despite all his years, he still hated two parts of being a jotunni knight. Waiting for a battle to start and walking into the darkness of a trap. This was the latter. Greyfell expected that he'd find a horde of zombies waiting for him, it the shadows of the trees.

Greyfell reached the bottom of the clearing and the *Talisman's* right boot hit the earth. He found nothing but trees and shadows. He removed the stirrup and released the cable. Two stiff tugs and the steel line lifted into the air.

"You're clear *Talisman*," Mikella said. "Good hunting."

"Roger that, *Folkestone*," Greyfell replied.

The airship ascended and disappeared. They would be close, not straying far. If he needed help, or an extraction, they'd be three minutes away. Three minutes felt like ages during the fight.

Greyfell glanced around him. The light being bounced from Hesiod shot dark shadows across the pine forest. Like most forests throughout the empire, a coniferous old growth forest covered the area. The old temple and the unpleasant history kept people from settling the area, leaving the forest choked with underbrush and dead fall. No forester had visited in twenty years, and it showed.

Opening a hatch by the *Talisman's* hip, light blasted out from a lantern. It wasn't something a part of his machine, but an attachment they used when necessary. Unlike other lights, it wasn't fueled by oil, but rather by crystals and glass lenses.

Why must I go in at night?" Greyfell asked, not expecting a response.

"We are here, as is the enemy. What happens if we don't take action against this necromancer? The longer we wait, the stronger he'll become."

Greyfell grumbled under his breath. She was right. If he was raising an army of the undead, then he needed to stop him sooner than later. Waiting would mean he'd have to stop more zombies.

He marched along a pathway, narrow and winding around massive pine trunks. Foliage hung close enough that the pine needles brushed against his shoulders. His hip light causes more harm than good as it cast strong shadows amongst the trees. It allowed him to see the trail that his massive machine marched up. More than once, he could step around a fallen log or dead growth.

Then he stepped around a tree and stopped. The forest ended, and the temple stretched ahead of him. It was like something kept the pine forest to encroach on the ancient site. He refused to consider the possibilities. It wasn't like he believed it.

"Why didn't you drop me here?" Greyfell asked.

As if to answer his question, a dozen zombies appeared from the darkness. Each one carried a hand weapon like a mace or a sword. Three, which held behind the others, wielded massive bows as long as he was. A tiny red crystal the size of a thumb lay embedded in the forehead of each zombie.

"Nevermind, *Folkestone.*"

Greyfell stepped forward, pulling his massive two-handed hammer from its holster. Gripping the shaft, he prepared for a fight by closing his visor. This act enclosed him further, closing off his field of vision - as if he watched battles from the inside of a tin can like he did as a child. Unlike the helmets of the standard knight with a single eye-slit, the visor of the *Talisman* lay covered with them. His face lay from the helmet, narrowing his vision further. Multiple slits gave him the largest field of vision while still having some sort of protection.

The three archer zombies shot at him, the arrows bouncing from this thick armor with clangs. Their aim was excellent, but inefficient. The arrows wouldn't do anything unless they jabbed inside his visor. Another shot clanked against the top of his helmet.

He stepped toward the zombies as they ran at them. Unlike most enemies he faced, who'd scream as they charged, these moved in silence. For most, screaming built courage to face death. For these undead, it was as if death had removed that requirement.

Using his hammer like a club, he struck at the first. The business end smashed bone and rotten flesh, sending the remains to tumble amongst the tall grass. He smashed the head of a second before another volley of arrows bounced across his helmet. The third hit the slat of his visor before bouncing away. Another inch higher or lower and he'd have met his end.

At least it will be in battle.

Greyfell charged across the field, bowling zombies over. He ignored most, while aiming at the archer zombies. They were the ones with the highest threat. Three more arrows flew at him. Two missed, but the third hit his visor's side.

Another inch.

He swung his hammer in three swift blows. He dropped one, then two, and finally the third. It was like he was in a training exercise rather than actual combat. The zombie archers lay scattered across the field, their rotting bodies lay in heaps and pieces.

He glanced behind him, and the temple complex stretched up a nearby hill.

"Well, shit," Greyfell said. "*Folkestone.* I think this is a bust."

Greyfell stared across the field at the temple complex. Dozens of zombies stretch up a hill toward the center and its mound. The ancients built the entire structure around a single massive hill which resembled a pimple threatening to pop. It resembled something man-made rather than a natural structure.

Old stones lay piled in rows, making up the foundations of ancient structures. They collapsed millennia before, with pieces being carted off by peasants throughout the years. A single street, with semi-covered paving stones and massive obelisks, lead toward the mount. Three more rows of tall stones formed rings on the hillside, with flat sections resembling roads. The top row of stones lay at the very top with a red glow emitting from its summit.

"Explain, *Talisman*," Mikella replied.

Greyfell explained what he saw. "I'll need help."

"Negative. No jotunni or draug in sight. Give it a try, and we'll be here if you need assistance. You'll be fine. It'll be fun."

He grumbled under his breath, glancing behind him. A crunch of a boot on gravel announced a zombie got close. He turned, swinging his weapon. The heavy hammer smashed into the torso, sending it to tumble into the tall grass. Two more stood behind the first. Greyfell stomped at the next, sending the corpse's body parts to the ground. He grabbed the skull of the last zombie with his massive hand. He squeezed and bones exploded into small chunks. The body dropped like a sack of potatoes.

Greyfell grumbled under his breath, lifting his hammer. At the top of the hill, the red light intensified, glowing deeper. A chill rose from his back as he stepped forward.

He moved into the ruins as two zombies charged. Two swings later and both lay on the stone covered dirt. If the zombies attacked as a single mass, they'd force Greyfell to retreat. Except they came at him in twos and threes. He felt like he was chopping at wood rather than fighting a genuine threat.

Greyfell marched through the ruins, leaving the zombies scattered behind him. Except every time a group attacked, it delayed him further and the red light glowed deeper and redder. He felt time slipping away.

"*Folkestone.* Tell me what's going on."

"We can't get close to it," Mikella replied. "Crosswinds have forced us away from the site. No way to get close."

"Crosswinds? It's a calm day."

"I don't think this is natural. It feels off and weird."

Greyfell grumbled once more. "So, I'm on my own?"

"I'm afraid so."

Anger flashed through his mind as he charged further upward. The zombies changed. At the flat of the temple, they carried maces and sword. Even if one got close, they weren't able to hurt him. These carried massive eighteen-foot-long pikes. Instead of attacking in twos and threes, they stood shoulder to shoulder in ranks. He counted six zombies wide and seven deep. The numbers frightened him.

The pike-wielders stepped forward at him in a slow march. The pikes formed a wall of steel points jabbing at his helmet with the closest few ranks jabbed at his helmet, forcing him to back up. He waved his hammer at the poles, trying to keep them away. His weapon wasn't long enough to reach the zombies.

"You stupid bastards," Greyfell yelled at the creatures.

Is this where I die?

Greyfell stepped back from the block of undead. Options drifted across his mind. The initial thought was to retreat and avoid them, but this would cause the monsters to pursue him. Option two involved charging and avoiding pikes to his face.

He chose the latter. He raised his weapon above his head. Greyfell charged toward the first sharpened ends. He swung his weapon at the poles, knocking them from the path of his visor. Four pikes jabbed at him, bouncing from the sides of his visor. He struck at the zombies, sending three toppling. He reversed the swing, taking out two more.

The beasts struck at his visor, a pike jamming into the slat. He grabbed the shaft and ripped it out. He shoved the butt end into the zombie and pushed. The creature toppled back from the front rank. Greyfell continued the charge, pushing deeper into the ranks of zombies. He swung his hammer in long, wide strokes. By being too close to the creatures, long weapons couldn't reach him. The ranks farther behind could hit him, except for the forest of pike poles. The chaos kept the sharp ends reach him.

Minutes drifted by as he knocked down more zombies. Then another pike slammed into his visor. Metal bent as the rusty, yet sharp, weapon came within inches of his face. He leaned his head back lest it were to cut him. He ripped the pike, snapping the shaft into splinters.

Greyfell glanced at his enemy while wheezing. From the over forty pike-wielding zombies, three stood carrying weapons. The rest laid strewn across the hill resembling a slaughter house rather than a battlefield. Chunks of limbs and body parts lay in piles and clusters. Every time his weapon hit a zombie, the corpse crumbled and scattered.

He charged at each surviving zombie. Three quick strikes and the last three zombies lay among its undead comrades.

Greyfell marched upward toward the summit. As he stepped, a wave of air — of wind — hit him. The blast pushed at him as if he walked into a hurricane. He marched upward, his foot half of what he could be making. He leaned into the wind to compensate. It was like someone was trying to push him down the hill. It lasted for a long moment before it ended. Greyfell almost fell forward as it ended.

He walked up the hill as three soldiers in draug stepped into view. One carried a thirty-foot-long pike with the other two shared a single rope. It was a standard tactic to take out a single, unprotected jotunni knight. The draug warrior with its pike planned to distract him, while two others would wrap his legs with the rope. If they could trip him up, then he'd be easy prey.

The pike-wielder jabbed his weapon at the gapping hole of his visor. The sharp end shot at his eyes. Greyfell knocked the pike away and stepped forward. He hoped to get close enough to drop the draug warrior. The two rope-weilder charged to either side of him with the rope taunt.

Greyfell jumped to his side attacking the closest roper. He swung his weapon, striking the man in the shoulder, who tumbled to the dirt with his armor dented. He raised his hammer once more and dropped it in the head. The helmet squished flat with blood, bones, and brains squishing from the cracks.

The pike shot at Greyfell's visor and jammed into the metal. It dented the side of the helmet inches from his eyes. He stumbled back from the man as the pike-wielder removed his weapon.

The second roper drop the cable and pulled a skinny, long blade. Not designed for chopping, but for stabbing into his visor.

Greyfell charged at the pikeman. He brought his two-handed hammer to the side, striking at the torso. The heavy weapon slammed into the draug's chest, sending him to tumble to the ground. He slid down the hill with its chest lay crushed like a stomped food can.

The last charged at Greyfell, with the draug jumping through the air. His foot landing on the *Talisman's* leg as he propelled himself and his skinny, long blade toward his face.

Greyfell grabbed the draug in the air as the blade swished near the visor. He tossed the armor-wearing soldier onto the side of the hill with a thud. With the dust settling into the dirt, Greyfell stomped into the man's helmet, squishing it flat.

He neared the top and the glowing red light of the summit.

Greyfell stepped up the hill, holding his hammer on the *Talisman's* shoulder. His arms hurt from exertion. The fight extended too long, and he needed to drill more. He was getting fat and lazy.

Almost as if on cue, a jotunni stepped in front of him. The machine stood a few feet shorter than his with longer arms — it would hit harder than the *Talisman* could. It resembled a massive version of a mythical dwarf with a beard included. It's flat, box-like helmet finished its look. Like Greyfell, he carried a two-handed weapon - a hammer with a narrow tapering point and a spike on the back end. It was designed to bust him from his armor.

Unlike fighting without the suits, he could taunt and insult his enemy. In a jotunni, it was near impossible to hear another unless you got within twenty feet of them. This was too close for comfort. With six-foot-long legs, it could cross that space in mere moments.

Having the high ground, the dwarven machine surged forward at Greyfell with the spike end facing him. If his faceless enemy could land a blow on his helmet, it would split his skull like a rotten melon.

Greyfell deflected the blow to send the weapon toward the ground. He side stepped and struck at the jotunni. His hammer met the shaft as the dwarf countered him. The fight stretched on as he felt himself losing ground. His opponent pushed him further down the hill, following the path he had taken. Greyfell landed a blow on the armor's flank, except it did minor damage beyond a dent. If he couldn't reach the knight himself, he'd have to damage the machine to stop him. This was easier said than done.

Nearing the hill's bottom, the dwarven jotunni remained relentless. It was like the enemy had an endless supply of energy that Greyfell didn't possess.

"Why are you doing this?" the dwarven jotunni knight yelled from his suit.

"Doing what? Stopping a mad man from diving into the dark arks? Because I'm getting paid."

"Fucking mercenary."

"Gordic. Never do any anything for free."

The dwarven jotunni knight yelled and charged. With twenty feet between them, there was little time to react. Then he saw his opening. The dwarven knight swung at Greyfell's helmet. He deflected the wild hay maker, forcing the weapon to land into the dirt. It sunk past its head into the soft dirt.

Greyfell stepped on the weapon's shaft with one foot and struck with his own hammer. The heavy weapon landed on the dwarven's helmet and squished it flat. Blood, bones, and brains flew from cracks in the metal as the jotunni fell forward onto its face with a thud.

He hefted his hammer back onto his shoulder and stared up at the hill. Greyfell marched up its slope for a second time. He wondered if he'd have to do it for a third time.

There can't be another enemy to fight.

Greyfell took a step forward as he regretted his life choices. Not all Gordics left to become mercenaries or bounty hunters. Some preferred a tranquil life of trade. They bought ships - either the sailing or the air kind - and made a living that way. Others became bards and storytellers. They wandered the villages and cities of the land juggling or playing instruments.

He reached the top of the hill after another climb. He took in what he saw. Parthalan Reis, the necromancer, stood facing him, hands raised. The man stood stark naked, with intricate tattoos woven and marking his skin. Embedded into his forehead were five crystals of different colors. They emitted a faint flow, which wasn't noticeable. His long red beard and his body dripped from the blood of a young man laying before him in a circle made of a fine crystal powder.

Whoever, or whatever, the warlock attempted to raise, needed a human sacrifice to complete. The red glow of crystals shot into the air, resembling a beacon.

Greyfell took a step forward, raising his hammer to his shoulder. He had a hundred feet to the warlock and he could reach it in fifteen steps. Greyfell can bring the man down with shattered legs by swinging at his knees. No one, no matter what magic he used, would stand — or at least he hoped.

Parthalan cackled. "You're too late. The ritual is complete. Lohikaarme-ajdaho shall rise and I'll rule the world."

The ground rumbled and shook. It wasn't violent like an earthquake, but it was like a large airship landing nearby. The ground leveled off and stopped moving as fast as it started.

"He rises. He rises. Lohikaarme-ajdaho will be mine to rule and control."

Greyfell stepped forward — fourteen steps to go.

Then the ground rumbled once more. Greyfell found he couldn't get *Talisman's* feet under him. He landed on his arm hard as his two-handed hammer skirted away. Greyfell scrambled to get to his feet, but the ground shifted. He dropped to his knees once more. Sparks flew from the impact.

The cobble stone ground lifted, rising from below. The blocks split from each other, a claw burst from the ground. Then another broke through, sending debris to tumble from it.

A dragon, once long dead, clawed itself from its grave. Forty feet long, with two massive wings and four legs. Its wide, flat head with a reptilian snout hung on its long neck. Despite being thousands of years old, skin and flesh lay on its bones, yet rotting. Its wings lay shredded, torn and unable to hold anything airborne. An empty socket existed where its right eye should be. Compensating, the left eye darted sideways.

It stood on the ground, its feet on the edge of the edge of the earth it dug itself from. "Who dares to disturb my slumber?"

"It is I, your new master, Parthalan Reis. You shall obey me and I shall rule the world," the warlock yelled, his voice high pitched and ecstatic.

"Shut your mouth, nave. I am Lohikaarme-ajdaho and no slave," the dragon growled, raising one clawed paw and hesitated. "You're a fool."

The creature moved its head so its one eye could see the hilltop.

"I'm Parthalan Reis and your master by the right of magic. These crystals will compel you to listen to me. I order you to sit."

Greyfell expected it would've been rolling on the ground splitting a gut. Except the dragon's laugh boomed across the temple as it grinned.

"You mispronounced the ritual," Lohikaarme-ajdaho said. "I'm surprised you raised me at all with how your butchered the Drachenkin language. The spell would've worked better if you'd use this cryptic, guttural dog-speaking thing you call a tongue - It may have bound me to you. But now. All you've done is to raise me from the dead and gave me new life."

"I am Parthalan Reis and your master. You shall listen to me."

Lohikaarme-ajdaho laughed and, with a single swift motion, he ate the warlock. He grabbed the man in its mouth and snapped his head up. Parthalan's arms and legs wiggled to escape. Then the dragon bit down and he stopped. With a gulp, Parthalan was gone.

Greyfell took a step back, hitting the button for his tubeless. "*Folkestone.* Did you see that?"

"Our payday just got eaten. No corpse, no coin. The Duke won't pay us for our word," Mikella said.

"Whose fault is that?"

"Let's not lay blame anywhere. I think those bones will fetch a good price. We can grind them up into powder. Every court wizard in a thousand miles will pay a premium for it. Kill the dragon."

"I don't think so. Chances are that if we were to try, it'll eat me."

"Then we'll earn get no money from this job. Just a repair bill for the *Talisman.*"

Greyfell cursed under his breath as she was right.

"The crystals… the power." A glow emitted from the dragon's skin for a split second as a few square feet of skin and flesh healed. "I require more, then with my immense power, I'll rule the world as I did all those years ago."

Lohikaarme-ajdaho glared at Greyfell and the *Talisman.*

The zombified dragon stepped forward toward Greyfell with its rotting mouth in a hideous, lip-less grin. It resembled a walking skeleton rather than a living creature.

Greyfell raised his two-handed hammer and held it to his shoulder. If he was lucky, he'd be able to hit it in the head. Perhaps he'd be able to kill it in a single strike.

"Puny human in a tin can," Lohikaarme-ajdaho growled. "You have many of those crystals. I can sense it. The power will heal me. I need them. Give them to me now and I'll let you live."

"I'll have to think about it," Greyfell replied.

"There is nothing to think about. I need them and you're going to give them to me."

Greyfell raised the massive hammer above his head as if to answer.

"Foolish human. I am Lohikaarme-ajdaho. A dragon of the Qadimgi-Ajdaho-Shahri. The ancient order of the fire drakes. No one can stand up to me. Submit and I will make you the king of the slaves. I'll topple these nations like the insects they are. Then, after I retake my lair, I'll have you as its steward."

"No."

"Excuse me?"

"No." Greyfell shouted the word, drawing out its two letters.

"So be it."

The dragon stepped forward, sucking in a large breath. Its chest expanded and glowed red. Its skin cracked and sagged as its connective tissue broke. Fire exploded from its lips as it shot at Greyfell.

The flames careened at him as he moved *Talisman's* arms in front of his visor. They wouldn't stop fire from turning him into charcoal, but it was something. Darkness and shadows disappeared from the area, being pushed by the new mini-Aether.

Except the flames didn't reach the jotunni. They stopped three feet from him. He felt the heat, but it wasn't enough to burn him. It was closer to standing next to a hot stove.

The fire stopped, and the darkness returned. Greyfell's night vision disappeared, the dragon the only being in view.

"That was disappointing," Lohikaarme-ajdaho said. "I need another crystal. Give them to me."

The dragon charged at Greyfell with its wings out to the side and its mouth open. It snapped at him, trying to get the Talisman's helmet in its mouth.

Greyfell stepped back, trying to get enough space to swing his long weapon. Except the dragon pushed at him, not letting him. Greyfell dropped the hammer, letting it fall away. He grabbed the dragon's jaw with one hand and punched the creature with the other. He struck once, then twice, aiming for its good eye.

Lohikaarme-ajdaho's chest swelled up once more. It prepared itself to send a wave of flame at him. Sparks erupted from its mouth as flames welled up at him. Greyfell jerked the dragon's maw from his face over his shoulder. The fire burst, sending the searing heat away from him.

"Greyfell," Mikella said. "Respond. What's your status?"

"I'm a little busy at the moment," Greyfell said as the fire stopped. "Don't talk to me unless you can help."

"Excuse me?"

"I'm trying not to die." Greyfell punched the dragon a few times more in the eye.

Lohikaarme-ajdaho stepped back, smelling the air as he shook his head. The beast growled under his breath. It raised its wings and flapped, attempting to fly. He ran to the hill's side and jumped. The creature stumbled along the ground like a wounded seagull.

Greyfell ran down the hill, pulling his two hand weapons from their holster. One weapon was a hammer, the other a mace. They didn't have the weight as the two handed, but it lay discarded behind him.

The dragon stumbled and collapsed along the ground as the uneven ground tripped him up. The beast slid halfway down the hill, landing in the pile of zombie corpses.

"Crystals," Lohikaarme-ajdaho said, as it ate a head.

As the beast did so, small parts of the dragon began healing. Square inch by square inch, the dragon regenerated. It still had hundreds of crystals to go, unless it found a larger source.

He jumped and landed on its back. He slammed the weapons at it as hard as he could. Greyfell felt more like a toddler attacking a troll. The weapons were taking chunks from its flesh, but he felt like he wouldn't be able to stop it.

"Hit it in the skull," Mikella said, through the tubeless. "It's still a zombie."

Greyfell grunted, sliding from its scales. The wings lay in his path as the dragon flapped, pushing him to the side. Greyfell ran around the wings as he attempted to get to the beast's skull. He charged at it and slammed his mace on the side of its head. The blow cracked the skull but didn't do any other damage.

The dragon raised its front leg and slammed his clawed paw against his chest. The blow sent Greyfell tumbling down the hill. Greyfell rolled and picked up speed. He saw the ground, then the night sky, in rapid succession. He closed his eyes as bile rose from his gut.

Greyfell crashed against something large and stopped. His head spun as he tried to stand up. His machine functioned, except its right leg jerked and stuttered. Its internal controls suffered major damage. Glancing to the side, he hunted for his weapons. They had slipped from his grip during the tumble.

The object which stopped his roll was the remains of the dwarven jotunni. It still lay where it had fallen. Its heavy hammer with its spike lay next to it. The weapon invited him to grab it.

Lohikaarme-ajdaho stood on the side of the hill, consuming crystals and regenerating. Every time it consumed one, bits of its flesh grew. Almost at random, the creature gained body parts.

"I need more," Lohikaarme-ajdaho said, spreading its wings.

The dragon jumped from the hill's side, coasting down at Greyfell. The dragon flew with its unrepaired wings, leaning to the right as it coasted down at Greyfell. As it turned off course, it flapped its wings, hovering in the air. If they were in one piece, the creature could fly and cause havoc in distant land.

His sole chance for killing the beast with the weapon. If he got lucky, he may hit the beast in the skull before it collided with him. The blow would kill it, except the timing would have to be perfect.

"Fuck it," Greyfell said, raising his weapon with the spike aimed down.

Greyfell slammed it into the back of the dwarven jotunni. He aimed for the crystal apparatus. Its heavy armor turned the sharpened end but left a dent that cracked the metal. Swinging once more, the spike burst into the apparatus, cracking the glass inside.

"What are you doing?" Mikella asked.

"Shut it," Greyfell replied. "And you may need to get some distance."

Lohikaarme-ajdaho glared at him with its good eye. It smelled into the air and grinned its lip-less smile.

"There are more. I must have them."

The dragon ceased flapping and glided toward Greyfell. It held its wings in close to its body like an arrow descending to its target.

Before Greyfell could hit the armor plating a third time, the beast body-checked the *Talisman*. The machine tumbled to the side, its legs tumbling over a short way. He landed on his front with a thud. He stayed down under the wall in the hopes it would protect him.

"So much crystals. They are mine. I will rule the world."

The dragon dug at the metal armor, bending pieces. It worked at a feverish pace, its addiction controlling its movements. It wasn't away of the danger that lay underneath it.

"I'm almost there. I can feel the power."

A crack reverberated through the night's darkness. Like calm preceding a storm. Dust and debris replaced the land around Greyfell as the crystals touched. The explosion sent waves of concussive force to blast around him. The explosion obliterated the wall he hid behind, sending rocks tumbling through the air. It was as if a massive spirit swung its arm scooping anything in its way and tossing it away.

Dust and debris covered the area as Greyfell hung in the *Talisman's* harness. Sweat dripped off his face as small rocks, bits of dragon flesh, and bones fell around him.

"Greyfell respond," Mikella said, over the tubeless. "Please respond."

Greyfell didn't register the words. They felt like gibberish to him as his ears rang and squeaked.

"*Talisman.* Respond."

"I'm here," Greyfell replied. "Or at least I think I am."

Greyfell forced his jotunni to stand up as the dust cleared. The blast wiped clean of stonework, corpses, and underbrush. Where the dwarven machine and the dragon lay existed as a small crater. He searched the area, hunting for weapons or anything of notes.

He found chunks of dragon flesh and bones. Except none of them were larger than his fists. Most lay scattered across the entire temple complex. He couldn't find any of his weapons.

"We're coming in for a landing," Mikella said. "I need someplace safe to land."

"Understood. I'm headed to the top of the hill. I need to find my hammer."

"Roger that. We're coming in."

The *Folkestone* landed on the top of the mound, with its landing struts sitting in the grass. Greyfell waited for them by the dragon's tomb. He stood next to his jotunni, with it at a knee, allowing him to dismount. He had found his two-handed hammer — the one he left at the top. The two smaller weapons and the dwarven's hammer were missing. He held the clawed front leg of the dragon in one and his eyeball with the nerve stem still attached.

Alf walked from the ramp as the crew spread out. They would salvage the area, perhaps they's find something of value. Greyfell didn't suspect it would be much.

"Do you still want to leave?" Greyfell asked.

"You want to stay?" Alf replied.

"I'm staying. At least until I earn enough."

"So, you're never leaving?"

"Perhaps."

Alf rubbed at his nose. "I guess I'm staying too. Though you'll owe me."

Greyfell lowered his voice. "I'll give you a barony when we get back."

"A title you don't have yet."

"I'm an Earl of an empty land. I can make you a baron of an equally empty one."

Alf shook his head, stepping to the *Talisman*. "You better keep your word. And no taxes."

"No taxes."

Greyfell walked toward the *Folkestone*, rubbing at his arm. Mikella stood at the top of the ramp. An angry glare lay plastered across her face.

"How do we ell this crap? I wanted a body to butcher," Mikella yelled.

"I'm just glad that I survived."

Mikella shook her head as Greyfell walked by her. "How about we consider the next mission? I'm sure we can make money with that one. A duel sounds easy compared to this."

"I hope so, for your sake."

About Nathan Pedde

Nathan Pedde hails from the dark recesses of Vancouver Island in Canada. Living with his wife and two kids, he has had the career of an author. He's worked in film and television, a gas station, a restaurant, engraving, restoration, and logistics. He's been writing since elementary school and has earned a BA from Vancouver Island University.

Curse of the Scaled God

By Axel Quintana

Seven warriors known as the Rout slay the mighty dragon Farrow, a battle hard fought but with no one dying. With their victory the seven, Wulf, Belle, George, John, Iseult, and Turin lead by the mighty Sieg have access to Farrow's immense cave of treasure and plan to pack up everything there. Their celebration is cut short as Sieg discovers a strange mystical ring, beginning the slow process of the group descending into chaos. Each night Sieg is faced with nightmares of a flaming beast escaping an endless sea of black shadows and during the day she becomes too lethargic to move or feel. All while discord befalls her group, arguments over what to do with the treasure, old grudges coming to a heed, things are getting violent and Sieg's feels unable to deal with it. Could the monstrous dragon be pulling their strings from beyond the grave?

Curse of the Scaled God

By Axel Quintana

There are few beings like the dragon Farrow. Body as mighty as a mountain, hellish scales like jagged snow-tipped peaks, and wings capable of blotting out the entire sky. From his hideous toothy maw, he breathes death that kills the earth and from his eyes black as coal pits he incinerates all he gazes. A destroyer of life, his claws rend the world and reduce it to nothing, his tail splits the very oceans and heavens apart. He is a monster; he is a God.

He is very, very dead now.

It was a hard-fought battle, a spectacle of such violence and brutality that it will be told for eons to come. There his corpse lays on his own hoard of gold, larger than even he, defeated by a group of warriors known only as the Rout. Lead by a warrior known as Sieg and her comrades Wulf, Belle, George, John, Iseult, and Turin, they beheld the creature's gruesome corpse, in a mangled mess of bloody chunks and burning viscera. The 7 cheer, taking the moment to rest, to feel satisfaction and pride in their accomplishment. Though they soon move on to their prize, the treasure.

Surrounding them on all sides, cacking their feet in layer after layer of gems, jewels, prized artifacts, weapons, armors all stacked in a massive hoard of gold unlike anything they have ever seen in their lives. It is time to begin excavating all this treasure out of this cave-castle.

The 7 start with the dragon itself, razing strip-mining its corpse, tearing off claws and scales to be sold or made into weapons, armors of the highest quality. They do not care that they are desecrating a corpse, after all Farrow was a monster, a murderous beast, friend to none, no one would ever shed a tear for him.

As Sieg tears off a plate, she gleams something sparkling towards Farrow's neck. Oddly it's a human sized ring tied around his neck, almost completely out of sight by scales the size of shields edging over it. With the sheer incredulity of a creature with a neck as thick as several towers tied together wearing a miniscule piece of jewelry, Sieg found herself fascinated by it. Pulling it from the string, she holds it between her fingers, its made of smooth green stone and enshrined by markings she is unfamiliar with. She has no way to decipher the value of this ring, but it was wrapped around Farrow's neck, that alone is enough. A trophy, the first of many as she fits the ring across her finger.

But as it slid across to the base, she felt a sharp prick on her finger and then the feeling of warm blood. The ring cut her finger, and she's not sure how because it's completely smooth, no edges or sharps points. The sullen warrior puts on an annoyed grimace, before waving off the oddly painful cut to fling the blood into the air. As she continues mining for any remaining valuables on the dragon's corpse, she doesn't notice that her blood has touched the ring, and the symbols glow a faint green light.

That night Sieg dreamt of green light, shining in the darkness. Pulsing rays an ugly emerald as if trying to escape the icky black shadows, surrounding it like waves. And beneath the swirls and waves of black and green, she feels as if she can hear something, like the flapping of wings.

The spear woman Wulf can be considered the group's accountant. Talented with numbers, she has always handled the logistics of their adventures, managing finances, supplies, and always knowing the exact cost of any purchase. Practical to a fault, she constantly tells the group where their money should go, stopping them from gambling or partying, what they should buy or replace, leading to numerous fights with Iseult and George who refused to give up their treasured weapons, even in the name of practicality.

A grim humorless woman without any sentiment, she cares little for companionship, but she is good at her job and is one of the finest warriors to have ever held a spear, so they bear with it, at least Sieg does. Any fight that happens from Wulf's frugality, Sieg would force it to end, as she does with any inter-conflict among the Rout.

Here Wulf is at the hardest work she has ever done, overwhelmed by Farrow's immeasurable treasure, a hoard of glittering gold that seems infinite. But Wulf calculates it all, nonetheless, dividing an equal share for the 7. All that's left is to steadily load them onto a system of self-driving caravans making back and forth trips, unloading their haul at an agreed upon location. A system made possible only by the magics of the sorcerous knight John.

Success deserves celebration, so the 7 have gotten together around a fire and indulge in all the food and drink they have, and whatever weird discoveries they uncovered in Farrow's cave. The dragon managed to collect quite a few rare wines and beers amidst his stashes. Sieg helps herself to one such bottle, taking a deep swig of something she's not sure what it is but its certainly delicious. Wulf doesn't drink or eat anything, she's still busy filling her ledger with everything she's uncovered, though focusing primarily on her portion of the stash. She never was one to enjoy a good meal, for reasons that always confused some members of the Rout, she has a severe aversion to eating.

Turin though is quite the opposite. Brimming with a youthful exuberance, he shoots around filling everyone's cups as he takes a seat next to their leader. Turin has been the happiest over their success, having never stopped smiling once Farrow took his last breath. Next to him also sits Belle who always did appreciate his company the most out of the 7, sharing in his joy with a well-done slab of mutton. The rest follow suit.

John sits with a loud thud, chattering endlessly about what he'll spend his portion of the treasure on, and bragging about being the one who landed the killing blow on Farron (he didn't). Taking a large seat himself that left Iseult and George to sit next to each other, to their mutual disgust. They were quick to argue and tried to force someone to make some space until Sieg gave them the look and they immediately clamp their mouths. Sitting knee to knee with great difficulty, the circle was complete as the 7 sit warmly and feast by the fire. Some wait for their leader to speak but she remains silent, instead looking at her new ring brimming with a greenish gleam.

Eventually they talk about their dreams now that they all have become vastly richer. John as always speaks first, boasting how he will have endless lovers, an army at his command, being able to buy everything he wants. He even mentions buying his own country, earning a derisive snort from Sieg, finding the very idea of "buying your own nation" insulting, not that John notices, too in love with his own voice to notice anyone else.

George and Iseult would talk over each other, saying how they will support their respective countries Liadda and Cuvernal, using the mammoth wealth to help ascend their homelands to glorious new heights. Though when George began talking about the faith of his patron God the Immolated Man, Iseult was about to scream and pull out her sword towards him. The only thing that stopped her was a look from her leader, she knew that if her hand pulled out that sword, she would lose it.

It was then when Turin decided to speak up. Unlike his comrades his words were not filled with pride or greed. In his dream the treasure is not for him, he intends to give it away to others, to support his family and help his home thrive. It was why he became an adventurer in the first place, to find some way to ease his people's struggling. A truly noble and kind-hearted goal, Turin did not have a selfish bone in his body. Though his sharing would produce some backlash from the group.

"That's what you're going to do with your share, just give it away?!" John asked him, completely baffled by what he just heard. He couldn't comprehend the idea that someone would just give away the treasure they fought so hard for to total strangers. At least he could presume that John and Iseult's plans have a veneer of selfishness, earning them high positions of power and authority. John calls Turin's dream a waste of their time and effort, saying he shouldn't receive anything if he's just going to give it away.

Quick to defend himself, Turin pierces through John's complaints by calling him selfish, someone incapable of love or friendship. There are some snickers from the circle, though its unsure whether those laughs are towards John quickly backing away or towards Turin for implying that they are all friends. Turin never could realize that ultimately the bond between the Rout is a professional one, most of them wouldn't really call each other friends. "Who are you to make fun of anyone? From what I remember you were busy hiding far in the back when Sieg finally killed that monster." Turin declares John a coward, calling into question his abilities as a warrior.

Braggart that he is, John is a capable sorcerer so he will not stand to be insulted like this. His wounded pride ensures he won't go down without making more of a fool of himself and dragging someone with him. So, he and Turin argue to the spectacle of their comrades, some annoyed at having to witness their idiotic squabbling, while others giggle finding the display hilarious. As Sieg witnesses the 2 arguing like children, she considers putting a stop to it, like she did with Iseult before. Whenever she ended any dispute among the 7, that was it, they knew to drop it regardless of what they are feeling. But Sieg doesn't say anything, she just lets it go on.

"John will never draw his staff, no need to interrupt a petty spat" she thinks, if it won't get violent why get involved? After all they have finally defeated Farrow, their quest is done. She doesn't need to keep the peace among them anymore, all that needs to be done is to wait for the caravans to finish hauling the treasure, and that will be the end of it. So let them bicker, it doesn't matter.

The two argue for some time but eventually night hits and they must sleep. Heading back to their tents, Sieg sees Turin walking towards her after Belle gave him a kiss on the cheek, telling him his "fight" with John was hilarious. Turin didn't understand what she meant, but regardless he thanked her anyway. Now he stands outside Sieg's tent, looking up at her with grateful eyes.

"I just wanted to thank you, for everything. For bringing me to this crew, for giving me this chance. Now that its all over I just wanted to say thank you Sieg." Turin offers her his honest appreciation and gratitude, truly grateful for being a member of the Rout and to Sieg for allowing him to join all those years ago. Surprised by the sudden display of gratitude, Sieg can feel a small smile forming on her lips, and to that she offers him her hand. He takes it, gripping tightly as she brings their hands up to their faces, and reciprocates with an even tighter grip upon his palm.

"It has been an honor Turin."

That night she dreamt of green fire blazing within the darkness. Then she saw something, coiling and slithering amidst the flames and shadows.

"It seems Turin had an accident." A sobbing Belle says, kneeling to a body buried under a mound of gold, with only the upper half of his head sticking out. Sieg can recognize his red hair and green eyes, open and unmoving like a statue. It is Turin and he is dead.

Sieg asks what happened, but no one can explain. They just found him like this, they can only assume he was trying to take some coins for himself and accidentally caused the large pile to collapse on-top of him. Though no one heard any noise so this must have happened when they slept. Belle makes an outrageous show of grief, openly crying and screaming Turin's name, demanding to God why he took him away as she grasps at the pieces of the pile. She does so with such exaggerated movements, her arms flailing through the air and her head shaking madly, that it feels like she is putting on a skit.

Ignoring Belle's grief, Sieg quickly shoves her hands into the golden mass and begins digging. Shoving fistfuls of coins aside and dragging Turin's body for all to see. Iseult makes a quick inspection; his body is cold, bruised with numerous welts and broken bones, which could only have been caused by the sheer weight of all that gold on him. So many questions arise, when did this happen, why was Turin gathering coins, did he die immediately, or did he lay there in pain calling out for help? So many questions, including a very obvious one, but only one was voiced out loud.

"So what about his share?" John said it first, confused, and half-hearted but he still said it. He gets some ugly stares, but Wulf quickly responded, "It will take a bit of time, but I can easily recalculate all our shares to an even 6."

An ugly feeling wells up inside Sieg, to already talk of money over their comrade's fresh corpse. Holding his body, she looks at the other five arguing amongst themselves and she wonders whether she should press this issue, confront each of them over Turin's death, discover the truth

But suddenly that feeling went away and she found herself engulfed in a dreadful state of ennui, the will to fight leaving her body. Suddenly the body of Turin felt too heavy to carry and she gently placed him on the ground, breathing a deep sigh that encompassed all the mourning she was capable of for him. Feeling something wet on her palms, she realizes that her hands are covered in his blood, the green stone ring on her finger slathered in red. It glows again a green light, brighter than before and somehow heavier.

She stands up and turns towards her men, standing taller than any of them, and looking through them she says. "Wrap up his body and put him on one of the carts. Send him to the agreed upon location for our corpses. After that we continue loading up the rest of the treasure as fast as we can. Any questions?"

Her eyes are an empty blackness, but none dare speak, they would rather not risk the fire returning. So, they all move on and go back to work without a word.

The rest of the day went by very solemn, an oppressive weight filling the air. The remaining 6 did their work, but they all kept their distance, unwilling to look at each other. The only sound is the cheerful humming of Belle, who even whistles a merry tune from her lips along with skipping in rhythm. The death of Turin seems behind her, despite the show she made earlier, she even plays with the gold a little bit before storing it, pretending to give them little voices and performing odd skits where they prepare to go on vacation and say goodbye to family.

Sieg always found her an odd person, she's quite competent with a dagger and bow, and her work ethic is stellar which make her little idiosyncrasies bearable. What soon gets her attention is the sight of George kneeling in front of a wagon, holding a candle in his hand uttering a prayer in an aria, his voice sounding like the chirping of doves. The flame on that candle burns with a warm glow, it feels like its embracing you with the softest hands. As he performs some kind of ritual, she remembers that that's the wagon Turin's body is stored in.

"What are you doing?" She asks in a terribly frustrated tone, the very act of checking in on someone greatly annoying for her. There is a pause as George finishes whatever prayer he's doing, of which he then lays the candle next to the body and gives Sieg a tearful look, the black markings around his eyes running across his cheeks like tears of oil.

George could barely get the words out, like he was about to choke on his own tongue. "Forgive me master. I was…. I was just performing last rites for him. I just couldn't let him leave without someone praying for his soul."

This is unexpected, but if he goes back to work afterwards, she sees no problem with it. As she prepares to leave George calls to her again, this time with a question of his own. is there any way we can divert the intended portion of Turin's share to the people he intended to give it too?"

She freezes in her step, and so Sieg looks at him with an eye that pierces into his soul. And George does not back down, he is sincere in this, which astonishes her to a degree as she knows George and Turin were never particularly close. Feeling the kindness radiating from this man, Sieg could only breathe a deep sigh as she tells him no. There is a sudden ping in her heart, but it subsides just as quickly, as she explains that as much as she would like to give Turin his share posthumously, she has no idea where she would send it. No one else knows either, Turin never managed to tell anyone where his hometown is before he died, so its sadly something they can't accomplish even if they want too.

Gloom falls on George's face, the melancholy cascading across his eyes and he begins to softly weep but he understands. He thanks Sieg for answering honestly, and he drops the issue, turning back to continue his prayer for Turin, calling upon the Immolated Man to bless the flame of his candle while singing another beautiful aria, his voice so sublime he sounds more like a tender poet than a hardened warrior.

Sieg finds herself chuckling at the thought, though that laugh disappears when she see's Iseult just standing like a statue, staring at George. She is practically seething with rage, radiating such pure contempt for him that it looked like the gold around her was melting. When Sieg passed her by, she turned towards her leader, and said with a voice filled with so much sneering scorn she spat out every word. "Look at him, why do this now? He never cared to flaunt his God with the many others that died before. Why give a man who's not his own, the prayers and rites of his people's pagan God?

Iseult's hand rests on the pommel of her sword, her fury compels her to confront George, but she freezes the moment she hears the silence of Sieg's steps. She does not dare to turn around, but she knows that Sieg is looking at her with those eyes of hers, black-black eyes that can gaze into the very core of your being and command it to do whatever it wants. Iseult lets go of her sword and stares at the ground in indignant shame as Sieg makes her way to her tent, Iseult not realizing that Sieg never looked at her, her back facing her the entire time. Sieg just didn't feel like turning, if anything the pause in her steps was more so her being tired than anything relating to Iseult.

The dreams of black return, and the green continues to burn brightly against the shadows. Now she sees the tips of great wings flapping against the flames. If she looks closely, she can see something else too. The wings are rotting.

The next day they discovered the dead body of an apparent thief. Belle found him and killed him by slitting his throat. According to her she saw him hiding in a far-off corner of the cave trying to steal some treasure, and then attacked her when she discovered him. She theorizes that he's the one who murdered Turin, as she found him rather close to the area of Turin's death. As convenient as it sounds, there's nothing really to disapprove of this notion so everyone goes along with it, and they quickly go back to work after dumping the thief's body outside. The only other thing of note was that the thief was carrying 2 holsters of the same size, one had a particular curved dagger with an X symbol at the base, the other was empty. Sieg wondered where the other dagger was.

Another dream, another nightmare. Great plumes of fire escaped from the miserable shadows, an assault of pure hatred and brutality birthed as a scorching ugly emerald inferno that would have reduced anything it touches to not even cinders. They were an endless symphony of fire, never stopping even as the darkness seemed to be trying to extinguish its might. Then under the smother of the void, the chorus of flames breathed a sound akin to a muffled roar, it almost sounded familiar.

Since the day began Sieg has been wracked with a terrible migraine, like something is banging from the inside of her skull with a metal hammer. She had hoped to get along with this smoothly as they have finally excavated over fifty percent of the total treasure, but that hope died once she sees George and Iseult getting into another argument.

Over what no one knows, only that Iseult is now screaming at him with a level of ferocity that has never been witnessed, her voice becoming hoarse and coarse like a banshee. Out from her maw she calls him every vile word in the book, liar, bastard, murderer, with such ferocity that George always kept his hand on the blade. Eventually he gets fed up and throws her the object he was holding, a sword wrapped in red cloth covered in the symbol of a golden cross.

Catching the sheathed blade, the sight of it is almost enough to bring Iseult to tears. But just as the smallest beads of sadness escape her eyes, her fury returns, and she holds the weapon towards him in accusation of his sins. "Giving me this changes nothing. It doesn't change what you did, all your sins! It doesn't change who you are!" Iseult screams so violently and without restraint, that the earth around them seems to quake, akin to the vicious roar of the great Farrow.

George simply stands there confused, for all the years in their petty rivalry, he never understood why Iseult hated him with all her being. Every time he tried to ask her and find some peace with her, she would always swat away his hand and threatened to cut his throat. He can't take it anymore, the holy warrior stands his ground, and looks her square in the face, eye to eye, and demands her to explain why she hates him.

For a second one could believe Iseult would shoot fire from her eyes or explode from sheer fury just to kill George. But instead, she gives him the coldest look anyone had ever seen and responded "Gladly."

It all begins with a story she says, of love long past and the joys of youth. Of a woman a solider who dearly loved a man named Tristan, a minstrel whose life was dedicated to the art of music. His lute an adorable oak carved thing and to hear him sing was to be embraced by the softest cloud in all the world. The woman loved him dearly, a man with the kindness of a saint and the joy of a child, there was no one else like him. Days were good until one day she left on a campaign, to her dissatisfaction she was called forth to fight on Cuvernal's behalf as her soldier, and so she left the man she loved as they both wept deeply for each other, the woman hoping to return to him once the battle was over. Only she never did.

Just as when she arrived at her home on relief, she had found that her city was being invaded by the holy burning men of Liadda, the entire land being burnt to the ground in a blazing inferno. As she cut her way through an endless horde of fanatics, she was met with the sight of her home in scorching ruins and the dying body of Tristan, his beloved lute destroyed and an infernal stab in his gut. As she held him in her arms, his final words, all he could tell her was about the man who killed him.

There was a long silence between the two, a void of sound or movement, the rest of the group just staring waiting to see what they will do next. Eventually George offered his response. "So that's what this is all about? You think I killed your husband?"

For a first she did not look at him in furious rage, but instead she smiled a smug contemptuous grin. "Did you?" She said mockingly. A giggle was then heard, coming from Belle who suddenly laughed a goofy grin and repeated Iseult's question in a gleeful exuberance.

"Of course not!" He yells to everyone, not just to Iseult but his allies as well. He is quick to explain that even when he was enlisted, he was never part of the campaign against Cuvernal. While not to say that he was never in battle, he was never in the raids against the cities of Cuvernal, and thus he did not kill Iseult's husband Tristan.

Iseult then laughed, an ugly sneer as she pointed her wrapped weapon towards the blade by George's side. "That weapon tells a different story." George's personal saber, with a golden guard and a black blade wrapped in burning spots, the only one of its kind and she declares this is the weapon used to slay Tristan. She states that before he died Tristan described the blade that impaled him, and his words painted a picture she could never forget. George putting a defensive grip over his swords pommel, begrudgingly responds that's impossible and continues to deny that he was ever in Cuvernal, he was stationed at the borders of his home far from Cuvernal.

Iseult demands he admit it, and George refuses to admit any validity in her accusations, remaining steadfast even as he feels everyone's eyes piercing at his hide into his soul. As he looks toward his eyes, he witnesses the ugly mocking grins from John and Belle smiling from ear to ear, but from Wulf and Sieg their faces completely and utterly still, a look of pure apathy like they don't even care. He's not sure which is worse.

Fed up with Iseult's tantrums and the stares of his comrades George declares he is done with this and turns his back towards Iseult. "This discussion is over. Iseult I'm sorry for what happened to your husband, but I didn't kill him."

The sight of him walking away from his crimes, the fury returns to Iseult's eyes. She grips her sword, but she freezes in place, suddenly remembering the gaze of Sieg is upon her. A claw of fear tears at her neck, threatening to cut off her head if she takes one step forward, keeping her in place from doing what she's desired for years. Seeing him get farther away its as if an empty cliff is between them expanding with every step.

She can feel the misery she felt seeing her love die, the rage she felt, the hate, the inconsolable pain happening all at once, everything she experienced on that day returning from the deepest pit of her mind, burning all inside her in a horrific storm of dragon fire. Cheeks stained by her tears she turns to look at her leader, and the sight of her causes something to snap. There was no fire in Sieg's eyes, no drive, no command telling her to keep herself in check, its like she isn't even looking at her, like she doesn't care.

A demon roar escapes her lips as she tears her sword and skewers George in the back through his heart. Even when George realizes what's happened to him, the screaming doesn't stop, the holy warrior falling before he could gaze at the sight of Iseult's vengeful face, teeth and gums barred, lips cracked, and skin tearing around her orifices, distorted by the pure catharsis of finally killing him.

The fire returns to Sieg's eyes and without any thought, she instinctively closed the gap between them in a single step and lops off Iseult's arm, her sword already drawn. Iseult didn't feel any pain from her parted limb when her entire world starts spinning, instead noticing that she's flying in the air. When she lands with a clumsy wet thud, she realizes that she is just a head, Sieg having already separated it from her body before she could comprehend the motion in an invisible stroke.

When Sieg's mind returns she is presented the sight of George and Iseult dead on the floor, George slumped over his own prized sword with a frightened look on his poor face, and Iseult's headless corpse falling backwards on that wrapped blade that started this all, leaving behind only pools of their own blood.

She finds herself breathing fast, her heart beating a mile a minute, and when she looks down, she sees her hands covered in blood. It's their blood, and as she brings her fingers deep into her palm, the green ring glows again.

In the black night and the green fire, a roar is heard again. Loud and deafening but still…. familiar. She's heard this sound before, like a million lives screaming as they died to the onslaught of the detonation of a million bombs. Wait this can't be, she shouldn't be hearing this, he should be dead.

The only sound that was heard is Belle's giggling, snickering whenever she exchanges eyes with Sieg. Days not even halfway through but Sieg already feels exhausted. The bodies of their fallen holy man and avenger have since been wrapped up and sent to where Turin's body is, but it feels like Sieg should count herself among her fallen comrades. She is lethargic, her body sluggish with slouching shoulders and dreary lidded eyes, she has to push herself to supply the wagons with the remaining treasure. They are so close.

John was currently in the middle of a mental breakdown. The death of no less than three of his comrades in only a handful of days has turned the already fearful man paranoid, afraid that he's next. He has become more hostile, yelling whenever someone gets near him and always keeping a hand on his staff.

"I know something is wrong here. I'm next, I'm next I tell you. They won't take me, I'll be the last one standing." He whispers to himself, always keeping a steady eye on his comrades. Watching like a rabid hawk, waiting for when they pull something.

Their glorious triumph over Farrow has turned quite sour. What should have been a victory lap taking the treasure they earned has morphed into a miserable experience. The remaining Rout wonder if more of them will die before the final piece of gold is taken.

Black talons swipe at fire. The flickering flames altering around the claws, a dance of green and black that she's not sure how many blades there are. Ten, twenty, 40, massive butcher blades the size of an entire man moving at impossible speeds, able to annihilate bone and disintegrate flesh with ease. They move almost like they are looking for someone.

Sieg woke in the middle of the night, the dreams make it harder to sleep. Doing something productive with her time, she is loading up more treasure on the remaining wagons. They are just on the cusp of finishing, one more day and their mission will finally be over. Might as well start finishing it now.

As she motions a self-driving wagon to leave, she hears a scream in the dark. Heading back to the tents she sees by the faint firelight the sight of John stumbling out of his tent in a mad panic, hysterically screaming that someone's tried to kill him.

"I knew it, I knew it! You are all trying to kill me, to keep the treasure for yourselves! Liars, tricksters, thieves!" He shrieks at the top of his lungs, the entire cave filled with his hysterical screaming, so distorted it sounds like the ugly moaning of a dying animal. He drops to the ground desperately pawing and reaching for his staff, too stricken with fear to remember where he last had it.

When he witnesses Sieg in the shadows, fearful screams escape his lips, he acts like he just encountered a monster. "Stay away" he shouts, terrified of his leader with a level of terror she has never seen from him, even in their battle against Farrow. As she steps forward to question John, he rapidly crawls away like an insect, rambling incoherently. Amidst the dark he throws something at her feet, a curved knife with a bloody blade, the blood still fresh and glistening even in the dim of light.

This knife looks familiar, but before Sieg can give it more thought she notices a torrent of flame coming her way, with the intent of disintegrating her head. Quickly dodging she sees that John has found his staff and the glowing obsidian crystal at its core has been activated, signifying that its in battle mode. John declares that no one will stop him from taking the treasure, not even Sieg and thus he commences another spell, this time shaping the very air itself into a blade to tear Sieg's body in half.

As the air lunges towards her like the pinchers of a mantis, Sieg even in the dark can see the motions of the incoming invisible air, and quickly takes to the side narrowly avoiding losing her head like Iseult. Her body moves faster than her mind can comprehend what's happening, instinct completely taking over the motions of the limbs as she reflexively heads towards the last place she left her sword, her tent which is unfortunately next to John's.

She moves like a phantom, her feet barely touching the ground as she ebbs in and out of the very darkness around them, dodging everything John throws at her with nary a scratch. The sorcerer screams in impotent rage, wondering how its possible for a human to survive the mighty onslaught of magic he unleashed, a force he claims to be unmatched by any warrior.

His frustrations reaching its peak, he readies his most powerful spell, raising his staff into the air as a ring of emerald gas swirls around the staff's core. This proved to be a great mistake, as when he began charging his Hail Mary, it paused the rest of his attacks, providing the perfect window for Sieg to slip past him in a single motion. By her bed she grips the handle of her sword, and before John could turn, she already has it unsheathed, and his head rolling on the floor.

The sorcerer's body collapses to the floor, his staff shattering upon the ground, and the light inside it fading into nothing. Sieg looks at the body with dead eyes, taking several minutes before her mind becomes alive again, and she realizes what's happened.

Another of her warriors is dead.

And the second by her hand.

She drops her sword, her hands shaking and twitching. She's not sure how it came to this, why, all she can remember before is John screaming in terror, and even that memory is faint in her mind. It feels more like a dream than something that really happened. Feeling the taste of metal on her tongue, Sieg notices that she has her hand pressed to her mouth and its covered in John's blood. Revolted from the taste of blood in her mouth she realizes that the ring is once again slathered in blood and is glowing so bright. Such an ugly shade of green, she remembers seeing this exact shade in her dreams every night, in the emerald flames that blaze against the darkness.

Before she could ponder this thought more, a feeling of drowsiness begins to take hold of her body. When the first yawn comes in, she feels a wave of smoke coiling around her body, and she recognizes this gas, it's John's deadliest spell, a sort of poison gas. While she did kill John before he completed the spell, the first stage had already begun producing a gas that was in the process of morphing into something fully lethal. And what was produced is a very effective sleep gas that can knock out even the most bloodthirsty warriors, Sieg recalls as her face touches the cold hard ground.

Despite her best efforts, sleep takes hold of her, and she can do nothing but wait for her eyes to close and for the darkness to embrace her.

An eye is staring at her. Unblinking and immeasurably massive, it shines a hideous green light as that black pupil shakes with squelching tremors. Her body is frozen in the air, surrounding her the darkness and this unholy eye, it stares at her radiating a horrific contempt. It hates her she can tell; this evil ugly eye says nothing but its like she can hear it in her mind just how much loathing it feels for her. Hate, Hate, Hate, Hate.......

She wakes up, still tired, her body not receiving an ounce of rest as she shields her eyes from the sun coming through the cave entrance. John's body is gone, and so is the rest of the treasure, carried off in the last of the wagons. The spell used to animate them should still work even if John's no longer alive to maintain it, all it seeks is to finish its task completely.

"Good morning, our glorious leader."

Wulf stands over her, spear in hand, radiating a look of pure contempt. Feeling her life is in danger, Sieg quickly scurries away from her and brandishing her blade against her. The spear-woman mutters some expletives under her breathe as she motions the rest of her spear to come into view, brandishing the impaled corpse of Belle on its end.

She throws the body in front of Sieg, dropping with an ugly thud and splattering her with blood. Driven silent Sieg tries to wipe some blood off her face, as Wulf dangles a glowing necklace from her fingers. "Our little scout was wearing this hidden around her neck." A metallic rusted spike hanging from a chain, glowing a reddish-pink color. "I did tell her to be careful with what she finds. Shame she never could take my advice."

"You.... You killed her." Sieg utters as Belle's lifeless eyes stare at her, Belle still smiling even in death. Wulf brings down her spear towards the body, akin to a predator showing off its kill. "Oh don't fret, she was trying to kill me. She also snuck into John's tent and tried to kill him." She says this so casually, not a single emotion or inflection could be parsed in her voice.

She guesses that she attempted to knife him in his sleep, but when he suddenly woke up Belle managed to slip back into her tent leaving Sieg to take the brunt of John's panic and finish him off. Belle would then attempt to knife Wulf in the back when the latter investigated what happened, but Wulf saw it all coming and killed her before she could try anything.

Why did she do this? Wulf doesn't know, nor does she care, she always found Belle an annoying unstable little runt. "But you." She utters in a hoarse voice before aiming the tip of her spear against Sieg. "This is all your fault you know."

A bizarre accusation, Sieg finally collects herself and stands against her last remaining subordinate. "Explain." The warrior demands.

Her lips move, shaped almost like a smile, Wulf never smiles. "You ask me why, I thought you stopped caring. It certainly seemed that way." She brings up her actions from before, whenever there was an argument, she would just let things be instead of settling them like she always did. When John mocked Turin's dreams, when Iseult confronted George at swords edge, she just sat out and did nothing. She could have stopped them, prevented things from getting worse, but she just let it all happen with a blank gaze on her face. Feels like their glorious leader had decided to finally wash her hands of them.

Sieg couldn't find a response, for she realizes Wulf spoke the truth. She has been slacking in her duties, there were several times when her position as peacemaker was necessary, and she didn't do anything. She just let it all happen, knowing it could go bad because she didn't feel like it, she remembered feeling that it would have been a hassle trying to stop them.

Turin, George, Iseult, John, Belle, their lives were her responsibility, yet despite always accomplishing her duty as leader before, she decided to shirk her duties to them. Yet Sieg couldn't come up with an explanation why. The reason for her inexplicable apathy escapes her, she thinks and thinks yet she can't come up with any explanation, as if there are holes and gaps in her mind.

Her subordinate staring her down, Sieg tries to apologize, but she wouldn't have it. She holds the spear to her neck and chuckles, a sound so foreign coming from Wulf.

"No apologies, it's too late for that. Since it's just the two of us, and you are the reason why all our comrades died, your position as leader of the Rout is now rendered null. I no longer have any reason to be loyal to you." Her hand gets tighter around the spears shaft, Sieg knows what's coming next. "Thus, I will kill you here and keep the treasure of Farrow for myself."

The next move almost took her head off. Wulf thrusted the spear faster than the blink of an eye, with such strength and force that the air around the blade collapsed into a vacuum. The closest Sieg has ever came to death in recent memory, the pure martial skill and power of Wulf concerns her far more than the darkest magics John could produce. The former leader of the 7 could only barely dodge that first strike, ducking to the side the moment Wulf finished speaking, but not without the spear taking a good chunk of skin off her shoulder.

Sieg ignores the pain, her body doing everything it can to stay alive against the warrior in front of her, she can feel her palm getting sweaty around the handle of her sword. Waiting for Wulf to make the next move, her survival instincts shout from every corner of her body as if she was facing a mighty predator instead of a human, telling her to run away and live. But she won't, she knows Wulf will never let her escape, Sieg could never outrun her so a fight to the death is the only resolution between these two.

Wulf takes another step and closes the distance between them in a mishappen blur, the white glint of her spear making another move towards her head. Blitzing through the pain in her shoulder, Sieg deflects the spear with her blade and with a quick change of hands thrusted towards Wulf's gut. The spear-woman is quick to regain her balance though, for with a simple twirl she sidesteps Sieg's attack and drops the spear over her shoulder, with the intent to slice her in half. Sieg's sword rises to meet her spear, and a hail of sparks explode from the clashing blades.

And so, the battle continued, a back and forth between two warriors who could only be considered each other's equal, neither one ever getting an edge over the other. The exchange of blows is endless, no moment spared, no action given any thought, an onslaught of steel on steel, the clanging of metal echoing throughout the cave. A dual of pure instinct vs pure skill, Sieg's body always moved faster than her mind could think, reacting against the most polished and refined motions of Wulf's attacks with instantaneous reflex. Sieg always moved perfectly, even with the lethargy that has poisoned her mind, her body refused to fall behind.

But eventually the dual reaches its inevitable crescendo. Sieg felt herself getting slower, more and more cuts forming on her body, less and less she's keeping up with Wulf's moves. Her body is falling behind, even pure skill and instinct cannot hold up an apathetic mind against a woman of focus, commitment, and sheer will. She was too much.

So, with her back against the cave's entrance, eventually her body makes a pivotal mistake and she's opened up to the final strike. The spear comes one last time, but in that moment, just before the sun rises beyond the ceiling of the cave, a stray ray of light peaks in and hits the shining white blade.

It was only for an instant, but Wulf's sight was gone, taken by the lone beam reflecting into her eyes. Her spear wavered, missing Sieg's body and nicking only skin, and in that moment an opening was made. For the first time Sieg was aware of what to do, and so she commanded her body, bringing down her sword across Wulf's chest.

Spear clanging on the floor, Wulf drops to her knees, her limbs no longer under her control. Sieg is quick to grab her, and so she holds her subordinate gently in her arms, looking into her face and not at the bloody crevasse within her chest. Sieg tries to say something, anything, but the words fail to come out of her mouth, the only noise is her stifled breathing.

Wulf begins laughing though. Still such an odd sound coming from her, but also beautiful, Sieg never expected her to have such a nice laugh. "Heh funny way to die. I like it." She utters a joke, with nary of resentment or anger in her voice, just amusement over what's transpired. Looking into her leader's eyes, they share a laugh, an awkward stilted laugh but laughter all the same. Wulf kept laughing, all the way to when her eyes finally closed, and then...... Silence.

"Thank you hated warrior." Farrow lays there in the black void towering over the flames in all his hellish glory. He is whole, alive as if he never died at all. That ring is wrapped around his neck again, shining brightly, and for a moment it was like she could see the faces of her, and all her comrades etched into its stone frame. He then looks at her with those lifeless black eyes, their shape an odd curve, almost like he's smiling. A twisted mockery of a grin, and what follows is a sound she has never once heard on this Earth. She thinks he's laughing. "It is time."

She opens her eyes, and her mind returns, all her passion, all her strength. She remembers events of the distant past, of fallen kingdoms and slain parents long since avenged. The bodies are gone, she sees the final caravan carrying away Belle and Wulf. She's alone, there is nothing left, no treasure, no comrades, only the black stone and the hideous corpse of Farrow.

Loneliness and regret washes over Sieg, with the pit in her stomach she realizes she misses all her comrades. Wulf, Belle, George, John, Iseult, Turin, she never did think of them as friends but still they were brothers in arms, going through so many adventures and battles together, yet now they are all gone.

At a loss of what do now, the earth begins shaking, the violent quake ripples throughout the cave as the ring explodes in a burst of light. Blind for who knows how long, when her vision returns the blood slathered ring is destroyed, dispelled into shattered fragments on the ground.

What follows is a terrible silence, a certain tension in the air as if waiting for something, something that's just about to happen. An ember forms on one of the shards, it then touches the ground and suddenly it becomes a blazing trail of fire, burning with such a hideous emerald green shade that its painful to look at.

The trail then makes its way across the cave, heading towards the dismembered and strip-mined corpse of Farrow, rocketing through any stone in its way. Sieg knows whatever will happen is nothing good, but there's no way to stop the flame, all she can do is wait and witness what's going to occur next.

The flame touches a broken claw first, and another detonation occurs, this time one of pure flame, the sight of it so incandescent that she can feel her skin burning and the blood on her body flaking into nothing. When the flames die down, she is witness to a sight that can be considered the Devil's miracle, the body of Farrow reanimated, moving with sickening wet sounds, things breaking and snapping in place with what remains of its desecrated corpse.

Green flames cover and replace what's missing, scales and digits all restored with the same emerald flame in her dreams. Somehow it looks even bigger than when it was alive, as a shroud of living inferno from the tips of wings and tail to encompass the entirety of the cave. Looking down at her those eyes have become solid green, staring at her with that same smiling curve. It doesn't roar, there is no need too. All that's left is to finish the final death.

Sieg beholds the great lich as it prepares to strike her. She takes a quick glance behind her to the opening of the empty cave, for a moment she wonders but she figures its pointless. So, she draws her sword with dried blood, and noticing the spear of the fallen Wulf still beside her, stomps on its end into her hand. She then glances at the lich, weapons ready.

"Come."

About Axel Quintana

Born in Havana, Cuba before moving to the US at a young age, Axel Quintana grew up with a love of reading books, mostly comic books. Living in Miami Florida all his life, he currently studies at Florida International University to get his Masters in the English Writing and Rhetoric program. While reading comic books, manga, fantasy and science fiction books, watching movies, and drawing whenever he has free time. Growing up with works like Marvel Comics, DC Comics, Dragon Ball, and Warhammer 40K have inspired him to take his hand at crafting his own stories. While managing his studies he works at his campus bookstore to help pay for his tuition and finances. He hopes to slowly improve his writing by delving into any genre he's interested in and taking up any opportunity to prove himself a writer.

The Wrath of the Bride

By Fulvio Gatti

The village is plagued by attacks from the Striders. Will the warrior Gaelandra and the animal expert Jarrod be able to understand why those raids happen, fast enough to save both the humans and the invading creatures?

Fulvio Gatti

The Wrath of the Bride

By Fulvio Gatti

The swift ocher figure disappeared behind one of the stone shacks. *Darn, they are quick*, Gaelandra thought. *This won't be easy.* She controlled her breath as she crossed the yard, going around the small building to anticipate the Strider.

The next thing she saw were savage, yellow eyes. The creature looked surprised, the scales around its beak darkening. Claws snapped out of the front paws as it shifted between its running, four-legged pose and the bipedal attack stance.

Gaelandra let out a Kavedian war cry, unsheathing her sword and charging the Strider. She bent her wrist, putting the blade before her face, in time to prevent a black claw from ripping her forehead skin. *I appreciate the good aim, but I've got too many scars on my face already, bitch*, she thought, flashing the creature a fierce gaze.

She pushed it back with the sword while her right hand—the free one—slammed in the middle of the Strider's neck. It winced, struggling not to fall, and exposed a portion of its chest, below the front plaque of its body shell.

If it weren't so quick with its claws, she could grab it and toss it against the stone wall behind them. A hard enough surface to bang its head against to get an immediate knockout. Any other move, with the shacks so close to one another, would be ineffective and dangerous.

Her best choice—she considered while dodging a bite from the deadly beak—was to bring the Strider out in the clearing for a proper fight. One that Jarrod could see, from his seat on the fig tree, to later comment in his naughty way.

Her eyes framed an undefended zone among the wiggling claws and beak. She crouched and kicked the creature's ankle the very moment it was leaping on her. Then she spun away as the Strider collapsed on the ground, screeching in pain. She rushed to the middle of the clearing, looking for Jarrod and recognizing the large branches of the fig trees.

Her partner waved a short arm, and she couldn't help but smile. She turned her back on him and struck a heroic pose. The Strider was running toward her, all the scales on its head now a shade of brown.

The attack found a competently wielded blade on its way. The Strider made a furious scream, purple blood dripping from its jaw. Gaelandra hopped back to put some distance between the attacker and her, trying to understand what Jarrod was yelling.

She took a few more steps towards the large tree, but she had to swivel back, stretching her arm and sword above her head, ready to prevent the menacing beak from reaching her. She groaned as her brain identified Jarod's single, repeated word: *Sword.*

Gaelandra roared and threw her sword. It slammed on the Strider's beak before bouncing down. Feeling that it wasn't enough, she kicked into its head as hard as she could. The bone cracked and the creature fell to the side. Gaelandra turned to the fig tree, bursting with rage.

"Really? You want me to go barehanded?" she yelled at Jarrod. "And what else, maybe? Drop my armor and fight all naked?"

"That would be a dream!" Jarrod shouted back.

It was then that a sting in her calf made her flinch. Gaelandra hated herself for omitting the armor on the back of her legs. She twirled to smack her fist on the animal's head. It anticipated her move. Both sides of the sharp beak sunk into her arm, cracking the light metal cover and making their way into her flesh.

"Gimme back my arm, you moron!" Gaelandra screamed, turning the pain into rage.

She stabbed the eyes of the creature with two fingers of her free hand. She kept pushing hard and wet filth came out, having her grimace in disgust. The creature eventually let her go, making upset moans and drawing its head back.

Gaelandra slipped her leg out of the claw–*ouch*–and then flipped on herself. It was not the years of military training, but self-preservation instinct which saved her from certain death.

Her wounded arm ached as the wrist held the massive beak away from her face. She swung the other arm, getting scratched many times by the claws while the whole, powerful body of the predator loomed on her.

Gaelandra threw her knee up, banging it against the shell. She did it again and again, nothing but a deaf sound coming through. And then her eyes were able to identify the recent cut on the creature's neck.

Ignoring the claws ripping into her flesh, she stretched her arm to sink her fingers into it.

More slimy, purple blood, a hideous smell, and no time for loathing.

Gaelandra waited until the creature loosened the pressure on her, to push it to the side with all the energy she could gather. The Strider fell on its shell, claws grasping into the air. She used the momentum to take control of the fight.

Feet on the shell, all her weight over the opponent, she yanked its higher limbs away while closing her hand into an iron fist. She punched the creature on the face so hard it snapped. She hopped on the shell, shaking the large body, then punched it again and again. A gurgle grew from the creature.

"It's your choice, pal," Gaelandra hissed. "I'll keep smacking you until you pass out."

Soon the creature below her stopped moving. The warrior took a deep breath, her wounds burning, eyes darting around to make sure the opponent was truly out of the game.

"You've fought well," she eventually smiled. "We could even become friends."

Gaelandra had seen many villages throughout her years in the army and traveling with Jarrod, but she must admit that Ailanto was pretty unique.

Seen by the boat they had arrived with, the tall hill it was built on emerged from the forest it was surrounded by on three sides, to later reveal the bunch of houses on its top, evenly divided between the rocky and the wooden ones, with the cultivated land, a stockyard and an orchard to complete the picture.

From the shore, they had climbed a carved stone staircase covering most of the hill perimeter, reaching the core of the town. Jarrod had also mentioned noticing, from the boat, some narrow holes in the rock.

He said they were the entrances to the caves the town was famous for, but Wanda—the town counselor who had come all the way to Nicie to ask for their help—had not offered any further information about it.

"You're not very talkative, huh?" Wanda asked, her eyes focused on fastening the bandage on Gaelandra's wrist.

"Not really," the warrior replied.

They sat on a trunk by the side of the field where two strong men, under the detailed instructions of Jarrod, had just tied the Strider and taken it away.

"You haven't even told me what you think of our town," Wanda insisted.

Gaelandra shrugged. "It seems like a quiet place."

Wanda's face darkened. "It was, before the Striders."

The counselor moved a strand of gray hair away from her forehead, then cut the last piece of fabric. She carefully put away all her sewing tools.

"Anything else?" Wanda asked.

"I think I'm fine, thank you for your assistance," Gaelandra replied.

The warrior stood up, noticing the broken branches below the fig tree. Bringing Jarrod down had been quite an endeavor, after the fight.

"Shall we go to the laboratory, now?" Gaelandra suggested.

"All right," Wanda replied, leading the way to one of the wooden buildings by the edge of town.

The large door creaked as the counselor pushed it.

"Keep the vibrations to minimum, please," Jarrod said. "Delicate analysis is going on here."

He finished pouring a purple, dense liquid into a vial. He brushed some white dust over it before putting it to the side. He took a small hourglass from a pocket of his robe, tapped his nail on the glass—making it ring—to check that the sand moved, then flipped it.

A dozen small dishes and cups were carefully distributed in front of him on a low table, close enough for his short arms to reach them.

He looked up just to briefly wink at Gaelandra. "Hey, honey. Missed you." Then glared at Wanda. "Can you tell the dumb guys in the corner they can go? They don't listen to me."

Two tall villagers, one stockier than the other, stood by the wall, giving worried glances to the Strider on the right half of the table. Its beak and legs were tied by the same, strong ropes that kept it on the table, but its belly moved slightly.

"It was your idea to keep it alive," Wanda retorted in an annoyed voice. "I even wonder if two men are enough, in case that monster wakes up."

"He won't wake up for days, I gave him an herbal sedative."

He trotted to the creature and caressed its head.

Gaelandra, at the sight of the deadly beak so close to his partner, had to keep from drawing her sword.

Jarrod looked at ease. "Also, it's a boy, not a monster."

Wanda pursed her lips. "I don't think knowing that will give us back the cattle we lost, or good ol' Barney."

"You still have no proof the vanished guy was eaten by a Strider," Jarrod pointed out. "Maybe your uncle just wanted to leave the town. Give me a few hours and I'll tell you if these cuties like human flesh at all."

"Seemed quite hungry to me," Gaelandra objected.

"I wonder who isn't, when seeing a pretty thing like you," Jarrod smirked. She blushed and looked away.

"It's still a problem I need you to solve, shorty," Wanda said. "Even better if you're quick."

Jarrod sighed and raised his index finger. "I seem to recall telling you, back in Nicie, that jokes on my height are funny only if I'm the one who tells them." He squinted. "For anything else, you hired us because all the hunters and cutthroats already failed at stopping the Striders. So, this time we do it our way." He blatantly looked around. "Speaking about pressure, I don't see your boss anywhere."

"You're summoned in front of the board tomorrow after lunch at the Town Hall. The Priestess herself will be there too." Wanda frowned. "Will you have something interesting to tell them?"

"Civil and religious power in the same meeting, I'm thrilled!" Jarrod replied, straightening up to his short height. "Now, if we're done with the bickering, I've some research to do. Please leave my lovely lady here, she's the only one who can drag me to our not-so-delightful guest shack once I've collapsed after a long day of work."

"Make sure he doesn't kill himself," Wanda ordered her men before leaving.

"Was I maybe a bit rude?" Jarrod asked Gaelandra, his tone sweetening. "I can't stand the people who expect to kill any creature which happens to be different from them."

Gaelandra crossed her arms and smiled down at him. "I've seen you behave much worse than that."

Jarrod blew her a kiss.

———————————

In the middle of the night, Gaelandra heard a thud.

She was already out of bed, dagger in hand, before recognizing the steps of an intruder. Her trained eyes saw how the back window curtains were open, then found a small figure.

She launched against it, pushing the intruder against the wall while checking for any weapon in their hand.

A shrill voice yelled in pain while a small artifact banged against the ground.

"Who are you? What do you want?" Gaelandra asked.

As the light went on—Jarrod had uncovered his box of fireflies—she was surprised to see a skinny young girl with long auburn hair in a brown robe.

"I guess it's a bit too late for home delivery," Jarrod commented.

Gaelandra's alert evaporated. There was no way the newcomer could escape their guest shack, so she stood back.

"I must warn you!" the girl stated in a trembling voice.

"For now, you only woke us up," Jarrod objected.

Gaelandra hushed him before focusing back on the visitor.

"Warning for what?"

"The Bride! You must not disturb her!"

"Which bride? Someone from here?"

"The Bride is everything! We must respect the Bride!" the girl continued. It sounded like a chant she barely knew the meaning of.

Gaelandra crouched to collect the artifact the intruder had brought with her. It was a sharp rock. She handed it to the girl.

"You came with this, in our home, by night," she said, calmly. "You intended to hurt us, didn't you?"

"We are afraid!" the girl exclaimed, on the brink of crying. "You're not like the others. The caves are not safe anymore! We must stop you! You can hurt the Bride!"

Gaelandra put her hands on the girl's shoulders.

"If that's what you fear, I can swear you now. We are not here to hurt anybody." She glanced at Jarrod in the bed, blanket covering him up to the chin. "Neither people, nor animals of any kind."

Jarrod tilted his head and flashed her a fond gaze.

"You will not?" the girl asked. She sounded hopeful.

"You may not know about it but the word of a former Kavedian soldier is always a word of truth. You can trust me."

"Gae?" Jarrod asked.

"What?"

"Is this some silly religious crap of yours, maybe?" he wondered. "Hiring a local girl, having her break in during the night to scare me and make me repent for my sins?"

Gaelandra sighed. "This has nothing to do with my beliefs."

The girl seized the occasion to launch herself to the opposite window.

Gaelandra jumped after her, grabbing her heel. The girl wiggled and freed herself, hopping off and disappearing into the night.

"See? Now she's gone!"

"You heard the girl? She mentioned the caves."

"So what?"

"They offered us to visit anything but those."

Gaelandra struggled to keep calm, hoping a good fight would begin soon. The stern gaze of the two-dozen white haired people, crowding the room and sitting behind a stone table, was much heavier to bear than the injuries from the brawl with the Strider.

Still, it was something they had to go through. The warrior was happy she had only to stand there while Jarrod did all the talking. Counselor Wanda was the only other one standing on their side of the table.

The Mayor looked overweight and easily annoyed. To his right, still as a statue, sat a thin old woman in a black decorated dress and a bonnet on her head: the Priestess.

"I'd like to make a formal request to visit the caves, Mr. Mayor," Jarrod asked the supreme authority at the end of a detailed report about his research on the Striders.

"Those are no place for strangers," the Mayor was quick to react.

"With all due respect, I insist," Jarrod said after a smirk to his partner. "There is a chance that Striders come to town out of some consequences from the mining activities."

The Mayor seemed to ponder, his eyes going from Jarrod to Gaelandra, to later reach the Priestess.

"Your Holiness Ydhati, I'd like to hear your opinion too," he said. "The caves, after all, are a sacred place."

The Priestess tilted her head slightly and below her bonnet, a pair of piercing eyes shimmered.

"The Bride is everything. The Bride will know," she said in a deep voice.

"So, do you think we can arrange that, Mr. Mayor?" Jarrod asked.

"Discipline, please," the Mayor replied, dry. He looked at Wanda. "Counselor, you're the one who requested the strangers' assistance in the first place," he said. "If granted access, would you go with them in the caves?"

"I don't think it's the best course of action, Mr. Mayor," she objected. "I'd feel much better if we also considered defending the town from further raids. We can't afford any more deaths."

Jarrod seemed to be about to speak, but he remained silent. When Gaelandra looked at the council, she shivered. All the eyes were on her. She took a step closer to her partner.

"We all saw your formidable fighting skills, lady warrior," the Mayor said to her. "While your associate visits the caves with Counselor Wanda, would you be interested in training some of our citizens, so that we will be less helpless?"

Gaelandra thought that the events had just taken an interesting turn.

"How deep do you want to go?" Wanda asked, her voice louder than needed, echoing in the narrow tunnel.

Jarrod crouched to study a glimmering in a niche. He moved his box of fireflies close to a small rock and it flashed back. He groaned as he identified it as nothing but gold. He collected his box and trotted back to the exploring party.

"Until I see something worth noticing, I guess," he replied.

The path was dimly lit by oil lamps, with a rope attached to the wall as an emergency handle where the ground became too steep. Jarrod walked right behind Wanda, with the two-armed villagers closing the line.

They went through many tunnels all similar to one another.

"Tell me, are we going in a circle for a reason?" Jarrod asked.

"There's not much to see, here," Wanda replied. "I think I told you."

"What about the spice mines?"

"I don't know what you're talking about," Wanda said, walking faster and leaving him behind.

Jarrod stopped.

"Come on!" he said, raising his voice and letting his frustration burst out. "It's no secret you export spice. You need to feed your village, after all!"

Wanda kept giving him her back.

Jarrod calmed his tone. "Would you bring me there? Please?"

Wanda sighed. "All right," she turned, mildly convinced. "The Mayor put me in charge, after all. Only, be careful with where you put your little hands."

They walked back to the last crossroad then took a smaller tunnel, so steep that Jarrod grabbed the safety rope and didn't let it go for all the descent.

The other bad news was that oil lamps were fewer and fewer as they went. As a result, when they reached the bottom, the only light source was Jarrod's fireflies.

"How can your miners work in the dark, down here?"

"You'll see."

They did their best to walk straight on, even if they could see very little. Even though the ground was less bumpy, Jarrod almost slipped two times. He shivered in his clothes, recognizing an excess of humidity along with a distant, familiar scent.

A dim blue light slowly brought the surroundings back into view.

"This is nice."

Illumination was provided by small cracks all over the wall, while the ground was covered in a soft layer of moss. Hue and intensity of the light changed, following a mysterious rhythm. The two villagers seemed as amazed as Jarrod was, while Wanda simply grinned.

"It's not always been like that," she explained. "The believers consider it a place sacred to the Bride, so they kept others away. A few years ago the Mayor promised the Priestess to build a new temple, if they'd let others mine for spice."

"I don't seem to recall such a building, out there," Jarrod objected.

"It will come, once they've earned enough revenues to cover all the construction expenses."

Jarrod chuckled. "Seems legit."

He put his box of fireflies down and stepped closer to one of the shimmering cracks. He touched it, feeling it was cold, but not as cold as ice. He brushed a corner with his index and then put it on his tongue. The taste was bitterish.

"That's it, you wanted to come all the way down here to get high on spice?"

Jarrod glared at her. "This flavor. I seem to recognize it but cannot identify its source."

"I knew spice was tasteless," Wanda retorted.

"Not in this unrefined form, maybe..." He flinched, recognizing his mistake. "Forget everything, it is tasteless, but there is a strong smell in here. So strong it confused my taste buds."

"There is no smell!"

"Believe me, it's there," Jarrod replied, excited. "If you were..."

A big tremor interrupted him. The blue light from the cracks went dimmer while the ground rumbled below their feet. Small rocks fell from the ceiling. A large one barely missed Jarrod.

"What's that?" he hollered. Then, realizing it was over, he frowned at Wanda. "An earthquake? Here?"

"I don't think so. I'd say one of the tunnels above us has collapsed," she explained. "Which is weird anyway, I haven't seen this happen in years."

They decided to climb back up the steep tunnel as fast as they could, to later walk their way back into the larger galleries. After a turn that Jarrod recognized as close to the entrance, they found a brand-new wall of land and debris. Two lamps had broken, and the oil made the ground shimmer.

"Isn't it too close to the entrance to be a cave-in?" Jarrod asked, getting no answer.

The villagers tried to dig through the debris with little result.

"Listen, what if someone wasn't happy when we came here?" Jarred insisted. "What if they tried to bury us in on purpose?"

Wanda frowned. "It's a small town. Who should do something like that?"

"I think the believers don't like my partner and me. One of them even visited us in our guest home."

"Why didn't you tell me?"

"It didn't seem important, then," Jarrod lied. "Come on, it's a huge network of tunnels, I'm sure there is another way out."

He focused on his sense of direction and started walking on his own. After some hesitation, the others joined him. He chose a chamber with impressive stalagmites, many different tunnels reaching it, deciding to count every time the path led them to cross it.

On the twentieth time, Jarrod groaned in despair and sat in a corner.

After some discussion with the villagers, Wanda came to sit by his side. She made some lines on the ground and didn't talk.

"Shouldn't your kind be at home in a cave?" she asked in an amused voice.

Jarrod felt tired to get angry. "I don't know about my *kind*," he replied. "I have a good sense of direction because I've experience in underground environment."

Wanda squinted. "May I ask you a question?"

"As long as it's not too personal, I'm still working for you, so happy to answer."

Wanda chuckled. "It's personal, but it has to do with the job," she clarified, playing with her gray bang. "We gave you a place to sleep and fed you, yes. But you didn't ask to be paid. Why?"

Jarrod scoffed. "I certainly don't expect to get rich dealing with wild animals *without* killing them."

Wanda studied him. "And that's all?"

"Be content to know that I did very bad things, in the past, and with my beloved Gaelandra I'm trying to make amends."

Short, painful splinters of his previous life flashed behind his eyes. A wild nature park as big as a region, full of life in all its diverse forms. An underground laboratory, where he could experiment and study the results. Suddenly something snapped as his memory gave a name to the familiar smell in the spice cave.

"It's pheromones!" he exclaimed.

"It's what?"

"Down there, among the spice. The spice extraction might release some gas that happens to remind closely of the pheromones of the Striders. When did the Priestess allow you to dig?"

"A little more than two years ago."

"More or less when the creatures started hanging around here," Jarrod considered. "I told you there was a plausible explanation. Animals don't quarrel, nor do religions or politics. They just go where their instinct tells them to."

Wanda looked impressed, but still clueless.

With all his energy back and a boost of enthusiasm, Jarrod stood and brushed the dust from his pants. He'd just remembered another weird thing.

"Is it possible that some minor tunnels are not open? Like the one leading to the spice mine, only blocked by rocks?"

"Maybe," Wanda replied.

He urged the exploration party to follow him a few steps back. He briefly feared not being able to find the right place again. But then, his trusted fireflies lit up a part of the wall that looked less solid, in a brighter color and soft under the touch.

He was able to scratch some earth away with his nails, so he asked the others for help. The villagers started working hard, using their hands and improvised tools, digging a small hole that eventually grew before their eyes.

Thanks to further shoveling, what was first a niche revealed itself as a narrow gallery. The men kept digging for a while, but there didn't seem to be a way to enlarge the opening further.

"It's too small to get inside," Wanda complained.

"Not for me," Jarrod objected. "Now, don't be a nuisance and let me enjoy as my biological disadvantage is for once pretty convenient." He gave Wanda a smug look. "Would you be so kind as to wait for me in front of the main entrance, until I come back with reinforcements?"

———

The sun was setting when Jarrod was eventually able to return to their guest shack, kicking each and every small rock he found on his way in an attempt to reduce his annoyance.

After a short trip on his own across the tunnels, the rescue mission had been simple and effective. The same he couldn't say about the rest of the day.

He found Gaelandra doing push ups on the floor. She flashed him a glance.

"Hey, good to see you. Can I finish before properly greeting you?"

"Whatever."

"What's wrong? Not happy I'm exercising?"

"Not happy you're still dressed."

She swiveled and as a result her top rose a bit, showing her toned belly. "If I strip now, you'll let me have a bath on my own later?"

Jarrod sighed. "You're always the one who gets the best out of our deals."

Gaelandra completed her exercises fully nude and Jarrod's mood dramatically improved.

Later on, as he was finishing cutting some carrots for himself, a steak for his partner roasting on the fire, Gaelandra came to sit on the bed while chanting the refrain of a Kavedian war song.

"How did your training go?" Jarrod handed her the dish with her dinner.

"Not bad, I guess." She took an immediate bite of the meat, then grimaced after burning her tongue. "There's no time for in depth training, so I just tried to see how many of them could handle a stick without breaking their own bones."

"How many?"

"Eight, with a possible ninth if the guy stops combing his hair after every move."

Jarrod finished munching a carrot. "How much are we screwed?"

"It depends if our believer friends find us first," Gaelandra replied. "Were you able to tell the Mayor they tried to bury you alive?"

"Nah," Jarrod commented, upset. "He made me wait all day in the lab, I had the time to prepare three full pots of fake Strider pheromones out of mushrooms and flavors, and he didn't bother to show up. And even if he did, he'd tell me I have no proof that it was the believers."

"You deserve it," Gaelandra teased him, swallowing a big chunk of steak. "You should be kinder with people who have faith."

"I have faith in something, honey."

"In what?"

"Your Holy Butt."

——————

Gaelandra woke up at the first scream.

She identified it as nothing but a distant noise, difficult to tell from the wind or any other source not indicating immediate danger.

It was day, quite surprising since she was used to opening her eyes at dawn. But these had been exhausting days. She felt like she was hearing something again, but she had to put a hand on Jarrod's nose to reduce the volume of his snoring. She recognized the scream of a Strider.

She'd already put her armor on when someone knocked at the door. Wanda looked surprised to see her fully dressed.

"There is... an emergency," she stammered.

"How many?"

"Striders?"

Gaelandra nodded.

"I haven't counted them, I was running."

Gaelandra grabbed a bowl of water and splashed it on Jarrod. He made a startled face, his eyes darted around while the stomps on the outside came in loud and clear. His eyes focused on the bowl.

"You're crazy? How am I going to wash myself now?"

Gaelandra tossed Jarrod his clothes.

"You don't."

She went back to Wanda to give him time to get dressed.

"We're almost there," she said.

Someone was being mauled by a Strider, according to a sudden, terrifying scream.

"Let's go to the lab," Jarrod ordered, trotting to the door, the left leg of his pants half wrapped, exposing his hairy calf. "I may have made a mistake with the artificial pheromones."

Gaelaedra was quick to lift him and fix his pants.

"Now you tell me they're coming because of you?" Wanda wondered.

Jarrod looked away. "Errors are part of discovery," he muttered.

Gaelandra led the way across the yard, finding everything too quiet. The fastest way to the laboratory would send them out in the open, so they'd better stay between the wooden shacks until they reached the stone buildings. The laboratory was the third to the left, the only wooden one in the block.

"Wait!" Wanda trotted behind the warrior, who was already a few steps ahead. "I hoped you would assist us with the defense!"

"Those who can't fight should leave the village now," Gaelandra said.

"Is there no other way?"

"There is, but you need to buy us some time," Jarrod intervened. "The village is not lost yet if I can use those pheromones right. I never do wrong... twice."

Gaelandra and Jarrod exchanged a nod. She unsheathed her sword and took cover between two wooden shacks, the others right before her, her senses on high alert for any threat.

"Gae..." Jarrod whispered.

"What now?"

"Be careful."

A Strider turned the corner and charged them.

Gaelandra halted, spread her legs in defense position, her sword ready. Apparently, the animal wasn't smart enough to read those signals, since it reached her with rabid energy.

A single swing of the blade had the head of the Strider roll to the side as its body collapsed.

"Go!" Gaelandra ordered, throwing herself across the same alley the dead Strider had just crossed.

"Such a pity," Jarrod commented, looking at the dead animal, his breath short.

"Tell me again," Wanda groaned. "How is it you've not been eaten by a wild animal yet?"

Terrible news awaited them in the clearing after the block of wooden shacks. Gaelandra was able to quickly count five Striders—but more may be out of sight—all variously focused on villagers.

Two human corpses were on the ground, but a group of villagers were keeping a creature busy with sticks and stones. On the other side, a skinny girl was swinging a sword bigger than her in front of a confused creature.

Gaelandra ran by the side of the girl, handing her one of her daggers while taking the sword.

"The wrong weapon makes you a dead warrior," Gaelandra quoted from her training.

The girl smiles grateful.

The warrior tossed the large sword at the Strider. The animal dodged the weapon. Still, the distraction was enough for another pupil of Gaelandra to collect the sword and join the fight. Both Jarrod and Wanda muttered in awe, until the warrior urged them to speed up.

A lonely Strider was scratching its claws against the wooden wall of the laboratory, trying to break in. Gaelandra took a running jump and locked her heels around the strong body of the animal. They fell on the ground, raising dust as they growled at each other.

The warrior saw Jarrod seizing the opportunity to trot at the door. He fiddled with the lock until it slammed open. Gaelandra scanned around, seeing more creatures were coming and the fights with the humans being horribly brief.

"Do you want me to keep protecting you or can I take care of them?" Gaelandra asked Jarrod. She punched the Strider's head so strong that it seemed to abandon his spine.

"Go!"

Jarrod jumped in.

The main pot Jarrod had cooked the pheromones in, the day before, was upturned, its content spilled in a small pond on the floor.

The greenish mixture was solid enough he could collect it in a little time. Only, a Strider was smelling it at that very moment. As the creature raised its eyes, Jarrod saw the wound on the neck he'd so carefully healed after the capture.

"Oh, hey, my g-good friend," Jarrod stammered. "R-remember me?"

The Strider growled softly at him, as Jarrod realized the only reason the deadly beak wasn't on him yet, was because the pheromones were confusing it.

A glance back made Jarrod decide that leaving the lab was out of question—they'd find him anyway, and this was not the time to run—so he frantically went through his pockets for help.

When he found both the fire striker and the flint, he decided he wasn't dead yet. He remembered using a wood spoon to mix some of the ingredients. He couldn't see it on the table. It was out of reach anyway.

He almost jumped as he saw an abandoned broom in the corner. The Strider grew upright, snapping its claws out. Jarrod dashed toward the broom, focusing on nothing besides his destination.

As Jarrod put his hand to the tip of the broom, it trembled. The Strider had bit the other end and the short man had to hold the wood stick with all his strength not to lose it.

Only when the creature seemed to lose interest in the broom, nothing but one claw still into the wood, Jarrod dared to grab the fire striker and the flint.

"Listen, I don't want to harm you, pal," Jarrod began, hoping to distract the creature from his hand moves. "I'm just setting up a little show."

The first spark did nothing.

Jarrod flinched as he felt the tool suddenly heavy. The creature had let it go. The bottom thudded against the ground.

Jarrod struggled to stay focused and produce a new spark.

Once more, nothing happened.

The yellow eyes of the Strider were on him as it prepared to attack.

The spark burst into a flame.

Jarrod cursed as he burned the tip of his fingers.

He rolled the broom to bring the flame closer to the creature.

The Strider's leap turned into a horrified stumble.

"Fire! Majestic friend of man against all the impolite animals!" Jarrod cheered.

The Strider was back on four legs, carefully studying the threatening flame.

Jarrod took a step ahead, pushing the creature back. He kept moving, cornering the animal until he was pretty close to the pond of pheromones, with the table right behind.

Holding the burning broom, he grabbed the pot trying to gather the liquid. Screams from the outside reminded him there was much more danger looming than the single creature in here with him.

Jarrod tossed the burning stick to the Strider, having it retreat in a corner. His hands free, he was able to put most of the pheromone mixture back into the pot.

"I seem to have mistaken your species, since this appears to be drawing males like you," he considered aloud. "So if I add a couple of flavors, I might be able to create something that scares you all to death."

He thanked whichever minor and nonexistent god for having left all the ingredients he needed on the table, along with the untouched two other pots.

Three times, with quick moves, he added smelly liquids or ill-colored powders to the mixtures. A puff of smoke came out of each pot as he hoped it would work.

He soon realized that neither the burnt smell, nor the crackle, came from his pot. He winced as he saw how the wall was on fire, flames spreading quickly across the wood.

Jarrod grabbed the closest pot with both hands and dashed toward the door.

He almost stumbled against the Strider going the same way.

He crouched on time to avoid a bite, then he realized the creature was now between him and the exit. The three other walls were burning, and the fire was reaching the ceiling as he watched.

"Here, monster!" a familiar voice came from the outside. "Short man doesn't want to harm you, but I do!"

Wanda was swinging a broken tree. She had blood on her clothes and a wild gaze.

Her stunt distracted the Strider for a split second.

Jarrod slipped below the creature's limbs, gaining his freedom as the shack creaked hard.

The smell of pheromones was overcoming. Jarrod realized he had left his pot behind. The fire had eaten it with all its content.

He stood and turned in time to see the shack collapsing. Burning debris ran over both Wanda and the Strider before Jarrod's horrified eyes.

#

Gaelandra sent seven Striders to the grave before hearing the voice of Jarrod, reminding her that *they were just animals, there was no need to be cruel.*

She groaned at him while out of rage she ripped a small tree off its roots. She pulled it into pieces and kept three strong branches, sharpening their edges.

The sight of three brand new, almost perfect wooden pikes soothed her.

She handed each to a different villager while she ran around to group the few remaining people.

When she smelled the smoke, she turned to the laboratory. She screamed and rushed to it as she saw it was burning, an oddly green colored cloud into the air. When the shack let out its last crack and collapsed in on itself, she feared for the worst.

Jarrod was right out of the burning havoc, his dirty face and the messy hair giving him a badass look. She dragged him away.

"What happened?"

"Wanda. She's gone."

Gaelandra felt a chill. "She saved you."

Jarrod gave her one of those sad looks that made her want to hug him hard. She controlled herself, pointing at the smoke.

"What's that?"

"It's the pheromones."

"It's bad?"

Jarrod squinted. "I'm thinking that maybe..."

A tremor interrupted him. They exchanged a puzzled glance, then the ground started shaking so hard that a crack opened below their feet.

Gaelandra was quick to lift Jarrod to safety.

"These *are* male pheromones," he said.

"So what?"

Gaelandra scanned around, seeing that the Striders were fleeing as much as the last villagers. Two wooden shacks were swallowed by the ground under her eyes, as the tremors continued, and larger cracks opened.

Jarrod banged his palm against his forehead. "Oh! I'm so, so stupid! I should have checked more specimens! Of course they are all males! Of course!"

Gaelandra slapped him. "What are you saying?"

"The female..."

"Where's the female?"

Jarrod locked his eyes into hers. "Take me on your shoulders, now!"

Gaelandra was quick to execute, even if the tremors made the operation more difficult. She slid by one side to avoid a brand-new crack as Jarrod's short legs hung from her shoulders.

"Villagers! Everybody! Listen to me! Leave the hill now!" he started screaming as loud as he could. "Run to the forest or the shore! Leave this place if you want to survive!"

Understanding her partner's intent, Gaelandra ran across all the streets of the town that were still intact. A couple of times she had to jump across holes as they opened.

She brightened, seeing her pupils taking control and leading people to the shore.

A family took a leap into the forest. She hoped that they'd land on the trees.

"Gae, careful!" Jarrod cried to her as she took a wrong step into an opening.

The fall was brief.

Her boots landed on a coarse surface, with bulges and scratches here and there.

It differed from the ground in its color, which was the darkest shade of green, while it felt much harder to break. Then this new floor tilted and Gaelandra had to grasp at one of the bulges not to fall down.

"This way," Jarrod screamed, pointing at the forest below. "Let's climb down before it shakes us off!"

Not certain she was understanding, but trusting her partner, Gaelandra ran across the floor that was now almost vertical.

There was a low barrier by the edge, she was able to hop on it, find balance and eventually jump down.

She fell among the trees, spiky plants scratching against the few exposed parts of her body. She flipped, softening the impact. She cheered as she realized she was back on solid—but soft—ground.

Only then she realized Jarrod had left her shoulders during the fall. She scanned around, saw a small body and crawled to him. Apart from some bruises, her partner seemed all right. His eyes were wide open, staring in the distance.

"The Bride," he announced, amazed, pointing his short index finger.

Gaelandra turned and saw it.

A fifty feet ocher creature, with a huge shell wrapped around its main body and a beak so strong it could wreck a building, stood where the town had once been. It made loud growls, each step shaking the ground.

Gaelandra eventually recognized the stone buildings still on the outer surface of the creature's shell. The Bride had been there, all this time, buried underground and disguised as a hill.

"It was not gas smelling like pheromones," Jarrod considered. "It was actual pheromones!"

"Should we leave?" Gaelandra wondered. "It's gonna stomp on us to death."

Jarrod gave her a disapproving glance. "Wait and see."

Gaelandra had to look closer to notice three Striders who had reached the paws of the Bride. They looked up and made acute sounds to get attention.

"She's their mother?" Galeandra wondered. "They will… grow up and become as tall as she is?"

Jarrod chuckled. "It's quite a different kind of love, the one you're about to see, my dear. But you are right to call the giant creature a 'she'. Because it's indeed a female. Their female. All my messing with pheromones accelerated a very simple process that was already on its way."

Gaelandra's jaw dropped as she saw the Bride come sitting on the ground with all its titanic body. The ground shook one last time. Then, one after another, the Striders left their shells behind and entered the many openings all over the coarse ocher skin. They all disappeared into her, a loud harmonic moaning invading the air.

Gaelandra flinched at seeing Jarrod standing up by her side. He offered his hand.

"Come on, honey," he said with a grin. "Let's give them some privacy."

Jarrod helped Gaelandra up, but the warrior was still puzzled.

"We are leaving?"

"Going anywhere but here, I guess," Jarrod replied. "It's quite clear our work is over. There will be eggs, or something. But Striders won't bother the people in this valley anymore for a while. I'd say a hundred years, more or less, until the Bride goes in heat again. Hoping this time, the Priestess and her believers would be a little clearer in telling the villagers what's so special in their hill." His eyes shimmered. "The circle of life, ain't it awesome?"

"But the village is destroyed!" Gaelandra objected.

Jarrod made a funny face. "This is why I don't ask people to pay us. I can't guarantee that the best solution doesn't have other, heavier costs."

He started trotting into the forest, reciting a limerick about the food chain.

Gaelandra took one last look around. The Bride was back in its shell, and all was quiet, except for some voices in the distance. Below, the sea kept reaching the shore, forming regular waves. Even the smoke was gone. It left room for a sky so blue, it seemed to wait to be populated with new, stunning wishes.

About Fulvio Gatti

Fulvio Gatti is an ESL speculative fiction writer, cultural project manager and journalist from the wine hills of Piemonte, Italy. His short stories in English can be found in pro magazines (*Galaxy's Edge*), anthologies, webzines and as podcasts in USA, UK, Australia, Canada and Europe. His first indie-published collection, *The Record Store at the Edge of the Time Stream*, is available on all platforms, while his Italian novel *Il Protocollo Scilla* was a finalist at the Urania Award in 2021. He believes his best co-creation, with his wife Filomena, is their brilliant daughter.

On a Wing and a Prayer

By Jena Rey & J. R. Handley

What was supposed to be a routine training mission for 3rd Platoon's 4th Squad turns into a nightmare. Instead of a quick jump and a smooth return, they land in a bizarre world filled with monsters that defy imagination.

Each soldier must confront their deepest fears while navigating this perilous terrain. They quickly realize that survival isn't just about strength; it's about teamwork and courage.

Can they find a way back home before it's too late? Or will they become just another victim in this strange new reality? It's a fight for survival on every front.

On A Wing and A Prayer
by Jena Rey & JR Handley

First Sergeant Perry droned on, but I focused on his words taking notes in my small green leader book. Had to set the example for my Joes like a squared away NCO. As the squad leader, I wanted to inspire my soldiers to exceed the standards.

"Staff Sergeant Short," Perry said, interrupting his presentation and catching my full attention. "Based on the murmurs coming from Private Buchannon, your troops have questions. Why don't you report to me with her, then we can clear things up."

"Roger, Sergeant," I said, my voice curt. I was loud, my words echoing off the walls as the rest of the platoon turned to stare at him.

Fuck me, I thought, *it would have to be the woman foisted off on me that causes me heartburn. Why did my rifle squad become the dumping grounds for our platoon? I can't even perform corrective action on this fuckwit without risking a SHARP complaint.*

After that politely public ass chewing from Top, I tried to listen attentively. I really did, honest. Unfortunately, this drop was the fifth since we started our two-week annual training. This time we were hitting the landing zone and marching to the live fire range. Shoot, move, and communicate. You know, infantry shit. We were mixing our jumps for qualification with getting our weapons qualification covered.

When everyone funneled over to the staging area, I waited with PFC Buchannon and her fire team leader, Sergeant Martinez. When I looked at the feisty Mexican NCO, I saw his barely constrained rage. He never wanted her on his team, but she'd reported her last two team leaders for being inappropriate with her, and they had to put her somewhere. Every time one of her sergeants performed spot corrections, she cried wolf.

Ugh, why couldn't we get one of many of the competent female grunts? Why did I have to get this soup sandwich?

"What do you have to say for yourself, private?" Top asked.

"No excuses, First Sergeant," she said.

"Were we boring you? Were we interfering with your club schedule?" First Sergeant Perry said, his voice quiet and cold.

"No, First Sergeant," she said.

"Will you stay true to your pattern? Are you going to report us too, Private?" Perry asked.

"Excuse me?" she asked, her snide attitude shining through her words.

Fuck me, what I wouldn't give for some good old fashioned wall-to-wall counseling.

"I think I was pretty fricking clear!" snapped First Sergeant Perry.

"Roger, First Sergeant. I'm good to go, First Sergeant," Buchannon said, her voice wooden as she stood at a lackadaisical parade rest.

"That dog just ain't gonna hunt," Perry said. "We're going to make a soldier out of you if it's the last thing we do."

There was a tense silence, as I stood at parade rest next to the leader of Bravo Fire Team. After several more stifling seconds, Top looked over at me and nodded.

"I expect you to get the situation squared away, Staff Sergeant Short," Perry told me.

"Understood, Top," I replied. "But, just once, can you give me the easy Joe's?"

"Where's the fun in the? Besides, your LT's on Six's shit list. Alas, your platoon gets all of the problem children. This cherry butter bar doesn't know what to do with an infantry squad. You get to be the dumping ground because you're the newest squad leader. Congratulations, welcome to the club. Now, here's your soup sandwich. Get a move on."

We had to hustle to prepare for our jump after leaving the briefing. Luckily, we weren't your average Nasty Girls. No, even with our screw up, my guard unit was a squared away outfit. We were a well-oiled machine. I settled, mentally running the training and before I knew it, the jumpmaster stood up.

"Time warning, 10 minutes!" the jumpmaster shouted.

Shit, already? Get it together, Ian. Can't fuck it up now.

Shaking my head to clear it, I checked my equipment, though I'd already done so when we boarded. But there was no such thing as being too prepared. The mission would still kick you in the teeth. Looking around, I saw my squad doing the same thing.

"One time advisory, 30 seconds!" the jumpmaster advised.

Here goes nothing, I thought.

"Get ready!" the jumpmaster shouted, his voice louder this time.

"Outboard personnel, stand up!"

"Inboard personnel, stand up!"

"Hook up!"

"Check static lines!"

Everyone moved with experienced precision as the jumpmaster shouted each command.

Gritting my teeth, I pushed back my fear of heights, my stomach one solid knot. I know, who in the Sam Hell goes airborne when they're afraid of heights? Me, that's who. I must be a masochist or something. I shuffled toward the door, more of a waddle than a march under the weight of the shoot and my gear. I reached the door, with the wind rushing by, got the signal and stepped out into the wild blue yonder.

One Mississippi.

Two Mississippi.

Three Mississippi.

Four Mississippi.

I was yanked hard by the chute as it caught the air, and my descent continued. Everything was normal, until the sky turned wonky, and I saw flashes of psychedelic colors where the afternoon sky should be.

"Shit!" I shouted, startled by an updraft.

I started spinning, the motion continuing until my vision blurred and my stomach lurched. It was all that I could do to hang onto my risers. My equipment was still there, I felt its comforting pull. I hoped that it stayed that way, the paperwork for lost equipment would be a pain in the ass.

"What the—" I heard from Specialist Brooks off to my right. If I could hear him, we were too close.

The sound faded away as the wind pushed us apart. I looked around for the rest of my squad, but I couldn't see past the end of my parachute harness. Neon colors flashed as electricity crackled through the sky.

"First Sergeant, that you?" I shouted, when I saw what I thought was his silhouette.

"Son of a—," I heard, as the unmistakable tenor of First Sergeant Perry's voice cut through the strange sky.

White electricity arced across the technicolor sky. The high voltage current struck Perry. His body spasmed, and I could swear I saw his bones as his body lit up. The current didn't stop, hitting another soldier, this one from 1st Squad. When the next man was struck, I saw an x-ray visage through him, more pronounced than what I'd seen with Top.

Looking down, I saw a dark inky flatness. It wasn't the ground, I didn't think. It looked more like a pool of crude oil that bubbled with a frothy malevolence. *Shit, this isn't good*, I thought. As I stared at it, a chill ran through my body. Time slowed; well, it felt like it did. I watched the darkness inch closer, inch by inch.

Then it changed.

The spinning spiral picked up speed, sucking him in. As he got closer to the vortex, he saw other members of his squad pulled to the same location.

"Think, Ian, think," I muttered to myself.

Shit, I thought, but there was no time to think of anything else. The wind from the inward funnel picked up speed, sucking me in. My world blacked out and I ceased being aware of anything. When I came too, I found myself still hanging from my parachute rigging. Looking around, I saw the sky was clear... but I didn't see the massive drop I should have seen. There were only twelve other chutes in the sky.

This has to be a dream, just a dream.

My mantra couldn't change reality, though. I looked down and saw massive tracts of woodland. The tree cover was dense. I almost couldn't tell that I wasn't seeing rolling grassland. At this height, the ground was a fuzzy blur. I was trying to do the math to figure out how quickly I'd hit the dirt when reality smacked me in the face. I'd drifted too close to Specialist Leclair. Our chutes intertwined and our descent picked up speed.

"Aghhh!" screamed Leclair.

"Calm! You have to stay calm," I shouted at him.

As I spoke, I tried to assess the situation and ignore the fact that the ground was closing at an alarmingly fast rate. Our parachutes wrapped around each other. I tried to break them free, but nothing worked. After the fourth time I tried, I knew I had to take another path to safety.

"Leclair, look at me!"

He focused on me instead of the chute failure.

"Grab your K-bar, cut your rigging. When you're clear, deploy your reserve. It's the only way!"

Once LeClair nodded, I pulled out my pilot's survival knife that hung from my flak jacket. With a grim resolve, I began cutting the rigging. I silently cursed myself for not making my K-bar easier to access. Having that larger blade would've been nice, but I can't have nice things. I didn't have time to lament the loss or how it would've made short work of my rigging.

I sawed back and forth, my hands going numb as I cut through one line after another. It felt like minutes were passing, but I knew it was only seconds. Once I was down to my last line, I looked over at Leclair. *Fuck me, he's only halfheartedly trying to free himself. Does this kid have a death wish?*

"Get it together! Cut the lines, deploy secondary," I said, gritting my teeth in frustration.

Grunting, I cut the last strap. In just under a second, I started falling away from my chute. I fell away from our tangled lines, watching the distance between Leclair and myself increase exponentially.

"Do it, damn it!" I shouted at the flailing specialist.

A gust of cold wind hit, pushing us apart. The wind hit me first, buffeting me to the side. Seizing the moment, I pulled my reserve chute. There was a momentary pause, and then I lurched as the canvas deployed and caught an up draft. It yanked me up, knocking my head back, putting distance between the flailing Leclair. I said a silent prayer as I gritted my teeth.

Wish that I could steer this bitch, I thought. *I need to stay close to Leclair, keep that kid in the game.* I could still see him, though the winds were pushing us apart. The kid was still only halfheartedly trying to free himself.

"Saint Michael, protect him," I murmured.

I knew there was nothing I could do for him, as much as I wanted to. Instead, I focused on my other responsibilities. I was still an NCO, and I had troops counting on me when we hit the dirt. Looking around, I counted 11 other chutes that were successfully deployed. We were all drifting in this strange new environment.

I had to fight off a wave of nausea. I knew that it was the stress of everything. I tried not to imagine what was going to happen to Leclair. I could tell that he didn't have time to deploy his secondary chute. He was a dead man falling, and it crushed me. I'd spent too long in Golf Company, 2nd of the 143rd with him. Fuck me, I'd been there last month to celebrate the birth of his daughter.

Think, Ian, think. What's next? Okay, landing… where can we safely hit the dirt? Crashing through the canopy is going to break bones.

Looking around, I tried to find a place to land. We had minimal steering, but our new chutes were supposed to allow for some control.

"Hopefully the R&D guys aren't blowing smoke," I muttered.

With laser like focus, I tried to reassess the situation and my surroundings. And then I saw it… an open field. It was slightly larger than a football field, but for the twelve of us left it would work. The clearing was in the middle of the woods, around what appeared to be a hill burial mound. With a landing zone in mind, I pulled on the straps to angle myself toward it.

While I moved, I reached for the flares that I'd snuck into my equipment. One of the perks for being an NCO, I inspected my own loadout. Pulling it out of my cargo pocket, I lit it and waved around to get everyone's attention.

"Over there, land there," I shouted as I tossed the flare towards the hill.

I watched the burning flare arc towards the ground. It hit the grass, making a targeting beacon for my soldiers. They seemed to get the message and began angling towards the site. A few of the troops made it faster than I did. I watched them land, zoning out as I tried to make plans for whatever was next.

"We're clearly not in Kansas anymore," I muttered.

Lost in thought, I zoned out until I felt muscle memory performing a parachute landing fall like I was born to PLF. One minute I was floating above the trees, the next I skipped across the ground, landing hard but within specs. I shook my head and bent to stowing my chute, while trying to get a good look around me.

"Sergeant Short, I figured I'd report in. Looks like your squad made it, minus Leclair. We picked up one random Joe from 2nd Squad, plus my gun team," Corporal Garber said, patting my shoulder.

"Did you see it, jefe?" asked Sergeant Martinez.

"See what?" I asked, used to my friend's informal title.

"The dragon," Martinez said. "I swear I haven't been smoking the wacky tobacky. There was a mother fucking dragon in the sky. I saw it when we were landing."

I burst out laughing, convinced that he was joking. This was all too weird for jokes. When other soldiers chimed in, affirming that they'd seen it too, I stopped in shock. Things went from strange to bizarre faster than I could process it.

A dream… I'll wake up. Just a dream, it has to be a dream.

"I can see the hamsters in your head spinning, Staff Sergeant. Why's this so hard to believe?" asked Sergeant Strother.

"I get it… I want this to be a bad dream. Maybe exhaustion? I've been working triple overtime. The new sheriff is on the war path, looking to cut the deputies by ten percent. I'll wake up at home," I said.

Shaking my head, I continued talking. "Fuck, I wouldn't be that lucky."

"We jumped into the sky above the Virginian mountains. We landed here, wherever here is. I'm pretty sure that the inky vortex that we fell through, well, we're not in Virginia, maybe not even on Earth anymore, Staff Sergeant."

I paused for a moment, thinking before I replied, "You're right, something is different. Right, we need to get a lay of the land. Figure out how to survive until help arrives. Our MREs won't last long, and I don't plan to starve to death in this godforsaken forest."

Help. I wanted to believe myself when I said help would arrive. If we weren't on our Earth anymore, what would help look like?

"Maybe the gods brought us here for a reason?" asked Private Winters.

Glancing over at him, I understood why everyone called the kid Hippy as a nickname. He was one of those New Age mystic types, into crystals and essential oils. The first time I'd seen him, I'd pegged him as the kind of weirdo who thought howling at the moon made him Wiccan. I didn't respond to him, focusing on what we could do over why we were here.

"Let's do this," I said. "We're going to defend the LZ, prepare for all eventualities. Hopefully, more soldiers from the 2nd of the 143rd will link up with us. But if we're all we've got, we'll do more than survive... we will thrive."

"Airborne!" came a chorus of affirmation from my *ad hoc* command.

"First, we're going to create defensible positions. Then we'll work on long-term plans," I said.

Looking over at the Alpha Fire Team Leader, I said, "Sergeant Strother, take two men and scout around us. Prioritize sources of water, we'll need that for long-term survival plans. The rest of you, let's get a good look around."

Dismissing the troops, I pulled out my leader book and sketched out a range card for a rough base. I focused on a plan to fortify the high ground. The hill in the open field where we'd landed was the perfect place to ride out whatever was coming. The only thing I couldn't cover was from the air, but fortifying a home was better than twiddling our thumbs as we waited to die.

In the back of my mind, I knew that the hill was a burial mound. I'd seen stories about them in a book I'd read once. I knew that we might be disrespecting the dead if we holed up there.I also knew we couldn't afford such sentimentality, not if it cost us our lives. If we were going to survive, we had to defend our position. Everyone knew that you took the took the high ground and cover, even a know nothing nasty girl like me.

With a plan in hand and Sergeant Strother out scouting for water. I called the Bravo Team leader and the machine gun team leader over. "All right," I said, "here's the plan for fortification. We're headed to the hill. First, we need to dig in. We'll start with foxholes; from there we'll begin taking out these trees. We'll use the logs to build something more substantial. Rome wasn't built in a day, and this defensive position won't be either. But we've got to start somewhere."

"Got a question," Garber said.

"Go on," I said.

"We need to build the foxholes with overhead cover. Especially with what we saw in the sky. We know that there are airborne threats. But how do we handle those? We've got three AT-4s and one grenadier. How are we going to handle aerial threats?" Garber asked.

"Yes, that's an important consideration. That will be phase 2," I said.

"What rotation do you want? What's the priority of work?" Martinez asked.

"What, no 'jefe' this time?" I asked, smiling. It was a weak smile, but it was a start. "All right, we dig hasty fighting positions for everyone. We focus on digging in Corporal Garber's gun. That 240 and the 249 are going to be our lifeline, at least as long as the rounds last. You good so far, Garber?"

"Roger. With two extra Joes, we can have the fighting position regulation ready by nightfall. Well, assuming there are no surprises when we get past the topsoil," Garber replied.

Nodding at him, I continued. "The next priority is digging in the positions for our SAWs. Then we'll get everyone else dug in.

From there, we can focus on overhead cover and sourcing food and water. That should keep us busy for a while. After that, we'll let the situation on the ground dictate."

"And then what? We need long term plans too, jefe," Martinez said, his voice quietly resolute.

"We don't know where we are. We don't know anything about the strange world," I said. "Other than here be dragons, of course. So we secure a base of operations, then we'll investigate further out."

As promised, we worked for hours and were able to get the first fighting positions dug in. The M-240 Machine Gun was positioned with aiming stakes and ready to cover its sector. We finished the first SAW positioned as well. We even cut down two trees to build air cover that we covered with packed dirt and native debris so it would blend in at a glance.

The work was hard and uncomfortable, but it gave everyone, me included, a focus that wasn't to panic or freak out.

We were working on the third fighting position for one of the SAWs when a shadow flashed overhead. I almost missed it in the gloom from the fading sun. I looked up quickly and saw the tail of a massive flying lizard. Yeah, it only took a moment for me to realize that it was a dragon we saw earlier. Well, maybe not the exact one but it was in fact a mother fucking dragon.

The beast didn't stop and bother us, roaring into the night sky. It was answered by another roar that was just as loud, though further away. The ground shook from the auditory assault from its bellow. Everybody stopped what they were doing and looked up in awe.

"Listen up, that beast is gone," I said. "Let's get ready for our night rotation. We don't have unlimited batteries for the NVGs, so use them sparingly. Only have one on at a time, you tracking?"

A chorus of 'rogers' and 'hooahs,' followed his question, so I continued. "I want a two-man guard rotation, changing every two hours."

As we finished, Strother came back and reported in. "Found a stream not far off, tomorrow we can carry it back."

"Anything else of note? I saw something clanking with Private Bowden's gear. What did you find?" I asked.

"A metal kettle. Not huge, but enough to boil water over the fire. There was also a cobblestone road on the other side of the river I found. It looked like something the Romans would be proud of. Clearly somebody lives around here. If we get to heaven, I'm gonna have a field day chatting with Tolkien about this place," Strother said.

"Good to go," I said. "We'll make a fire in the center of our position tomorrow. Water is a critical need for us, so you'll prioritize that at first light. You just missed a flyby from Pete the maybe friendly dragon."

"I heard it, sounded like King fricking Kong. Caused a few strange looking deer to take off. Oh, and we found a skeletal carcass of one of those creatures with three iron arrowheads in it. I brought those back as well, maybe we can use them. But there is undeniable proof of at least a medieval society here," Strother replied.

"Understood, you and Bowden want to take first or last watch? I need y'all fresh in the morning for the water party," I said.

"We'll take first watch," Strother said. "You've laid out fighting positions. We'll use the ones assigned to my Joes for our guard rotation."

"Negative, we'll use a roving guard for this. We've got to secure the entire perimeter and that can't happen with a static guard."

"Roger, Staff Sergeant. Then we'll be making a lot of noise, but we'll rove as ordered," Strother said.

"Can't be helped," I said. "Plus, everyone is beat. We need them rested, that's why we're doing two-hour stints. We spent all day digging foxholes and fortifying those positions. We cut down the trees and used the wood for overhead covering. I'm just glad Martinez insisted on bringing his collapsible pioneer kit."

"Me too," Strother said. "I thought for sure he'd regret humping that when we hit the LZ."

"Go eat, start the watch after you've devoured that MRE that Uncle Sugar so graciously provided," I said.

"Every day an adventure, every meal a feast," Strother said, smiling and nodding.

"Right. Now, get out of here before I find more work for you," I said.

"Will do," came the curt reply.

The evening was uneventful, at least until dawn. That moment just before sunrise was a bad omen, bad shit always happened just before daylight. Today was no different. That's when another roar echoed off of the trees. It blanketed the area in eardrum destroying noise. It was the best alarm clock ever. We were suddenly alert, adrenaline making us hyper vigilant. Looking up, I saw it. There were two of those draconic monsters flying toward us.

"To the tree lines!" I yelled.

I didn't need to make that order, everyone ran toward the tree line automatically. Looking over, I saw Corporal Garber struggling to manhandle the machine gun out of the covered foxhole. Rushing over, I dove in through the rear entrance and grabbed the bipod. It'd been jammed into the dirt to ensure stability when rocking and rolling.

Together, we got the 240 out of the foxhole and charged toward the wood line. We made it seconds before a massive dragon landed on the top of the fortified position. Luckily, we formed up in a half circle so we could fire without shouldering the risk of friendly fire. Sometimes the fates are kind, and in that second, I almost believed that was the case. Then I got lost in the shock of seeing the dragon up close.

I tried to think tactically, I really did, but it's hard when you're staring at the monster straight out of your childhood nightmares. The dragon was tall, bulky, and made of rippling muscles. It was easily a third of the size of a football field from tip to tail. The wingspan was just shy of those numbers too, but it was hard to tell with them tucked in while it sat in the clearing. Based on the size, I guessed it weighed several tons. I didn't ask the thing to step on a scale.

The monster perched itself on top of the burial mound where we'd set up our defensible position. It was a deep black creature with scales that reflected the light strangely, creating a shimmering effect that made it hard to focus on. The monster had a pair of strong hind legs tipped in huge talons that left deep gouges in the soil. The front two limbs ended in clawed hands that were just as strong, but seemed like they had opposable thumbs.

As I watched, it extended wings that were leathery and grey. Every time it moved, the earth rumbled underneath my feet. Those moments of awestruck observation ended with a sickening finality. The dragon turned, its tail sweeping behind it. The appendage crashed through one of the nearby trees with a loud crunching sound. For a moment, time stood still, and a silent stillness hung over the clearing. I watched with bated breath as the tree fought to remain standing. And then everything changed.

The tree toppled over, slamming into the one next to it. There was a crashing sound, as more trees toppled over, one after the other like a row of dominos. And then I heard the sound that shook me to my cold dead heart. A pain filled scream echoed from nearby, ending in a gurgled choking sound. And then there was silence again. The treeline offered protection, but also death.

"Sound off!" I shouted, desperately wishing we had comms.

"McShane, here!" came the startled yelp of a female paratrooper. The young private sounded almost hysterical, except she was winning her fight to hold it together.

"Brooks, here!" shouted the alpha team SAW gunner. The squad automatic weapon was a scapple under his skillful use.

"Sparks, here"

"North, here."

"Garber."

"Grousset."

"Buchannon."

"Strother, too,"

"Bowden,"

"Martinez here, jefe."

Shit, shit, shit, I thought. *Winters, my hippy dippy grenadier is missing.*

As they finished sounding off, the dragon lifted its head and roared. The beast bellowed out a plum of fire that shot into the pre-dawn sky. The danger the thing represented was clear and present, I knew we couldn't live and let live with this thing. Even if we waited it out, it would come back. It was time to take the beast off of the chess board of life.

"Open fire!" I shouted as I took aim and put three rounds into dragon's face.

There air was torn asunder with the sound of fury, as my squad put rounds into the monstrosity. Not a single one of those penetrated the tough scales. And then I heard the glorious buzz saw sound of the M240 firing short bursts of death. It repeated itself, as it joined the fray. I added more rounds, rejoining the fight. They had little effect on the beast's body, so I closed ground and shifted my aim to the face. Sighting intentional, I put three rounds of M4 fury into the dragon's eyeball.

I watched the eye explode from the impact of my rounds, spraying a dark viscous liquid. A small rivulet of blood dripped out of the ruined socket. It roared, its front talon tipped claw slapping at its face where I'd shot it. More rounds smacked into the lizard-like face, but they bounced off, flying into the early morning sky. I'd been lucky to get the angle right once. It probably wouldn't happen again.

I pulled the trigger again, but no rounds flew toward the dragon. Shit! I was out of ammunition, the magazine dry. With practiced ease I pressed the button that released the empty mag as I opened the pouch on my chest for a resupply. The discarded magazine landed with a clatter on the forest floor. I pulled out a full magazine and slammed it into the magazine well with more force than necessary.

While I reloaded, I heard the firing continue around me. The beast wasn't done, the pain I'd inflicted causing it to thrash around. Its tail flapped around behind it, knocking over more trees. None of them were close, thankfully. I said a silent prayer of thanks for that small blessing and put more rounds on target.

The dragon leapt forward, reaching out with its clawed hand and snatching up Specialist North, the gunner from the weapons platoon.

"Robin, use your grenades!" Garber shouted from his place near the captured specialist.

The A-Gunner pulled a grenade off of his flak jacket. He threw it at the dragon, but in pain and panic he didn't pull the pin. The baseball size explosive bounced harmlessly off one of the dragons' nostrils. Cursing to myself, I remembered the AT4s our riflemen carried. Standing near me was Private McShane, her anti-tank weapon slung across her back.

I let my rifle drop to my side, the sling catching it and taking it out of my way. I took two running strides over to the female paratrooper. My breath was coming fast, even though I hadn't run far. I had to do something before we all died.

"Stand still, I'm taking your AT4," I told her.

As I spoke, I unsnapped the anti-tank weapon from her back. She hadn't secured it very well in the haste to evacuate the burial mound we'd chosen for our defensive position. That sped up the process of freeing the weapon, for which I was grateful.

Stepping back to my original position, I went through the process to prepare and arm the portable recoilless rifle for use in record time. I brought the weapon into the firing position, sighted the dragon, and waited for a chance to get a decisive shot.

"Buchannon, your AT4!" I shouted, hoping she'd join the fight with the more destructive weapon.

While I waited, the dragon shoved Specialist North into its mouth. The paratrooper was still struggling to free himself, and I heard him cursing and screaming. The dragon bit down into his soldier with a sickening crunch. Blood sprayed. The young soldier stopped struggling and went limp.

Another one of my soldiers, hearing the word grenade, ran forward. I watched Private Bowden throw his grenade, hoping it would do what our rifles couldn't. It landed at the dragon's feet and exploded, sending shrapnel outwards.

My ears rang, but I was focused on the battle in front of me and ignored the pain as best I could. I studied the area around the dragon and was frustrated that the grenade didn't do much damage. There were some puncture wounds, though, so I knew it could be hurt. I saw blood trickling from the wound site, dripping into the thirsty soil.

"Fuck yeah!" I shouted.

While the beast thrashed in pain, Bowden threw a second grenade. It landed almost on top of where the first had exploded. The grenade went off, sending shrapnel into the same wounded patch of scaly skin on the dragon's lower leg. That caused some cheering from my men, breaking up the normal vulgarities of a firefight.

The explosion caused the monster to roar in pain. It dropped the lower half of North to the ground, clawing for the nearest soldier. The dragon flapped its mighty wings, sending a gust of wind outward. The force knocked me down, grit in my eyes and nose, but I managed to quickly regain my footing.

I watched as the dragon lifted several feet into the air, but it didn't stop my paratroopers from keeping up the barrage. It lurched forward, exposing its underbelly to me, and I fired my anti-tank weapon. Years of conditioning helped, and I remembered to shout 'backblast area clear,' before depressing the trigger. I heard the high explosive round shoot out of the barrel and smack into the dragon's lower belly. That area was the same grey as the wings and looked like it had less scales than the rest of the dragon.

It felt like things were happening in slow motion, as I watched the round slam into the dragon's weaker underbelly. The beast let out a roar of pain, making me smile in delight. I watched with grim satisfaction as the explosive round penetrated the dragon's stomach. The anti-tank round did its job, exploding and sending chunks of flesh everywhere. It sprayed the dark, viscous blood onto the thirsty soil of the hill. It wasn't a fatal wound, but it'd done the most damage so far.

Shocked and in pain, the dragon dropped to the ground with a mighty thunk. The force of that landing caused the burial mound to cave in, and the dragon fell into the depression it'd created. Sensing victory, Specialist Brooks ran forward. He charged up the hill and stood there, with his SAW in position. I anxiously watched as he opened fire with the squad automatic weapon. Brooks sprayed the wounded dragon, emptying a drum into the beast.

Brooks was a good paratrooper, setting the standard of excellence. I was positive that he was firing rounds into the unarmored underbelly, though I couldn't see it. The dragon wasn't out of the fight, as it lay there roaring in pain. The beast let out a burst of liquid flame from its maw. The fluid incinerated the young soldier, coating him in molten death. One second the gunner was standing there, firing at the monster and the next he was rolling on the ground screaming in pain.

I watched in horror as my soldier died in front of me. Brooks had tried to extinguish the flame, using the stop, drop and roll we'd all learned in school. It had almost no effect on the dragon's fiery liquid breath. The coating reminded me of the napalm I'd seen in historic videos from Vietnam…except more grizzly and macabre.

My soldier, my paratrooper, screamed until his voice went hoarse. Then we all watched as he twitched in his death throes. While he was dying, I tossed aside the empty AT4 tube and brought my M4 up. Then I started advancing, and ordered the rest of the survivors to join me.

We advanced slowly up the hill where the dragon still slowly thrashed around. I lowered my rifle, holding it in place with one hand, while my non dominant hand grabbed a grenade from my rigging. Bringing it up, I pulled the pin with my teeth and threw it. It landed in the depression and rolled down into the crater before exploding. The dragon squealed in pain, and I knew I'd sent shrapnel into its already wounded stomach. Without pausing my advance, I pulled my second grenade and tossed it into the crater after the first.

The rest of my squad were out for blood. They advanced up the hill with me, firing into the beast. Other soldiers began pulling and throwing their grenades, causing a cacophony of explosions that made my ears bleed. I didn't care, I just kept advancing.

"Get some!" came a shout from McShane, advancing beside me.

I heard similar sentiments from other soldiers as we pushed ahead. With my last grenade thrown, I brought my weapon to bear. I put rounds at every part of the exposed dragon. As I crested the hill, I sensed that the battle was almost over. While up there, another one of my riflemen, Private Bowden, brought his AT4 out. He primed it and had it ready, looking for his own pound of flesh.

Hells to the yeah, I thought, as I watched the young man take the initiative.

When we were all at the top of the hill, the beast opened its mouth again. I could tell that it was preparing to spit flames again, and so could the soldiers near him. They all tensed, ready to react to whatever happened, but we all kept putting rounds into the dragon. When my mag went dry, I tossed the empty container at the dragon and reloaded, hoping to keep the thing focused on me.

Before the dragon could discharge whatever caused the fiery breath, it swiped outwards with its thick talons. The claws ripped through Martinez and Grousset like a hot knife through butter. One minute they were standing there, firing at the beast and bellowing their war cries. In the next moment, their bodies were cut in half and flopping onto the ground.

Fuck me, not Al, I thought in pain. I'd been the best man at Albert Martinez's wedding and attended his sisters quinceanera. And now he's dead, a casualty of a fight we didn't want in a place we didn't intentionally come too. There wasn't time to dwell, though. The beast wasn't out of the fight yet, though I didn't know how that was possible given the ordinance we'd pumped into it, and I couldn't let it hurt anymore of my men.

The dragon turned its head toward where Bowden and Strother stood. The young rifleman fired first. His AT4 shot forward, the recoilless rifle round slamming into the opened maw before exploding. It went off inside the beast's throat, finally able to do significant damage. The wound was devastating, almost decapitating the beast. Blood, dragon flesh and scales rained down on us.

I realized it was dead as my blood lust faded. Gritting my teeth, I restrained my primal desires to keep damaging the thing and shouted at my men, trying to be heard above the chaos.

"Cease-fire, cease-fire," I roared.

My order was passed down the line, my men and women gradually losing their battle lust. The firing along the line died down, until silence returned to the clearing. When my Joes were done, I looked around and tried to figure out what was next. Exhaustion made me shake, feeling as though I'd aged years in the last few minutes.

"Alright, we police the field and consolidate. Then we're going to bury our dead. They deserve at least that," I said. The reality of the losses were setting in, not only for me, but for everyone. I wanted to offer the dead more, but I knew the best thing we could do for them was to live on.

Everything was a blur of pain and exhaustion. We managed to dig a large grave for the five soldiers we lost fighting the dragon. I wished we could hunt for Leclair's body, but that would come later. With the hole ready, we stripped the useable before we buried them. I didn't think a resupply would happen; I was sure none of the rest of the 143rd Airborne would find us, even if they'd survived. We were well and truly on our own.

As we finished the quick ceremony for our dead, Specialist Sparks asked the question everyone was thinking. "What do we do now, Staff Sergeant?"

I didn't want to say it out loud, knowing that I might destroy the morale of my soldiers. "I'm not sure where we are, but it appears that it's somewhere medieval. Something not quite the Earth we left. Wherever we are, I don't think we're going home. So, what do we do? We survive and thrive. We fortify this hill, and we prepare to make this place our bitch."

"How?" McShane asked. "We don't have unlimited ammo, and we burned through a lot of what we carried taking out one dragon."

"She's right," Bowden said, interrupting the female paratrooper. "We heard another dragon overhead yesterday. We know that there are more of those things. If it took all of this to kill one beastie, we'll be screwed when the next one lands. We only have one AT4 left, and it took two to take out this dragon."

"I am aware of our situation," I said. "We're going to have to go native, learn to live off the land. Learn to make the weapons of our ancestors and build this place into something worth fighting for."

"Staff Sergeant, I saw evidence of habitation yesterday," Strother said. "Maybe we can find trade partners if we're going to build up this place."

"Will we try to join some local tribe?" Garber asked.

"No, we'll make our own home and let others join us," I said.

"Then what do we call our new home?" Garber asked.

"Fort Defiance. We'll honor our Virginia ancestors and Georgie Washington himself," I said.

"Why not Camp Dragon Shit?" said a laughing McShane.

I tried to keep a straight face, I really did... but I couldn't help but laugh with everyone else. It felt good, like we could really make this work if we could work together. "For that, you get to help strip the beastie and field dress it. If it can be eaten, then you're going to cook it for us."

"Better you than me," said a smirking Buchannon.

Glaring at her, I said, "You just volunteered for the shit detail, Private."

Looking over at Strother, I continued speaking, "Let's get to building our home."

About Jenna Rey

Writer of the weird and the wonderful, Jena Rey has long been a fan of science fiction and fantasy and becoming a writer in this genre was a natural step! She's been writing for nearly 30 years with 20 books in print. She finds inspiration in the rocky mountain landscape where she lives with her family, fuzzy sidekicks, and the voices in her head.

About J. R. Handley

J.R. Handley is a pseudonym for a family writing team. He is a veteran infantry sergeant with the 101st Airborne Division and the 28th Infantry Division. His family is the kind of crazy that interprets his insanity into cogent English. He writes the sci-fi while they proofread it. The sergeant is a two-time combat veteran of the late unpleasantness in Mesopotamia where he was wounded, likely doing something stupid. He started writing military science fiction as part of a therapy program suggested by his doctor, and he hopes to entertain you while he attempts to excise his demons through these creative endeavors. In addition to being just another dysfunctional veteran, he is a stay-at-home parent, avid reader and all-around nerd. Luckily for him, his family joins him in his fandom nerdalitry.

Our web page is http://www.jrhandley.com.

Ashes to Ashes

By Jordan Campbell

The fires of judgment burn hotter than the coals in a blacksmith's forge. So too does the all-consuming desire of revenge. When his family, and many other innocents, are killed in a horrific attack, Sayad has one purpose left in life--destroying the dragon he knows to be responsible, whatever the consequences. A bounty hunter by trade, Sayad is facing a monster unlike any he has ever fought before. A creature of absolute nightmare, the embodiment of evil. But he is not alone--a mysterious stranger who has his own history with the dragon is by his side and Sayad is going to learn just how far some are willing to go into the fire in the name of righteousness.

Ashes to Ashes

By Jordan Campbell

Ashes rose up slowly, so slowly that Hope could almost count them. The preacher always lit a fire at the beginning of his sermon, and he would speak and pray and sing, all while the fire burned. The sermons could take a long time, so the fire always burned down to nothing before he was finished.

Hope struggled to keep from fidgeting. The preacher was not boring, not really, but the pew she sat in was hard and her legs ached. Her brother and sister never fidgeted, but they were older and bigger, so they probably had more practice. Hope did not want to sit in the pew. She wanted to go into the forest and explore. She wanted to climb the tallest pine tree, as high as she could and see as far as she could. She wanted to wade in the shallow creek in the grove near her family's house. She wanted to take her doll exploring too. But it was the Sabbath. Even after the service was over, she would have to follow her family straight home. She had her doll in her pocket though—not that Hope could take her doll out to hold, since she had to mind the preacher and the sermon.

The preacher raised his finger, pointing directly ahead. Hope was pretty sure he was not pointing at her, specifically, but at the congregation as a whole. She could not twist her head to look around, since that would be also be fidgeting and her mother would disapprove.

"Repent, my children! Repent! The fires of judgment are hotter than even a blacksmith's forge and they will never, ever be extinguished!"

Hope smiled to herself. Her father was the town blacksmith, and he kept a forge that he never extinguished completely. The blacksmith's forge had to always have some coals in it, so it could burn extra hot. Just the thought of the forge and how hot it could get made Hope feel hot and sleepy. The preacher had been beseeching them for almost three hours already. Hope closed her eyes and it got hotter and hotter inside the stuffy, sticky chapel.

"I say to you, repent!" The preacher declared. "The fires of judgement are not like any that man would know!"

"I think I know a thing or two about fire."

Hope raised her head up so high, she hit it against the pew behind her. Everyone was looking around, trying to find out who was speaking. It was a voice she had never heard before and given that almost everyone had come to her father for smithing work at some point, she knew almost every voice.

The roof shook as something *huge* slammed into it and Hope fell out of her seat and onto the floor.

Everything hurt. Hope coughed and cried and coughed some more. She lifted her head. Every single thing she could see was on fire. The pews and the pulpit and the walls and the ceiling burned. People were on fire.

Hope choked on the ashes.

————————

There was nothing left but ashes. Sayad closed his eyes and the ashes crunched and shifted under his boots. He could pretend they were icy patches of slush, not yet melted from the spring thaw. Spring thaws meant life; ashes meant death. But when Sayad closed his eyes, the stench of burned flesh and charred wood and ash burned his nose.

The survivors had moved the bodies of the slain away. The chapel had been the largest building in Soldier Township, doubling as a school and a meeting house. Over one hundred people had been in here—more than three dozen of them children—and the fire had consumed them all. The stones that had been the church's foundation lay broken and charred and scarred with claw marks.

The Serpent had done this. Sayad gritted his teeth and clenched his fists. Everyone knew the stories of the Serpent. He'd heard tales around the campfires from mountain men, rumors whispered in taverns and pubs from travelers, horror stories proclaimed by miners and loggers who swore off the miles and miles of land where the creature was said to live. No two stories were the same. Some told how the Serpent could not be slain by arrow or spear. Others recounted how the Serpent glided through the skies swifter than a falcon. Still other tales recalled how the Serpent could eat a full-grown bull in a single sitting, bones, and all. But all the stories agreed that the Serpent kept to itself, thanks be to Providence.

But burning a chapel down, on the Sabbath? This violated every law there was, every sense of decency. Sayad flexed his fingers, so stained with ash they were black as pitch.

"Oy!"

Sayad looked over his shoulder. A broad-shouldered man with thick jowls and beady eyes was glaring at him. Sayad recognized the town's butcher. Sayad shifted his weight to face the butcher directly. He was in no mood for confrontation, nor for condolences from a man he knew to be cantankerous in the best of times. The butcher was itching for conflict, Sayad could read it in the man's body language, see it in his eyes, but decorum dictated that he show restraint, for now.

"I'm..." Sayad bit the inside of his cheek. He glanced again at the ruined chapel before turning back to the butcher. "What is it you want?"

"I recognize you," the butcher grunted, crossing his arms. He was as ash-coated as Sayad and his eyes were extremely bloodshot. "You were here last autumn. You're that bounty hunter, the blacksmith's cousin."

"I *was* his cousin," Sayad said sharply. His fingers curled into a fist so tightly his knuckles cracked. His resolve was solid, but his composure was weakening. Jude had been more his brother than his cousin, and about the only blood relative Sayad had any love for. His gaze lingered towards the path that led to the ruined chapel. Jude's body had been whole enough to be recovered and wrapped in a blanket. The body of Jude's wife, Beth, had only been identifiable by the ring she wore on her right hand. Two of their three children had been found as well.

"Aye," the butcher spat on the ground, which Sayad might have thought would be considered profane, had there been anything left of the chapel. "He was a good sort."

"I won't be staying long," Sayad said. "I...have business to attend to...elsewhere."

There was nothing left for him in this town, so Sayad would travel. Where to go then? West to the desert? South, to the sea? Sayad's stomach tightened into a knot. No, he wouldn't go west or south. He'd go north, to the mountains, and he'd find the Serpent.

"What do you make of that one? The loner?"

Sayad followed the butcher's pointing finger. Dozens of blanket-laden bodies lay along the path that led from the chapel through the rest of Soldier Township. Beyond the bodies, men clustered together in small groups. Beyond them, a man stood in the exact center of the path, staring towards the horizon. He was impossibly tall, nearly seven feet if an inch from what Sayad could tell, and his shoulders were nearly as broad.

"I don't much care for strangers," the butcher said. "Why would a stranger be here?"

"I'm here," Sayad grunted. "And I haven't been back in this part of the country in months. What's it to you?"

The butcher muttered something else profane. Scowling, Sayad walked away from the ruined chapel and the dozens of wrapped bodies. Others gathered around the ashes: Farmers who had tended their crops before attending the Sabbath services and had missed the massacre; a shopkeeper who hadn't set foot in the chapel at any point trembled where he stood in the ashes. Horrified mourners wept and wrung their hands over the bodies of their loved ones. Others, stunned by grief, stared out at nothing. But the giant hadn't moved so much as an inch, his stoicism unique. Loath though he was to admit it, Sayad could not shake the feeling that the stranger knew something of the Serpent.

Sayad walked, almost without meaning to, getting closer and closer to the stranger. It was impossible to judge his age. The stranger's skin was darker than most of the surviving townsfolk. He wore unusual clothing, with no buttons or zippers, but folded around him, like a tunic. Sayad was still several paces away when the stranger spoke.

"You're going to need my help, Sayad."

The stranger spoke in a surprisingly soft voice and Sayad stopped short. The stranger knew his name? The stranger turned on his heel and faced Sayad. Muscles rippled through the man's odd clothing and the glint of a weapon's hilt was visible at the man's hip. Sayad craned his neck so he could look the stranger in the eye. The stranger held out his hand.

"You want revenge," the stranger said. "You want to kill the dragon."

"The Serpent killed every member of my family that was worth a damn," Sayad barked. "What's it to you?"

"I have history with the dragon," the stranger said. "But you won't be alone, Sayad."

Sayad raised an eyebrow. He was alone *now*. He had wrapped Jude and Beth's bodies himself, and two of their children, Josiah and Sarah. There was a third child, a little girl named Hope. But surely, she was among the unidentified who had been grouped together. There was nothing that was going to get Sayad his family back.

But killing the dragon, getting revenge for the sake of his family. It consumed Sayad where he stood. This stranger was willing to help him do it? That was enough for Sayad, for now at least.

"When do we start?"

————————

Even at this distance, the ashen stench of the spent forge was enough to force Sayad's face into a grimace. He struggled to keep his composure as he got his bearings. His cousin, ever the blacksmith, would not be greeting him from atop a hearth of red-hot coals.

Sayad tied his horse, a chestnut stallion named Morgan, to the hitching post outside his cousin's shop. Morgan nickered, but there were no children to come up to him, eager to offer him pets and carrots.

The blacksmith's shop was unnervingly quiet. He would never hear Jude hammering again, nor the children's laughter. The forge's fire was silent and cold. Sayad's breath hitched. Jude would never light that forge again. Jude's apron, blacked and creased from years of toil, hung from its hook. Sayad's fingers trembled as he took the apron. It was too heavy to fold easily, but he could make use of it. There was no sense in letting it go to rot from moths and rodents.

Sayad's eyes brimmed with tears, and it wasn't just from the ash-stained apron. Rage burned in his belly and Sayad pressed himself forward. He had more business to attend to. The shop was a stone's throw away from the rooms that Jude and his family had kept for their home.

Sayad was a bounty hunter. He roamed the countryside, tracking and killing animals that wrecked homesteads and farmers' livelihoods. Occasionally, he tracked down bandits and thieves. His needs weren't Jude's needs. As a hunter, he did not need a house. But there had been a place at the table for Sayad when he'd broken bread with Jude's family. There had been a cot for him to rest in. There had been a chair for Sayad to sit in, where he would regal Jude's children with stories of his hunts. There had been a tiny sliver of home the rare chances he'd gotten to be here. But that was no longer the case.

Sayad walked down the steps into the cellar, his boots pressing hard against the earth. There were a few lanterns, dimly lit, but it was still enough to see by. Jude had fashioned several weapons for him over the years, in exchange for Sayad providing the raw materials. Two spears and three quivers of arrows lay on one table. Sayad gathered them up and looked around the cellar. The stories said that arrows could not pierce the Serpent's hide, but Sayad prided himself on his ability to shoot beasts through the eye. Not even the mightiest of beasts could survive a rod piercing their eye through to their skull.

A sword was propped up on the wall. Sayad didn't usually use swords—they were too cumbersome to use in hunting most of the sorts of animals he was paid bounties on, but it could be useful against the dragon. The sword was sheathed, and Sayad took care tying the scabbard and belt to his hip where he could reach the sword more easily. Armed as heavily as he could be, not counting what he had on his horse, Sayad trudged out of the cellar.

The stranger stood nearby. He ran his fingers against the muzzle of a magnificent stallion two hands higher than any horse Sayad had ever seen. His own mount, Morgan, nickered and Sayad ran his hand against his horse's flank.

"Mount up," the stranger said, not unkindly. "We can make several miles before nightfall."

"If we're going to be working together," Sayad said, "I want your name. I don't work with people I don't know."

"My name is no concern of yours," the stranger responded. "Whether you believe my intentions are pure or not is no concern of mine."

Sayad's fingers curled around the reins and tightened until his hands hurt. He did not like it, but he likely needed the stranger. The Serpent had killed his family. He stole a glance towards Jude's house. *It's not a home any more…it's just an empty building now.*

"You will have your chance for vengeance," the tall stranger said. "You will not be alone in this."

He pointed and Sayad followed his direction. He was unsurprised to see the butcher approaching them, leading a donkey, with at least a dozen knives glistening from belts wrapped around his chest. He came to a stop when he was within arm's reach and glared at Sayad.

"Why are you so surprised?" The butcher shifted his weight and the knives clicked as they moved with his body. "I lost family to that damned dirty lizard too. I've done my share of hunting and tracking so I'm going no matter what you say. We ain't been introduced proper. What'll I know you by?"

"Sayad," Sayad said. He didn't bother with his surname. "And you?"

"I know who I am. Call me Messer," the butcher said shortly. He turned to the tall stranger. "But I don't know who you are."

"Enough," the stranger said, turning his head away. "We ride."

———————————

Ashes and smoke congested through the roads of Soldier Township and it made their travel slow. With the chapel burned to ash and dozens of dead, the townsfolk scattered across the town, bewildered at best, devastated at worst. A few men had gotten their hands on a keg from the inn, but their drunkenness was the furthest thing from rowdy debauchery. The men drank in enormous gulps rather than sips, none of them speaking more than a few words. One of them raised his tankard slowly, but didn't do more than nod at Sayad, Messer the butcher, or the tall stranger. One of the drunks took too large a gulp of the ale and broke into a coughing fit that soon turned into a wrenching sob.

"Poor bastard," Messer muttered. "He was the preacher's father. He was always a mean cuss, but seeing him like that?"

Sayad kept his eyes forward, focusing on a stretch of trees in the distance. The further they got today the better. The stories of the Serpent were widespread throughout the region, but a creature of that size would struggle to hide anywhere but in the mountains. He would get his revenge. Hell itself would not be enough to keep Sayad from tracking down the Serpent and taking its hide. He wanted to find the monster so badly he could taste it.

They rode through the town, passing the shops and the townsfolk who had clustered together. Sorrow and grief could drown even the strongest man and they were one another's lifeline. Near everyone recognized the butcher and more than a few waved tear-dampened handkerchiefs.

"We'll kill that bastard good and dead; you hear?" Messer called. "That's a promise."

The hills surrounding Soldier Township were the dull shade of brown just turning to green, as was typical of early spring. But Sayad could not remember a time when an early spring day was this quiet. Birds did not chirp, insects did not buzz, small rodents did not chatter or scurry about.

The three riders traveled mostly in silence and as they rode, Sayad's mind turned towards the Serpent. Just how strong was this creature and how were they going to be able to kill it? With the weapons he had gathered from Jude's cellar, and those which he had already, Sayad had four spears, a sword, five quivers of arrows, one bag full of black powder, and a single flintlock.

The snapping of wood broke Sayad out of his daze and he turned his head. Standing upright just to the side of the path was one of the most hideous creatures he'd ever seen. Seven feet tall, dark skin and only a handful of patches of fur, thin enough he could count the beast's ribs. The first animal he'd seen in hours, and it was a mangy, starving bear. The bear roared, its jaws glistening with saliva and Sayad bellowed as his horse bucked.

"Shit," Messer swore as his own donkey brayed in distress. "Steady, steady! Whoa!"

The bear got down on all fours and started towards them. Its run was little more than a limp, which gave Sayad ample time. He rolled out of his saddle and grabbed one of his spears. The bear was far larger than a man, but the spearhead was nine inches of steel, sharpened to a pike. He would face the bear down and then dispatch it with his sword. With its limp, it was not nearly so dangerous to outmaneuver. Before the bear reached him the stranger stood in front of Sayad, his arms outstretched.

"What are you doing?" Sayad shouted. "You don't have a weapon! Fall back!"

The stranger did not so much as flinch as he slammed his fist into the bear's snout, knocking the brute to the side with a single punch. The bear bellowed in pain and rage, but the stranger did not hesitate. He darted faster than a man his size should be able to do and climbed up the bear's back. The man was nearly as tall as the bear, if not quite as wide, but he wrapped his arms around the beast's neck. The bear reared up, but the stranger was tall enough that this didn't have the same impact it would have had Sayad been the one on the bear's back. But then, Sayad had never known any man strong enough to fight a bear in fisticuffs. Sayad gripped the shaft of his spear so hard, splinters cracked into his palms.

"He's open," the stranger called. "Do it now!"

Sayad ran forward, gripping the spear with both hands, and plunged it into the emaciated bear's belly. Blood splashed down through the wound as Sayad shifted his arms and pushed the spear deeper into the bear's chest, until the shaft snapped in two in his hands. The gash across the bear's belly and torso was nearly two feet long and blood poured out rapidly. The bear bellowed again, more agonized than ever before. The stranger slid off the brute's back, ran to the side, and wrapped his arms around the bear's neck again. With a single twist of his arms, the bear's neck broke.

The bear was still alive, but it would not be for long. The battle, while brief, had been brutal. There was likely more blood on the ground than there was in the bear's body and the angle of its neck was *wrong*. Sayad's eyes narrowed and he drew the sword at his belt. With a single slash, he put an end to the bear's suffering.

"Good man. Pity it had to happen this way," the stranger said. "But it's better for you now. Clean your sword, Sayad. There's a good man. Gentlemen, let's get moving."

It was over as quickly as it had begun, and the stranger acted as if nothing had happened. Sayad clicked his tongue and tugged the reins and his horse steadied to keep pace with the stranger and Messer. He glanced back at the bear's body. It had only cost him one of his spears but that did mean he had one less weapon to fight the dragon with.

How strong was a dragon's hide? Sayad had taken down boar and wolf and bear over the years. But what was fur and skin compared to armored scales? With the stranger, did that even matter? Sayad shook his head fiercely and bit the inside of his cheek until he tasted blood. He would not allow himself to let doubt enter his mind. And what to make of the stranger? He *strangled* the bear as easily as a farmer would wring a chicken's neck.

The sun was low on the horizon, the sky-stained orange—far, far too much like fire—when the tall stranger raised his hand. It was still unnaturally still, unnervingly quiet of wildlife, and the crackling of a nearby brook seemed loud as thunder as a result.

"We can stop here for the night," the stranger said. "You both have bedrolls, yes? I'll have no need for one. We can have a fire and then tomorrow we will continue into the mountains."

Sayad and Messer nodded and dismounted. Messer grunted and looked for large stones to set up a fire pit. Sayad squinted against the setting sun and lifted his equipment away from his horse.

"Thank you, Morgan," Sayad murmured. "Let's get you some water."

Sayad led all three mounts to the brook and let them drink. The stranger's enormous stallion drank more at once than any horse that Sayad had ever seen before. The horse nickered when Sayad placed a hand on its flank.

When the horses were watered, Sayad led them back to the others and hitched them up to three different trees. Messer had gotten a small fire going. he raised his hands to the flames. Even in the low light, the callouses from decades of gripping knives and cleavers were clearly visible.

"There's salted pork and beef here," Messer offered, holding up a large sack. "Help yourself, there's plenty."

Sayad had not eaten since before he had arrived at the chapel and his stomach lurched at the thought of eating. But he'd need food…he'd need as much strength as possible when it came to facing the Serpent. He took several pieces of the dried meat out of the bag and chewed them one at a time. Messer shoved a particularly large piece of salted pork into his mouth and ate noisily. The tall stranger turned his head away from the food.

"Thank you, but I have no need of it. We've traveled twelve miles today," the stranger said. "If we keep this pace, we should be facing the dragon tomorrow."

"Didn't feel like twelve," Messer grunted. "But that's impressive, considering when we started. We'll be able to make it through the mountains at that rate…but where is it hiding? There's a lot of mountains to choose from."

The stranger stiffened. Sayad considered this reaction. He inhaled slowly through his nose and exhaled through his mouth. He took a bite of pork, his teeth grinding against a particularly large grain of salt. The stranger was enormous, as large a man as he'd ever seen. How could he not need to eat? Especially after wrestling that bear and breaking its neck? Across from him, Messer fingered a knife and glanced at the stranger. He glanced back at Sayad and nodded, gripping his knife more steadily.

"It goes beyond that."

The tall stranger's voice had grown rigid. Sayad and Messer turned their gaze to him. The tall stranger was still standing and at this angle, he appeared even taller than before. In the fading twilight, he was pantherine in his mannerisms. Slowly, the tall man raised his head and locked eyes with Sayad.

"The dragon despises humanity. The attack on the chapel was not the act of a predator. It was not food, it was hatred. Killing all those people, he did it because he relished doing so—why else were none of the fallen consumed after the chapel burned?"

Sayad's innards turned to ice. The beasts of the fields and forests were cleverer than many gave them credit for, he knew that well enough. But they acted on instinct. Even if a wolf or bear took to preying on livestock, it was because it was easier than hunting deer. A wolf or bear developing a taste for human flesh was of a similar cause. But for the stranger to speak of the Serpent as if it could plan and conspire? Sayad wasn't sure he wanted to know how it was that the tall stranger thought this way. Messer, on the other hand, did not linger in his bewilderment.

"He? You speak of these things as if you know them as people," Messer said. He raised himself to his full height, which wasn't particularly impressive. "I think Sayad and I are entitled to some damned answers! We've been following your lead. Who the hell are you and what the hell do you know?"

"Who I am is none of your concern!" The fire in the pit erupted into the air, twice the stranger's height. The tall stranger turned his back on them both, staring out at the ever-darkening sky. "What will happen will happen, let that be said. I told you I would lead you to the dragon and I will, make no mistake of that. As for what I know? I know the sound a panther makes after it sinks its fangs into a lamb. I know how the air thins to nothing at the top of the highest mountain. I know the bloodlust that drives the Serpent, do not doubt me!"

Nobody spoke and for the longest time, the only thing that could be heard was the crackling of fire and in the distance, the rushing of the water brooks. The unnatural silence that had haunted their trek here was still present. There was no hooting of owls or cries of foxes, not even the ribbiting of frogs in the brook.

Sayad did not sleep that night. Across from him, Messer fidgeted and grunted, trying to keep sleep at bay. The tall stranger still stood, not moving so much as an inch, as the fire faded away to ashes.

The next morning was much the same as the first day had been. With the tall stranger leading the way on his abnormally large stallion, the three men traveled along the path through the mountains. Nobody spoke, the previous night's argument fresh in their minds. Sayad had a hundred questions, most of them concerning the tall stranger and his motivations, his background, his intentions, but every attempt to voice them failed. The words caught in his mouth; his tongue too heavy to articulate speech.

"How are we going to fight it, anyhow?" Messer asked as they went down a game trail that conspicuously had no trace of game on it. "Does the Serpent have any special weakness? Silver, maybe?"

Abrasive as Messer had been up to this point, that was actually quite a fair question and Sayad held his breath as he waited for the tall stranger's answer. The tall man was pensive for a moment, as if considering how to phrase what he was about to say, but then he finally nodded.

"The dragon has no particular weakness to any metal," the stranger explained. "He is tremendously strong in most respects, but it will not be impossible to subdue him. He can be cast out of this land and prevented from returning."

"But can it be killed?" Sayad asked, almost too quickly.

"He is not something divine," the tall stranger replied. "He is mighty as beasts go, but that only goes so far."

"Oh, I'm mightier than that, I should say!"

The voice was unlike anything Sayad had ever heard. It was thunder given speech. It was a force of nature onto itself. It went beyond hearing–Sayad's senses were blasted on every side by the declaration. Messer covered his ears and his own mount reared up on his hind legs, throwing the butcher from his mount. Sayad's hands trembled as he gripped the reins until the leather bit into his palms. His eyes shut of their own accord and bile rose in his mouth.

"You so-called champions of men, face me! I want to look into the eyes of those foolish enough to challenge me!"

Sayad's eyes opened without meaning to. To his left, Messer was on his hands and knees, backing away and trying to stand at the same time. His horse continued to buck and rear up, the sacks of salted meat pounding against its flanks. Sayad's own mount whinnied in distress and any attempt to whisper reassurances to Morgan died in Sayad's throat. Powerful gusts of wind slammed against Sayad on every angle and a shadow obscured the sun. Messer cowered and swore. The tall stranger did not flinch.

The Serpent landed in front of them. It was impossibly large. As wide as five oxen standing flank to flank, thrice as tall, a thick neck that could have stretched to the loft of any barn, the Serpent was a creature of absolute nightmare. Its head was almost serpentine, but twisted, thicker and rounder. A maw of long white teeth clashed against the obsidian scales and the blood-red eyes. It was four-legged, with claws that were wider than a brown bear's paws and the talons clicked against the earth. Two wings spread out, as long as the dragon's body on either side, thin and batlike. Sharp ridges ran down the Serpent's back and its tail ended in a ball of spines a foot long if an inch.

To think anyone would have thought that such a creature could be reasoned with. This was a monster beyond comprehension.

"Hello."

It was wrong for such a beast to be able to form human speech and Sayad desperately fumbled with the bow lashed to his horse's saddle. It was the wildest of wild chances, but he had to at least try. For Jude, for Beth, for their children, for every other soul this terrible beast had destroyed.

"Hold fast, Son of Seth. I have business with this one!"

The Serpent gestured towards the tall stranger, who stood unflinching, his dark features twisted into a grimace.

"We do have business," the tall stranger said. His hands curled into fists. "It is time we settle it."

"Is that any way to greet your own brother, Uriah?"

"Brother?"

Sayad staggered in his saddle and let the arrow he'd notched fly. It flew harmlessly past the Serpent's shoulder and the dragon laughed. Sayad fell to his hands and knees, his knuckles pressed hard against his bow. Messer groaned, falling backwards. The tall stranger, that was to say Uriah, took a step forward.

"We share a sire," Uriah said, his voice matching the dragon's, at once thundering and yet soft as silk. "We do not share a father. You rejected Father when I ran to Him."

"You call him 'Father,' while you serve as a good little slave! So it has been these many, many years! Do you yet tire of it, brother?"

The Serpent exhaled sharply and a jet of fire, as orange as a sunset, erupted from its jaws. Sayad flung himself to the ground and Messer rolled to the side, the flames passing over them. Sayad gasped as the heat bored around him at every angle and he coughed terribly. The heat from the flames parched his throat. Just as quickly as it started, the heat dissipated, and Sayad tilted his head. The Serpent reared its head back and laughed again, as terrible a noise as Sayad had ever heard.

"You cannot hope to best me, Uriah. You know as well as I that I am immortal."

"Liar!" Uriah shouted. "I will best you!"

"You can certainly try, brother. I shall be waiting for you, as I always have. You know where to find me."

"First, the girl!" Uriah shouted. "Tell us what you've done with that girl!"

"Does that little brat truly mean that much to you? You humans are all alike. Weak, pathetic, vermin. It is all the better to watch you burn. I have watched your kind crawl along in the mud since before the sea parted. I'll make sure the wretch dies painfully. Maidens were always the tastiest."

The Serpent spread its wings and flapped hard, the air pressing Sayad back to the ground. His nose scratched against one of his arrows and Sayad choked on coppery blood. The dragon rose higher into the air, again obscuring the sun.

"I'll be seeing you all soon. Are you ready, yet Brother?"

Sayad blinked thrice to clear his vision. He rose to his feet slowly. Messer was on his hands and knees. Uriah stood, rigid as a tree.

"Messer?"

"I'm alive," Messer grunted. "I'm not sure whether that's a good thing, but I am alive. As for the Serpent, what was that about you being his damned *brother?*"

"That is a matter of no importance," Uriah said. "Are you injured? Sayad, you are bleeding."

"No!" Messer shouted before Sayad could respond. "Tell us what the hell you've gotten us into! Dammit, now!"

Sayad's fingers curled around his sword. Messer was right, they both deserved answers and Uriah had not been near forthcoming enough. What was this talk of a child in the dragon's clutches? The tall man stared at the butcher and the bounty hunter and sighed deeply. He reached for the hilt at his waist. Sayad paused. He had noticed the hilt before, but the way it was positioned…how could the man not risk stabbing himself in the leg, even by accident? The man pulled the hilt free, and Sayad blinked in surprise: the hilt had no blade. It was little more than a handle in that case.

"I am Uriah," the man closed his eyes and inhaled slowly. The swordless hilt in his hand vibrated and a moment later, a narrow beam of flame erupted from it. The man, if he was a man, held the flaming sword out lengthwise. "Son of an angel, as it was written, I am among the last of the giants of old. The dragon, or as I once knew him, Azazael, is one of the other scions of my sire."

"So, is he a man who can turn into that *thing?*" Messer asked, drawing one of his own cleavers. The cutting knife was sharp enough to take fingers, but against either Sayad's sword or the flaming blade Uriah held, it was not so impressive. "I hate witchcraft."

"So do I," Sayad muttered. He held his sword out, the blade vibrating in his grip. "Keep going."

"Make no mistake," Uriah said. "It is not magic that drives me and Azazael is no man. Whether he has a soul or not, I do not know, but he has never walked among men as I have. I am not my brother, and I am not my sire."

"And why should we trust you?"

"Because I'm your only chance to best him," Uriah said. "Just as Azazael has lived these many centuries, so have I. I need not sleep, but I have spent one thousand nights on the peaks of icy glaciers. I have trekked into the lowest valleys, submerged myself into springs of water hot enough to melt steel. I have seen every cave. I have fought in ten-score wars, and I have faced Azazael more times than I can count."

"You've tried to kill him?"

"We have both tried to kill each other," Uriah said. "Where we have fought on every plain, every field, in the mountain and the valley and the waters. It should not come as a surprise to you that most weapons cannot harm him."

"The stories I've heard say that arrow and spear cannot pierce the Serpent's hide," Sayad said. He looked across the ground. There were still many of his arrows spilled and one of the spears he'd picked up from Jude's forge lay on the ground.

"And yet you brought them," Uriah said. "That would surely lead to your own demise, Sayad."

"That is not…I would say that…" Sayad's response broke off and the back of his neck burned. His sword felt very heavy in his hands all of a sudden and he took a step backwards to reposition himself.

"There is more to it than that," Uriah continued. "Look back to what Azazael left behind."

Sayad turned back. There was a small object on the ground. Sayad took several steps back, never taking his eyes off Uriah, until he was level with the object. He glanced at it again. It was a doll, stitched from cloth and linen, stuffed with fibers.

"I recognize this," Sayad said slowly, reaching down to pick up the cloth doll. He lowered his sword. "This belonged to Jude's younger daughter, Hope. But Hope died in the chapel, with the rest of her family."

"You never did find her body."

"We didn't," Sayad answered. "I didn't, that is to say…but…but…"

"There were plenty of bodies that were too badly burned to identify," Messer interrupted. "What are you saying?"

"It's a tale as old as time," Uriah said. "The dragon took the child. As bait, as a trophy, because he wanted to spite me. I don't pretend to understand why Azazael does what he does."

"But why my niece?" Sayad asked. "Why Hope?"

"Why not?" Uriah asked. "What do you know of the child?"

Sayad paused. Of Jude's three children, Hope had liked him the best. Her elder brother Josiah and her sister Sarah had been older than she by several years. Josiah had been able to forge tools almost as well as his father but had no skill in hunting or tracking; Sarah had been softer, disliking it when Sayad recounted stories of his hunts. But Hope had admired Sayad. She had loved exploring the groves of trees near her family's home. She was bright and inquisitive and a delightful child.

Could Hope still be alive?

"If you've been fighting that dragon all this time," Messer interjected. "Then why is it that it's still alive, surely, you should have been able to beat him by now."

"Much of it comes down to timing," Uriah said. "He and I are different in every way save one: We can only be bested permanently when the moon obscures the sun in totality."

"The dragon can only be fought at night?" Messer asked. "That's not going to be easy at all, with how dark its scales are. It's black as pitch, it is."

"He means during a solar eclipse," Sayad said. "Don't you?"

"Correct," Uriah said. "But the moon only ever fully obscures the sun for a few minutes at a time. If Azazael and I do not slay one another then, then the best you can hope for is for one of us to banish the other, and even then, that is only temporary."

"Then when's the next eclipse?" Messer demanded. "You can fight the Serpent and we can go in and grab Sayad's girl."

Sayad's breath hitched. This all came down to whether Hope was still alive or not. She had to be. He squeezed the cloth doll so tight, his fingers hurt.

"In thirty hours."

———

It was another day's travel before the three men came near the Serpent's domain. The mountains stretching towards the sky were still capped with snow, the thaws not yet complete. The brilliance of the snow reflecting against the sun made the dragon's presence all the more apparent. One of the mountains had been charred black, great jets of fire pressing hard against the stone over who knew how many years. Sayad had seen it before in his journeys through these mountain passes, but he had never dared venture up the peak.

"Is that his lair?" Messer asked. "This seems almost too easy. How do we know it isn't a trap?"

"Azazael knows we're coming," Uriah said. "We cannot refuse to fight one another. Whether it's merely pride and hatred driving us, I cannot say. But across the ages, we have never failed to face one another."

"I still don't like it," Messer said. He reached down and pulled up a long flower with white petals. "This here is oleander and its poison to most critters. Why can't we just poison some game and see if the Serpent takes the bait? Or Sayad's arrows—they're barely enough to scratch the beast, but even a scratch of poison would not be nothing!"

"What makes you believe I did not think to try that myself?" Uriah shook his head. "It has to come down to the two of us. Sons of Adam bearing witness to our fight is something that has happened before and we have both had allies on occasion over the centuries. This is not something I am entirely unfamiliar with."

The mountain the Serpent resided in was, as far as Sayad could tell, if not the tallest, then certainly the steepest. The trail that led up the mountain was not suitable for Morgan, to say nothing of Messer's mount or the mighty stallion Uriah rode. Given what he now knew of Uriah, the thought occurred to Sayad that the half-angel might not actually need a horse to travel long distances.

Sayad held up his hand and dismounted, guiding his horse to a tree. He did not tighten the hitch. If things went especially badly, if the Serpent was victorious, then he wanted Morgan to have a chance to escape to safety. Sayad's fingers lingered over his supplies. He still had Jude's smithing apron. It was the slimmest of chances that they would prevail in this measure. But there was still a chance. If they could rescue Hope, then it may be a comfort to her if Sayad wore the apron that Hope's father had always favored. Sayad was facing the dragon for the sake of his family. With that in mind...there was no reason not to wear the apron. He glanced at the sky. It seemed somewhat darker than it should for this time of day, as if it were approaching dusk rather than midday.

"We must make haste," Uriah said. "There are only a few hours left before the eclipse."

The mouth of the cave was not merely scorched black. A thick layer of ash, several inches deep, spread out deep into the entryway. Sayad's boots pressed deep into the ash. It cracked under his boots, just like the ash at the chapel. He took a few more steps forward and Messer was at his side. The cave was drenched in darkness, with no other openings that Sayad could see.

"I'll take the lead," Uriah said. "You two must be ready to take Hope away from here."

The three men walked in near synchronization, Uriah's sword providing the only illumination. The silence that had been all too present along the trails was all the more overwhelming here. There was no whispering or chittering of rodent or reptile; there wasn't even the dripping of water from stalagmites.

The cave was warm as well...too warm. The heat was all too familiar, so much like the dragon's breath that Sayad could not help but choke. The brightness of Uriah's flaming sword cast heavy shadows on the black stones, and it was as if the shadows were one. Sayad stumbled over one particularly large rock and nearly lost his footing. A large hand grabbed him from behind and yanked him back.

"We're close," Uriah said as Messer steadied Sayad. "Azazael has a habit of keeping his prey in his nest. It entices him, keeping his victims as far away from freedom as possible. Look around now. What do you see?"

They had come to a rounded area. In a human structure, it might have been an antechamber. Or the sanctuary of a chapel. Here, however, it was the nest of the Serpent...a den for a viper. Or the King of Vipers. Sayad looked around the nest, the light from Uriah's sword his only aid. There were several stones, but here also there were fallen logs. The stench of charred wood was strong here, mixed with mildew and grime.

"I don't see anything," Sayad shook his head. "Nothing that tells me where Hope is."

"Look again, hunter," the half-angel whispered. "She is here."

Sayad squinted, irritation bubbling alongside panic over not being able to find Hope, but then it struck him between the eyes and shame nearly overcame him. Messer gasped and Uriah gave a small nod.

"There!"

Not even a stone's throw away from them was his niece. Hope was so filthy with ash and dirt that Sayad had missed her presence entirely, mistaking her for just another stone. She trembled where she lay, curled with her knees to her chest. Her clothing was in tatters, with both sleeves torn away and her legs bare from the knees down. Her hair was gone, singed and torn away. A hundred cuts and scrapes lined her arms and legs, tiny terrors inflicted by the dragon. Her feet were bare and covered with blisters, several of them torn.

"Uncle?"

Her voice wasn't even a whisper and Sayad wondered at first whether he had heard it at all, or whether he had simply given her voice to the movement of her lips. The little girl was pinned down under the skeletons of several of the Serpent's prey.

Sayad darted forward, Messer a step behind him. Sayad wrenched the skeletons away, snapping the bones like twigs. How sadistic was Azazael to surround Hope with the skeletons of his old victims? Finally, Sayad was able to drag his niece away. Hope gave a tiny sob and flung herself into his arms.

"I've got you, Hope," Sayad whispered as the little girl clung to him. His grip tightened while hers slackened. She slipped in his arms, and he wrapped her up with Jude's apron. The heavy cloth might have weighed more than Hope did. Messer clapped a heavy hand on Sayad's shoulder.

"We need to leave," Messer said. "We're boxed in here. If the dragon shows up, then we're as good as dead."

They walked back the way they'd come, Sayad careful to keep Hope away from the ashes as best he could. She was bleeding and Sayad did not like the thought of ash getting into her open wounds. The cave's entrance was a beacon of light that matched Uriah's sword. Every step was a step closer to the outside, to safety. A shadow obscured the mouth of the cave and dread turned Sayad's innards to ice. It was much darker now than it had been when they had entered the cave. Hovering above them was Azazael. The dragon's claws clicked against the stony trail almost lazily.

"We settle this now!"

The dragon's fire roared down on them and Sayad stumbled backwards, pressing Hope tighter to his chest, shielding them both with Jude's blacksmithing apron. The heat was muted this time and the apron held true, but Hope's terrified screaming was the worst sound Sayad had ever heard.

"Face me, brother!"

"Not yet!" Uriah shouted. "You know as well as I that we cannot hurt one another until the sun is darkened in totality! When the moon blocks the sun, when day turns to night, then you will bleed for what you have done!"

"It starts now!"

No sooner did the dragon say this than the entire sky darkened to a point where it might have been night. The sun was obscured by the moon, a disc of black illuminated by a ribbon of white. It was too dark to go down the trail, for surely, they would fall off the mountain and be lost. Sayad turned back to face the two terrifying figures.

Hope screamed, clinging tightly to Sayad. Her grip slackened and Sayad stumbled. It was too dark for him to move any further without risking falling. Even as Azazael and Uriah fought, flames shooting out this way and that, Sayad could not see the edge of the cliff.

Messer swore. He had lost most of his knives somewhere along the line, but not all of them. He staggered where he stood, falling to his hands and knees. Slowly, he got back to his feet.

Azazael beat his wings and powerful gusts of wind pressed hard against Sayad, Messer, and Hope. Uriah did not so much as blink. The Serpent snarled and dove down, jaws wide. Sayad had no easy way to get to any weapon with Hope so close. Messer was not so limited. He turned and locked eyes with Sayad.

"I'm going for it!" Messer snarled. "Snake, I challenge you!"

The butcher had a knife in each hand, and he ran as fast as his legs could carry him. Azazael was only a few feet off the ground, within Messer's reach. He slashed and stabbed and jabbed and cut as fast as he could. The Serpent snarled and turned his long neck to reach for Messer. The butcher screamed as teeth and fire consumed his body. Azazel shook the man like a rag doll and threw him. Messer's body slammed hard against the side of the mountain, and he did not get back up.

"Murderer!"

Uriah slashed with his sword and though it was flame it struck as steel and he drew blood as Azazael drew back his leg. Azazael roared, loud as thunder, and swept his spiked tail towards Uriah. The man moved with a fluidity that his height and bulk should have never allowed for, but he was as nimble and graceful as a deer and dodged the spines easily. The dragon snarled and lunged at Uriah, biting down, and catching him by the sleeve. The fabric ripped and Uriah fell backwards, but he was on his feet again before Azazael could take advantage. He stabbed the dragon in the side of the face, the blade cutting against the Serpent's chin. Scales tumbled down from the dragon's skull, clattering against the stone and the dragon let out a great jet of orange fire.

Uriah was ready for the fire and held his sword out directly in front of him. The half-angel and dragon continued fighting, oblivious to the presence of the humans. They matched one another, blow for blow, neither of them giving so much as an inch, both of them moving so quickly it was nigh on impossible to keep track. Uriah slashed and cut and diced, running as fast as his long legs could carry him, while Azazael fought with fang and fire, claw, and spine. All of this happened very quickly, as both knew that if the other did not fall within the eclipse, then the fight would start again all over. After the longest minute that Sayad could imagine, Uriah slashed down hard at

Azazael's chest, tearing open a gash a foot wide and three feet long. Not even the Serpent could ignore an injury like that.

Azazael could not ignore the injury, but he was not incapacitated either. He roared and slashed down his claws, knocking Uriah back to the ground. Azazael snarled and slashed out with his tail, the force so strong that Sayad and Hope were knocked down. Something small and hard pressed against Sayad's back. Arrows, a spearhead, he did not feel especially wounded, so he had not been pierced. But what was pressing against him…what else had he stowed? The flintlock!

Sayad got back to his feet, pulling the flintlock from his pocket. He did not use the weapon often, but it was the best option he had. He aimed the flintlock at the open wound in the dragon's chest, croaked out a desperate prayer to Providence for his shot to be true, and pulled the trigger. The flintlock burst and a metal ball shot out faster than any arrow could fly. The metal round pressed against the gash, hardy enough to truly worsen the injury. But it was the opening that Uriah needed.

Fire, white as the snow, erupted from Uriah's sword, mixing in with the orange of Azazael's breath. The two flames danced around each other, acting on their own accord. The flames took on shapes of their own: the white flame from the half-angle resembled a lion, the orange was even more serpentine than Azazael. Uriah was inches from the dragon's chest, and he plunged his flaming sword into the gaping hole, piercing the dragon's heart and spreading fire through the blood. Azazael roared louder than ever before and the flames, white and orange alike, spread out in every direction. Sayad struggled forward and Uriah turned to look at him. The flames obscured every feature, but Uriah nodded his head and Sayad knew what it meant.

"Farewell."

The fires burst, the heat vanishing, but the force was mightier than any wind Sayad had ever felt. Sayad was knocked backward and shut his eyes just as the sky lightened and the moon left the sun, daylight beginning to return.

Sayad was not sure whether he'd lost consciousness, or whether he'd been knocked out for a few minutes or days, but slowly he got his bearings again. Hope was trembling, on her knees, her tiny hands clinging to his. Sayad's vision cleared as he took a few steps forward, Hope still clinging to his hand as a lifeline. He wrapped his arms around her and lifted her up. Hope buried her head into his shoulder.

Messer's body lay against the side of the mountain, his knives melted against his skin, but his expression looked strangely peaceful. Sayad bowed his head at Messer. There was no trace of Uriah or the dragon. The holy flames from Uriah's sword and the infernal flames from the dragon had consumed them both. Sayad stepped forward, shifting his weight careful not to put undue stress on Hope. His niece was *alive*. Sayad's boots shuffled against a thick layer of snow-white ashes.

"Let's go home, Hope."

Sayad had nothing else to say as he led his niece down the mountain. There was nothing he could even think to say. Nothing of the battle remained but ashes.

About Jordan Cambell

Jordan Campbell was born in Santa Cruz, California and moved to Maine at the age of eleven. Long fascinated by fantastical tales, Jordan has read more books than he can count and has been telling stories and creating worlds for nearly as long as he has read them. Dragons in particular have been among his favorite monsters to read stories about. Jordan is excited to bring his stories to the world.

The Scourges of Ojunland

By Sevanna Wells

The young, hot-headed Regan is chosen by lottery to give up all of his animals and food to feed the local dragon and save his starving village for one more year. When he realizes that he and his father will starve if he obeys, Regan elects to fight the fearsome beast instead. If he can beat the dragon against all odds, not only will he receive fame and fortune for his father, but he might just win the heart of the girl he has always yearned for.

In his fight against the beast, Regan realizes there is more to his village than he realized—and the dragon isn't the only thing preying on the people of Ojunland. If he truly wants to save his people, Regan will have to become more than he has ever been.

The Scourges of Ojunland

By Sevanna Wells

Regan's heart dropped with despair when he opened his palm and saw the iron coin inside. The crudely carved profile of a dragon stared back up at him; they had lost again. Seven years in a row.

Regan's father, Mathiak, didn't say a word when he saw the coin. Other villagers around them sighed and muttered with relief upon finding generic silver coins in their palms.

The village elder's shrill voice pierced the air. "Who bears the mark of the monster?! Who has been chosen by the dragon?!"

Regan closed his hand, and his fist trembled.

"Regan," Mathiak urged.

The other villagers looked around, whispering to each other. The sea of relieved expressions became uncomfortable and shuffly. Regan stopped to look at the fair Vidanye. She smiled, relieved, at the coin in her mother's hand.

Regan thought perhaps he would have been wealthy enough this year to ask for her hand in marriage. *Now I will have nothing,* he thought bitterly, *and she will not have me.*

"Bring forth the mark!" the village elder demanded. The elder's son Yarov caught Regan's eye and gave him a smirk, as though he had expected this.

"Regan," Mathiak repeated.

Regan marched up to the elder's podium and gave the elder a defiant glare. He threw the coin in the mud at the base of the podium and forced his way back through the crowd, who began to whisper and mutter at his passing. His jaw and fists tightened with every comment.

"Mathiak was chosen *again.*"

"Do they even have anything left?"

"… they'll have to brave the mountains or starve."

Regan ran up the hill and back to his tiny hut. He stopped to look around their meager farm. The last cow would definitely be taken. All of their stored meats, emaciated chickens, and slaughtered pigs would also be sent. His gaze fell on his beloved dapple mare Enja. He stroked her neck; he couldn't think of a way to keep them from taking her.

Regan heard his father hobbling up the path with his cane.

"This is unfair, Father," Regan growled. His father limped up to the hut, and Regan followed, his tone escalating. "We have borne this burden for seven years. They should redo the drawing."

Mathiak sighed.

"You think I'm wrong?" Regan pressed. "Say it is by chance that the heavens have taken Mama away, and then stripped us of our possessions year after year."

"It is possible," Mathiak said. He didn't sound convinced of his own words. "We may have earned the wrath of the heavens somehow."

Regan glowered but did not respond. He couldn't think of anything his father could have possibly done to lose everything. Mathiak had always been a saint. He should have been installed as the village elder years ago.

"We are going to be beggars and slaves now," Regan said. He opened the trapdoor to their cellar and peered inside; he could barely make out the last two sacks of salted pork. That would only sustain them for a week.

"While we are still alive, we still have a choice."

"What choice?! We do not have the means to cross the mountains around us, nor the ocean. We have nothing left. We will either lose our land, our *freedom*, or starve."

Mathiak gave him a patient stare, as though this fact did not bother him.

Vidanye will not have me if I am nothing to have. I would rather die than be a beggar in front of her for the rest of my days.

Regan stopped, remembering the conditions associated with the mark of the monster.

"We have nothing to lose, Father."

Mathiak's eyebrows rose.

"We are not sacrificing our remaining possessions." Regan stood and ran to the door. "Stay here, Father. I will return." He ran out into the night.

Thunder cracked in the sky above, an ominous warning against Regan's mad idea, but the idea thrilled him. He would either gain all of the glory and power possible for anyone in this forgotten corner of the Empire, or he would die.

He burst through the door of the elder's great hut, dripping with rain and unable to keep the insane, bewildered smile off of his face.

The elder frowned when he saw Regan. "Bring your sacrifice in the morning. You are too late to supply it at this time."

"I will not bring a sacrifice," Regan said.

The elder stood, his frail frame suddenly menacing. "You cannot refuse."

"I choose the alternative," Regan said. "I will slay the dragon."

The elder's eyes widened. "Regan, you have no training, and you have no weapons."

"How can you forget the speech you repeat every year?!" Regan demanded. "The town is to supply the sacrificial hero with supplies and shower his family with everything they have."

The elder shook his head. "You are serious about this. You know this is certain death, regardless of what the villagers supply you with. We are not equipped to fight this dragon."

"When the imperial trader comes next week, I will have the villagers buy his finest weapons."

The elder sighed. "You do not have enough fear, young man. But I suppose this last sacrifice would be everything your father has. If it is to sacrifice for his lasting comfort, I understand your intent."

Regan lowered his head. *I should be doing it for my father, but if it were my father, I would ensure that I live. I'm doing it to have Vidanye, and a real future in this corner of hell.*

The elder dismissed him for the night and told him to rest, but Regan could not sleep. While he was terrified, he was also proud. He felt a surge of hope for the first time since his mother had been eaten by the dragon. Perhaps his father would regain a sense of purpose as well.

The night passed quickly and slowly all at once—as though Regan expected it to be his last night alive, even though the sacrifice wasn't even due for another three days, and the dragon probably wouldn't notice for longer than that.

Regan went to the decaying village square to announce his intent. The village elder had notified the greatest gossips in the early morning, and now everyone was watching him and whispering. The elder raised his elderly, withering hand.

"Villagers of Ojunland," he called. "It has been so many years, and I realized we have forgotten the alternative to sacrifice."

He was met with a sea of confused expressions. Regan's stomach churned, but his chest swelled. He couldn't decide if he was elated or terrified— whether he should cower or stand proud.

"Young Regan Seawood," the elder said. He paused, giving Regan a questioning look. *It's not too late to rescind,* his eyes seemed to say, but Regan stared at him—unwavering despite the terror slowly creeping up on his resolve.

The elder nodded, resigning to Regan's intentions. He turned back to the crowd. "Instead of giving meat sufficient to feed the dragon for a year, Seawood will attempt to slay the dragon--,"

The rest of the elder's words were lost in the commotion. Some cheered, some gasped, one fainted. Many just stood in place, frozen by a sudden wave of ideas and implications. Many others shouted, although Regan could hardly understand them. The terror overwhelmed his sense of purpose at their sudden reactions, and he crumpled in place.

"Silence!" the elder called, although only some of the crowd quieted. The elder's son Yarov bellowed wordlessly, and the crowd began to still. Many were still whispering and fidgeting.

"Young Regan here will attempt to slay the dragon." The elder nodded affirmatively, and the crowd began to whisper more. "His family—his father, I suppose—is now under the care and protection of every villager here. Ensure his father has enough food, drink, and comfort. The Hero's Hut will belong to his father."

The elder gestured to his son, who had turned beet red. Yarov currently cared for the Hero's Hut and had likely taken it up as his primary residence. Regan felt a little vindicated taking it—he had never liked Yarov.

"Bring the conditions," the elder said. "It has been so long; I do not recall them all."

Yarov nodded and ducked away. He glared at Regan as he slinked back to the elder's hut.

Regan looked up to find himself surrounded by villagers clambering for answers.

"Do you have any weapons?!" one man called.

"What possessed you to do this?"

"Why would you waste yourself? You will only satiate the dragon for a month at best if he eats you!"

Regan stumbled away from them, but they just kept coming. He had never been cornered by the entire village before, and suddenly he wished to be facing the dragon rather than this chaotic onslaught.

"Leave him alone!" a familiar voice commanded. If it had just been anyone, the villagers wouldn't have listened, but Vidanye held sway over the people of Ojunland. Some of the more timid people backed away immediately, some just stopped to look at Vidanye. She circled the crowd and brought Regan to his feet.

"I'm sure he will have time to answer questions," she said sternly, and the rest of the villagers backed away. "If you have any desire to help him succeed, choose your words carefully."

Regan dusted himself off, then looked up to see Vidanye's face right in front of his.

"You have gray eyes," he said suddenly.

She tilted her head and grinned. "Pardon?"

He shook his head, trying not to get lost in studying her. She was radiant from a distance, but up close she was … intoxicating.

"I mean, thank you," he said. He pulled away from her and stood behind the elder's podium. "You are right. I'm sure I'll be able to answer all of your …" He paused, eyes lighting on her golden curls, her elegant hands. He swallowed. "Everything."

She eyed him, smiled, and walked away.

A fist wrapped around Regan's shirt collar, and he struggled.

"Don't look at her," Yarov sneered. "Don't talk to her. Don't even think about her. She's mine; do you understand me? Your fate lies with the dragon as it is."

Regan steeled his expression. *We will see who she chooses.*

Yarov shoved him and took the Great Tome of Tradition to the elder's podium. The elder nodded gratefully, and Regan glowered. Many in the village considered Yarov to be their pride, their greatest strength. He wished for the day he could expose Yarov as a conniving rat.

Regan had never felt so sure about anything as he did when he signed his name on a dusty old contract. He noted the "on pain of death" passage. Once he signed, he couldn't turn back. He looked up at his father, but Mathiak's expression was unreadable. He probably should have consulted his father first.

The elder read the passage about offering a hero instead of a meat sacrifice. Regan ignored most of it; it would be applicable to his father. Besides, as discussed, the night before, the traditions the elder was droning on about would ensure he received all of the resources he needed.

"In the event that our hero is slain by the dragon--,"

Regan's heart dropped at the statement, and murmurs and shouts rippled through the crowd again. The elder demanded silence, but no one heard him. He waited until the exclamations died down.

"In the event that our hero is slain by the dragon …" The elder paused, and a thrill entered his tone. "His family is to be forever marked and shamed. They will be stripped of the property provided to them by the village, and their bloodline will be considered cursed by hubris."

Regan's brow furrowed, and his face burned. That didn't sound right. That couldn't be right; the hero's family should be comforted following his death. He had done this because it guaranteed his father's safety, and that the village would help him even if Regan did not return.

For the first time that day, the air was deathly still. All eyes turned to Mathiak, but he still did not change his expression. He just stared up at Regan, as though accepting that his fate now rested on experience his son did not have.

Regan turned away from him. How could the elder have not known about this?

"Let him take it back," a voice called from the crowd. Shouts arose from the other villagers, protests against breaking a tradition contract and defense in the Seawood name.

Regan looked to his father one last time for a response, again with no luck. But as he searched harder, Regan realized something. He had not told his father anything about his plan to fight the dragon, but not once had Mathiak looked worried, irritated, or blindsided like he had so many times during Regan's childhood.

While his father was impossible to read, Regan chose to interpret his peaceful expression as trust. Trust that Regan could truly slay the dragon.

Regan stood, not breaking eye contact with his father. It stilled the thrashing of his heart. The villagers all looked at him, still whispering and gawking at each other.

"I've accepted the contract," he said. "There is no need to relieve my family of my promise. I only ask for your support in slaying this dragon. With your assistance, I will rid our village of this torment!"

The corner of Mathiak's mouth turned up, and Regan swelled; his words had penetrated the villagers. A scattered chant— "Regan! Regan!"—started in the middle of the crowd, and soon a great roar of support filled the air.

Regan turned to the elder, now flush with excitement, but the elder did not seem so pleased. Regan's brow furrowed; perhaps he was still worried for the fate of the Seawood family.

"If you succeed," the elder said, no longer trying to keep the villagers' attention, "you will take eighty percent of the dragon's treasure. Twenty percent will be distributed amongst the villagers. Word of your conquest will be sent with the imperial trader, and you may be summoned to the Imperial Seat to be awarded the title of Dragonslayer."

Leave this horrendous village. Take my father anywhere he desires to go. Perhaps, if he is no longer in the place where my mother died, he will be happy again.

Regan nodded.

The elder raised his hand, and the villagers slowly quieted.

"Begin preparations at once," the elder commanded. "Bring the greatest weapons and provisions we have. Our hero has a long journey ahead of him."

The elder's words started a whirlwind of activity. For the next week, Regan was never alone. The two blacksmiths in the village measured Regan for armor; the women of the village showered him and his father with new tunics and fresh bread; Yarov sneered at him every time they passed each other. Every minute, it seemed a new villager sought the attention of the town hero.

The villagers flocked the imperial trader's gilded carriage when it arrived, and the entourage of soldiers accompanying it pushed them away. Regan thought about approaching the trader and explaining the situation, but he'd had enough of his fellow villagers to last a lifetime. So, he sat by the elder's podium, watching the villagers spare none of their meager expense to support his family.

At least, if he died, this moment of glory would give his father one more joy before it was all over.

"Regan?"

Vidanye's voice made him jump, and he scrambled to his feet. Her delicate smile widened, and she gave him a polite nod.

He cleared his throat. "Miss Talon."

"Please," she said. "You can call me Vidanye."

Regan just stared back at her, scared to say her name lest it would embarrass him.

"May I sit down?" she asked.

Regan backed away and gestured to the podium. She descended to a sitting position like a swan taking to water, and Regan swallowed. How could anything so graceful and beautiful have happened to this emaciated, gray village?

"I'm sorry I have not provided your family with a token yet." She brought out a sheathed knife from behind her back and handed it to him. He accepted it, and almost opened his mouth to ask what he was supposed to do against a dragon with such a tiny knife.

She cut him off before he could speak. "I know it doesn't look like much," she said. "It is crude and cheap, but I specialize in herbs and poisons, not smithing. It is coated with a potent venom from the mountain serpents. If you are capable of wounding the dragon or exposing any of his flesh, one stab from this dagger would surely be his end. And be certain to use the dagger; if you don't, the healing properties of the dragon's blood could repair any other wound you give it."

Regan's eyebrows rose, suddenly envisioning this delicate woman in front of him braving the mountain paths and wringing the life from deadly snakes. He blinked. "I ... you did this yourself?"

She smiled but did not answer him. "Why do you take this task on yourself, Regan?" she asked. "Is it really worth the shame of your family, turning your father into a pariah, if you—don't come back?"

Regan's chest swelled. He could not dwell on the idea of his father's demise without shrinking into despair and anxiety. "We would have starved anyway, being the recipients of the monster's mark for seven years. I have given us a fighting chance."

"You could have become the servants of another's household," Vidanye suggested. "That surely would have been less drastic, and you might have climbed back to success."

Regan shook his head. "It's too late for that path now. I would rather die than see my father reduced to slavery for his food with no way to help him."

Vidanye nodded, quiet for a moment. She spoke again. "What will you do with the treasure when you have it?"

"Leave this place," Regan blurted, although her stunned expression told him her might have kept that idea to himself. He twisted her dagger over and over in his hands, looking for an explanation that would justify him in her eyes. "It is so desolate here. And my father hasn't been happy since ... since my mother passed away. We don't have a future here, and it has always been his dream to leave this place."

Vidanye cocked her head. She looked a little disappointed, but Regan couldn't imagine why. Perhaps she was hoping he would say that he planned to compensate her for her contribution.

"Don't worry," he said. "A fifth of the treasure goes to the village, so you'll definitely get some."

Vidanye laughed. "Of course."

"Viddy!" Yarov roared in the distance. "Viddy, my love!"

Vidanye peeked over her shoulder, then ducked behind the podium. "Don't be fooled," she hissed, her eyes narrowing. "There is no love going on there. He thinks that being the elder's son entitles him to any woman he wishes. Unfortunately, I think my parents are of a like mind."

Regan knelt by her, and he waited for Yarov's voice to pass before continuing. "I knew he was a conniving son of a--,"

"Speak of him and he shall come," she warned. She gave him a half smile and opened her mouth to speak. Then she shook her head.

"I should go before he finds us," she said. She stood to walk away, but Regan grabbed her hand.

"Vidanye," he said. She looked at him, her expression now unreadable. Regan wondered at how stone-faced the people in his life could be. Perhaps he was drawn to those who knew when to show their feelings.

"If I return ..., would you consider ..." He sighed. "I want you to come with me when I get back. Think on it."

He stood and ran away before Vidanye could respond, and he didn't dare turn and face her again. It had been a ridiculous request. Vidanye's family was wealthy and revered—she had no reason to leave.

The mountain passes looming over the village, blocking any simple exit from the village area, would be too treacherous for a woman like her, anyway.

Regan resolved that he probably didn't need to talk to her again before he left. He would be taking Enja and the men who offered sacrifice to the dragon each year the next day; he could avoid her until then.

Any dragon fight would be easier than trying to talk to Vidanye without slipping up.

Still not inclined to interact with any curious, zealous, or cynical villagers, Regan slipped over to the Hero's Hut to see if they had readied everything for his father to live there. He heard Yarov barking orders. Regan crinkled his nose at the sight of Yarov with his arm looped around the shoulders of a very uncomfortable Vidanye; he must have found her just after Regan left.

You wait. After I slay the dragon, I'll get rid of you too, coward.

Regan crouched in a scraggly bush when he noticed what Yarov was directing. Crews of villagers struggled to drag iron chests the size of ponies out of the Hero's Hut. There were four such chests.

What are you up to, Yarov?

Regan wanted to creep up for a better look, but he couldn't find any better cover closer to the hut. Perhaps the elder would know.

"Yarov?" Mathiak called.

Regan ducked behind a line of trees as his father limped up the path to the Hero's Hut, bearing a small sack of belongings. Yarov gestured for the villagers to hurry, and they scooted the iron chests out of sight. He also shooed Vidanye into the forest, and she followed the villagers out of sight.

Those chests couldn't move too far by the time Regan had to leave in the morning.

Yarov and Mathiak struck up a conversation, and Regan snuck around to the path. He walked up behind his father and put his hand on the older man's shoulder.

"Regan," Mathiak said. "Yarov was just moving the rest of his belongings out of the Hero's Hut."

"Interesting," Regan said. "I thought the children of the elder were supposed to *tend* to the hut and keep it in livable condition, not use it as a private residence. Or, perhaps, a storage space."

Yarov glowered. "There are no such rules. Besides, I felt that keeping it a relevant location was the best way to tend to it. I would never remember to tend to it if it served no purpose at all."

Liar. "Sensible conclusion," he said through gritted teeth.

Yarov nodded curtly to Mathiak. "I'll send my men to retrieve your larger items."

Mathiak waved a hand. "That won't be necessary. We only have a table and a few animals; Regan and I will bring them."

Yarov turned away without another word and disappeared into the forest where his chests and men had gone. Mathiak led Regan back to their old home, but Regan kept glancing behind him. If he lived, he would learn what Yarov was hiding. If he died … well, it probably didn't matter.

Their little cart was almost too small for their table and chairs. Regan hooked up Enja and didn't look at the old property. All of his hazy memories of his mother lived in that house, but the future mattered more in that moment.

"Regan," Mathiak said as they crested a small hill. He stopped when they reached the top and stared out into the distant gray ocean. Perhaps in a less desolate place the ocean would be harder to see—and more pleasant. Here, it just represented one more impossible barrier. "I have something to talk to you about."

Regan stopped Enja and stood beside his father. He'd been dreading this conversation, and he didn't want his father to have to start it. The guilt he had been suppressing since the day of announcement bubbled up in his chest. "I'm sorry," he said. "I acted rashly, and I thought they would take care of you after my death."

Mathiak chuckled. "No, my son. That is not what I wanted to speak to you about."

Regan's adrenaline slowed, and his guilt faded to confusion. "No?"

"I think you are doing what needs to be done. Our village has been actively feeding a young dragon, making it stronger, trying to delay the inevitable. One day, the dragon will no longer be satiated. The treasure it collects as it travels and the food it eats that we willingly provide it will not be enough for its insatiable greed. Do you have a group of fighters that will go with you?"

"They are only sending guides. They're meant to report on whether I lived or died," Regan said bitterly.

Mathiak stared at him. "You're fighting the dragon alone?"

Regan's heart plummeted. Mathiak hadn't known his son was condemning them to death.

Mathiak and Regan continued in silence to the Hero's Hut. Regan halted Enja on the crisp grass and unloaded the furniture. The hut was much bigger than their old home, and the floors were even made of stone. Regan stopped to take it in, but Mathiak grabbed his arm.

"If you're going alone," Mathiak said, "I must teach you all that I know."

"I've already received training from the best fighters in our village, Father."

Mathiak shook his head. "Our best fighters don't know everything." He grabbed Regan's sword from his belt.

"What are you doing?!" Regan reached for the sword, but his father spun out of the way. "Father, you're going to hurt yourself."

"I can do without using this appropriately for a few minutes." He threw Regan's sword to him and raised his cane like a weapon.

Regan thought he had learned how to fight, but even with a bad leg, Mathiak somehow knew more. They sparred for what felt like hours—and when daylight crept through the windows of the Hero's Hut, Regan realized it actually had been hours.

"That will have to be enough," Mathiak said when he saw the sunlight. He grabbed Regan's shoulder and sat him down. Regan didn't realize how exhausted and sweaty he was until he slumped, grateful, in his chair.

"This dragon has no weaknesses," he said. "It hasn't fought with other dragons. There are no chinks in its armor, and we didn't create any. You will have to kill it through the roof of the mouth or the eye." Mathaik sighed. "I should have told you this years ago, but ... I didn't think you were old enough." He pulled a black string with a pearl pendant from his pocket.

Regan's brow furrowed. "We don't have pearls around here anymore."

"No. I kept one before the elder sold them all ... and I gave it to your mother." Mathiak breathed heavily, more emotion stinging his eyes than Regan had seen in many years. "She gave it to me as a good luck charm when we took the village's best fighting men to confront the dragon." He shook his head.

"Mother ... fought the dragon. With you," Regan said.

Mathiak nodded.

"And she died there."

His father didn't look up at him.

"How did you get away?"

"I saved her. We both fainted before the village found us, and she never awakened." Mathiak tapped his leg. "I suppose I've endured this for so long that you didn't have a reason to question it."

You were going to orphan me. You both could have died up there.

Mathiak gave Regan the pearl. "Perhaps your mother can defend you better from beyond the grave than I can," he said. "Don't worry about me in your final moments, should this dragon be your end. Every day I've had with you is time I did not deserve for nearly abandoning you—and for being unable to save your mother."

Regan placed the pearl in his own pocket, new irritation and confusion added to the gathering storm in his body.

He did not speak to his father again, even when he left in front of the entire village with his small entourage of guides. He caught Vidanye's encouraging smile—at least someone still believed in him.

The guides were slow, hesitant, whispering behind his back. The cragged, gray pathway had no forks, so Regan just charged ahead.

Let's get this fight over with.

He didn't have the same brash confidence he'd had when he volunteered for this. Now his determination simmered in his stomach, ready to boil into a rage driven by his will to live. His will to avenge his mother, preserve his father, protect his helpless little village.

He dug his heels into Enja's side, and she charged up the mountain. Her lungs swelled and contracted between his legs.

"Even if you kill me," Regan hissed, "I'll get you first."

Enja turned a corner on the trail and scrambled to a halt. Regan clung to her back, struggling to keep his balance. Her ears pricked higher than Regan had ever seen them, and her nostrils flared.

Regan followed her terrified gaze to a massive void, a larger cavern opening than Regan thought could ever exist. It soared over him like a mountain. Logically, the rising sun behind his back should have illuminated the cave—but it was pitch black.

Chills raced up Regan's spine. Involuntary dread gripped his heart. A hiss filled the air, or perhaps just his mind, and he thought he saw the shadows of the cave racing towards him, ready to swallow him whole. He jerked Enja's reins, and she backed away from the cave. The illusion faded, but the pounding of Regan's heart was very real.

This wasn't just a giant, impenetrable predator.

This was a monster of genuine, malicious evil, capable of things Regan couldn't begin to understand.

"Well?" one of the guides called, his voice shaking. He hadn't even come around the bend in the trail. "Go on. Kill it."

Regan frowned. *Cowards.*

He thought about his father's advice—and the dagger from Vidanye at his side. He couldn't confront the dragon exactly. He would have to surprise it, stab its eye before it could sense his presence. It would take just one shot, and that would be all the time he probably had.

Having a plan stilled his nerves. He dismounted Enja and grabbed her halter. She gave him a worried look, not shifting her head away from the cave.

"Protect my father for me," he said. "Wait around the corner for me for two days. If I'm not out by then, I'm not coming back." Regan didn't expect her to understand, but hopefully she would be smart enough to figure out if he had died or not. He pointed down the trail, and she hesitantly backed away from him.

Regan faced the cave and drew his sword in one hand and the poisoned dagger in the other. He tiptoed into the gigantic void, swallowed almost immediately by the darkness.

He turned around to look back at Enja, but he could only see a faint glimmer of light, like he had walked straight into a screen of inky smoke.

He had no way of finding the dragon without light.

"A sacrifice?" a voice hissed in the darkness.

Regan froze, then dove to the side of the cave. He found a crevice in the darkness and burrowed into it. A wall of blinding fire erupted from the back of the cave, so long it spewed out of the mouth of the void. Regan could barely make out Enja's terrified whinny over the roar of flames.

When the fire ended, Regan held his breath. Loud footsteps rocked the cave, and he shrunk down.

The dragon sniffed the air. "Nothing," she mused.

All was silent again.

Regan waited for what felt like hours for a sign of the dragon stirring. He couldn't imagine she'd gone to sleep; he couldn't even hear her breathing.

She might be baiting.

"Is he dead?" one of the guides muttered from outside the cave.

"Maybe he and the dragon got each other," the other said.

"Go on. Check on him."

"I'm not going in there!"

"Well, we can't say he's dead if he isn't. And if he got the dragon, we can take some of its gold and get out of here."

Greedy cowards.

"We both go in on the count of three. One …"

Regan pinched his mouth shut, praying the dragon wouldn't hear them. Perhaps she *had* gone back to sleep.

"Two …"

Something rustled in the blackness. Regan strained not to shout a warning, and he covered his ears.

The dragon whooshed past him. No matter how hard he pressed his palms against his head, he could still hear their brief, terrified screams. He squirmed, forcing the thought out of his mind that he would almost definitely share their fate.

He lowered his hands slowly. He hadn't heard Enja scream; maybe she had survived and run away.

The dragon sniffed again. A smacking sound followed, like she was licking her lips. "Meager," she said. "Perhaps it is time to end the misery of your village, little sacrifice."

Regan's heart pounded. The dragon chuckled.

"Yes, pitiful snack. I know you're here. I can smell your fear, the pumping of your blood." The dragon's hand slammed into the cave wall right above Regan, and he bit his tongue to keep from yelling.

"I'm close," she said. "You've found a nice little hiding place, haven't you?" Her wings shuffled. "You'll have to come out eventually. Better to be eaten now than starve where you sit. If I have to smoke you out, I will."

The cave went quiet again. Regan allowed himself small breaths, but he couldn't take the deep, loud ones he wanted. He had already lost any element of surprise he hoped to have, and he thought there would be at least enough sunlight in this cave to scope out her position.

Now he didn't know what to do.

The dragon let out a disappointed grunt. "You're annoyingly patient," she said. "How lucky you are that I've just eaten, and I won't break my own cave on top of you in a violent rage. Perhaps you will come out before you get crushed to death."

This time, Regan heard her walk away. A *whoosh* echoed through the cave, and light sprang up at the other end of it. He waited in his cavity for what seemed to be an eternity before moving again.

Regan peered outside of his cavity; certain he would see her coming now that some meager light had filled the space.

He paled when he saw the dragon. He thought she was a boulder at first, or an outcropping in the cave. Lying down, she was nearly as tall as the entire cavern. She probably had to duck her head to walk through it. He couldn't tell if the orange light of the fire she had made was depicting her color accurately, but she appeared to be a deep crimson.

Regan bit his lip. The cave was long, and he had no guarantee of finding another cavity to hide in. She had nearly smelled him out as it was, and when she got hungry again, she would do more to find him than he could survive.

He had no way of knowing if she was asleep. She had been patient when the guides were waiting to see if he'd died, and she knew he was in her cave.

An idea struck him, but he wanted to wait a little longer. He ducked back into his cavity, fingering the dagger at his side. Maybe if he could feint the dragon into showing if she was awake—he didn't know if dragons slept during the day or night, and neither had anyone at the village.

Regan scooped up a handful of rocks from the ground, although these rocks were unusually smooth, light, and tube-like. He speculated that they might be bones, and he nearly dropped them. He covered his mouth to keep from blurting in disgust.

He glanced up at the dragon one more time, then threw the bones and pebbles as far towards the mouth of the cave as he could. He looked at the dragon for a reaction to the sound, but she didn't give one.

Regan's pulse quickened. She was asleep, so now he had to make this quick. He sheathed his sword and stood out of the cavity, disturbing as little rubble as possible. He pressed a hand against the cave wall, creeping quickly and carefully. The faint light helped him avoid some of the bigger obstacles, but the dragon still seemed so far away.

The mountainous creature stirred, and Regan froze. She let out a massive sigh, then shuffled.

He didn't know how much longer she would be out. He probably didn't have time to be careful anymore. Adrenaline powered him forward, and he couldn't slow down. He sprang towards the dragon, victory enclosing on him faster than he could process it.

He slowed right by the dragon's face. Her eye was almost the size of his entire head, but he had confidence in Vidanye's poison. He raised the dagger and plunged it towards the dragon's eye.

Before he could make contact, her eye snapped open. She swung her tail and flung him into the cave wall. Regan yelled but was cut off by the impact of stone against his back. The air rushed out of him, and he collapsed to the ground. The dragon leered over him as he struggled to regain his breath. His heart pounded, making it even harder to inhale.

The dragon chuckled, revealing jagged, stained teeth. She grabbed Regan with her talons, and he scrambled helplessly for his weapons. He found his sword, but the poison dagger slipped from his fingers.

No. No, no, no. Not like this. No. He gripped his sword, knowing it was futile. At least he would die like a warrior, and maybe take down the dragon if his sword injured her throat.

"Scream, why don't you?" the dragon teased. He met her golden eyes, and they stunned him. He recoiled. He didn't notice his breath had returned until she sighed.

"Annoying to the end," she said. "A little smarter than most." She opened her mouth and lifted him to her teeth.

Regan's heart pounded, and the heat of her breath washed over him. He heard the gurgle of fire deep in her stomach; he scrambled to make peace with the way he had left things. He thought of his father, of Enja, of Vidanye.

Vidanye.

Steam and smoke built up in the dragon's mouth, and Regan coughed. Her grip relaxed so she could drop Regan into her mouth, granting him an opportunity he hadn't expected.

He didn't have the knife, but the fleshy roof of her mouth was vulnerable to him.

Regan thrust the sword upward into her skull. The dragon roared and struggled. She swung her head, and Regan tumbled from her mouth. He let go of his sword; it was still stuck in her mouth. She swayed until she crashed to the ground and lay motionless.

He gasped and swallowed, not sure if he had succeeded. He stood cautiously and walked to the dragon's side. He scooped his dagger up from the ground and crept to her eye. He prodded her, waiting for a reaction, but the pooling blood under her head and the lack of movement told him all he needed to know. He didn't even need to use the poison.

Regan breathed a shaky sigh of relief, then exploded in cheers and yells. He slammed into the side of the cave and immediately regretted the ache that reverberated through his torso. His face flushed. He sank against the wall, staring down his victory with ramping pride.

He had slain the dragon. He had rid his village of the greatest terror possible, and he had done it alone. He hated to think that he now had to tell his father that the sparring they had done didn't matter in the end, but perhaps his father would be too happy to see him to care.

Regan drew his sword from the dragon's mouth and moved to clean it— but he needed proof he had accomplished his task. He swung his sword at her gums, breaking a gigantic tooth loose. He pried it the rest of the way. It came up to his hip, the size and sharpness of a foreign blade.

Perhaps I will make a sword out of this.

Regan slung the tooth over his shoulder and sheathed his sword. He thought briefly about looking around for the dragon's hoard, but it would be futile to try and carry it all back now. Perhaps if the village had believed in him, they would have sent a cart, but they obviously didn't anticipate he would make it back in one piece.

Regan smiled coldly. Power and pride surged in his stomach as he thought about the shock on their faces, then about the relief on his father's face. Regan's heart pounded—what would Vidanye think? Would she be surprised? Giving him the dagger seemed to be an act of faith on her part; she'd had to put a lot of effort or money into the poison.

Regan didn't see Enja. Panic struck his stomach; had she been consumed by the dragon fire?

He whistled, and after a quiet moment, he heard a neigh in response. He sighed with relief; not only had his companion been smart enough to survive, but he wouldn't have to drag the massive dragon tooth back to Ojunland all on his own.

He didn't make it back until dawn. He saw his little village from one of the peaks in the trail. As he descended, a small crowd gathered at the farthest end of the path. Distant heads, so small from up on the mountain, wiggled around as though looking for him—or probably the guides sent with him.

Regan frowned. Perhaps he would not even return to them at all, just get his father and Vidanye and leave this place. Their cynicism and cowardice didn't deserve the salvation he had won for them.

He sighed. His father did not need to brave the mountains, and Vidanye had not consented to leave. And how would he feed Enja? A vast wasteland might be between Ojunland and civilization, for all he knew.

No. The villagers could share in his victory as long as they gave him what he needed. And if they helped him gather the gold, he would distribute it as promised.

Regan relished in the gasps of excitement and amazement as he drew near to the village. He didn't mean to puff himself up; they didn't know what they were cheering for. They thought he had rid them of an annual sacrifice. But his father had made a point—the dragon would have run the village to destitution and then attacked them all.

He had saved their lives, protected his father, ended the sacrifices, and satiated the gods.

Enja raised her head and tossed it at the cheers, as though she was proud too. Regan patted her neck, then raised his arm and shook his fist.

"Regan! RE" the meager group chanted. Other villagers poked their heads out of their homes, and soon a crowd had swarmed around him. They reached up to brush against the dragon's tooth. Some of the sillier villagers squealed with delight and shock; others just stood back and nodded to each other.

Enja forced her way through the growing crowd, and Regan led her over to the Hero's Hut first. Mathiak sat on one of their chairs in the crisp gray grass, his eyes bloodshot and his face gaunt. He didn't look up when Regan rode up the path.

Regan dismounted, confused at the state of Mathiak. "Father?" he asked.

Mathiak looked up, and his eyes widened. "Regan," he whispered.

Regan held out the dragon's tooth. "I brought this back for your, Father."

Mathiak hobbled out of his chair and grabbed Regan's shoulders. "You—you survived." His voice tightened. He embraced Regan tightly, and Regan dropped the tooth. He hugged his father back. There was nothing more to be said.

Mathiak marched with Regan and Enja to the elder's podium, with what seemed to be the entire village trailing behind them. Mathiak beamed at everyone, occasionally grabbing Regan's hand and raising it for everyone to see.

Vidanye stood at the podium, and Regan smiled at her. But she just stared at the ground. She gave him a quick worried glance, and he frowned.

I came back alive. What is wrong?

The elder didn't look too pleased either, but he said nothing until Regan stopped in front of his podium and the villagers quieted down. He raised his hands, then gestured at Regan.

"Ojunland," he said. "I present your hero!"

Mathiak urged him to step up to the podium. Regan did so but didn't take his gaze off of Vidanye. She kept shooting him tense, terrified glances. Had someone threatened her? Had something happened while he was gone?

The elder kept talking to the villagers, something about safety and glory and praises. They chanted his name more. Vidanye shook her head at Regan.

"Yarov!" the elder called. "Bring my mantle! In honor of Regan's success, Mathiak will be the new elder of the village."

Regan's eyes widened. This wasn't part of the deal. He looked at Vidanye, but her eyes were closed.

Yarov and the elder couldn't possibly be pleased.

Regan relaxed. What could the elder do to him? He had slain a dragon, and he had more combat capability than anyone in this village right now. Vidanye had good reason to be worried, but she didn't know everything about Regan and what he could do.

The elder sighed. "Where is my son?" He shook his head. "We will get the mantle later. Seawood, does it please you to address the village?"

Regan looked at Vidanye. Perhaps now was not a good time to declare that he wanted her for his wife, but he could give it a try.

At least this would tell every other man in the village to back off, even if she needed some time to think about it before she would accept.

Regan stood at the podium and opened his mouth to speak, but a cold dread washed over him. He startled; it felt like what he had experienced in front of the dragon's cave.

Vidanye lunged for him. "Regan!"

He opened his mouth to tell her something was wrong, but he couldn't finish. Cold despair gripped him uncontrollably, and he writhed to get rid of it. Vidanye grabbed him and wrestled him over the edge of the podium, and the world erupted in flames.

Villagers screamed, and the podium began to smoke. The elder cried out— but he sounded elated. No longer gripped by fear, Regan looked up at the sky.

Yarov was on the red dragon, sitting behind its head.

Regan paled. Vidanye's voice came back to him: "The healing properties of the dragon's blood could repair any other wound you give it." He turned to her for answers—and found guilt. He stiffened.

"You knew," he whispered.

Vidanye grabbed Regan's arm and hoisted him to his feet. "Yarov and his father have been making deals with the dragon. They have its treasure." Another spew of fire blew from the dragon's mouth. Regan grabbed Vidanye and raced into the forest.

"Find him!" Yarov ordered, and the dragon roared in response.

"They have been the ones feeding the dragon instead of finding a way to destroy it," Vidanye said as they dodged trees and Regan scanned for a hiding spot. "I would have told you, but they threatened my father."

"Threatened? What could they do to him?" Regan pulled Vidanye under a felled log just as the dragon spit more fire into the trees behind them.

"Come out, Seawood!" Yarov demanded. "Face death like a man!"

"You got the coin every year at the command of Yarov," Vidanye whispered. They watched the dragon arc around at the top of the trees, then fly off, still watching for them. "He was always jealous of you."

"Jealous of me?"

"You are better than him, and part of him knows it," she said. She sighed. "I had hoped you'd poisoned the dragon, but when I saw that you still had the dagger, I knew the dragon was still alive. Yarov left to confirm its death." She buried her face in her hands. "All is lost now. They will not preserve the village for anything."

Regan grabbed her shoulders. "I still have the dagger, Vidanye. I will save Ojunland if I die trying."

Vidanye's eyes glistened. She looked away. "I can't ask you to sacrifice yourself again. I can appease Yarov if you escape."

Regan shook his head. "My father said that we should be done running. Some other sorry family will be Yarov's victim if we don't finish this now."

"I thought you hated Ojunland."

Regan nodded. "This place is desolate and forgotten, but it's not bad enough to abandon to the dragon." He drew his sword and felt for the poison dagger at his side. "Take care of my father, Vidanye."

Vidanye grabbed his sleeve. "I'll go with you. If you survive and you decide to leave this place, take me with you."

Regan smiled sadly. "It will comfort me in death to know that you would be there for me. I have long admired you, Vidanye, and I hope you find a man that will care for you and treat you well."

Vidanye squeezed his hand, then finally let him go.

The dragon screeched.

"Seawood, you coward! Come out!" Yarov demanded.

Regan raced back to the Hero's Hut. The dragon spotted him on the path and swooped down to follow him, roaring and spitting flames.

Regan ducked into the Hero's Hut, and a tower of fire followed him inside, splitting the roof with its force. Regan snatched up his father's hunting bow and three arrows; maybe he could shoot Yarov off of the dragon's back.

The roof creaked and began to cave in the middle. Regan leaped out of the side window as the entire structure collapsed, whining and popping as the fire consumed it.

Regan stood and turned to face Yarov and the dragon. Yarov pointed at him.

"Get him," he ordered.

The dragon dove for Regan and opened her mouth. Regan ducked and rolled to the side, and she swept past him.

"How could you miss him?! Get him!"

"Hold your tongue, or I'll eat you too!" the dragon retorted.

Regan nocked an arrow to his bow. The dragon wouldn't necessarily stop attacking him if he killed Yarov, but at least he would only have one enemy to deal with. Both would have to die for Ojunland to be truly safe.

The dragon swooped again, extending her talons this time. If her mouth didn't catch him, her claws would. Regan ducked behind the smoking remains of the Hero's Hut, then raised up just enough from the ashes to shoot at Yarov.

The arrow sailed right over his enemy's head.

"What are you doing?!" Yarov screamed. "He almost took my head off!"

The dragon only growled in response. Perhaps they would tire of each other.

Regan nocked another arrow, aiming a little lower this time. The dragon saw it coming, and when the arrow loosed, she dropped out of the sky. Yarov screeched in surprise but did not rebuke the dragon.

Regan grabbed at his quiver and only found one arrow. He looked back up at Yarov, but the dragon was circling and shuffling. He had one shot, and he needed the dragon to be close. He stepped out from behind the rubble of the Hero's Hut.

"Hey!" he called out. "Come down here so I can finish what I started!"

The dragon screeched and dove for him, claws extended again. Her mouth gaped open, and fire lit her chest. Regan raised his bow, ready to trade Yarov's life for his—and then he spotted an empty space in the dragon's row of jagged teeth.

The tooth I took.

It would get the dragon and Yarov on the ground if he could hit it.

Regan bit his lip and waited for the dragon to get a little closer. He waited until he could see the veins in her wings, and he loosed the arrow.

It struck her raw gum, and she roared. Regan rolled to the side, and she crashed into the dirt. She tumbled until she slammed into a nearby tree. She scrambled to her feet to shake herself off and grab fruitlessly at the arrow jutting out of her mouth.

Yarov lay in the path of her fall, not moving.

Regan didn't know if he was dead but didn't want to waste time checking. The dragon plucked the arrow out of her mouth like a needle and threw it aside.

"What are you?" she sneered, approaching Regan. "Why do you think you have the privilege of defeating me?" She opened her mouth, and fire raced through her chest and up her throat again. Regan cowered behind a tree, which quickly lit on fire around him. He ducked away and kept running.

"It's hopeless now." The dragon grabbed a tree behind him and uprooted it like a simple weed. "You defeated my little ally, and you tricked me once, but you won't be so lucky this time."

Enja appeared out of the trees and almost knocked Regan over racing to his side. He mounted her and dug his heels into her flanks. The dragon swiped at Enja with her tail, but the horse was just a little faster.

The dragon snarled. "I'll eat your little horse, too."

Regan circled back around and drew his sword. He didn't have a plan now.

Enja pawed the ground impatiently.

The dragon's lips curled to reveal her teeth. "Go on. Charge at me."

Regan patted Enja's neck. "It's over. You can still get out of here. I'll take care of the dragon."

Enja tossed her head, as though gesturing to the dragon.

Regan chuckled sadly. "Thank you for coming for me." He sat up. He wouldn't go blindly into the dragon; maybe he would figure out something while he charged. But the dragon's golden eyes were losing their patience.

He urged Enja forward, and she galloped at full speed towards the dragon. He raised his sword, ready to plunge it into anything he could reach. The dragon opened her mouth—

Instead of fire, a mighty scream erupted from the dragon. Regan turned Enja away from the dragon's face. The beast twisted and flailed her wings, inadvertently turning a tiny rip in her wing into a full-length tear, all the way to her wing bone.

Mathiak stood on the other side of the dragon, sword in hand.

Regan gasped. "Father!"

But he was too late. The dragon swung her tail, and Mathiak slammed into a tree. She grabbed him and began to squeeze.

"Put him down!" Regan screamed. He urged Enja, and they plowed through the dry grass towards his struggling father. He leaped from Enja's back and began climbing the dragon's scales in his terrified fury.

The dragon threw his father and turned her head to bite him. He swung out of her reach, too high off the ground to turn back now. She reached up with her hind claw to swipe him off, but he had reached the back of her neck. She strained to grab him, and finally caught his torso with her claw.

Regan drew Vidanye's dagger and hurled it at the dragon's eye. It stuck in her pupil, but she did not slow. She gave him a triumphant smile.

"Your ridiculous little needles are no match for--," She paused. She blinked, and her eyelid caught on the dagger. She dropped Regan and struggled to get the dagger. It was smaller than his arrow had been, and she could not pinch it. She wriggled and screeched, tried to take to the sky, anything, but soon the poison overtook her. She swayed and collapsed to the ground.

Regan's chest heaved. He waited for what felt like an hour; he thought he had killed her once. He didn't want to make the mistake of falling for her tricks again. He briefly wondered if Vidanye had actually poisoned the dagger.

When he had recovered from his short fall, he wandered over to the dragon. All the light was gone from her eyes.

The poison had been good enough.

Regan looked around the forest. Villagers poked their heads out from behind trees. When he spotted Vidanye, she raced to his side and squeezed him close.

She didn't have to say anything. Regan didn't really want to talk.

He pulled away from Vidanye and scanned the forest again. Many villagers had come to gawk at the dragon, but then he spotted what he was looking for. Mathiak lay in a pool of blood, unmoving.

Regan walked to him; running felt pointless. He knelt by his father's body.

"I wouldn't have killed the dragon without him."

Vidanye lowered her hand onto his shoulder, and he grabbed her fingers. A rogue tear escaped his eye.

"And he wouldn't have done it without you," she said.

"Seawood, sir," a voice interrupted.

Regan looked up. The village blacksmith, Erik, nodded to him.

"The village elder was accused of treason, sir. In line with Yarov being involved with the dragon and all." He paused. "And—well, he didn't like that too much. He's gone, sir. Fled into the mountains."

Regan stared at his father's body. "Why are you telling me this?"

"You've been selected as the village's new elder, sir. I know you're just a kid, but … the men and I are pretty sure killing a dragon is more than we've ever done."

Regan turned to Vidanye. She just smiled in response.

He had a fleeting vision of running into the mountains with her, escaping Ojunland. But it didn't really feel like an escape anymore—the elder and his son were no longer in power, and the dragon no longer loomed over his land or his people.

"I suppose I don't have a reason to refuse," he said.

"And one more thing," Erik said slowly. "I never liked keeping secrets, and—well, Yarov was keeping the dragon's treasure in some chests I made for him. I don't know where they are now, but that gold is yours."

Regan's eyes widened. He had forgotten about the chests. Yarov had stolen the dragon gold.

His first act as elder was to distribute the gold. He distributed eighty percent rather than twenty; even after building a new home for him and his bride Vidanye, he wouldn't have enough space for all of it anyway. With the dragon gone and Yarov's corruption removed from Ojunland, they entered a period of prosperity beyond any villager's imagination. Crops and goods from the sea flowed from Ojunland through the imperial trader.

Regan presided over Ojunland with his wife for forty years. When he felt too worn, he turned the title of elder to the villagers and allowed them to select a new elder for themselves. When the imperial trader came that summer, he bid farewell to his children and their children, finally free to roam wherever he desired with Vidanye at his side.

About Sevanna Wells

Sevanna has always been obsessed with fantasy and dragons. She loves reading, music, art, science, history, and all other things academic or creative, but writing stories is her true passion. She has her bachelor's degree in family studies. She lives near the Rocky Mountains with her husband and children, spending as much time reading and writing as possible. When she can't be in her books, she is often daydreaming, spending time with family, or attending writing conferences. Her other published work is in the anthology The Dragon's Hoard 3.

Fire in the Land of Wolves

By Jesse James Fain

Rune Red Eagle, monster hunter and renowned warrior, has found himself leader of the Flying Iron Raiders, infamous air pirates sailing through the skies of post-civil war America. Rune cares not for preying on the weak, his inner spirit craves to prove himself the strongest. The apex. When a nightmarish creature has a king's ransom of a bounty placed on it's head, Rune and the Raiders set out to face a deadly dragon, and discover dark secrets in the Virgina hills. The Muscogee Berserker must face down the brutality of nature, and the darkness of man.

Dedication: For Dad, who fought a battle he could never win.

Author's note: Kaccv is the Muskogean word for Cougar/Mountain Lion sometimes translated as "tiger", I have preserved its spelling in the story, but an English pronunciation or writing would be something close to "Kotch-shu" (Fellow southerners say it with me, Coach-Shoe)

Fire in the Land of Wolves

By Jesse James Fain

The light alone was bad enough through the barn style doors of the mechanics shop, before the crowd of feral children came pouring in as a tide of squealing torment. The Old Man followed behind them, flanked by the older of his scions and rescued children. Normally it would be like pulling teeth to get them all out of bed and off to work, but the excitement over the sleeping warrior in the loft had them up bright and early.

"Uncle Rune, Uncle Rune!" They cried while they danced, as if the man could have possibly slept through their invasion. They paid no heed to the fact he flew from his rest with an axe in one hand and a heater in the other, snarling like a panther. The moment passed when he realized it was his family, and not some bounty hunter or bandit. He shared a moment of recognition with his second father. The Old Man saw his scars, especially the internal ones. That recognition destroyed the embarrassment and shame Rune felt drawing down on his nieces and nephews. The Old Man knew his own share of rough awakenings. He didn't blame his adopted son.

"I couldn't hold 'em back anymore, Son. They want to hear about the dragon. Granny's about done with breakfast too."

Rune tossed a shirt on and stored his weapons into fine leather holsters, then passed a brush through his long, raven black hair. He headed down from the loft, through the sea of spare parts and steam engines, and out to the main house for breakfast at the old oak table of his youth. When the table was set, it was Granny herself who asked him for the story with a warm smile. She sat a hot plate and a cold cup in front of him and requested the tale.

"Alright, Bubba. Tell us about this dragon."

Rune drank first, but the glass of water in his hand failed to offset memories of flame. Seeing the anticipation on all their faces, he began to speak.

———

Rune Red Eagle rode with the fires of Muspelheim behind him. His feather and bone covered steam cycle tore through the forested hills of Virginia with reckless speed. Smoke poured from the exhaust, unable to match the black cloud of the conflagration that chased his heels. There was fury in his bright blue eyes, feline pupils betraying the rage and focus of Kaccv, the inner beast.

The fire seemed sentient, chasing him across the trees and over the grass. Great gouts reached for him with all consuming fangs. The black stained sky swirled and twisted with heat driven currents. Over the popping and hissing of the burning trees a constant shove of air echoed and the shadows solidified into an enormous form. Brown and green scales reflected the firelight off the building sized serpent as it flapped its powerful wings and stalked the fleeing hunter. Rune cut through the trees at lethal speeds. Man and machine outperformed the natural world in the pursuit of survival; fleeing faster than the panther, wolf, or elk could run. The dragon raced behind him, the gods' chosen avatar of rage and predatory hunger.

At the top of the next ridge the bike twisted, and Rune's left hand snapped the heater from his belt. Floating at the top of his iron horse's gallop, the Muscogee Berserker let loose with the steam pistol. The bullet smashed flat and ricocheted off the bony ridge of the monster's head. To the dragon, it was no more than a powerful sting. It bellowed with wrath and leaned up to the sky with a great breath, showing its blue under scales. Light flashed in its mouth a split second before flame rushed past its fangs in a blistering line. Rune's wild ride fell over the crest of the hill, shielding him from the wrathful blaze. Muscles strained to steer his prized machine, he throttled down again and rode for his life. On the dragon came, shaking the forest with the winds of its passing and the vibration of its roar.

They rushed on for frantic seconds, hissing fire and screams of fury chased the rumbling motor and the occasional crack of a steam pistol. Rune let out his own demonic calls and guttural roars, cursing the fiery beast in three languages. The steam cycle mounted another ridge, and suddenly the land cleared into nothing but knee-high grass. The hunter tore across the field at full speed, throttle down and determination glaring out from his feline eyes. The dragon sensed an opening, and poured on speed, no longer content to leave the gap between them, it pushed even harder to catch the fleeing beast man that had harassed it from its nest.

The tree line Rune raced towards was dense and littered with thick brush. Bushes and vines weaved an impenetrable mass of vegetation from thick green to bright white. In the face of that mass Rune braked and turned with all his might, stopping before the wall of branches and thorns. Nearly laying the bike down, he turned to face the onrushing beast, and drew his steam rifle from its long leather sheath on the side of the bike.

For a moment, two pairs of inhuman eyes met, rage eternal clashing from multiple founts as fire met bestial fury and headed for an inevitable clash. There may have been satisfaction or even respect in the dragon's eyes. Its snarl twisted slightly as the chase came to an end, but what that meant no man or man like thing could know. The dragon swooped on, and as it closed in those final moments, the brush came alive.

Out from the brush, barrels extended, first one, then ten, then fifteen, and lastly the great bores of steam cannons. Scarred and rugged men leaned from behind trees or rose from root covered dips with rifles and blades. Their leather jackets and worn jeans marked them as raiders and brigands. Grimly, the pack of air pirates sprang their trap, so many wolves ready to face the great beast of a dragon. Rune, as their Alpha, led the most dangerous of prey into the ambush.

"Fire!" He roared over the sizzle of the flames and the rush of dragon's flight and reaped a reward of cracks as the Flying Iron Raiders let loose.

Steam cannon shots the size of melons blasted out and smaller rifle bullets slammed into the dragon from horn to tail. From the left and right of the raiders ambush line, great steel bolts, designed for grappling other airships and reeling them in, spiked into the dragon's flared wings with hellish force. One simply tore through, while the other stuck deep.

Anguish and flame poured forth from the great monster in equal measure. Wings damaged beyond flight; the pull of the chain stripped it from its balance on the drafts. The legendary monster fell into the clutches of two legged wolves. Men died as the dragon fell, its holocaust of heat striking one last vengeful blow that seared the flesh and life from the raider's bones.

Rune descended on the Wyrm with the gravity of a shooting star. Kaccv called for blood and flesh tearing; the ultimate proof of who the real apex predator was. Rune howled; fangs bared as he charged the beast with a great spear from the back of his cycle. The ground shook and burning men flailed. The smell of charred meat added to the smoke of maple, cedar, and pine. Bloody but untamed, the dragon lashed with wing, tail, and claw as it worked to right itself and recover from the shock of so many wounds. Earth flew and charging men crumpled from the great thrashing.

Rune took two great leaping steps, once… twice, and with another battle cry from the demon within, plunged the spear into the chest of the struggling beast with all his inhuman might. As the dragon began to scream, the hunter slammed both triggers down on the hilt of the weapon, and the steam stored in the handle erupted from small slits all along the broad-leafed blade. Pressure hammered through the body of the dragon, shocking organs, and shoving blood in great gushes from the dragon's mouth and nostrils as its pierced lung exploded. The dragon lay still at the devastating wound, its head falling to stare at Rune with a final, baleful light that slowly left its eyes.

Covered in flecks of scalding blood, Rune loosed a great hunting cry. His arms spread wide in flexing triumph under his duster and holsters. The animal spirit and the man both reveled in the rush of winning the ultimate contest. Some of the raiders cheered, others tried to tend to the burned and crushed. Few wounded men survived. Dragons only dealt in killing power, be it fang, claw or fire.

A fiery haired elven woman, wrapped in sky blue silks and a black corset, wondered over. She was clearly used to Rune's display. Thin scars dotted her hands and face, long turned white and almost unnoticed at a glance. She stood comfortable with the air rifle cradled in her arms, and patiently waited for her captain. Rune wrenched the mouth open on the dragon's massive head and began roughly hacking out one of its great fangs with an axe from his belt, his father's axe.

"We lost ten men. Martinique, Jenner, Vasquez, Corio, Helene, Zachariah, Ali, Gabriel, Bobby, and Gerald. Most of them burned… Dimitri didn't make it?" She offered Rune a rag for the blood.

Rune hopped down for the carcass of the beast, his fangs retracting, eyes changing back to round pupils, and hair thinning slightly. The look he gave her was full of concern and reverence. His head shook as he took the cloth and cleaned most of the gore away.

"Thank you, Fay. something got Dimitri. We split to try and find a path up the mountain. I heard a scream and a shot, but all I found was blood. Please have the men see to their graves. I can speak for any that followed the Spirits or the Aesir."

"They aren't going to want to wait long before going for the horde. Did you find it?"

It was a dangerous question. Over the past few months, Rune had cemented his rule over the Flying Iron Raiders with strength and the promise of the $100,000 bounty on the dragon. Still, every fool knew that dragons hoarded treasures. This very beast was accused of raiding one of the Confederacy's gold reserves during transport, now that Richmond and D.C. had given up on destroying one another.

"I found it, at least part of it. The dragon claimed one of the nearby mountains as a roost." He gestured back through the roaring flames. "Shining metal sat under its wings when it took my shot through the hole in the mountaintop. The horde will be close."

The surviving men gathered around their captain and first mate, some with sadness, most with something much sharper in their eyes; hunger, avarice…greed. Rune could feel it, the pulse of dark desire for blood and riches radiated off his wolves in human skin. Every one of the men and women looking at him now was a practiced killer for plunder and pilfering. It was in that plundering that Rune had come to lead them a few months hence. Slaughtering a quarter of their number before dueling their best sword, and their first mate to the death. Captain Mitchell had struck a deal and then betrayed Rune, paying for the treachery with his life, and leaving Rune to lead his gang of air pirates.

"Between the bounty and the horde, we'll all be living the high life." Cortez gave a half gold smile from Rune's right, "Especially with us cutting down on the split." The man had been handsome once, but some battle or addiction aged him too fast. His blond hair once lush now greasy. His brown eyes cold instead of warm. The comment hung in the air, pregnant with foreboding in Rune's mind. He'd led these killers to this moment because it was his best chance to survive, because he was capable of it. When the time came to part the fruits of their violent labor, Fay was the only one of them who would be kind enough to stab him in the front instead of the back.

As the captain, his share was bigger than the others. Eliminating "The split" meant eliminating Rune himself, and then Fay. Kaccv hissed and roiled in his chest, better to kill them all now the Beast said. If these wolves chose to be snakes, he would simply skin them all. The rational part of him won over, and with a sigh of inevitability, easily disguised as the weight of grief, he gave Cortez a nod.

"They died bravely in battle; they will live on with The Spirits or in Odin's Hall. Let's get the graves dug and the trophies collected. For the horde, we need to talk as a crew…"

Rune said the words with a circling hand gesture, waving everyone in. While might always made right, raiders and pirates across history had rules for making choices.

"Something killed Dimitri. Something willing to spend time right next to a dragon's nest. We go back into those burning woods, we have the fire and whatever that is to contend with. $100,000 dollars means none of us need to work for years..." Rune let the implication hang.

"If we skin this big beast and sell the parts, that's worth as much as the bounty alone." He continued after looking at them all. "So we need to make a choice, as a crew. Are we all going into those flames for the gold? Or are we taking the sure money and sailing off to warm beds and full bellies."

"I don't want to take years off, I want to never work again," Cortez piped in.

"Death does that easier than money," Fay added from Rune's side. "Captain has a point. It's enough for all of us to live on for a long time. Dragon's sure money, paid in lives enough already."

"Never took you for a coward, Fay, Captain Red Eagle drops Brightline and suddenly you've lost your spine?"

"I'll show you your spine if you call me a coward again." The elf woman quipped. Rune cut them both off with a sharp hand gesture before Cortez could retort.

"I'm not asking either of you alone. I'm not asking myself alone. This is for the entire crew to decide. Let's bury our dead, and then we take a vote."

They argued as they worked, cliques forming, and even the occasional scuffle breaking out. Rune stepped in several times to keep the peace, making the work of burying the dead take all that much longer.

The circle was tense around the ten new holes, and Rune asked a simple question.

"Are we going for the horde?" and held up his right hand.

"Aye!" The cry came from most of the Flying Iron Raiders. Rune dropped the right and raised the left.

"Nay!" It was clearly softer, but the cooler headed side of the crew spoke then.

Rune couldn't help the feeling of impending betrayal as the choice was made, but he proclaimed it all the same.

"The Ayes have it, we head to the mountain."

The *Martha's Revenge* made short work of the trip back to the mountain once they got her in the air. Rune hated the name of the ship but hadn't risked the time or the political capital among the crew to call a vote over it. At this point nobody even knew who Martha was, Mitchell had taken the meaning behind it to his unceremonious end. It mattered little at the moment, soaring high over the black choking plumes of the burning forest. It took all the remaining crew's skill to make sure they avoided the brutal heat and swirling embers until they got close enough to drop Rune and half the men down. Fay would stay with the rest to have the ship ready at their signal. With flashlights, torches, and thick canvas packs, they climbed down from the airship on vast cargo nets and followed the captain to his discovered path.

Rune led them up great switchbacks and through the green needles and broad leaves. The normal sounds of wildlife were sparse in the wake of the fire roaring much to close for the Raider's comfort. Rune thought several of them would have changed their votes if they had seen the deadly flames the way he had before deciding to risk the adventure.

Worse still was the feeling of being watched that came on suddenly about halfway to the overlook Rune used to antagonize the resting dragon. They would have to work from there to try and find some way down into the open topped cavern the great beast made its home. As they stalked through those eerily silent turns, accompanied by only the crackle of flames and their own footfalls, Rune's senses were on high alert. He scanned constantly for the thing he could feel watching them. Fire and the predatory musk of the dragon filled his nostrils; while the lack of the birds, squirrels, and occasional leaf crunches set Kaccv on the tip of his powerful metaphorical paws. If Rune had fur, it would have stood up all the way down his spine. The rest of the killers around him could feel it too, less gifted in their senses and woodcraft, but aware all the same that something was wrong.

With the sun high in the sky over the green hills and smoke waves, they finally made it to the wide opening that revealed the hole in the side of the mountain. Black stone dotted the inside of the hundred-foot fall to the cavern floor, signs of the dragon's breath and meals littered the floor and walls, along with scatterings of metal, a ruined battle wagon, engine parts, and even small gold pieces. The pirates peered, scanning for any way to reach the lair.

It was Cortez who found the passageway on the far-right side of the cave.

"There, that's a tunnel!" a scarred and tattooed hand pointed the way.

"Looks like it's coming up from deeper, though. Might have an opening back down the mountain." Henry said from next to Cortez, then spit tobacco juice down into the pit. The massive railroad man dipped at every chance. His size, dark bronze skin, and warm chocolate eyes were the Spaniard's total opposite. He turned to Rune, who was once again disturbed by some unrecognized piece of information. Something about the cavern was different from before.

"You said Dimitri went down the holler?"

Rune nodded, blue eyes only giving his crewmate the smallest of glances. His eyes roamed the shadow strewn tunnel entrance.

"Henry, how far can you toss a stone?"

"You've seen the boys, and I throw a ball around, Captain, I've got the best arm on the crew. Baseball would be lighter, so a stone the size of a small biscuit oughta fly 'bout the same."

Rune plucked a stone from the nearby dirt he thought was about right, checked the weight, and handed it to his crewman.

"That lump at the front of the tunnel, it wasn't here before." Rune gestured to a dirt covered pile of bumpy cloth near the tunnel. "Hit it."

Henry gave Rune a smile before stepping back two steps and hopping into the throw. The rock sailed from the big man's grip out into the open area and plummeted down. With a single skip it crashed into the offending lump, which moaned softly in the low winds, and twitched just enough to reveal a mangled face. A face they all knew, Dimitri's.

Guilt hammered at Rune's inner thoughts like they were hot steel. He'd wrongly written one of his Raiders off for dead. While the cutthroat crew wasn't shy in its motives and lack of morals, Dimitri had been loyal. Rune led the charge back down and through the secondary path with a heater in hand, hellbent on saving the man.

It took too many frantic minutes to find the blood. The crew spread out around the spot, searching for clues. Rune stared at the blood; a pint's worth scattered on the grass. Earlier, Kaccv had been howling at him to prioritize prey over pack, and the relentless pressure of leading his murderers agreed. The dragon could have flown off to hunt at any time. He had to act and get it to the ambush.

Rune threw the introspection away then, using the anger to summon the beast within. His eyes shifted, and teeth twisted into sharper shape. The colors of the world became crisper, and the smells amplified.

"I've got blood here." Bozman called and Rune met the man in a flash. A tracking predator awakened, Rune could now see the small flecks of vitality on the grass and leaves, and the light drag marks in the dirt. There was more blood beyond, misted around the air and trees. It mixed with Dimitri's blood. That heater shot had found its mark in something.

The crew took up the trail, weaving through brush and root until the green was so thick it fought against the light of the sun. There in the dark they found the cave entrance, and more of their friend's red life-water. Flashlights, heaters, and blades came out from sheaths and pockets. Armed for dragon, Rune led the way into the darkness.

The tunnel before them was wide enough for a wagon, not big enough for the monster they felled earlier, but enough for multiple men to comfortably walk shoulder to shoulder. It twisted and turned, slowly leading them into the depths of the mountain. Rune stopped them when he noticed the flash of a reflection in the darkness and crept forward on silent feet. For a moment the wonder of the sight before him struck the gravity of the hunt from his mind.

A vast cavern opened before him, full of great geodes of shining crystal. Amethyst and ruby pillars sparkled at him. Giant cracked stones revealed massive slabs of luminescent minerals. The vast room glittered from floor to ceiling with the earth's natural splendor.

Rune waved the crew forward as he stepped into the crystal garden, and discovered what could only have been a curated footpath. Shaking off the shock of the moment, he noted other paths, and candelabras that held deep red candles or torches to provide the wonders with light. Suspicion killed what wonder was left in the beast man then. These were the works of men, not dragons. There should be no men here in the deep woods and the darkness under the dragon's den.

The Flying Iron Raiders lived up to their name, snatching gems and crystals that looked valuable while prying loose any stone that could be levered out to carry away. More than once, some reflection or twist of the light gave the guise of something moving. Rune himself detected something in the shimmer and shadows, but nothing made itself known.

The crew made their way forward and the crystal monoliths cleared suddenly, opening to a grand room full of dark wood pews and fine carpets. Carvings of dragons and demons adorned the walls. Dark, red curtain shrouded doorways lined a second story balcony. The cathedral felt cold and cruel despite its splendor of crystal and warm colors.

Rune's wariness reached a crescendo when his eyes fell upon the large stone offering table laid before the front of the pews, and the dark ruddy stains that painted its oaken legs. Through all the oil, leather, and sweat of his crew the smell of long settled blood rang clear in his animal senses. Beyond the alter, the cave back was open, a wide torch lit tunnel with the barest amount of natural light creeping into it from beyond. Rune opened his mouth to give an order, when a red robed figure swept out onto the balcony above and cut his command off with a question.

"What fools would dare to disturb the Temple of Torrcarath?" The man asked from behind his crystal mask, his posture matching his offended tone. He looked over crew before his eyes fell to Rune.

"I am Rune Red Eagle, and these are the Flying Iron Raiders," The Muscogee man declared. "We mean no offense in intruding, but one of our men is injured in the cavern above. We were only searching for a way to him and found this Temple. We would gladly take leave of this place once he is returned to us."

Cortez gave the shortest of scoffs at that. "Speak for yourself, I've got a treasure to find. Let's just bury the god botherer."

"Shut…up." Rune hissed, doing his best to subtly gesture to the crew to take a better look around. He could hear them now, though it was much too late, the slight fall of boots and the lightest scrap of claws on stone and crystal.

Men came from the balcony doorways, long waving blades gleamed in their red gloved hands. reptilian heads the size of watermelons peered with bright and malevolent eyes from the top of the geodes, and crystal monoliths. All of the crew shifted slowly, instinctually adjusting to not bunch up or get in each other's way. The violence in the air was growing thicker by the minute. It turned every breath into a battle of will.

"We know you, Rune Red Eagle, and your sins against the church. Your trespass is nothing to the crime of slaying Torrcarath's messenger. You come here to steal life and our sacred treasures. You will have neither. The gold and jewels belong to the dragons." Rune made one last attempt at diplomacy.

"If you know us, then you know the price we can reap. We can return gold and gems. You lost a dragon, don't lose more." The man in the crystal mask only gave a more vicious grin.

"Dragon blood stains you. Sacred life wasted on your visage. There is only one fate for all of you... Dea-" Rune's steam pistol shot slammed into the man's upper chest and cut the end of his proclamation short.

Rune's battle scream shook the walls of the crystalline church as he changed targets and kept firing. Dragonlings launched from the shadows and heights with fist sized jets of fire pouring from their lips. Cultists fell to the crack of steam weapons as Raiders fell to the fire and claw of the lion sized reptiles. Bozman screamed in terror and pain as one of the beasts bore him to the floor. Blood ran from his arm, chest and belly. The dragon ravaged his left arm with a shake of its horned head but failed to see the gleaming steel of the Arkansas Toothpick in the other. The raider plunged the blade with all his might over and over again, mixing the blood of man and monstrosity, he roared out in anguish again as the draconic blood seared his flesh with its heat.

Henry saw the monster leaping for him and swung with his boarding axe as the beast pounced, cleaving an arm from it as it dropped to the floor past him. Ignoring the burn from the spray of crimson, he swung in a circular step. As the monster howled, the gigantic man smashed his axe into the beast's spine between its small wings.

Cortez met the rushing cultist at the foot of the stairs with cutlass and dagger, sadistic glee in his eyes and a death's head grin on his face. He deflected the cut of one waving blade with his sword and slashed the man's throat with the dagger, feeling another cultist carve a line across his ribs as he danced aside to use the crumbling fanatic as a shield from attack. Another of the crew rushed to even the odds, but a jet of flame dropped him screaming from brutal burns.

Rune emptied his pistol into one of the beasts savaging his crewmates and drew his second axe to dance with a pair of cultists.

"Yee Naaldlooshi" one of them whispered in recognition and fear at the sight of Rune's bestial features. Rune knew had been called the name before, though it was the language of the Navajo, and not his southern people. He knew no real name for what he was, his father and uncle might have known, might have taught him, but the Blue Coats had taken that from him, and now only Kaccv could tell him what he was. Kaccv didn't care for names, only to prove he was the deadliest.

Rune had no fear of knives. He smashed through the first man's guard in a furious rush and cleaved through his jaw with the second strike of his father's second axe. The blade ripped jaw from face, snapping the head aside and dropping the man into a screaming ruin. Kaccv's predator senses launched him aside when the other cultist pulled a gnarled wand from his robes and gestured with an arcane cry. The panther demon inside him screamed a single thought.

"Sorcery!"

Thunder and blinding white light rattled every living thing in the cavern, a bolt of brilliant lightning lashed from the fanatic's relic. A raider was blasted from his feet in the bust of electric power. Rune snapped up from the floor in an instant and sent his left-hand axe sailing into the chest of the spellcaster. He chased the throw, splitting the caster's skull to be sure of the kill and wrenching his throw weapon from the corpse.

Blood ran through the room, weaving its way through the sparkle of crystals in the firelight. Raiders fell to plunging knives, ripping fangs, and thundering magic. Dragons and cultists both spewed flames. Bozeman was somehow on his feet dripping from a dozen wounds, covered in purple burns from the dragon's blood, and slaying fanatics at Cortez's back. The Raiders were growing thin, dangerously thin, but so too were the number of worshipers in this beautiful nightmare of a church.

Rune danced with the last visible dragon, its long neck lashing over and over to snap at him. He watched with furious calculation, and slipped left or right as the jaws came in. Finally, he saw the spark of light in the back of the creature's jaws and leapt forward. In aiming its fiery breath, the beast had forgotten its defenses. Rune slapped the beasts head to the side as the spew of flame began and followed with a vicious strike to its neck. The flames washed over one of the cultists circling Henry, who used the distraction to strike another opponent down with his ferocious power. Rune struck into the dragon's thick neck and was rewarded with more tiny burns from the near boiling blood. The dragon did not die, but clawed at him, ripping ragged wounds across his belly, but the warrior simply struck over and over again with his tomahawks, trading blows again with the dragonling, until the head fell from the beast.

Rune hissed in fury from the burns and looked up to what remained of his expedition. The claw wounds on his chest and stomach slowly began to clot and mend. In all that blood covered crystal, only Bozeman, Henry, and Cortez were on their feet. Every other Flying Iron Raider that walked into the cavern was dead or dying. Cortez walked over to a twitching cultist and slit his throat with a casual quip.

"Looks like you needed a better god, or a better blade." His eyes reveled in the crimson wash. He leaned up from his victim and gave Rune a half smirk.

"I've always envied you for that trick," His bloodstained weapons gestured to Rune's rapidly closing wounds. "Hard to kill a man that can heal like that."

"Had its own price."

"Like what?"

"Dead parents and being ugly enough to scare children when I'm angry." The bloodthirsty pirate studied his captain's face.

"I always hated kids anyway."

"Maybe I'll find a blind wife. Now quit jabbering and let's see if anyone is still alive."

"Aye." All three men answered. The triage was fast, only Merrick had a chance to live, burned but still breathing. They wrapped him in torn shirts and the cleanest cloth that could be found. Rune took one last solum look at the man before he headed past the brown streaked stone altar and into the wide tunnel beyond. A series of ceremonial torches lined both walls, leading past red tapestries of draconic and demonic figures engaged in slaughter or ceremony. He chased the sliver of light he saw before the fight. The sun was brighter around the bend, and Rune found himself emerging into the partial afternoon light and finding the dirty lump that was Dimitri. Rune saw the mess one of the dragonlings had made of the man: broken limbs, blackened eyes, and ravaged guts. It was a miracle he was breathing. Henry, Cortez and Bozeman followed a moment later. They looked at the ruined man with a mixture of worries.

"I hate to say it boss, but it looks like he's played his last inning." Henry said.

"Game over, man." Bozeman said solemnly.

"We'll wrap him up like Merrick and get him back to the *Revenge*. I saw men live through some nasty things in the war."

"Have you found the treasure? There was nothing but a wounded dragon and some living quarters back there." Cortez's eyes roamed the basin, "Some of this looks valuable or useful. That might be some Spanish coin over there." he jutted his chin at a metal pile.

Rune's teeth gritted. "Spread out and make it fast. We find it in a few minutes, or we don't find it all."

Cortez sneered at that but leapt immediately into his search. They spread over the cavern, pocketing the occasional coin or necklace, shifting quickly through steam wagon parts or broken engine refuse. The dragon clearly doomed more than one trip. It was Henry who found the horde.

The massive man pulled back a wall of vines and revealed the gleam of gold. He let out a whistle and the other men came to join. Beyond the vines were piles of ornate chest, shimmering gems and ornate weapons. The dragon and its cult clearly gathered for decades.

English, French and Spanish coins, ornate breastplates and even black powder flintlocks from before the age of steam lined racks and piles. Tired eyes full of joy, even Kaccv beamed at the spoils of a successful hunt. The men filled their packs quickly, strapping on ornate scrolls, and weapons to the outsides. Their packs filled with loot shockingly fast.

"Going for another pack!" Cortez blurted and dashed away back to the cavern below. Rune didn't like the delay, but the ship would take time to get here, to get crew on the ground and get help to them. Cortez could enjoy his gold collection. The man was vicious, but they only had to make it back to civilization and sell their riches before he was rid of the bastard.

Rune walked out into the debris filled hollow, taking one last look around before fishing in his duster and producing a flare launcher. He checked the chamber, made sure the flare was in position, and aimed it into the sky. With a powerful thump, the sparkling red flare shot off into the open air. *Martha's Revenge* would be watching, and sail in close now that the treasure was found. Rune stowed the launcher and took a deep breath. He struggled to relax now that the work was done. The *crack-pow* of a steamer shot interrupted him, and he turned still feline eyes to the source of the sound.

Cortez stood over Dimitri, one of the long torches from the church in his left hand, and a heater in this right. A neat new hole punched through Dimitri's forehead, the back of his head drizzling blood from a larger wound. Rune stormed over, axe and pistol filling his hands, but somehow Cortez met him with his sadistic grin and waved the torch threateningly.

"Hold on now, Captain," The pirate said, shifting his pistol hand vaguely in Henry's direction when he emerged from the vine shrouded horde.

"What the hell are you doing, Cortez, scared he was bit by a vampire or something?" Henry hissed, but it was Rune who answered.

"Cutting down on the split. I'd bet we won't have to worry about carrying Merrick out anymore either."

"Merrick stopped breathing on his own," Cortez shrugged and gestured to Dimitri.

"And I was doing him a favor. A man that wounded and tore up is in hell and just going to suffer until he dies anyway. If I'm ever that way. I expect you to do the same for me."

Rune almost accepted the view, even respected it. It was probably even true that Dimitri would have died or been crippled all the rest of his life. they might have dragged him to the ship only for him to bleed out or die from infection. The logical part of Rune could have played it off. Could have accepted that what was done was done for treasure and peace. Kaccv would not have it, and when the reason came Rune could not abide. Cortez was not the master of life and death here, not the man in control. He was not leading this pack. He had violated the pact that held the vicious men and women together. There was only one price for that, as the priest in the crystal church said. Death was the cost of betrayal.

Cortez saw the look his companions gave him and brandished his weapons with more determination. "Not so fast, I've got the drop on you both, and you... I've found your weakness, my monstrous friend. The claw wounds sealed in short order, but the burns, those bloody burns, have stayed since this morning. Your black magic might ignore my pistol, but flame marks you true."

The betrayer took a breath and his face softened, but no denizen of earth would ever know what offer or placation he was about to give. A vicious line of fire consumed half of him with a great growl as the air was sucked in around it. Broad and powerful, the scarred face of another adult dragon spewed flames and wrath from the top of the wall above. Red and brown, wider and more powerful than the beast they had slain earlier, the walking and flying nightmare tried to burn them all to ash. Henry dove for the safety of the treasure cove. Rune scrambled for cover behind the battle wagon, and shot back, aiming for the beast eye, only to see bright flashes of fragments as they smashed flat instead of penetrating.

"*Stupid!*" Kaccv and Rune's collective conscience agreed. What idiots they all had been. Him for trusting Cortez when his instincts screamed not too, and all of them for missing the obvious. *"Kits are made from two!"* Every one of the raiders had seen the clutch of dragonlings and not realized young would have both mother and father. Rune holstered the pistol, unable to harm the beast, and filled the hand with his second axe.

There in the heat of the flame, his thoughts turned to his father and uncle. When the Blue Coats came to their Alabama home, his family had gone out to meet them. Word of Sherman's war crimes had already spread from Georgia. The people of Cathedral Caverns had chosen to make the invaders bleed instead of waiting for mercy or the sword. They left that day knowing they could not win. His father, affectionately called Lamb by all the Europeans who could not pronounce his real name, led the men in their skirmishes. His uncle and his mother followed in tow. His mother, Kaja, sang, loud and long the whole morning before they went to a war they never wanted. They had all died. All accept Rune.

Rune made the same choice in the face of the dragon. To make the beast bearing down on him bleed until he died by burn or bite. Kaccv agreed and they both rumbled his chest in a deep growl. Would The Spirits take him to the land his father dwelled in, or would a Valkyrie take him to see his mother in Odin's Hall? Fire spent, the dragon crashed down into the cavern, senses hunting down the warrior. It smelled him, taking only the smallest of moments to track his unique scent. A prayer to his ancestors and their gods was his last thought as the dragon loomed over the smashed wreckage.

A great boom sounded, then another. So close to him the dragon's roar shook his very bones. Henry had come back from the treasure trove with muskets in tow. The dragon lashed its head around to him, losing all trace of Rune in the pain of the gunshot's shallow wounds.

Feline blue eyes wide, rage and determination on his features, Rune launched from his cover. Inhuman speed and dexterity carrying him up the wreckage in three bounding steps and into the air. The shrill scream of a mountain lion on his lips, he buried both axe blades into the broad back of the great beast and began to rend.

He alternated the axes, chop after chop, burying the blades in with weight and power the soft lead bullets could not match and ignoring the constant pain from the sizzling blood that flew. The dragon spun in rage and pain, twisting its great head to see what demonically foolish thing was hurting it. Henry fired again, then once more, and came charging out from the treasure cove with his own axe. He hacked at wing or leg as the great monster turned. Rune lunged aside as the gigantic jaws of the beast came for him; burnt carrion breath filling his nostrils. He tore skin on the beast's rough scales but slammed another axe into the flesh of the creature to gain a hold. Now by the base of the wing, he decided he could take the sky from the monster if nothing else and savaged the tendons at the base of the wing with a great hack.

It wasn't enough; it never could have been. No regular axe or sword could cut wide or deep enough into this great serpent that had seen mankind's first fires. It spun with sudden ferocity and its long tail smashed Henry from his feet, as Rune was launched from the dragon's back to slam into the cave wall. The railman turned pirate rolled and bounced along the stone floor in an ironic facsimile of the stone he tossed a few hours before. Rune's ribs and spine cracked against the inside of the mountain. His ears rang and blood poured from them. He struggled to find the catlike balance he knew only a moment before, trying to make his broken body work by sheer will. He knew already the crushing would be mending, but in that dreadful moment nothing would work, the grip on the hafts of his weapons a miracle itself.

The dragon sensed its prey was injured, shook itself, then turned its head to Henry, and with a few great strides hovered over the fallen man. It opened its great maw with a flash of light and breathed out the hellish inferno from within. Rune wanted to throw his axe or draw his heater and empty it into the beast. He wanted to save the broad, dark-skinned man that had fought so bravely, but the first battle Rune had ever fought already taught this lesson. No matter your power, you can't save everyone. He hadn't saved anyone. Not now, not then.

His vision cleared just in time to watch Henry's skin slough away. His spine aligned and his ribs cracked back into place just in time to blunt the feeling of the wind that carried Henry's incinerated organs. His feet held his weight just as Henry's bones turned black. Rune was whole again, as Henry became nothing. Burned, blood soaked, with blades ready, Rune set to make the dragon bleed again.

The *Martha's Revenge* drew blood for him instead. The ship floated in above the scene to let loose with a full broadside. Its gun crews fired with over a dozen cannons at a time. The heavy artillery smashed into and in some places through the gigantic beast, laying it low with an agonized roar. Rune heard a cry from above and watched a long spear fly out into the air. He tracked it like a caracal hunting a pigeon and leapt up to snatch the weapon from the air. The steam cannons did grim work on the great serpent, and so Rune rectified another mistake, and put crew first.

He found Cortez wheezing and twitching from the burns, delirious from half his body being scorched. He kicked the traitor over to look him in the eyes and balanced his spear one handed to draw his steam pistol. Cortez tried desperately to speak. It didn't work. Didn't matter anyway. Rune knew exactly what was just.

"You'll either die on the ship or be crippled for the rest of your life." Rune snarked. "I'm going to do you a favor. Make sure you don't suffer and go on this way. After all, you did it for Dimitri. You'd expect me to do the same." Rune then pressed the barrel to Cortez's forehead. He waited a moment to see the panic in the bastard's eyes before he slowly squeezed the trigger.

Rune hadn't been able to save anyone, not then, not now, but he had avenged them, He looked to Henry's charred bones, and promised to carry the song of his life into the world.

———

"Two full grown dragons! The radio only said one!" Jeremiah, one of his nephews, roared with enough excitement to shake the table. The outburst earned a stern eye from Granny and a chuckle from The Old Man. He couldn't blame the boy. Rune's exploits were all over the radio shows. So far, it was as much nonsense as truth. His mirth dropped when he saw the look in Rune's eyes. The Old Man could almost watch Henry burn again in that reflection. He stood, and clasp his son on the shoulder, meeting that horror washed gaze.

"It's done now, son. Done and gone. You did them proud." The warrior shook himself once, and the haunting past faded.

"Tell you what, buddy, go grab the leather satchel out of my left saddle bag." Rune said to Jerimiah as he polished off a biscuit and honey. The young boy did his best impression of a lightning bolt while the rest of the family started clearing dishes from the morning meal. Rune being home didn't make the work go away.

Jeremiah was back a few minutes later with the satchel, struggling to carry it. Rune rose to help his adopted nephew and dumped the contents onto the table. The children all gathered around in wonder. A journal and a bone knife were tied together, along with a collection of teeth, two the size of a man's hand and one almost as big as a dinner plate. The largest item was a claw almost big enough to be a short sword.

"Dragon teeth!" the children cried.

"Go ahead and pick them up but be careful. they are sharp enough to take a finger." Rune warned. He let the children play for a while, even The Old Man and Granny taking a look at his trophies. In the end it was his adopted father that brought an end to the spectacle.

"Alright, everyone out to the shop! Those wagons won't fix themselves!"

Reluctantly, all the trinkets and trophies were stored away, until only the long claw remained. Little Shawna carried it over to the table and sat it before the monster hunter.

"Uncle Rune, what is that?"

"That's a Kraken claw, Honey. big nasty beast that lives in the ocean. look like someone crossed a squid and a shark."

"Are you going to tell us about that monster too?"

"I sure will, but not right now. Some stories are best saved for another day." He kissed her forehead and walked out to join in the familiar comfort of building machines.

About Jesse James Fain

Jesse James Fain is a Science Fiction and Fantasy Author, Editor, and retired powerlifting champion. Jesse's extensive experience in martial arts and weapons training leads to vibrant martial tales of revenge and combat that bring a taste of reality to fictional battles, along with a humorous southern twist from growing up with the kind of family polite towns pretend don't exist.

Jesse began his life in Metro Atlanta, torn between the worlds of nerddom and athletics. Traveling between the sands of Arrakis and the grassy fields of The South's most holy game, Football. He found his true loves in Powerlifting and MMA, winning two WABDL world championships. Jesse would go on to instruct in martial arts and get a degree in Political Science with a minor in History from Berry College. Outside of writing, he would do absolutely nothing with it.

Inspired by classic authors like Lovecraft and Howard; he decided some D&D campaigns might make decent stories. This began a lifelong passion for crafting heroic stories and dark worlds. He now resides in North Georgia, penning great tales of battle and revenge for you to read while still bouncing back and forth between fantasy and real-world fighting.

You can find more about Jesse, and his tales at Outlawauthor.com.

We hope that you enjoyed this title and look forward to many more to come. Please, leave us a review! Reviews matter to all our authors.

Take a look at some of our other award-winning series at https://threeravenspublishing.com/series-universes/

Visit us at https://jrhandley.com and sign up for our newsletter for the latest and greatest news on upcoming titles and events.

Other series and titles you might enjoy.

James M. Ward

Wolfoid

You can also keep up to date with J. R. Handley and his cohorts on the Blasters and Blades Podcast at https://www.youtube.com/c/BlastersandBladesPodcast.

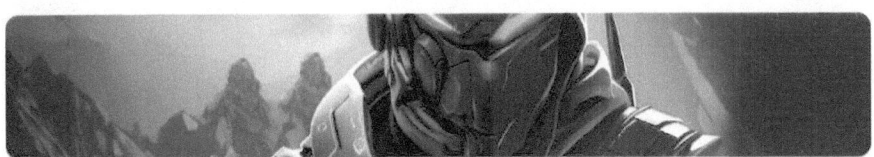

The Blasters and Blades Podcast

@BlastersandBladesPodcast · 532 subscribers · 540 videos

The Blasters & Blades Podcast ...**more**

podcasters.spotify.com/pod/show/blasters-and-blades **and 12 more links**

Subscribe
